RUBY

RUBY

THE LAST PSION BOOK 2

Maxwell Farmer

Podium

Podium

Recap of Events

Kiru was a half-elf who lived along the outskirts of the Kingdom of Blades. Raised by his mother, he dreamed of becoming a powerful cultivator warrior. His mother had taught him well and he was making great strides. Unfortunately, he was prone to getting into fights, and after he started one with the local duke's son, Ambrose, his body was left crippled, and his fire mana core shattered. Hope was not all lost for Kiru, however, though he didn't know it yet. After Ambrose sent an assassin to finish him off, he and his mother fled their small village to hide in the woods.

It was there Kiru learned that he was the son of the previous king, Ruken Chromebane. Ruken was labeled as a tyrant who manipulated others using a taboo mana: mental mana. Kiru's mother told him that Ruken had been wrongfully accused but did in fact possess the power to cultivate mental mana, a power that he had passed onto Kiru. He was a psion. This was his inheritance and responsibility.

Centuries ago, the Great Alliance made up of various nations on the continent had fought a war known as the Draconic Campaign against Nidhogg and his dragon army. The Great Alliance pushed them back, but it was only due to the secret powers of the psions who ruled the Kingdom of Blades. Now, with a psion no longer on the throne, the dragons were set to return to bring ruin and devastation to the continent.

At only sixteen, Kiru was given nine years to figure out a way to use mental mana to restore his ability to walk, reach the heights of cultivation, recover his father's lost artifacts spread throughout the various nations of the continent in order to make him stronger, and reclaim his rightful throne before the dragons were set to return. Though the task was daunting, Kiru pushed forward with the aid of his mother and William the imp, a familiar he gained over the course of his adventures. He eventually discovered a way he could move again through Telekinesis. Using that technique, Kiru practiced magically manipulating his body like a puppet, even going so far as to call his path "the Path of the Puppet Master." He still couldn't feel anything below his neck, but this allowed him to go about his life with a semblance of normality. After two years of steady cultivating and practicing away from civilization, Kiru reached greater heights than he had ever achieved before.

Unfortunately, the Assassins' Guild was still under contract to kill him. Kiru's mother sacrificed herself to save him and eliminate the threat, leaving him only her armor and enchanted storage ring to remember her by. Realizing it was time, the newly minted Gold-ranked cultivator emerged from his isolation to join the Royal Academy, the nearest place where one of his father's items was located.

The psion managed to keep his cultivation type a secret and gained entry into the academy as a student under the label of fire mana cultivator and Defunct, the term for a cultivator who couldn't use any techniques. He discovered that the cultivators there were operating under many different political agendas, and he needed to be careful not to draw too much attention to himself. Kiru also learned that his father's item was located below the stadium where the annual Warrior Games were held, and it was only accessible once a year to participating students who were part of a team of four. Over the school year, Kiru managed to gain allies for his team and even grew to trust them enough with his secret heritage. Their team name was Pandemonium, and they were certainly a force to be reckoned with.

There was Brunhilda Lightsworn, a dwarven paladin within the Order of Valhalla who served the Vasir. Her goddess was the minor deity, Hlin, goddess of protection, and Brunhilda's goal in life was to help her become a major deity within the pantheon. Next was the gold drakonid rogue, Zhaden of Clan Ironclaw. Unlike most gold drakonids, he used dream mana rather than fire mana, which gave him the ability to create powerful illusions. His goal was to elevate his clan's status among his race by joining the elite peacekeeping force within the Great Alliance known as the Fangs. Last among them was Mutt, a blind orc who loved two things above all else: hunting and fighting. When they first found him, an immoral cleric at the academy had been performing unspeakable experiments upon him; he had sworn loyalty to Kiru for rescuing him. Mutt was a powerful fighter, and all he really wanted was to have increasingly challenging fights.

The four cultivators formed a team called Pandemonium, and, with the backing of Niajar J'sarko, the academy's head librarian, they became a force to be reckoned with. Kiru also received training from a skilled Defunct, Giiyam, a stoic, half-orc groundskeeper and the only Defunct to have ever won the Warrior Games. Giiyam taught him how to fight with the exotic hook blades called Fu Tao, using the Cruel Mantis style. Along with Telekinesis, Kiru gained two more techniques:

Telepathy and Subjugation. He also discovered that, whenever his familiar, William was brought back inside his core, he had perfect recall. The last part aided him in learning and retaining extremely complex data quickly, such as becoming fluent in numerous languages and taking in over a thousand tomes' and scrolls' worth of information.

Pandemonium fought hard and eventually succeeded in winning the Games amongst the first-year combatants. Kiru even got some well-deserved payback against Ambrose, who was also participating, by somehow turning the noble's lightning-based technique back on him with a well-placed punch.

Their trials weren't over, however. Before Kiru could claim the first of his father's artifacts from the prize room beneath the stadium, two more obstacles were in his way. Firstly, he had to *not* draw the suspicion of Van Blaine, the murderous usurper who had killed his father. The psion only just managed this, but he wasn't able to avoid the king's awareness entirely, being forced to have a conversation with the winged cultivator and pretend to promise to serve in his guard. The next challenge was the former headmaster, Niazen J'sarko, Niajar's brother. The elf lost his position to the librarian due to Kiru's victory and wasn't happy about it.

Niazen revealed that he'd had the heads of two dead psions surgically grafted to him years ago and planned to add Kiru's to his collection. Kiru and the rest of his friends would've surely died had not Giiyam come to save them. The half-orc revealed that he had once served Ruken and would do so for Kiru as well, sacrificing himself to allow Pandemonium to escape. Kiru protested but was carried away. Fortunately, however, he was able to get his father's artifact, an orb of Psyslime, a metal controlled by the psion's Telekinesis that was able to form a wickedly sharp blade.

With the item in hand, Kiru was greeted by a projection of his father who encouraged him to continue his quest. The psion and his friends agreed on the importance of Kiru's mission, and they all fled south toward Mutt's homeland, the orc nation of Imakandi, to find the next artifact.

RUBY

CHAPTER ONE

Clues

Van Blaine and his soldiers walked amidst the rubble. During Round 2 of the Warrior Games, he had heard a loud rumbling under the stadium floor while the second-year students were fighting. The winged king had suspected something was wrong. He couldn't tell for sure, however, as the powerful students competing had displayed an impressive range of abilities. Multiple times, their techniques shook the very ground and made the arena tremble slightly. Still, the vibrations seemed random and much stronger than any mere second-year at the academy could produce, despite their higher cultivation ranks.

His suspicions were confirmed when he received word that the first-year contestants—including that half-elf boy he'd so graciously taken under his wing—hadn't returned from the prize room. Deciding to investigate further, he joined the second-year victors down there, where they found that part of the room had caved in. After that, they began digging. Sure enough, they discovered a corpse.

Niazen J'sarko? he thought to himself in sheer shock as he took in the sight of the elf's crushed body amidst the stone debris. At first, Van Blaine was confused. His mind was rattled as to what in the abyss had happened. Why was one of his loyal vassals dead, and in the prize room of the academy he had supervised, of all places? *The blasted elf was an Emerald. Who could've had the strength to kill him? More so, who could've had the strength to kill him and avoid my detection? He couldn't have died from a mere accident, could he?* But then, as his guards began to uncover more of Niazen's body, he nearly froze them on the spot in his fury. There, attached to one of the elf's shoulders was another head, ruined and stitched on like some abominable science experiment.

It wasn't just the freakish degradation that the elf had done to himself but whose head he'd used. Van Blaine's eye widened and, without thinking, he pulled down tighter on his odd conical helmet crown. It was one of the Mad Tyrant's warriors, another one of those accursed mental mana users Van Blaine had killed nearly twenty years ago. To think that the tyrant's influence would go so far as to corrupt this elf so long after the king had killed him!

That still didn't answer the question as to where the boy and his team had gone. With steadily mounting anger, he ordered his guards to continue searching. They found a second psion's head that had clearly been cut off of Niazen's other shoulder based off the evidence of a crushed stump of odd flesh the dead elf had there. At that moment, finding the first-years became of secondary importance to him having a long, painful conversation with the J'sarko Clan. If Niazen had succumbed to this foul, corrupted path, who knew how many more had been under his influence?

The king clenched his fists as frost began to spread out on the ground from where he was standing, "I'm going to wipe out his entire clan . . . at least his boy and brother," he muttered to himself. After he managed to get his anger under control, he saw that his guards had found something else. A hook blade—like the kind the half-elf used, with the inner edge lined with sharpened trollstone—was found wedged between two large boulders. It was nicked and slightly bent, but its quality was undeniable.

This must have been what the boy acquired from the prize room, he thought to himself. But he was still left without answers. Van Blaine didn't like not having all the answers. *Where are the students? Or at least, where are their bodies? How did Niazen, a soldier I promoted myself, become so corrupted? Are there more of these abominations walking around my kingdom? Also, why had Niazen attacked the first-years in the first place?*

Fear gripped the winged man's heart. He quickly took off to find his wife. Despite her being a foreigner, her beauty and sharp mind were unmatched in his experience compared to any other bride he'd been offered. No one truly knew her power and capability, and she was a proven tactician who actually ran the kingdom's entire military, her rank second only to himself. She also ran the kingdom's covert enforcers, the policing division that kept the peace and eliminated any would-be usurpers and troublemakers.

Van Blaine furrowed his brow as he neared the door. He could hear a strange hissing or whispering noise, like that of a dying mouse.

"Darling, what troubles you?" his wife asked him after he opened the door, a goblet of wine held in her right hand.

The king cocked his head to the side. "Were you conversing with someone? I swear I heard you saying something."

"Oh, just talking to myself, darling. You know how I get when I don't have my strong husband around." She cooed and gave him a wink.

"Oh, right." He remembered that she was prone to this. He often woke to her animatedly talking to herself on the balcony connected to their bedchambers. *She's an odd one, but the beautiful ones always are,* he thought.

Van Blaine then remembered why he'd come to find his wife. "Xiomara, something isn't right." He proceeded to explain his findings. He watched her untroubled face begin to show increasing concern until a scowl developed. As beautiful as his wife was, when she was unhappy, the looks she gave sent chills up his spine. When she was angry, her face could contort into something almost monstrous, the death mana she cultivated temporarily altering her features. *Good thing she won't be mad at* me *this time,* he thought as he continued his explanation.

"As you no doubt suspect, my dear, the evidence is irrefutable. It's clear that the influence of that blasted Chromebane has reached far deeper than we feared. Round up the J'sarko Clan and summon the Inquisition. Dead or alive, I will have that boy and his team found. Any possible remnants of the Mad Tyrant mustn't be allowed to exist," Van Blaine ordered.

A predatory smile grew on Xiomara's face. "As you command, my king."

CHAPTER TWO

Life in the Wild

Two Months Later

Kiru and the rest of the party stalked carefully across the savanna grassland. The afternoon sun beat down hard, but they still managed to keep their breathing in check. They were downwind of their intended prey, an antelope that had strayed away from the migrating herd in favor of exclusive rights to a thick patch of grass to munch on. That decision would be its last mistake.

The cultivators continued to stalk, getting closer to the unsuspecting creature. Zhaden was already adept in stealth, so he took point. Meanwhile, Kiru was holding his own, whereas Brunhilda was . . . well, she had room for improvement.

The paladin, in her heavy armor, took a clunky step forward, accidentally snapping a twig underfoot. The antelope popped its head up, its eyes bulging as it quickly scanned its surroundings. The party all crouched, but the creature's instincts appeared to not trust what it heard. It quickly turned in the opposite direction of the cultivators and bolted. Both Brunhilda and Kiru were too far away, but Zhaden was not. The gold drakonid jumped out of the grass and flung three daggers. Two hit their mark, striking the animal in its chest and shoulder. They bit into the flesh and drew blood, but the creature's hide was too thick. Neither was a killing blow.

The rogue was about to run after the creature when it took a sharp turn by a large tree. As it went under its shadow, Mutt descended, ambushing the beast from the treetop. The blind orc's large maw bit into the antelope's neck. His fangs crunched down on the vertebrae in its neck and lacerated its jugular vein. The antelope squealed at the sudden attack. It had been knocked off its feet and began scrambling in an attempt to get back up despite the orc still biting down on it.

Mutt growled and violently jerked his head to the side, breaking the antelope's neck with an audible snap and killing it on the spot. Kiru and the rest of

Pandemonium grimaced at the noise as they jogged up to the orc just as he was spitting out the antelope and wiping the blood from his mouth.

"Damn, Mutt! That's some jaw strength you got there!" Kiru exclaimed.

Despite—or perhaps due to—his blindness, the beast cultivator's other senses were far more advanced and had easily compensated for that disability. Mutt licked the blood off his hand, then smiled as he looked over to his allies. "Haha, yeah, Boss! I don't know which sacred beast cores I ingested back at the academy, but one of them was clearly a strong biter." The orc's carefree attitude came out clearly in his tone. That attitude also caused him to address almost everyone by a nickname, opting to go that route instead of having to remember their names. To Kiru's joy, Mutt had remembered his name instead of calling him "Sword Guy" like he had when they first met. The psion also noticed that Mutt extended that same courtesy to those important to him, but old habits die hard. Though Mutt did remember Kiru's name, he often still called him "Boss." The only person Mutt consistently called by their name was Brunhilda.

"You three did good today. You almost actually caught one of these things without even using some fancy technique. Well, besides you having to move, Boss." Mutt added. Kiru gave the orc a slight nod in understanding what he meant. It was because Kiru had to use his Telekinesis technique to help him move. "You remembered to be downwind and targeted an isolated prey." He raised a finger. "But your stealth could still use some improvement, particularly you, Brunhilda. You sounded like a warthog digging through a dead log looking for bugs."

The purple-haired dwarf paladin blushed at the criticism. "How am I supposed to be stealthy, eh? I be wearing plate armor, for crying out loud!" she replied indignantly.

The orc chuckled good-naturedly, unperturbed. "Nah, I can't buy that excuse, Brunhilda. Even the mightiest of beasts such as the dire saber leopards have to rely on stealth out here in Imakandi." He gestured to the expansive plains with sparse trees around them.

Kiru's mission to recover his father's lost items, reclaim his throne, and prevent another global war had been going well so far. He'd acquired the first item—an orb of Psyslime that could morph and change shape to his will—hidden in the Kingdom of Blades. He had also managed to gain a small party of trustworthy allies. Still, it hadn't been without its hiccups. Their former academy headmaster wound up being some sort of monstrous abomination with multiple heads and had tried to kill them. Plus Van Blaine, the man responsible for killing Kiru's father, had taken a personal interest in him. The young psion truly hoped that the winged man would assume he'd died, but he wasn't betting on it. As such, the party had avoided taking any major trails as they'd traversed through Imakandi, homeland of the orcs.

Their current plan was to keep a low profile, get to the orc's capital, and use Mutt's family connections to help them locate the precise location of Kiru's father's second artifact. It hadn't been hard to avoid any civilized areas so far. Imakandi was massive—by far the biggest region in The Great Alliance. Mutt explained that the northern territory of his nation, where they currently were, was the biggest of all the territories. It was also ruled by the Thrar'fang Tribe, a savage clan currently at peace with the ruling M'Baku Clan but were *very* territorial about trespassers. They decided that blazing a new trail south would be the safest, and even though it had been two months, they were close to crossing into safer ground.

They quickly dissected the dead antelope, wanting to get all they could before predators could become interested. After months of training, Mutt had helped the others become much more efficient in the gory tasks of butchering. They removed an impressive amount of the creature's meat and stowed it away in their storage devices, such as Kiru's enchanted ring, before heading out. The special storage items fortunately had a preservative property that prevented any sort of decay as well as eliminated the items' weight, a win-win by all accounts.

Pandemonium continued their trek for another couple of hours, led by Mutt to keep them clear of danger with his bestial senses, before they made camp for the night. They found a small cluster of tall trees, an island itself in the grassland. They were also near a fast-flowing river about a hundred feet down the muddy cliff face below. They started cooking the meat, and the party took some time to relax.

Kiru took in a deep breath of the fresh air. A subtle breeze was blowing across the savanna, making the long, brown grass shift like waves of water. Despite being out in such a wild place, free from towering structures and artificial light for two months, Kiru's breath was still taken away when he looked up in awe at the innumerable stars in the sky. Neither the Royal Academy, with its grandiose stone architecture, nor the small mining town he grew up in had ever had such a clear and breathtaking view of the sky above.

About a month into their journey, the party noticed that the sky had gained a subtle purple tint regardless of whether it was day or night. When they questioned Mutt about it, the blind orc just shrugged. He was unsure as to why that was the case. Everything else so far within the orcs' homeland had appeared normal as far as the environment and the behavior of the creatures were concerned.

"Master, can I come out now? I'm bored."

Feeling safe to do so, Kiru complied with his familiar's request. With a flex of his will, Kiru summoned William from his core. A red ball of energy formed in front of Kiru's head and transformed into an ugly little imp. Kiru had grown accustomed to the hideous-looking demon, but his appearance could still be unsettling. The small, wingless demon's most distinct feature was his skull, or lack thereof. Instead of the expected horned head, William's skull was missing from the middle of the forehead up, exposing his brain for all to see.

"Hahaha! Hello, fools!" he declared to the others as he landed on the ground.

"Little shite," Brunhilda grunted.

"Palabitch," the imp responded in kind, trading insults as a form of greeting. The demon and paladin still butted heads, but they had a truce going for the moment.

Zhaden just gave a subtle nod to the overconfident little demon.

"Oh, hello, little dude," Mutt replied with a grin.

William turned to face Kiru. "Master, it's been two months! When are we gonna get back to civilization? I'm tired of us not fighting anybody! All we do is walk, avoid animals, and occasionally attack some scared creature that doesn't even want to fight back." the bloodthirsty imp pouted.

"Don't worry, little guy. If all goes well, we should be in my clan's territory by tomorrow," Mutt said. "Though I don't know if we'll be fighting anyone there. Well, maybe my sister." He chuckled. "She's always so serious. We used to fight all the time! She's real tough!"

"Yes!" William cheered, then turned to face Kiru. "Master, that sounds like a worthy opponent. When we get to Mutt's territory, we should fight his sister immediately. Someone who was an opponent to the orc is a worthy foe we must conquer!" He grinned as he squeezed a fist in excited anticipation.

Kiru's heart raced in alarm. That was exactly what he *didn't* want to do. "What? No, William. She's his sister. We want her to be an ally, not an enemy," the psion said.

"Yes. Once you defeat her, she will be your ally by being your servant. Then, this land will be yours."

Kiru rolled his eyes and shook his head.

"You want to defeat my sister? Good luck." Mutt said through a mouthful of cooked antelope meat. "Besides, that's not how rulership is obtained in Imakandi."

William put his hands on his hips and looked back at the orc. "Oh, then how *does* one rule here?"

"I'm also interested in this," Zhaden added, his harsh voice sounding like a hiss, as always. "You are part of the noble family here, are you not?"

Kiru was also wondering how the orc nation was governed. Based on how intently Brunhilda was focusing her attention on the conversation, he could tell she was interested as well. Mutt hadn't disclosed too much about his family or the politics of his homeland. From what the psion did know, he was somewhat of an outcast, sent off to the Royal Academy in order to become stronger and better serve his family. Despite that, Mutt didn't really seem to care that much about that, from what Kiru had seen. He only ever seemed serious about fighting, hunting, or protecting his friends.

The blind orc let out a loud belch, then gave an uncharacteristic sigh before wiping the grease off his mouth. "I'll be honest, guys, I don't like talking much about my heritage, just sticking to the basics. You know what I mean? Seeing as how we're not too far from my clan's territory, though, I guess it's time you learn about my family and people," he said with more seriousness than he'd ever exhibited before. "As I've told you before, I am part of the M'Baku Clan, who have ruled Imakandi since its founding after Ragnarok. There are ten main clans that live in Imakandi. Honestly, I don't remember them all, but I know of mine, the Thrar'Fang, the Tau, and the Jabari," he said, counting off his fingers. "Those are the big ones. Oh, and there's an ogre tribe, but they've isolated themselves to the wastelands for some reason I don't know."

Mutt seemed to realize he was rambling, because he focused back on the topic at hand. "Anyway, instead of inheriting rulership without question, after the head chief of our country passes, the shamans arrange a set of trials. Whoever wishes to rule has to qualify to compete in those trials, and then they have to both survive and succeed."

"So, will ye undergo the trial then when yer father passes?" Brunhilda asked.

Mutt gave a wry grin and pointed at himself, "Who, me? Nah, I'm not interested. All I want to do is enjoy the thrill of greater and greater hunts. Oh, and to help out the Boss, of course! I owe him."

The others just stared at him in stunned silence. Mutt had the opportunity to become the future ruler of not only his clan but an entire nation, and he . . . just didn't care. It seemed rather lazy or even selfish depending on how you looked at it. Perhaps, he was just magnanimous and selfless in not wanting to claim power?

"Um, I'm confused. Isn't it your responsibility to care for your people? Isn't that what your father would want?" Kiru asked.

The orc gave a sarcastic smirk and shook his head. "Truth be told, I don't give a damn what my father thinks. All he wanted was a 'worthy heir,' and when I was born blind, he wanted nothing to do with me. I was still part of the royal family but barely treated as such. My mother died when I was young, and it was only by the grace of my sister that I wasn't cast aside. Even most of the citizens shunned me, avoiding me like some sort of plague rat."

"I'm so sorry, Mutt. I-I didn't know things were so bad with your family." Brunhilda said.

"Pfft, family drama, right?" Mutt's casual attitude was back in full swing. "Well, anyway, though things aren't good with dad, Myev's always had my back. She was the one who taught me how to cultivate, fight, and hunt. Without her, I'd probably be as scared as a newborn puppy. Myev can kick my butt in a fight, but because of her training, I'm the best hunter in all of Imakandi. Even the shamans were forced to acknowledge how good I was and give me my first technique."

The nails on his right hand grew out to sharp points. "Fenrir's Claws." He retracted his claws and continued. "Anyway, when my dad realized that I actually *had* some potential, he stopped training Myev to focus on me. Let's just say, it didn't take. As I told you before, I love to hunt, so I'd bail and sneak out of the palace at night and travel the country looking for bigger and better game. The nice part about being blind: you can sneak out in the middle of the night, and the darkness doesn't affect you." Mutt gave a boyish grin.

"So, when my father had enough of my 'hunting trips' and wanted me to 'actually make something of myself,' he sent me off to the academy. You know the rest."

"May I inquire as to how are you able to keep so calm? I'm also a pariah of my people due to the type of mana I use, and it's been difficult not to harbor a grudge against some of my kin for their treatment," Zhaden said.

Mutt's toothy grin grew wide, "Sure, Stabby. My sister taught me that I can't control others, only myself. In other words, I can't rely on others to make me happy. That's up to me. So, I focused not on them and their petty biases, but on what I enjoy." He took a big bite out of his charred antelope leg, "And that is hunting and fighting. Pretty soon, I got so good that even if they didn't like me, they had to respect me. Haha!" He bellowed before taking another bite of the meat.

"Ye said the priesthood taught you a technique. Do ye follow a certain deity?" the paladin asked, a tone of excitement in her voice.

"Oh! Nah. Many of us orcs from Imakandi follow the tenets of the Beast Pantheon, though each tribe favors a particular beast. The tenets include living free and . . . huh, I can't remember the rest," he trailed off.

"The Beast Pantheon?" Kiru asked. He hadn't focused much on religion even when he was at the Royal Academy. So, he thought it wise to get some more information on who this nation worshipped.

"It be a group of sacred beasts who've accumulated enough mana and power to ascend to godhood," the dwarf answered. Kiru knew that being a paladin was a topic about which she was the foremost authority in their party. She continued, "Before Ragnarok, there were two main factions of gods, the Aesir and the Vanir. Afterward, the surviving remnants merged to make a new faction, the Vasir. The magic during that apocalyptic event had empowered many sacred beasts too, ascending them to godhood as well. They comprise the Beast Pantheon. Unlike the two previous factions, the Vasir and the Beast Pantheon are allies."

Both Zhaden and Kiru turned to Mutt to confirm this. The orc just shrugged. It looked like that was news to him too, which wasn't shocking given his poor attention to detail. William had grown bored with the conversation and began chasing small rodents around for food.

Before anyone else could question him, Mutt yawned as the last of the pink in the sky from the sun's light had faded, the color seeming more vivid due to the barrier's effect. "Welp, time for some sleep. We've got a big day ahead of us tomorrow with crossing over into M'Baku Territory. I'll take the last watch," he said, then quickly climbed up the large nearby tree with the speed and grace of a jungle cat.

Zhaden took the first shift. Brunhilda would take the second, and Kiru would go after that before Mutt would finally take over. It was when Kiru went to relieve the paladin of her watch that things took a turn.

CHAPTER THREE

Eye on You

Kiru let out a yawn and rubbed his eyes. The elven heritage his mother had passed down to him lessened his overall sleep requirements, but he still needed a solid six hours. He'd been staying awake a few extra hours each night to cultivate. When people slept and dreamed, there was a higher concentration of mental mana floating around. Needing it to literally move across great swathes of land every day, the young psion had to make sure he replenished as much of the magical energy as he could get. So far, Kiru had achieved a rate of one hour of cultivating the mana from dreaming minds to equal about three hours of movement for him.

While that helped with his mana stores, it definitely cut into his sleep, some nights winding up with notably less than the required amounts. Imakandi was a wild land, and the party's safety had been in question more than a couple of nights while traveling across the orcs' homeland. As Kiru shook himself awake and blinked his vision clear, he noticed it was still dark. The sky was mostly black and there was just the subtlest pink hue. Dawn was almost upon them.

There was a loud noise beside him. Startled, Kiru turned to find William obnoxiously snoring just inches away from him. Kiru chuckled slightly as he rolled his eyes. He then recalled his familiar back inside his core. Kiru could cultivate from William's dreaming mind too, so he nearly always summoned the imp before settling down for the night. William continued to sleep, oblivious to being turned into an orb of red light and brought back into the psion's core.

Besides no longer having to be subjected to the imp's snoring, there was another benefit. Back at the academy, Kiru had discovered that while William was inside his core, he perfectly remembered everything around him, down to most infinitesimal detail. This had helped the psion over and over again, with rewards ranging from remembering the answer to a riddle in a trap-filled tomb to trying out a sword form for the first time on an unsuspecting opponent. It also helped Kiru remember now where his friends were supposed to be sleeping and notice that one was missing. Concerned, he activated Telekinesis and stood up.

Kiru glanced around the campsite. Brunhilda was gone. Her sleep sack was empty. He didn't see any blood or signs of struggle. *Her shields aren't here either. She probably took them with her . . .* Still, he wanted to find her. So, he looked over the small cliff face and across the riverbed. To his surprise, he noticed the purple-haired paladin . . . sneaking? Yes, the armor-clad dwarf was crouching and without a doubt sneaking up on some frog.

Amused by the sight and now thoroughly interested, he quietly walked over to the path down to the riverbed and continued to observe Brunhilda. Carefully, he made it down to her level. When she was finally within a few feet of the frog, the dwarf quickly threw her hands down to grab the amphibian. But her lead foot sank in the wet sand and the noise alerted the frog. It let out a shrill croak and leapt forward, narrowly avoiding Brunhilda's attempt to grab it. "Shite!" She spat in frustration.

"Getting bored with keeping watch?" Kiru asked, breaking the tense silence. *Mutt and Zhaden should be far enough away that our talking won't wake them up,* Kiru thought.

She gasped, snapping her head up and grabbing one of her shields in one deft motion. When she caught sight of her friend, she let out a relieved sigh and placed a hand to her chest. "Oi! By Thor's Hammer, ye scared me there, Kiru." She took a deep breath and composed herself. "If ye must know, I was practicing me stealth," she answered, crossing her arms defiantly.

The psion smiled knowingly. "Really? I thought it was pointless to practice stealth while in heavy armor."

"Well . . . ye know, I . . . think Mutt may be right." Though it was dark, Kiru was pretty sure she was blushing. She had developed a subtle crush on the orc, the two main reasons Mutt hadn't realized it himself was because his blindness kept him unaware of the little looks she would constantly give him . . . and also he was just really oblivious in general. The orc liked the simple things and didn't really bother monitoring people's complexities most of the time. *It may be for the best that Mutt doesn't want to go into politics.*

His thoughts were cut off, and he was brought back to the moment when Brunhilda continued speaking. "And if I be better at stealth, maybe he'd want to spend more time with me," she said nervously while tapping her two pointer fingers together.

Kiru was surprised to see shy Brunhilda actually admitting her feelings out loud. "For the record, I *do* think it is good to practice, but why aren't you asking Zhaden for guidance?" he asked.

She smacked herself in the forehead. "Why didn't I think to ask the blasted rogue?" She looked back up at Kiru. "Don't tell anybody that I be doing this!" she punctuated, glaring daggers at the psion.

Kiru raised his hands up defensively. "Your secret's safe with me. Also, if you'd like, I can try and give you some pointers on your stealth. I'm not as good as the other two, but I've picked up a few of the basics from Zhaden."

A series of emotions danced across Brunhilda's face, embarrassment, pride, and hope being the most prominent. Finally, she agreed. "Aye, go on ahead," she relented. "Oh, but first let me get the frog. The little bugger be a good practice buddy." The paladin searched the sandbar for the creature for half a minute and eventually found it hopping away toward the muddy cliff face not far from the path where Kiru had come down. Not trying to be stealthy this time, she trudged on over and picked it up from atop a piece of muddy driftwood partially lodged in the dirt.

"Hmm, this driftwood be softer than I expected. Guess it's been here for a while," she said, then hammered her fist against it.

Kiru felt his eyes widen. Since Brunhilda was facing him, she didn't see the so-called "driftwood" moving—and not from her strike breaking it. No, the log *wiggled*. Part of the mud fell off from the movement, revealing a massive foot longer than the dwarf's body. "Umm, Brunhilda."

"Yes, Kiru?"

He raised a hand and pointed behind her.

She turned back to see the foot. The foot moved again along with the leg it was attached to. Then, the entire body moved. A thick layer of the muddy wall shifted, falling down to the ground to reveal a massive creature, leaning against the cliff. The humanoid monster wore nothing but a loincloth, revealing a large body of thick skin and fat. It had a surprisingly small head with one massive eye, which was thankfully closed.

Both the dwarf and psion froze. *That's a cyclops!* he thought. Kiru had read about them among the hundreds of texts he'd scanned in his time in the library back at the academy. His perfect memory recalled that the book, *Monsters & Mayhem*, said cyclops weren't the most intelligent, but that didn't make them any less dangerous. In fact, their small brains were also their strength in a way. Their lack of intelligence forced their bodies to contend with both mistakes and harsh environments causing them to evolve tough, durable bodies in order to survive, with skin strong as stone.

"*Oh, shit! Run, bitch, run!*" William said inside Kiru's mind.

Looks like the little asshole is awake. I'm just glad he spoke only to me and not Brunhilda. He figured that if he had, it might have startled the dwarf. He didn't want her to accidentally wake up the hulking monster before them.

The half-elf activated Telepathy and spoke to the dwarf: "*Okay, Brunhilda, I need you to listen to me and do exactly as I say. Don't speak. Just follow my directions.*"

She nodded her head in agreement, not daring to take her eyes off the sleeping behemoth.

"This is going to be a crash course in stealth. First, bend your knees slightly."

The paladin complied.

"Next, spread your arms out wide. Dispersing your weight makes your steps quieter."

She did so, still comically clutching the frog in her right hand.

"Good! Now, carefully turn and walk slowly to me, stepping from heel to toe. You don't need to be fast. You just need to focus on not making a sound."

With a literal sleeping giant threatening to wake up and squash her nearby, Brunhilda took the advice to heart. Slowly, carefully, she began to creep away from the unconscious cyclops. The dwarf was going at a snail's pace, and sure enough, she was getting away without disturbing the monster. Kiru stood at the start of the path leading upward, monitoring and encouraging Brunhilda with his telepathic coaching.

When she neared him, he almost slapped himself on the forehead when he remembered that he could use his Telekinesis on other people as well. He signaled for her to stop. Then, with a force of his will, he channeled his Telekinesis technique around both of their bodies. The two began to levitate and float up quietly. Kiru had to maintain his focus to not drop either of them.

Once they finally set their feet on the top of the hill in relative safety, they both let out a sigh of relief. A nervous chuckle escaped from both of them as well. Just as Kiru felt his pulse start to slow, however, the frog in Brunhilda's hand made its presence known again. Apparently, it had finally had enough of being held captive, letting out a surprisingly loud, shrill croak as its slimy body squeezed itself out of her grip and jumped away. Kiru's heart skipped a beat; the croak had been so pronounced the sound was still echoing. For what felt like an eternity, neither of them moved their bodies.

Kiru could see that Brunhilda wasn't completely still as her mouth moved in what he presumed was a silent prayer. The goddess Hlin didn't answer the dwarf's prayers this time around, however, as a loud, low groan came from below. Shortly afterward, the hulking monster emerged from the muddy cliff face nearby. It grumbled and turned its small head toward the source of the offensive noise. Its large single eye opened to lock on the pair of cultivators. The cyclops snarled, revealing a set of sharp, jagged teeth. Its breath assaulted the pair's nostrils, hitting them with a mixture of mud and rotten meat. They winced, and a hand the size of Brunhilda's entire body clasped the cliff edge with a loud crunch.

This time, Kiru *did* heed William's words and he ran. The pair of them took off, sprinting toward the tree where their allies were. If they had to fight a giant cyclops, they were going to need all hands on deck. The cyclops lifted itself up to their level and quickly began pursuit. With each stomp of its large feet, the ground audibly shook. Kiru spared a glance to see it had an entire acacia tree in one hand, wielding it like a simple club. The ground below continued to shake as each lumbering step sent tremors in its chase.

Those loud stomps awoke the sleeping orc and gold drakonid. Zhaden's reptilian eyes widened first in surprise, then in fear as he processed what was going on. Mutt, on the other hand, activated his Fenrir's Claws technique, turning both his hands and feet into clawed animal-like limbs. The orc roared, then jumped down from the tree and began running on all fours toward the cyclops. Zhaden shook off his shock and began running as well, his long legs helping him gain ground.

Kiru summoned William to his shoulder. "Keep an eye on that thing!" he ordered.

The little imp grumbled but did as bid from what the psion could tell, focusing on their six and the monster following them. Not long after, William proved his worth. "Duck!" he shouted.

Both cultivators dropped to the ground without question, a split second before a tree club whooshed right above their heads. They stood back up and took off running once again. But before they made it much farther, a large foot stomped right beside them with a *boom*—the cyclops was on them. Kiru was scared to fight such a foe but was resolute in his sense of obligation to protect his friends. He and Brunhilda gave each other a knowing look before bracing themselves as they turned back to face the monster. Kiru was relieved that she had come to the same conclusion as he had: they had no choice but to fight. Only then did Kiru process that Brunhilda had left her shields down by the river, as her hands were balled up into fists.

The cyclops shouted unintelligibly as it raised its club up high to smash the pair. To Kiru's relief, that was right when Mutt entered the fray. The beast mana cultivator leaped over his friends and slammed into the monster's abdomen, clawing furiously at its exposed belly. The cyclops groaned in surprise, stumbling a couple of steps back due to the orc's momentum before slapping Mutt, sending him flying about twenty feet to Kiru's right, his body skipping across the tall grass. "I'm good!" the orc shouted once he had finally landed.

Kiru nodded gratefully, then turned back to the cyclops. Mutt's claws were sharp, but the cyclops' hide was almost stonelike. Still, the orc was able to draw blood, carving out a small, exposed wound in its belly. It wasn't invulnerable.

The cyclops looked down at its abdomen and the blood on its hand. The one-eyed monster was clearly unused to being hurt because it scowled in indignant rage, then let out a guttural bellow. Zhaden had finally made it to the others and also joined the fight. The gold drakonid hurled a set of daggers. The cyclops used its free arm to block the blades. The knives bounced harmlessly off its stony flesh. It then charged forward, using the tree like a battering ram.

Zhaden, Kiru, and Brunhilda all jumped to the side, out of the way of the monster's mad dash.

"Brunhilda, since you don't have your shields, stay back and focus on support. Zhaden, keep its attention on you. Mutt and I will focus on bringing it down." Kiru sent telepathically. The psion let out an inward sigh of relief when they immediately complied. He wouldn't let them down. Brunhilda was their tank, but she wasn't fast, and without her shields, she'd be a sitting duck. Zhaden could serve as the primary distraction in a pinch.

The gold drakonid threw another blade at the cyclops, this one aimed at the exposed wound. It wasn't just any dagger, though, the thin, more elongated blade undeniably his enchanted Bloodstep Stiletto. The moment the weapon slammed into the exposed wound, the blood that touched the blade triggered its magic. In an instant, Zhaden was teleported right to the blade itself. Quite literally at the belly of the beast, Zhaden grabbed the dagger and began thrusting it in and out like a prison shiv. The smell of iron began to permeate the air, filling the psion's nostrils as small fountains of blood began to shoot out from the monster, drenching the ground beneath and coating the drakonid.

The cyclops roared again then, leaning down to try and bite the rogue in two. Kiru knew that his roguish friend was ready, and sure enough, Zhaden did a graceful backflip, pushing off the monster's body and avoiding its teeth.

To Kiru's left, Mutt roared and charged back into the fight. The cyclops, now truly frustrated, swung its club at the oncoming orc.

"Divine Shield!" the paladin shouted from behind the psion as she activated one of her three techniques. A column of holy light surrounded Mutt and intercepted the club. With a loud crash, it pushed it back and set the top of it alight in flame. It would eventually burn the entire tree club to ashes, but since it was so thick, the flames would take some time. Kiru rushed toward the cyclops, drawing out his Fu Tao. He sliced at the monster's thick legs as he ran in between them. His steel didn't break the skin. The other, however—the one made from the Psyslime—managed to successfully cut into the muscle.

The giant monster growled as it gritted its teeth, thick blood oozing from its wound. It then mule-kicked the psion with its uninjured leg, forcing the air from Kiru's lungs and sending him nearly tumbling over the cliff. Fortunately, he tucked his body in, rolled across the ground, and landed a good distance away from the cliff face. He shook his head, removing some of the dirt now caked in his black and red hair. Kiru grunted as he quickly stood up. It was out of habit versus any actual need, a perk of being unable to feel any pain. That lack of pain also aided him in not losing focus. He turned back to face the monster, and shook his head once again, this time to get the ringing out of his ears from that attack.

"Master, that was embarrassing. You're a conqueror, and that monster made you look like a little weakling." William said, brushing the shirt off his own shoulders. "I mean, look at it. Its tiny head is almost all eyeball. All you need to do is just poke it smack dab in the middle of it, and then it'll be easy."

The cyclops glared and began to trudge toward the psion, yet paused its advance when Zhaden activated his Duplication technique. Though the drakonid was behind the cyclops, he conjured two illusory duplicates of himself in front of the large monster. The cyclops cocked its head to the side and gave an unintelligible grunt, which sounded suspiciously like, "Huh?!" It only hesitated for a moment before swinging the burning tree down on one of the duplicates. The makeshift club went straight through the illusion, crashing into the ground with a boom.

Mutt then began crawling up its back, harassing the monster with a series of strikes.

It groaned and swiped at the orc with its free hand, not succeeding in hurting Mutt but protecting its head successfully, nonetheless.

William is right, its large eye is a weakness, Kiru thought. The problem is, the monster knew it, and it made sure to protect its vulnerable spot. With the only ranged attacks being Zhaden's daggers, they needed someone to get in close. Kiru gave his familiar a predatory grin as an idea struck, "You're right, William. We just have to poke its eye, and I know just the person for the job."

Before the imp could protest, the psion grabbed William and hurled him toward the monster with all his might. William let out a panicked scream as he flew through the air.

As the demon soared, Kiru activated Telekinesis on him. The psion had done this once before in a fight against an axe-wielding barbarian. William continued to scream as he flew. Familiars could die just like their masters, but Kiru was confident in his plan despite its recklessness. That was due to his Telekinesis. He could precisely aim the imp exactly where he desired him to go. Kiru telekinetically maneuvered him, and the imp landed square on the cyclops' eyeball.

The cyclops winced, then its large pupil locked with William's beady eyes.

The demon let out a high-pitched cry of fear before he began scratching at the eye out of desperation.

The monster's skin may have been rock-like but its cornea was not. It let out a deep, pained scream, and slapped at its own eyeball in response.

William gasped as the large hand came toward him and jumped off, leaping into some nearby brush to cushion his fall.

The cyclops continued to groan as it pressed against its injured eye. It began waving its burning club around wildly, afraid of being struck by an unseen opponent.

No one could get near the mad, blind cyclops as it flailed its burning club about. Kiru hadn't taken that possibility into account and was wondering if he'd made a wise choice in blinding it. None of the party had any ranged techniques, so they would eventually need to close the distance in order to kill it. The blinded monster's fear and pain caused it to move quicker, spreading the hot flames on its club across the dry grass underneath. Small pockets of fire started to build up from the swings, and they were quickly growing.

Mutt stuck his head up in the air and began to sniff loudly. He turned his head off in the distance and grinned. "Hey, you smelly monster, come get some!"

The cyclops, with its eye squeezed tight, was still blinded, but it turned its head to the noise. It began lumbering toward where Mutt was, swinging his burning club like a cane. Its thick skin was unbothered by the flames its club cast upon the ground in front of it and with each step, stomped out most of them underneath its feet.

Mutt began running away but at a controlled pace, making sure the monster was still following him. "Don't worry, I've got an idea!" he shouted to the others as he led the monster farther away.

The three others all joined back up and watched Mutt continue to guide the angered, injured cyclops. "Where do you think he's leading the creature?" the rogue asked before scanning the quickly growing flames.

"I'm not sure," Kiru answered as he squinted, following their path. "Brunhilda, I recommend going and getting your shields now," he said with obvious concern in his voice.

"Aye," the dwarf hastily agreed, then left to head back down to the riverbed.

Kiru knew Zhaden didn't have Darkvision, so there was no way he could see much outside from the light of the burning tree, which was getting smaller and smaller in the distance. Kiru did have the ability to see in darkness, but it wasn't as good as a full-blooded elf or dwarf. Still, he could easily make out what was happening as they quickly moved away from the fires.

Mutt was expertly leading the cyclops onto what looked to be a large, writhing mass. The orc let out a bestial roar toward it, and Kiru realized that it wasn't a singular mass at all, but a grouped-up herd of some kind of bovine creatures.

The orc's roar appeared to have disturbed the creatures because dozens of eyes all turned to face him at once.

Kiru's blood went cold as he saw the raw anger flash in the creatures' eyes. They glowed red in the firelight.

The beasts let out a collective howl and charged toward the orc and cyclops.

Mutt did a complete 180 and booked it back toward his friends. He managed to leap and roll out of the way of the blinded cyclops' club swing as well. He kept running for another hundred feet before stopping and turning back.

The beasts, which looked to be some sort of bipedal bulls, attacked the cyclops. A couple of them were sent flying by a burning tree club, but they quickly overwhelmed the monster like a swarm of vengeful ants, taking advantage of its previous injuries to rapidly overtake it.

The cyclops groaned, then began to let out pained cries as it was repeatedly gored and ultimately disemboweled. The flames were abruptly put out by the mass of beasts trampling over them.

Mutt placed both hands on his hips and laughed in triumph. Then, the cyclops' cries suddenly went silent. Mutt didn't seem to pay attention to it and continued laughing. With the monster dead, the bull creatures all looked up to the orc. Only then did Mutt seem to realize what had happened, and his smile immediately faded.

The beasts began to give chase once more. "Hahaha! What an imbecile!" William cackled, as he hopped back on Kiru's shoulder.

"Is he?" Zhaden asked as he watched what was happening.

"Yes," the psion answered Zhaden's question.

In his rush to try and get away from the creatures, Mutt was leading them toward the party! "Grab our stuff, now!" he shouted. Zhaden ran around the flames to quickly shove whatever he could into their bags of holding while Kiru went back toward where Brunhilda had gone off to.

She had come back up with her shield just as he made it to the ledge, "What's all the fussing for? Did ye think I couldn't find my own shields?"

Kiru shook his head, "No, worse!" He pointed behind him. While the flames had grown stronger, the literal stampede coming their way couldn't be ignored.

"By me goddess's purple hair!" she exclaimed, and they began running away. Kiru had been wrong in his previous assessment. There wasn't a dozen beasts. There had to be at least a hundred of them angrily stampeding in their direction. Fortunately, Mutt had gained some ground on the pursuers by running on all fours. He made it to the dwarf and psion the same time Zhaden did. Unlike the drakonid, however, the orc didn't stop moving.

"Keep running!" Mutt said in a desperate panic as he moved past them, continuing along the river's edge. Trusting that the orc native knew best, and not wanting to test that against a stampede of angry beasts, Kiru followed after Mutt. The rest of the party appeared to be of the same mindset because they almost instantly joined in the running. They ran with all their might, but they couldn't keep this pace up for long.

Brunhilda had undergone a risky procedure to save her life when she had been close to dying back at the academy. Her blood had been transmuted to trollblood, and it mutated her body to a degree as well. She had gained an increased regeneration rate, purple hair, and longer arms. It did not, however, elongate the dwarf's legs. So, while her changes were impressive, her speed hadn't improved at all.

The paladin knew it too, so that's why she spoke up. "Where we be going, Mutt? Shouldn't we try and cross the river?" The river beside them was slow moving but deep and wide.

"We're going downstream, Brunhilda. The river's too slow to lose the minotaurs up here," Mutt shouted back over his shoulder.

The bull creatures—apparently called minotaurs—were slowly but surely gaining ground on the party. They hadn't been at all deterred by the fast-growing
flames and were instead just running through them. They trampled over the burning grass with ease and put out the likely would-be wildfire in moments, their
eyes glistening with bloodlust as their anger pushed them forward. Kiru's ears
were filled with the rumbling of their hooves. He looked over to realize it wasn't
just the beasts' feet, it was the river as well. As they continued running alongside
the water, the river grew faster and faster, becoming louder as it began to rush
along even more violently.

"Uh, Mutt, how are we going to cross that? It's now a rushing rapid!" Kiru
asked.

"Simple, Boss. There's a bridge up ahead."

Kiru looked to see that there was indeed a rickety bridge there. Given different circumstances, he would *never* have considered this a legitimate option
for his friends. With his ability to use Telekinesis to levitate himself, he should
be fine, but they didn't have that luxury. Situations do change, though, and
Kiru was now considering the bridge to be their best chance. That option was
quickly taken away from them, however. As they neared, Kiru saw a surprisingly familiar frog on top of a rock by the bridge's edge. It seemed to narrow its
eyes and glare spitefully at the paladin. Then, while still looking at Brunhilda,
it opened its mouth and launched its tongue against one of the support ropes
like a whip.

Normally, that would be of very little consequence, but of course, the frogs
in Imakandi had a degree of danger that no other had. Mutt had told them
during their travels that the small amphibians in this land had a sharp spike on
the edge of their tongues, allowing them to impale their prey, or in this case,
cut a rope. The rope thinned, frayed, then broke with an audible snap. No longer fully supported, the bridge groaned loudly before completely collapsing
into and being swept away by the rushing river. *What had Brunhilda done to
that frog to make it so mad?! Note to self: never use a frog to practice stealth!* Kiru
thought.

"Okay, change of plan!" Mutt said with a mixture of exasperation and excitement as he made a sudden hard turn. He continued running but now at an angle
leading directly to the river. "We jump."

"We jump?" the others said in unison.

"Yes, we jump." This time, he pointed ahead of them. There was an abrupt
end to the river, and the noise of crashing water up ahead was louder than ever.
It was a waterfall!

"You can't be serious!" William barked.

"You've never dealt with minotaurs, have you?" Mutt asked. "Those things won't stop until either we're dead or they lose sight of us, little guy!" Mutt shouted back, frustration evident despite his pleasant nature.

Deciding having William out was one thing too many to deal with, Kiru recalled his familiar back into his core. All four members of Pandemonium made an abrupt stop once they reached the waterfall's edge. They turned to see the enraged creatures just a hundred feet away and closing. The blind orc stood in front of his allies, between them and the beasts, his clawed hands spread out wide as if to protect them.

"You sure about this, Mutt?" Kiru asked.

"Aye, are ye? This be more cockamamie than some of Kiru's plans," Brunhilda said.

Though he wasn't looking at the psion, the orc grinned. "Yep," he said, then turned and tackled his three friends over the cliffside and into the waters below.

CHAPTER FOUR

Welcome to the Jungle

The churning river tossed the members of Pandemonium back and forth as it carried them along. Kiru was pretty sure that he'd broken his arm because he'd heard an audible *crunch* as he was slammed into a large boulder in the middle of the rapids. It was one of the few times he was actually glad he couldn't feel his body. To say the river was fast-flowing would be an understatement.

The farther they went downriver, the more violent the waters became, flinging them about like they were ragdolls in the middle of a tornado.

Were the water any calmer, however, Kiru most likely would have drowned, pulled down by the sheer weight of his gear and wet clothing. But the current was so strong and the depths so varied and irregular that the party were inevitably forced up and even able to catch a breath of air to keep them alive from time to time.

None of them could tell how long they were being carried down the violent rapids in the dark of night. Thankfully it was almost summer in Imakandi, because the water would've been even colder and more violent at a different time of year. After what felt like hours but was likely only ten minutes or so of an adrenaline-fueled fight for survival, Mutt found a way out. The blind orc clicked his mouth and used echolocation like a bat. He then doggy-paddled ahead, using the current to accelerate his speed even further.

Then, with all his might, the orc reached up and sunk his claws into the bark of a tree overhanging the water from above. It was on the very edge of the rapids, hanging on to the side by its strong roots. Mutt climbed up and got himself out, shaking the water off his long brown mohawk before crying out, "Up here!"

Kiru's head was above the water at just the right time to hear him. Sensing a lifeline, he blinked his eyes clear and saw where the orc was. Just before he could be thrust back into the water, he activated Telekinesis on himself. The psion shot out of the water and landed on the prone tree with a wet *thunk*. He gasped and shook his vision clear. He saw Zhaden's gold scales glimmering in the light of the rising sun. "Here!" he called out and reached down to the drakonid. The lanky rogue clasped Kiru's hand.

Kiru groaned as both the drakonid's surprising weight and the force of the current almost pulled him back into the water. "Mutt, help!" The bestial orc simply reached down and grabbed the back of the rogue's wet tunic. He heaved him onto the tree with one hand. He was at Ruby, a whole tier above Kiru and Brunhilda, and it showed through his sheer strength.

Right after he similarly pulled Zhaden up as well, Mutt began snapping his head around frantically, sniffing loudly. "Where's Brunhilda?! I don't smell her!" he asked in a panic.

Kiru also began looking around. If Mutt's enhanced senses couldn't detect her, that wasn't good news. *Something must be obscuring his ability to find her*, Kiru thought. Both Kiru and Zhaden began hastily scanning the area. Though the sun was rising, it was still pretty dark out, so the drakonid's vision was limited. Despite that, Zhaden finally located her. "There!" he hissed and pointed into the water.

"Where?!" Mutt shouted.

Kiru could see where the rogue pointed. There under the water was a tuft of purple hair. Brunhilda was being pulled under the current, her thick armor holding her down. "I got her!" the psion shouted. "Mutt, hold on to me."

As soon as the orc put an arm around Kiru, his body went limp. Kiru stopped Telekinesis on his own body in order to more fully concentrate on using it on the dwarf. His head shook with the effort, but he was able to lift the paladin out of the water soon after she went past the tree. Brunhilda let out a violent cough as she expelled water from her lungs, then took in a sharp inhale of air.

"Get us to high ground. I'll carry her over there." Kiru strained. Both the orc and drakonid readily complied and the two gracefully climbed the tree with the psion in tow. Kiru continued his focus, channeling his mana and dragging Brunhilda across the air toward them. They quickly made it to safety, and the psion was able to bring the paladin to them soon after.

They all collapsed in a heap, sopping wet, their breathing heavy. The sun continued to rise, bringing more light and warmth to their shivering bodies, though, being at Ruby-level, Mutt and Zhaden didn't need as long as Brunhilda and Kiru to recover.

Kiru also asked Brunhilda to heal him as he was still concerned about his potentially broken arm. The skilled paladin gladly obliged with a use of her Healing Hands technique. Kiru's arm jerked as the bones snapped back into place. "Thanks," he said.

"Any time." She waved him off and the two began to explore where they'd washed up. Unlike the large savanna grassland from before, they were now on the edge of a large jungle. A strange, two-headed crocodile tried to ambush them, but Mutt quickly showed the animal who was boss. The orc turned it on its back, exposing its soft underbelly, and ripped out its heart. Two heads, but only one heart.

The orc also reached into the reptile's chest cavity and ripped out a small, round, crystalline gem. It was a sacred beast core. Mutt tossed it in the air and swallowed it whole like a snack. "Phew! That was a close one," he said cheerfully.

"By me grandmother's war shield, Mutt! Why did ye anger an entire herd of minotaurs?!"

"Oh, well, I heard the sacred beasts off in the distance. We could've handled the cyclops, but we likely would've been too exhausted to deal with the minotaurs on top of it. Minotaurs are really territorial, so I decided to let them handle the cyclops. Though I didn't realize just how many of them there were. My bad." The orc scratched the back of his head and chuckled nervously.

"You mentioned that name earlier too—what exactly is a minotaur?" Kiru asked.

Mutt cocked his head. "You don't know about 'em?"

Kiru flushed a little, "Um . . . no. I didn't read too much about sacred beasts in the library." Before learning about his psionic powers and heritage, Kiru had grown up pretty sheltered and isolated. His mother had kept him hidden in plain sight, raising him in the isolated mining town of Bristleton. It was right on the edge of the Kingdom of Blades, and it had no through traffic. Kiru had gained much of his knowledge and know-how from his internship at the academy library.

An unintended bonus from having William as his familiar was that Kiru had perfect recall. He could tell you the fifth word on the fourth line on the third page of any book he'd read if you asked him. So, to make up for his lack in knowledge and understanding, he began ravenously consuming the various books, tomes, and scrolls within the library. Unfortunately, the building was extensive and magical, so Kiru wasn't able to gain *all* the information within. One such topic was the sacred beasts of Alterra. Hopefully, he could rectify that deficiency here. With such a high volume of sacred beasts living in the orcs' homeland, the place must have contained a repository of in-depth knowledge on the topic somewhere.

"Well, minotaurs are a type of sacred beast that originates from Imakandi. They're strong but will leave you alone if you don't bother them," Mutt explained. "They are part of the great herd that migrates around our nation. If you try to hurt one, though, all of them go into a frenzy like those ones we saw. They won't stop until they either kill you . . . or lose track of you. Seeing as we weren't likely going to be able to kill a hundred of 'em, I thought jumping in the river was our best option."

The orc scratched the unkempt goatee growing on his chin, "Still, that doesn't deter people from hunting them. They are a worthy prey!" He chuckled. "I've only ever hunted one once in my life, and it was a straggler that had gotten too far away from the main group. That thing was still a tough opponent, and it was an old one. This group was young and healthy, and they killed that cyclops in seconds! How amazing was that?" he asked excitedly before his face grew pensive, "Though, that was also strange. Cyclops don't tend to venture that far north. I wonder why that one was even there."

"Perhaps we can analyze the ecology of your homeland after we figure where exactly we are now?" Zhaden hissed, frustration evident in his voice.

Mutt just smiled, "Good point, Stabby." He turned to face the dense jungle ahead of them. He sniffed a couple of times, then cupped his hands to his ears. "That's a jungle lark I hear." He turned his head. "And . . . a whispering serpent." Mutt's body went tense at the words. Kiru could see some of the hairs on his mohawk sticking out like those of a nervous cat. "We went south but too far west from our destination. We're not in the land inhabited by my clan." He snorted dismissively. "We're in Jabari Territory."

"That be a bad thing? Ye said that the tribes follow yours, right? If this be controlled by a different clan other than the really defensive ones we avoided, shouldn't this be better?" Brunhilda asked.

Mutt sighed, his typical carefree attitude gone. "Yes and no, Brunhilda. While the Jabari are not as savage as the Thrar'fang, peace has been . . . tenuous at best. They won't outright attack us, but seeing us in their territory without their permission could cause . . . problems for my clan. Problems I'd rather avoid, if you get my meaning."

Kiru could read between the lines. They'd unintentionally gone out of the frying pan and into the fire. The Jabari weren't a direct violent threat but a scheming political one. Kiru believed that to be the worse of the two options. "Well, let's get a fire going, dry ourselves off some more, eat that beast if it's edible, and get out of here as quickly as possible. The plan hasn't changed. We get to the capital to enlist the help of Mutt's clan to help us find my father's second item and resupply for more travels. Then, we have everything we need and leave before anyone starts asking questions about us."

"Uh, Kiru, do ye think we can have a day to clean and recover while we're there? I mean, I understand that time be pressing and all, but I'd *really* love a bath," Brunhilda said.

"I believe that would be wise as well," Zhaden added. "You warm-bloods have acquired a strong scent that the river hasn't managed to wash off."

"I don't care as long as we get out of here soon," Mutt said.

Kiru was surprised at the suggestion. They had been using the natural bodies of water to clean themselves, and he thought they were doing an okay job. He took a quick moment to sniff one of his armpits and found that he was wrong. "Okay, we can take a day to shop and use a bathhouse," the psion relented. "Zhaden, were you able to save our bags?"

The drakonid nodded and raised two bags, one like a duffle bag, the other like a purse. To Kiru's surprise, they were as dry as ever. *Gotta love enchanted items!* "Good, then the plan hasn't changed. Let's get a fire going and put on some dry clothes. If all goes well, we'll head out in an hour."

"If it's okay, Boss, I'd recommend we avoid the fire or eating the two-headed croc I dealt with earlier. We can get to the capital today if we hurry, and I don't want us to delay or draw any—" A twig broke off in the distance, and Mutt turned his head and flashed his teeth in that direction. After a few tense seconds, he settled down. "—unwanted attention." He growled.

Anything that could make the often-laidback orc tense, gripped Kiru's heart. "Sounds good. You're the expert here, Mutt," he said, trying to keep himself composed. He put a hand on the orc's shoulder. "I trust you."

Mutt seemed to detect his leader's nerves. "Don't worry, Boss. We'll get through this." The party changed into some dry clothes. Another nice thing about the spatial storage devices was that the items stayed in the exact same condition as what they were stored. In other words, no wet clothes!

Shortly afterward, Pandemonium began traversing through the dense jungle. Mutt took point, expertly navigating through the foliage. He climbed up trees, swung on branches, uprooted bushes, and crawled under impasses. The orc was in his element. The rest of the party . . . not so much. Where Mutt could climb up and swing from one tree to another to avoid an obstacle, the others were forced to go around it. Kiru was able to levitate himself over or around certain areas but didn't use his power on his friends unless requested. While in this foreign jungle, he wanted to conserve his mana in case any threats reared their heads. They were still going at an impressive pace, but not every plant was devoid of thorns, or poison, or in one particular case, a mouth and teeth.

By early afternoon, they made it to the edge of a large clearing within the jungle, at which point Mutt held up an arm to stop them from going any further. Kiru noticed that his mohawk had flared up once again.

"What do you detect?" Zhaden asked, his hissing voice lowered to an almost-imperceptible decibel.

Mutt's ears twitched slightly. "Something's coming. I smell cats." He paused to smell again, "And snakes."

The party didn't have time to question him further as there was a crashing sound from the forest across from them. To their left, what looked to be a bipedal lion adorned in a variety of bones and hides ran out into the clearing. The creature was an albino, its eyes solid red. Judging by the intelligence in its eyes and the aura of a Gold coming off it, Kiru knew it was no ordinary beast. *It must be another sacred beast like the minotaurs,* he thought. The lion creature had a look of fear in its eyes, and both of its arms were wrapped around its chest as if it were carrying something. Its mouth was wide open and it was breathing heavily.

"No . . . it can't be," Mutt uttered.

The sacred beast stole a glance back but didn't pause. It took a few more steps, and just as its head turned back for a moment, a perfectly timed spear flew out of the thick jungle. The weapon's arc matched the creature's trajectory, and it struck the beast right at the base of the skull. The blade pierced through its thick mane, straight through the back of its head, and exited halfway out of its mouth. The sacred beast coughed as it fell forward, and a few items fell off its person from the force of the impact. The spear tip embedded itself in the ground, leaving the beast impaled. It was dead before it hit the dirt, though it was cold comfort to the party.

Just then, a loud cacophony of hissing came from the area of the jungle where the spear had come from. Out came seven orcs. Though they were natives to Imakandi the same as Mutt, that was where the similarities ended. Their hair was short—shaved completely bald or kept very close to the scalp. They were well-groomed with clean-shaved faces. All of them wore sleeveless black tunics made from some sort of panther hide.

The other major difference was their skin. Across their arms and in a line from the bridge of their noses all around their head, were a set of concentric raised scars. If Kiru didn't know any better, he would have said they were reptilian scales. They all gave off the feeling that they were at Gold. Each held a spear, ornamented with fur and bone, and they all began to carefully approach the dead beast.

The feline's body went limp, and its arm slunk down, dropping something that landed softly on the grass. Under the shadow of the corpse, it was hard for Kiru to determine what it was, but eventually he saw it was moving under some sort of blanket. After a moment, the blanket slipped off, revealing a small, hairy, brown creature. *Is that a cub?* Kiru thought. After a couple of more seconds, he had confirmation that he was correct. Peeking around the covering was a tiny leonine face that undeniably belonged to a cub.

CHAPTER FIVE

Extremism

Brunhilda gasped and began to rise to the poor creature's defense, but Mutt put a meaty hand on her shoulder. "Wait. We're on their land. They're within their rights to hunt," he whispered.

She gave him a disgusted look and tugged her shoulder away. "I swore an oath to protect the innocent, Mutt." She spat, keeping her voice low. "I cannot abide letting these people kill an innocent little baby, even if it be an animal. Besides, yer always goin' on about havin' a 'good hunt.' What be so good about this?!"

The orc was taken aback, surprised at the truth and conviction of the paladin's words. Before he could say anything else, she took off out of the brush. She gripped both her shields and raised them, placing herself between the scarred orcs and the cub who was still cowering by the corpse of its larger companion.

The orcs were surprised by the sudden intrusion. They all hesitated for a moment before flashing their sharp teeth and growling as they lowered their spears at Brunhilda. They took a couple of steps forward but were visibly even more surprised by the rest of Pandemonium rushing out to join the dwarf. The orcs muttered in their native tongue and growled even louder.

Mutt then raised his hands up and said, "Wait," in Orcish, but before more could be said, the seven spear wielders attacked.

Kiru was taken by surprise at the orcs' speed. Mutt had told them over their months of travel that the people of his homeland were beast mana cultivators like him. As such, each one's technique was taken from the sacred beast that inhabited their nation. It became readily apparent that these orcs had been inspired by some sort of snake. They charged in a serpentine pattern, their bodies literally changing as they neared.

Zhaden, being the agile rogue he was, ran forward toward one of the orcs. His dexterity allowed him to duck under a spear thrust and get up close to his opponent. He wrapped a lanky arm around the orc's chin and placed a dagger against her neck. Normally, that would have been enough to subdue an opponent but not these orcs.

She dropped her spear and grabbed the dagger. Despite it cutting her palm, she forced it just far enough that it was no longer touching her neck. Then she activated one of her techniques. Before Zhaden's very eyes, the orc hunter's neck elongated until it had to have been at least six feet long. In a display of flexibility and power, she twisted it to face the opposite direction of her body. She gave a predatory glare at the drakonid and opened her mouth so wide that Kiru was sure it had to have been dislocated. Then, she struck. Her head lashed at the rogue like a whip. Zhaden let go of his dagger and rolled out of the way. His foot landed on one of the items that had been flung off the sacred beast. Zhaden quickly picked it up and lashed his tail from side to side. It looked like he would have to try a new weapon.

Two orcs went after Kiru. As they neared the psion, their legs morphed into a single large snake tail, accentuating their serpentine movements and making them harder for him to keep focus on. They lashed out at him, intermixing spear thrusts and whipping out their tails to try and trip him.

Kiru used Clean the Hoof to deflect one spear upward before slashing at the other one to his left with Hammer the Boards.

The snake-like orc recoiled before his blade could hit, then hissed and spun, whipping his tail at the psion's legs.

Kiru jumped over the tail but was instantly attacked by the first orc's spear once again. The psion was able to block the attack midair but was thrown back from the momentum of the blow. He landed on his feet, gritting his teeth in frustration. The fighting continued on like that for another half-minute, Kiru holding his own but with such unorthodox opponents, it was naturally more challenging for him. The reach of his opponents' weapons surpassed that of his hook blades, and the Cruel Mantis Style he'd learned from his tutor back at the academy was tailored to fighting bipedal opponents. The snake-like orcs were not the intended targets.

If only my blades were a little longer, he thought to himself as he deflected another spear thrust. Kiru then remembered that his Psyslime blade wasn't just a blade. It was in that shape because it conformed to his will. He expressly remembered the hologram of his father with the Psyslime. Ruken had made it fly around him and change shape with just a flex of his mind. Kiru didn't yet have that level of control over it, but as long as he maintained physical contact with the slime, it would change with ease.

Kiru smiled as an idea grew. When one of the two "snake orcs," as William was calling them inside his mind, came to stab him from behind, he spun and used his steel-bladed Fu Tao to catch the weapon in the hook of his blade. He then forced his Psyslime blade to change into a rope. Kiru whipped it out and had it wrap around the orc's torso.

The orc's eyes instantly grew wide upon being snared.

The psion then yanked and pulled the orc in close. In one fluid motion, he dislodged his Fu Tao and punched the orc square in the mouth with his guard.

The orc spit out a few broken teeth right before his eyes rolled back. As he fell down unconscious, his tail morphed back into a set of green legs.

One down, one to go, Kiru thought.

Of Pandemonium's four members, Mutt had the easiest time fighting. The beast mana cultivator grew up battling various creatures and cultivators like himself, so Kiru reasoned that was why he was able to dodge and parry their strikes. Mutt was also at Ruby, so he was naturally stronger as well. While Rubies could be easily taken out by a Gold, especially with superior numbers, if a Ruby supplemented their rank with enough training, the odds of defeat were much less likely. Luckily for Mutt, he *did* have the necessary training.

The blind orc activated his Fenrir's Claws technique. He slashed, punched, and kicked at his opponents, all without sustaining injury to himself. He almost got hit once by accident when Zhaden's opponent nearly collapsed onto him. The assassin had pulled out a rather deadly tool Kiru had never seen him use before: a garrote. Kiru grimaced thinking about how brutal a tool the sharp, thin metal wire was against an opponent with such an obscenely large neck. Once Zhaden got the garrote around his enemy, the snake-necked orc gripped onto it and began thrashing her head about violently as she was being strangled.

She ended up striking Kiru's other opponent in the back with her flailing head, causing it to stumble, thus unintentionally helping the psion defeat it. Brunhilda, focusing on protecting the cub, opted for the turtle approach. She took her two large shields and formed a protective shell around herself and the cowering lion creature. The spearmen struck at her repeatedly, using spear thrusts and tail whips, but the paladin was able to take the punishment. Still, as time went on, Kiru could tell from the speed of their strikes that they would be able to eventually get around her.

Kiru heard Mutt growl. The orc must have noticed the paladin in trouble. In response, he threw his two opponents into hers, forcing all four of them to crash into a nearby tree. "Enough!" he shouted.

Zhaden still held a garrote around his opponent. She was still conscious but visibly subdued, her face conveying defeat. Meanwhile, the other orcs—those that were still conscious at least—were slowly forcing themselves up.

Mutt dismissed all of his bestial enhancements and held his head up high, like the noble he was. It was the first time Kiru or any of his party had ever seen the orc act in such a way, and of his own volition to boot. It was clear that while Mutt didn't enjoy being a noble, the training was still there. The blind orc's pure white eyes seemed somehow to glare at the other orcs. "Do you know who I am? I am M'baku M'toon, son to M'baku Otto, your king," he declared in his native tongue. Kiru fortunately understood the orc's language thanks to his perfect recall from studying it at the academy.

The Jabari orcs looked at Mutt and then at each other nervously. Kiru could hear a couple asking their compatriots underneath their breath if Mutt was telling the truth. It was clear they didn't know for sure if Mutt was who he claimed to be.

Then a loud clapping echoed out from the section of the dense jungle where the Jabari had emerged from. Kiru couldn't tell the source, but he could sense both power and danger coming from it. It was a terrifying aura that washed over the entire party, a genuine threat likely far beyond their capability to combat. After a few seconds, another Jabari orc came out. This one was taller than the others and was adorned in many more bones, even wearing a giant snake skull on top of his head. His neck was long but not as exaggerated as the one Zhaden still had the garrote around, and it was completely covered in golden rings.

He gave off the power of a Sapphire. At what tier within that cultivation rank, Kiru was unsure. He hadn't been taught about the specifics of that rank, since he had only reached Gold back at the academy. It didn't matter, though. Even without his clan backing him up, the psion knew their chances of surviving would be slim-to-none if they fought.

"Ugh! What an ugly guy!" William called out inside Kiru's mind.

The orc truly looked like he was part snake. While the others had just a line of concentric scale scars across their faces, his entire face was covered in them, making his grin extremely unsettling to the psion. His teeth didn't help, either. Instead of the thick, bulky teeth most orcs had, he had multiple concentric rows of tiny, sharp teeth, while his canines seemed unnaturally elongated, reminiscent of a viper's needle-like fangs.

"So, the runt has returned home," he said in Orcish to Mutt.

Mutt audibly growled upon recognition of the figure. "S'Vol. What are you doing here?"

The heavily-scarred orc chuckled, displaying all his needle-like teeth in a monstrous grin. "I am Jabari Clan, M'Baku M'Toon. This jungle is my home. The real question is why are you here in *our* territory?"

"Don't avoid the question! We both know you should be in prison," Mutt barked back.

"Ah, just as straightforward as when we last met. It seems that your time in the north still hasn't helped you to control that insolent tongue of yours."

Mutt flared his teeth and growled even louder. He looked like he was about to throw himself at this S'Vol, when the latter raised a hand, "Still, I am more than happy to tell you why I'm here, M'Baku M'Toon." A malicious grin grew on the orc's face. "I am here because my fool of a brother and his family died in some tragic accident. My people, lost and without a ruler, wisely decided it was best to release me from my bondage and instate me as chief of the Jabari Tribe." By the orc's tone, Kiru had a feeling he knew what "tragic accident" meant.

"If you think my father will—"

"Oh! I haven't gotten to the best part." S'Vol interrupted. "Your father couldn't say no, seeing as he's dead too."

The color seemed to leave Mutt's face at the words.

S'Vol grinned. "Oh, yes. Not long before my brother's passing, that peace-loving orc died in a most dishonorable way." His grin grew too wide. "Two weeks ago, he succumbed to illness, like a weakling."

"Bastard!" Mutt shouted as he lunged at S'Vol.

The Jabari orc didn't move his feet at all yet still managed to catch Mutt by the throat. S'Vol *tsk*ed and shook his finger from side to side. "What a waste. Despite your lineage, your potential, you are a fool, M'Baku M'Toon. You and your sister should have accepted my invitation all those years ago, but instead, you chose weakness." He sniffed the writhing Mutt. "And you smell . . . odd. I don't know what creatures you took your strength from, but you've tainted your-self with some pitiful sacred beast cores. Ugh!" He scowled in disgust and threw Mutt back toward the rest of Pandemonium like he was infected with some kind of disease.

Mutt landed on his knees and coughed, trying to clear his throat. The blind orc was at Ruby, tying Zhaden for highest cultivation rank of the party, and S'Vol just made him look like a harmless puppy. The aura that Kiru felt was not a fluke, and it wasn't even at full power. The Jabari chief then projected his aura at the party, full-force.

Kiru and his friends all groaned as they were brought to their knees. *He's not Sapphire? No, he's an Emerald!* Kiru thought.

"Though you are a failure, M'Baku M'Toon, you should consider yourself for-tunate. With your father's death, the shamans have decreed that Ukufakaza is in effect. As such, you are not worth my time." He waved a hand and dismissed the aura that had been bearing down on the party.

They all took in a breath with much more ease.

"Take your pathetic group of outsiders and leave our jungle. You can even take the leokin whelp," S'Vol spat. "Just leave the adult's corpse here."

Mutt's nostrils flared as he slowly stood, hand clutching at his throat. He gave a wet cough before speaking. "You . . . killed a leokin? Why? How could you sink so low?"

This irritated S'Vol. The Jabari leader hissed at Mutt, "The strong take what we want, while the weak and the stupid die. Any sacred beast that crosses into our land does so at their own risk. We are within our rights to hunt them," he said pointing to the impaled creature. S'Vol's finger moved over to the rest of the party. "A right I can easily extend onto your friends for trespassing."

There was a heavy silence as the five just stared each other down, the tension clear in the body language of all of Pandemonium's members.

Eventually, S'Vol's grin returned and he pulled his hand back. "But as I said, you are not worth my time. Now go, before I change my mind."

The tension eased from the party, though Mutt still had a scowl. The little lion cub creature that Mutt called a leokin quickly sensed what was going on and hopped into Brunhilda's arms when the paladin knelt down to pick it up. With that, they left the clearing due west. Mutt was the last to go, making sure that he was standing between his friends and the Jabari. When it was clear that S'Vol and his tribe weren't going to make a move, Mutt let out one last growl before bolting into the jungle.

"A friend of yours?" Kiru asked, trying to tell a joke to defuse the tension as Mutt ran up to rejoin them.

"No, Boss," he responded seriously, all of his trademark ease gone. "I'll explain later. For now, we are in very real danger, and we need to get out of this jungle." Very much on the same page as the orc, the party all focused on escaping as quickly as possible.

The furry little leokin didn't make a noise, just clinging onto Brunhilda and scanning the surrounding area frantically, on the lookout for any hidden danger.

They continued to—as William would describe it—"haul ass" for another couple of hours, not stopping until they were at least a couple of miles out of the jungle and in M'Baku Territory. Kiru wanted to ask about the orc's father while they escaped but decided to wait until a better time to broach the subject. The psion knew the pain of losing a parent; it was a subject that had to be handled delicately. Instead, after feeling so powerless in the face of that Emerald, he was reminded of his own cultivation journey and his need to get to the next rank, Ruby. He just needed a fourth technique, and that's what had been eluding him. Mental mana techniques weren't easy for him to come by, either. *Maybe I really will have to make my own,* he thought.

After the party's hours of fleeing, they had finally made it safely into the land occupied by the M'Baku. Where the northern territory was vast brown savannah grassland and to the east was thick jungle, the land controlled by Mutt's clan was flush with rolling rocky hills covered in lush, green grass. Many boulders dotted the landscape, and the unobscured open sky gave a sense of freedom to all present. It amazed Kiru how the orcs' homeland could have such varied topography.

But one thing that all the places within Mutt's homeland that Kiru had visited had in common was wild, untamed splendor. M'Baku Territory seemed to call out, promising adventure. Kiru couldn't help smiling at the sight. If he had been here under different circumstances, he'd have been tempted to spend months hiking and camping in such a grand and wild place. He'd only ever heard about places like this from stories some of the village elders had told him when he was growing up.

The psion sat down on the ground and placed his back to a boulder. He then dismissed his Telekinesis, and his body went limp. In relatively safety, he began cultivating via the method he'd learned from William when he was just a Bronze. It was a variation of the base method those within the Great Alliance were taught.

The base or standard method involved passively absorbing mana from the environment through one's pores. As the core drew the mana toward it, the body naturally filtered the magical energy, breaking it down into its base form. It was an inefficient method as one couldn't improve the filtration process or direct the core to absorb more mana that way. A lot of times mana that could otherwise have been beneficial would be unintentionally filtered out as well. Any unabsorbed mana would then be excreted through the body's gastrointestinal system. The only notable by-product was a strange sulfurous odor to the waste. Kiru had been told by some residents of his hometown that was why the smell coming from the outhouse by the school in Bristleton for early cultivators was so horrendous!

William's method was a much-improved version of the base method. The first thing was that, instead of drawing mana through all of his pores, Kiru focused on only the pores in his head. William had taught Kiru that he should think of his head as "one big pore." Using William's method, Kiru was able to absorb mana both at a faster rate and at a better efficiency than the standard version. When he'd first learned it, the psion had reasoned that the reason his efficiency was much better was because there was less distance for the mana to travel to be filtered out, leaving more to be infused into his core. Based on Kiru's experiences, cultivating using the base method would provide him one hour's worth of simple movement for every hour cultivated. William's method gave ninety minutes of movement per hour cultivated.

And Kiru had found a way to improve on that even further. The psion had discovered that when he was around minds that were either abuzz with mental activity or in a dream-filled sleep, his rate of absorption was two times better, giving him three hours of movement per hour cultivated. That's why Kiru cultivated at night so often. The mental mana that came off his colleagues was more potent, and it helped him replenish his stores more easily. The same could be said for his time in the library. With many eager, intelligent cultivators spending hours researching and learning there, the place was rife with mental mana.

"I believe we are now in relative safety." Zhaden said, leaning against a large rock and scanning the surrounding countryside.

Mutt lifted his head and sniffed the air. "Yeah, I no longer smell the Jabari. We can rest easy for now."

"Good, then ye can tell us who in the abyss was that freaky-looking orc, and why did they try to hurt little Nom here?" Brunhilda asked.

"Um, did you just say its name is Nom?" Mutt asked, clearly thrown off by the moniker.

The paladin blushed. "Well . . . yes. A cute little furball like this has gotta have a name, right? And he seemed to feel more comfortable when I gave it some of me food," she said and handed the small little leokin a piece of jerky.

"Nom!" the cute creature said as it opened its mouth wide and took a big bite out of the snack.

"Yes, that's right. Ye like to go 'nom,' don't you?" she said as if it were a puppy, and tickled its belly.

The creature purred happily at that.

Kiru couldn't deny it though, the name suited the little sacred beast. As it chewed, it continually went "Nom," and even after it finished, "Nom" was the only thing it continued to say. Despite the tension of recent events, the little creature eventually provoked a smile from everyone in the party. Well . . . with the exception of one member.

"What an annoying little creature!" William grumbled inside Kiru's mind. *"If that paladin doesn't get a handle on the beast, it'll eat all our food!"*

"I suppose you can do better at 'handling the beast?'" Kiru mentally asked.

"Pfft! Of course," the imp said dismissively.

Kiru smiled. *"Then it looks like you're on babysitting duty,"* he sent, before summoning William from within him.

Nom appeared enamored by the sudden appearance of the glowing orb of light, its pupils growing large in surprise. In a matter of seconds, the little imp manifested beside Kiru.

William put his hands on his hip and looked down his nose at Kiru. "You want me to look after that ugly thing? You're wasting my talents." Despite Kiru's protests, William began walking on over to Nom.

The little leokin was curious about the small demon and crawled off of Brunhilda's lap, moving on all fours toward William until the two were just inches from each other. On all fours, it was already the same size as Kiru's familiar.

That didn't stop William from acting superior. He puffed out his boney chest in order to look bigger and pointed a sharp finger at Nom. "Listen here, Beast. I am William, Breaker of Wills, and you will listen to—"

"Nom," the little leokin said in declaration, promptly interrupting the demon's speech before biting the little fiend's tail.

"Gah!" William cried out. "Get it off me! Get it off me!" He ran in a panic, dragging the little sacred beast around behind him.

Nom, on the other hand, couldn't be happier.

Kiru began to laugh, and it seemed to be infectious because after a few seconds, the rest of the party started laughing too.

Most importantly, it visibly eased Mutt's tension. Some of his trademark casualness returned too. "Looks like the little guy found a friend," he chuckled before addressing the others again. "That orc was Jabari S'Vol. He was once a friend. His father and mine were allies, so we grew up together. Besides my sister, he was the only one who accepted me and helped me to overcome my blindness."

Mutt's tone then turned sad. "Five years ago, our clans had arranged for him to wed my sister. It was to be a show of 'unity' or whatever my father called it. I can't say it wasn't a good match. They both were ambitious, stubborn, and seemed to really care for each other. I reckon S'Vol's ambition is what drove them apart. He is—was," he corrected, "the second son of the chief of the Jabari Clan. As such, he was set to inherit nothing. S'Vol was like a brother to me, and he was competitive. He was the more powerful cultivator compared to his blood brother and he would tell me all the time of how he hated the idea of being seen as 'lesser' just because he was second born. The idea of it ate away at him until he was no longer the orc I knew."

Mutt sighed before continuing. "I offered for us to get away—for me, my sister, and him to live free without responsibility. To show his family that their approval didn't matter, only our own. Myev cared much more about 'duty' and 'tradition' than I did. So, she said no. S'Vol also said no. I discovered that he didn't want the freedom I craved. He wanted power."

The orc continued, "He forsook us and his people. One night, all of a sudden, we got word that he had disappeared, unable to be found by anyone in his clan. I had hoped he'd left Imakandi, but he opted for blasphemy instead. S'Vol sought out the Jormuns," he spat the last word. Nom even growled reflexively at it too.

"Who be the Jormuns, Mutt?" Brunhilda asked.

Mutt growled, "Cultists, extremists who worship a beast banished from the pantheon, Jormungandr. With them at his side, S'Vol attempted to assassinate my father in order to take the throne. Father defeated S'Vol and would've ended him had it not been for his friendship with the Jabari chieftain who happened to be S'Vol's brother. So, S'Vol was imprisoned and sentenced to work in the mines for the rest of his days."

Mutt bunched his lips and took in a big inhale through his nostrils before continuing, "But if S'Vol is free and in control of the Jabari Tribe now . . ." He trailed off, leaving a pregnant pause.

No one else said anything until he finished his point.

"It must truly mean that dark times have come to my homeland," Mutt said. "Last time I saw S'Vol, he was just a Gold and he didn't seem as snakelike. Now he's an Emerald, and I know he doesn't plan to stop there."

"I've heard of Jormungandr." Brunhilda added. "He killed Thor! I thought he be dead too . . . Why was he banned from the pantheon?"

"Honestly, I'm not sure, but I know it wasn't good. You can ask my sister once we get to my home," Mutt said.

"What is that thing S'Vol mentioned? That Ukufakaza? I've never heard of it before," Kiru asked, his perfect recall conjuring up the complicated word.

"It means 'The Proving.' It is the set of trials that I told you about to inherit leadership of Imakandi. It means my father really is dead," the orc answered.

"My condolences for the loss of your paternal figure, Mutt," Zhaden said, trying to console his friend the best he could. He had previously told the party that gold drakonid society raised the young as a collective. While they were divided into separate clans, the concept of one father or mother was foreign to the rogue.

The blind orc gave a slight smile, "You're good, Stabby. Truth is, he was a hardass and a bit of a dick. We didn't agree on much, but he was still my father so . . . Thanks."

Brunhilda wordlessly stood up and walked over to Mutt. Before he could ask what she was doing, she wrapped her muscular arms around him in a tight embrace.

Mutt was caught off-guard for a moment, but then his smile grew larger and tears started welling up in his eyes as he hugged her back.

Kiru and Zhaden also walked over and each put a hand on one of Mutt's shoulders, expressing their sympathy.

After a good minute, the blind orc managed to compose himself. "Thanks, everybody." He gave a loud sniff, then turned his head to Kiru. "Boss, this also explains the purple color all of you have been seeing in the sky."

"What is it?" Kiru asked, eager to know.

"It's a barrier. It happens every time there is a Proving. Imakandi is the territory under the protection of the Beast Gods. Back when it was founded, the gods ensured that no one outside of Imakandi could interfere with the rites of selecting a new leader. They did that by creating a dome of mana that would surround our entire nation—not just a city or a town but our whole nation—that would activate on their command. People can notice it from the inside but it's translucent from the outside. Until Ukufakaza is finished, no one is allowed in until a new High Chief has been chosen by the gods."

"But people can be allowed out, correct?" Zhaden asked, his eyes nervously scanning their surroundings like he was feeling trapped in a cage.

"Yep," Mutt answered. He then raised a finger. "They can't come back in once they leave until the Proving is complete though, Stabby. And before anyone asks, no, I don't know how the barrier is formed. I didn't care to pay attention to that part. I just know that it exists."

"Pray tell, what be the criteria for yer gods to choose a new leader for yer people, Mutt?" Brunhilda asked.

Mutt just shrugged. "Honestly, I don't know. When I was a kid, I was bored with most of it. I know there's usually a trial by combat part because I liked the sound of that, and I know that the timeline is different every time. It could be two weeks or two years for all I know. As for the rest, I can't remember for sure. Anyway, we should probably get to the capital. With Ukufakaza in effect, my sister is the new leader of my clan and the interim High Chief of *all* the clans for now. She should be able to help us get your father's item, Boss. I know your dad didn't tell you exactly what it is, but if it's in my homeland, that item must be strong."

"That can wait." Kiru said.

Mutt turned his head in surprise, "But the dragons. Boss, if we don't get those items, the world will—"

"The world has time, Mutt," Kiru interjected. Memories of loss, of pain, and of loneliness flooded him in a flash. Once he had felt utterly alone and helpless. It was only by the aid of his mother that he'd made it to where he was today. He wanted to be a man that acted as she did, to fight for those close to them, to put everything on the line to make the world a better place. He wanted to be a ruler that protected and uplifted others, to be someone who would make his parents proud.

Kiru's eyes welled up a little before he shook his head. "We still have the better part of six years to get them. We can't ignore what's going on here, though. This is your home. If it's in trouble, then as an ally, I must help. Besides, what good is saving the world if we let it fall apart before we can?" he asked rhetorically. He meant what he said, and by the looks on his friends' faces, they knew it.

They all smiled at each other, even Zhaden, despite the difficulty in doing so with his reptilian anatomy. Then, they looked west in the direction they were to go, deeper into M'Baku Territory.

A world of trouble and hardship was in store for them; there was no denying that. Despite that fact, together, they felt like they could meet it head-on. They would help stabilize this country and save the world. Their party would no doubt bring pandemonium to the multitudes of malicious powers in the world. It was in their name.

CHAPTER SIX

Family Reunion

After a few minutes of their skin soaking up the sun on top of one of the rocky hills they'd stopped at, much of the sweat had dried off the cultivators' bodies. After some recuperation and cultivating, the team, with Nom in tow, continued on their trek westward toward Imakandi's capital city, Dissé. The little leokin was keeping William on his toes, the sacred beast seeming to be the more physically capable of the two at the moment.

The countryside and rolling hills of the M'Baku Territory proved a much safer and enjoyable journey than either the Thrar'fang or Jabari lands. A strong breeze countered the sun's heat, providing pleasant conditions. In addition to that benefit, the ample rocky outcroppings made it much easier to spot potential danger, with the high vantage points to scout from. Zhaden was able to make good use of them whenever the party was concerned. Another bonus was that the green grass only went up to ankle height, making it unsuitable for large predators to use for cover.

Those two specific geographic changes helped the cultivators avoid multiple encounters with dangerous sacred beasts in the area. Mutt's hearing, smell, and sense of touch were also invaluable in helping them avoid threats. Early on in their trek across M'Baku Territory, as they were going down a deep slope, the orc raised his fist silently in the air.

After months of previous travel experience with Mutt under their belt, Kiru and the rest of the party halted. They knew that that signal meant a threat was nearby. They all stood still as Mutt slowly advanced toward a solitary boulder. He walked barefoot and spread his toes wide, carefully digging them in the dirt. He had previously informed the party that his sense of touch had grown so strong that he could detect vibrations with his feet. After a couple of seconds, the orc let out a subtle gasp, then activated his Fenrir's Claws technique. Before anyone could ask him what was happening, the orc jumped up in the air in the direction of the boulder, claws first. He landed in a grassless spot right beside the rock, with his claws buried deep inside the dirt. There was a high-pitched cry of pain and a couple small fonts of blood shooting up from the dirt and then silence.

Mutt gave a chuckle, then a groan as he hefted up what looked to be a mole the size of a man, covered in a layer of thin gray fur out from the dirt. Its head and neck were impaled in multiple places by the orc's claws. The orc dropped the dead creature in front of his feet.

"Well done! I approve!" William said, clapping his hands enthusiastically at the violent display. The imp on Kiru's shoulder then leaned into his master's ear and whispered, "You should really act more like this guy. More bloodshed is always the answer in my book."

Kiru chuckled slightly as he rolled his eyes at his familiar's words.

"Thanks, Little Dude," Mutt said to William. "That was a boulder mole. They're ambush predators that like to live under the large rocks present in my clan's territory. They are pretty dumb for sacred beasts, and we consider them pests. It would've bitten someone's leg off had I not spotted it."

After the orc's explanation, the party decided it was best that Mutt now take the lead instead of Zhaden. The gold drakonid was undoubtedly the most paranoid and on-guard of the group. Kiru wondered if the rogue inherited that trait from studying under the irrationally anxious Professor Ivan Zerkoff back at the Royal Academy during their Strategies I course. Whether that was the case or not, despite Zhadens' skill and paranoia, after seeing that he hadn't detected the mole earlier, Zhaden had no qualms with Mutt taking point. Kiru could still hear the rogue muttering to himself and keeping his eyes peeled for any potential threats. If he couldn't watch from the front, he would make sure nothing was going to get them from behind.

They also got to learn more about the leokin on their way too. Not from Nom himself, he was too busy trying to catch various insects or lizards to eat, or when he couldn't find any, chasing William around like the imp was his favorite toy. The first thing they learned was that Nom was indeed a "he." They were discussing that very topic, when the leokin promptly lifted up his leg and began licking his groin, highlighting that fact.

Mutt also gave them an impromptu lesson in the leokin overall. When Brunhilda asked about the type of sacred beast Nom was, Mutt was happy to explain all he knew. He spoke with a grin as he continued jog alongside the others, "Well, you know by now that some sacred beasts are smarter than others."

The party nodded as they trekked. During the months they had been traveling south, they had experienced the various levels of intellect different sacred beasts possessed firsthand.

Not getting any response to the contrary, the orc continued, "Leokin are like, super smart, though. Some I bet are even smarter than me." He chuckled.

"Well anyway, my sister told me that they only live in Imakandi and that they owe their evolution to the Beast Gods, somehow. Because of that, they are fiercely loyal to the Beast Gods and are the only ones who are allowed to serve as guardian shamans."

"What be a 'guardian shaman?'" Brunhilda asked, genuinely curious. As a paladin to a goddess of the Vasir pantheon, she knew only a little about the Beast Gods.

"Do you know what a shaman is?" the orc asked.

"Nay," Brunhilda replied.

"Uh, I guess you could call them 'priests.' Only, they're pretty different from the priests of your order, Brunhilda," Mutt explained. "Instead of keeping strict order, shamans focus on keeping the world in a more natural and free state. They ensure Imakandi is still a place where both orc and beast can thrive as nature and the Beast Gods intended. Guardian shamans do as their name suggest—they guard."

"What are they guarding?" Kiru asked, interested in what Mutt had to say.

"The First Temple, Boss. It's the first place established in worship by the Beast Gods. It's located in an isolated and hostile desert south of here. That's where the leokin live. So, that's why I was surprised to see one of them running in the Jabari jungle," Mutt explained. "Normally, no one would ever dare touch the leokin due to their statuses as guardian shamans, but S'Vol was right. In Imakandi, each tribe that controls a territory has the absolute right to hunt any animal or sacred beast that is within their borders. It's unfortunate, but the leokin, being sacred beasts, were fair game."

Nom whimpered in Brunhilda's arms, "Mutt!" Brunhilda said. "There be a youngling here. Please consider yer words."

"Oh! My bad, little buddy," Mutt apologized. They had stopped on top of another hill and let William distract the small leokin before Mutt continued his explanation, "So, just so you know, no one has ever harmed a leokin before due to it being undeniable sacrilege. Only those within the Jormun cult would even consider such an act. I don't know exactly where the First Temple is, aside from a general idea. Hopefully, my sister will help us get the furry little guy back home."

They continued on. After a few hours of travel, the sun had reached its zenith in the sky, indicating it was midday. That was when they finally made it to Dissé. The orc capital was set on the largest rocky outcropping they'd seen yet. It wasn't a mountain per se, but it wasn't far off, the main difference being it had a large plateau at the top rather than a sharp peak. There were multiple concentric rings around the outcropping, going higher and higher to the top. For a couple of miles in all directions, the land was flat with areas of grass and various tilled fields placed around. It was an ideal spot for a capital city. The way it allowed its inhabitants to use the natural environment to help spot an attack from miles away was ingenious.

It was obvious that they had manipulated the land surrounding the capital too. Many of the buildings that could be seen in the distance were made of various uneven stones with some mud-colored mortar holding them together. Likely the material was gathered by removing the rocks from the ground below in order to make the dirt ideal for farming. The odds of such a large plot of land being fertile and without the telltale stones every other place inside the territory exhibited, seemed astronomically low to Kiru.

Mutt grabbed a cowl and placed it over his head, both blocking him from the sun as well as concealing his identity. Being a prince, even given his history of being a black sheep, made Mutt a bit of a celebrity. He didn't want to attract more attention to their party than necessary. The party descended to the valley below. As they neared the tall, multi-tiered capital, they noticed more and more people gathered on both sides of the path. Some were clearly weary travelers—orc families looking tired and dirty, crowded around various cooking fires.

"Refugees," Mutt said quietly.

Kiru's pointy ears twitched. "From where?"

"Jabari Territory. I can smell it on them. I'm betting not everyone is okay with S'Vol's new position."

"Why do ye say that, Mutt?" Brunhilda queried.

Mutt pointed to one of his nostrils, "The nose knows, ya know?" When Brunhilda just gave him a deadpan stare, he continued, "They smell of three things: fear, blood, and snakes. Honestly, their scents remind me of a panicking rabbit cornered by a serpent." Kiru didn't have the nasal capacity to contest that claim, and from what he knew, neither did the others. So, he nodded along to his friend's logic.

The party continued, and the makeup of the people alongside them slowly transitioned from refugees to various vendors hawking numerous items, from clothing, to hunting equipment, potions, and cooked meat. William attempted to steal a kabob skewer from a dwarf hunter/vendor named Aurvangr Orynn, but Nom promptly swiped it away from him. The vendor was understandably upset, but when Kiru paid for it and two more, even giving the man a little extra coin on top of that for his "understanding," his demeanor immediately changed.

They got down to one of the main gates into Dissé. A pair of guards in tribal armor noticed the group of foreigners. There were very few non-orcs about, and they were all human and dwarf vendors. Therefore, being a mix of different races, Pandemonium stood out, despite their attempts to blend in. The guards crossed their spears, barring the party's entrance into the city proper.

"Halt! State your business for coming into the city," one of the guards said.

The party had already discussed their cover story. They needed to keep their identities a secret to try and help prevent word from reaching the Kingdom of Blades. So far, as far as they knew, they'd made a clean getaway. Kiru wanted to keep it that way. The barrier going up had been a blessing. It kept anyone from entering Imakandi for the moment, but it didn't stop information from being spread. So Kiru was ready with their story. "We were hired to escort a merchant caravan here. We'd like to get a drink and spend our coin before our employer goes off to their next destination," he said.

"Mmm, mercenaries then, huh? What's the name of your company?"

That caught Kiru off-guard. *Are you kidding me? After coming up with all this complex backstory, I forgot to come up with a name for us?!* he thought, fighting to keep any look of surprise from reaching his eyes. There was an awkward pause, but Zhaden came to the rescue. "It's Pandemonium."

The orcs had a puzzled look.

The drakonid just doubled down. "Our company's name is Pandemonium."

"Hadn't heard of that one before," one guard said to his compatriot, stroking his chin. "Where are you based out of, and who are you escorting?"

"We are based out of the Kingdom of Blades, and Aurvangr Orynn is our employer," Zhaden answered without skipping a beat.

The confidence and speed of the rogue's answers appeared to satisfy the guards. They nodded and uncrossed their spears. "Very well, but if you cause trouble, we'll make sure your employer hears about it."

They all just nodded and proceeded past the guards into Dissé proper. After they made it a good bit past the guards and into the hustle and bustle of the orc capital, Kiru spoke. "Damn, Zhaden. You really saved us back there. I didn't know you were so good at deception."

The gold drakonid looked a little offended. "Of course I am. I'm a rogue. I don't just deceive with my illusions. We were specifically taught to use our words to help us in that skill as well. Why *didn't* you think I would be good at that?"

Kiru opened his mouth, then closed it again. He actually hadn't given too much thought to it. Kiru knew the gold drakonid was paranoid and an adept fighter always keeping an eye out for danger. When it came to being a cunning conversationalist, however, Zhaden hadn't ever seemed particularly impressive. Kiru tried to answer Zhaden's question again, but before he could say anything, William spoke up.

"It's because you don't talk much, duh," the imp said, idly picking his nose. "You just watch things and hiss a bunch when you speak."

Zhaden looked shocked at William's bluntness, then looked at his friends.

Kiru shrugged, "You are rather quiet when it comes to anything other than discussing strategy or safety . . . which is undeniably a good thing for a stealth-based fighter."

"Aye, ye be very good at ambush fighting, but . . . ye be a man of few words," Brunhilda added.

Mutt nodded in agreement, "What they said, Stabby."

"I hadn't noticed. I will endeavor to aid in more deceptive matters in terms of espionage when the opportunities arise," Zhaden promised.

"Sure, thanks," Kiru said in gratitude as they continued farther into the city. The capital was jam packed with orcs. Even more vendors were present within the walls, with goods of much better quality than outside. There were also conglomerations of what Mutt said were various orc tribes grouped together in different sections. He could tell by their smell. Fortunately for everybody else who didn't have the orc's ridiculous sense of smell, there were tribal flags that helped to differentiate them. There were small clusters of humans and dwarves and a handful of gold drakonids present but no elves, as Kiru noted. The city was overwhelmingly Orcish. It was easy to hear the various conversations going on around them. The main topics were the loss of their king, Ukufakaza, and who the pantheon would deem as Imakandi's new ruler.

Being constantly reminded of his father's death seemed to really be getting to Mutt, the orc repeatedly pulling down his cowl to cover his scowling face. Even though Mutt and his father didn't have the best relationship, he was still in mourning. Losing the man who raised you, especially unexpectedly, had to be rough. Kiru didn't even know his dad, and upon learning about him, it still hurt. He could only imagine how Mutt was feeling.

As they moved deeper into the city, they continued further and further up, spiraling around the massive stone pillar it was built around. The streets were winding and could be pretty narrow in places during their ascent. Dissé was a bustling metropolis with orcs aplenty roaming about, selling their wares, tidying their abodes, or just living their lives. With the press of so many people, the air was close and smelled of a blend of sweat, spices, and oddly enough, what smelled like dog to Kiru. He had to be extra careful with using Telekinesis to move himself to make sure he didn't unintentionally knock over any unsuspecting orcs as he moved amongst the crowd.

The noise levels were chaotic as well. There was everything from merchants trying to get the attention of potential customers, to the sound of sizzling meat, and numerous animal sounds as well. "Wild" was the word that came to mind to the psion. Had they not been in the orcs' homeland, Kiru would've been seriously concerned about some kind of wild animal breakout.

At one point, most of the noise died down and was replaced by the voice of a rather thin, elderly orc. He was hunched over, had a long gray beard, and wore a tunic with a patchwork pattern, made from various animal hides. The sleeves were long—longer than his arms and made of a black-and-white striped hide. On his head was a headdress fashioned from what looked to be a minotaur skull on top.

The elder orc stood on a podium next to a small tent that served as a temple. The hide the structure was made from had a similar patchwork pattern to the orc's tunic. He was shouting about Ukufakaza as well as the glory of the Beast Gods to an assembled mass. Mutt informed the party that the elderly orc was a shaman of the people, which was obvious given that he was talking about their deities. Kiru couldn't help but notice the shaman pause to look at their party passing, but it was only for a moment before the orc began evangelizing to his people again. The psion didn't pay him much mind.

They continued their press upward, navigating through the maze-like streets. Kiru could appreciate the strategical advantage of the city's architecture and planning. Anyone who would ever try to besiege Dissé would have to go through miles of open terrain before even reaching the orc capital. It was the ideal choice for any major settlement, and the area they chose to make their capital couldn't have been better in the psion's opinion. Even after an opponent had successfully crossed the open terrain, they would either have to wage a slow campaign to take each section of narrow, crooked streets as they ascended while trying to avoid attacks from above, or try some way to get to the top first while avoiding attacks from below.

Kiru felt like they stood out more than he wanted them to, especially since the one orc with them was trying to keep a low profile and his prominent elf ears were drawing attention, so he readjusted his headband to cover their points. It gave him a small modicum of comfort, at least for the moment. Eventually, the party made its way to the upper tiers, finding it less crowded and with fewer buildings. This seemed to be where more upper-class orcs resided. Kiru assumed that based on how the buildings were in better condition, the citizens looked healthier and cleaner, and even the air was fresher. Also, there were two temples in this section. One was covered in various animal furs and bones, dedicated to the Beast Pantheon, just like all the others they had seen at every other level of Dissé. This one, however, was the largest building they'd seen here.

The other temple was markedly different. Unlike most of the other buildings, made with various uneven stones stuck together only by strong mortar, this one was made up of even walls of solid stone and an evenly measured pointed roof. The entrance boasted a number of tall, ornately carved columns. This structure seemed out of place, as if it had been dropped into the city from elsewhere.

Brunhilda gasped as she recognized the building and the symbol carved in the front part of its roof. When Kiru followed her gaze, he saw it was one of the main capital temples dedicated to the Vasir, the gods that the Order of Valhalla served. Hlin, the minor goddess of protection who Brunhilda followed, was one of the deities within the pantheon. The dwarf paladin's holy quest involved those temples. In order for Hlin to become a major goddess and be accepted by her brethren, Brunhilda had been tasked to put one of her shrines up within every major temple within the Great Alliance. Every major temple was located within the capitals of the nations within the Alliance.

The purple-haired dwarf had to visibly restrain herself from breaking away from the party to go over to the temple. "We'll get there." Kiru said. "Your quest is important too. After we're done talking with Mutt's sister, the temple will be the first place we visit." Kiru wasn't a fervent follower of Hlin like Brunhilda was, but, as with Mutt, he wanted to help. *If we can consecrate Hlin at this temple, we'll be one step closer to making her a major god. I bet she'll grant us major benefits from that too*, he thought.

Brunhilda smiled and nodded, comforted by the psion's words. Shortly afterward, they finally made it to the gated entrance to the royal grounds of Dissé. Six muscular orc guards standing at the ready, each wielding a shield in one hand and a sword or club in the other. As they got closer, the guards all drew their weapons in unison and lowered them at Pandemonium, their shields up.

"In the name of Regent Queen M'Baku Myev, go no further." The party all stopped at once, raising their hands up. Brunhilda had previously made a sling over her chest, in which Nom was currently sleeping, his belly full of meat. More guards then appeared from the nearby bushes and trees, making twenty in total, now surrounding Pandemonium. "The queen has decreed that, until Ukufakaza is over, no one is to enter the royal grounds unless they are part of the royal clan or given permission by them. Any who try to approach the grounds are to be imprisoned and questioned. Now, surrender your weapons and get on your knees."

Kiru hadn't expected such a hostile welcome. William growled, but with a sharp mental rebuke from Kiru, the imp just grumbled and raised his hands as well.

Mutt let out a growl too, but it quickly changed into a chuckle, "Nah, I don't think we're gonna do that."

The head guard bared his large teeth, "Who do you think you are, foreigner? Surrender your weapons or die."

"Funny, I've been gone for only a year, and now I'm a foreigner." Mutt then took off his cowl and stood tall. His back audibly cracked as he straightened it, increasing his height by a few inches, and his muscles bulged as he faced the guards. The way he held himself and the air of superiority that came off him was very different from the Mutt that Kiru was used to. He truly gave off the gravitas like he was some sort of orc noble in the psion's eyes. "I am M'Baku M'Toon, a member of the royal clan and brother to the regent queen, M'Baku Myev," he declared, his blind eyes looked off past all the orcs and still the words were spoken to them all.

The guards' eyes widened. "Prince M'Toon," the lead guard said in surprised recognition. Kiru figured he must've not noticed who Mutt was until he took off his cowl. The guards all immediately went down on one knee and bowed their heads. "Forgive us. We did not know. It had been reported to Her Highness that you had gone missing. We feared the worst."

Mutt sighed and relaxed his posture back to his regular hunched-over form. Mutt scratched the back of his head, "Ugh, I hate all this formal talk," he uttered under his breath just loud enough for Kiru to hear. "Alright, alright, all is forgiven," he said, his hands out in a placating manner. "Now, will you please lead me and my party into the grounds and let my sister know we're here?"

"Right away, Prince M'Toon," the guard said as he and the others quickly got back up.

Mutt just sighed again and wiped his face in frustration at their use of his formal name. He decided not to correct the guard, though. The large gate doors opened, and the party was led into the royal grounds. The grounds were made up of the flat area at the very top of the stone outcropping that the city was built on. With nothing else above them, all the cultivators were granted an unobstructed view of the clear purplish blue sky above them. Kiru was surprised to find a healthy covering of fresh, supple shortgrass on the ground as well as a number of large acacia trees. *How is such a fertile landscape possible atop such a barren foundation as the stone Dissé was built on?* he thought. The rest of the city lacked such greenery, the exception being the obviously tended farmland surrounding the orc capital. Kiru could even see a large, well-manicured garden off to his left containing a variety of strange-looking plants.

Inside the royal grounds, there were also a large number of orcs about in well-kept robes. From what Kiru could gather, they were mostly servants. To his surprise, very few guards were present. There were, however, a variety of sacred beasts, all of which appeared both larger and more muscular than their counterparts that the psion had seen out in the wild. A three-headed crocodile with intelligent eyes observed the passing cultivators from a shallow pond. A brown wolf patrolled the border side-by-side with an orc guard whose head only reached the beast's shoulders. A few eight-legged horses casually grazed on some grass in the distance.

Lastly, there was a minotaur a head taller and even more intimidating than the ones that had chased the party into the river. It was standing guard in front of a large palace at the center of the clearing. An intimidating axe, almost as big as the sacred beast's body, was strapped onto its back. It was fascinating to see all these intelligent, obviously dangerous animals all in one area coexisting peacefully. William gawked in open amazement at the scene.

"How is this possible?" the psion asked.

"The beasts? Eh, not sure." Mutt shrugged. "My sister will be the one to ask about things like that," he said, completely unperturbed. They continued forward, escorted by the lead guard who had defied them earlier, now visibly nervous, occasionally glancing back to Mutt. Eventually, they made it to the palace. Unlike any of the other buildings they had seen in Dissé, this one was made entirely of wood painted in browns and greens; where it wasn't painted, the wood was polished to a fine finish.

The party got up to within ten feet of the minotaur guardian. The sacred beast uncrossed its arms, took a couple of clopping steps forward, and put a hand to its weapon's handle. It had a thin layer of black hair on its obviously thick leather hide. It snorted loudly, the exhalation of air forcing all of their hair back. A palpable heat came off its hulking body. The guard that had been escorting the party signaled for them to stop, then went to go speak to the minotaur in hushed whispers. Kiru's elven hearing helped him pick up the gist of what was said, however. The orc was simply explaining the situation, saying he wanted to alert the queen in order to have her verify it was truly her brother in case this was some imposter.

The psion couldn't fault the orc's suspicion. It was fair enough to double-check and be sure. The party shouldn't have a problem, though. They were who they said they were, and proving it wouldn't be an issue.

"I can hear you, you know?" The two paused and looked over to Mutt. He pointed to his ears. "The benefit of being born blind made my hearing as sharp as a bandicoot mouse's."

The guard tensed and shivered as if caught in a trap. He slowly turned his head to look at Mutt and gave a nervous smile, "Uh, I will have to have the queen verify it, for her safety of course!" the guard quickly and nervously said, seeming to find any sort of excuse to remove himself from the situation.

Mutt rolled his eyes and sighed. "Fine. Go tell her."

The minotaur opened the heavy wooden door and let the guard in. The beast then closed it, crossed its arms, and stood back in front of it. The minotaur tilted his chin up at the party, signaling he wanted them to take a few steps back, and they complied.

After only a few minutes, the door opened again, this time from the inside by another minotaur. The guard came back out, still looking just as nervous. "The queen will see you now," he said, then quickly shuffled to the side to allow them to enter.

Pandemonium then followed the guard and entered the palace. Kiru decided to recall William before he entered, in order to prevent the imp from saying something that would upset the queen. Kiru didn't know the cultural etiquette of this place, and with William's lack of filter, he thought it was best to mitigate any risk. Also, William was prone to offending *anyone*, not just royalty. So he felt it was the smartest call.

The royal palace was more like an extremely large and majestic longhouse. It was mostly just a large central chamber with rooms off to each side and in the back. Multiple axe-wielding minotaurs lined both sidewalls, standing alert.

In the back of the main chamber, seated on a throne adorned by a wolf skull, atop a rising set of stairs, was a female orc. She was not alone either. Curled up around her throne was a large wolf that was black as night. Seated on one of the stairs in front of the throne was a boar who snorted out flames. On one of the throne's armrests was a rooster with blue and yellow feathers. To see such powerful sacred beasts all congregated together and focused on them, Kiru didn't know if he should feel impressed at the ability to amass such a force or intimidated at what it could do to him. In truth, he felt both.

Still, the sacred beasts weren't the most imposing things in the room. No, that was undoubtedly the queen regent. M'Baku Myev radiated power. There were only two things that signified she was Mutt's sister: her brown mohawk, which she kept braided and adorned with bones and beads, and her strong, distinct jawline. She wore a crown made of yellowed bone adorned with a blend of onyx and ruby gemstones.

Myev's clothing clearly opted for speed and function over protection. Based on the aura of power coming off her, though, it didn't seem like she needed much protection. She wore a sleeveless brown leather vest, a simple low-cut skirt, and a pair of interlaced sandals. Her face had multiple piercings made from sharpened teeth, and her entire right arm was covered in tattoos of various beasts.

The nervous guard had followed in behind them. "Your Majesty, I present—"

She raised her hand, interrupting the guard. "Leave us."

The guard nodded and quickly left the room.

Once the minotaur had closed the door behind him, she addressed the party. "I didn't know it was possible."

"What's possible, sis?" Mutt asked with casual ease, not bothered at all by the display of power before them.

It was interesting to Kiru how Mutt both sounded and carried himself so much differently than the other Imakandi orcs. They all had a distinct accent, which he lacked. *Why is that?* Kiru thought.

"That time would make you look even uglier." Both the siblings grinned and began to chuckle. Despite both time and distance, family could recognize family.

After their good-natured laugh, Myev's nostrils flared loudly as she inhaled twice in what seemed to Kiru like an exaggerated display. "As for needing to identify you, that was unnecessary for me. I could smell you a mile away," she said, tapping her nose. Myev was warm toward her brother but didn't leave her seat or elevated position, quickly eyeing the others and keeping a calculated distance. "We'd received word that you had died in some tragic accident after the Warrior Games. Father was furious."

"Nah, some weird guy with three heads tried to kill us, but we got away." Mutt's tone instantly went somber. "Is it true about Father?"

She nodded, then glanced uncomfortably at the others who'd accompanied her brother, locking eyes with Kiru for a few seconds. "Who are these outsiders you bring to my doorstep, Brother?"

"Oh! This is my party, sis! These are the cultivators I teamed up with to win the Warrior Games! This is Brunhilda. She's a paladin and tougher than a giant tortoise's shell. She may smell like a troll, but that's just cause she had to get a blood transplant—"

"Er-hem." The dwarf coughed loudly to interrupt Mutt, blushing furiously in embarrassment.

"That information isn't necessary, Mutt," Kiru whispered to his friend. The psion wasn't the most well-versed in talking to women, but even he knew saying someone smelled "like a troll" was never the right thing even if it was factual.

"Oh, okay." Mutt just shrugged before continuing, "Next up here is Stabby. He's real good at making illusions, though I can't see 'em, ha!"

"Zhaden of Clan Ironclaw, Your Highness," the gold drakonid hissed as he bowed.

"Last up is the Boss." Mutt slapped Kiru on the back. "He may not have enough meat on his bones, but he's one strong guy. He and the others helped me out when I was in trouble, and I owe 'em a life debt."

She raised an eyebrow. "A life debt? Truly?"

Mutt nodded.

Myev smirked, and in one quick motion, jumped down beside Kiru. She was tall—just as tall as Mutt was when he had good posture and a good half-foot taller than Kiru at his six feet. Myev cocked her head and studied the psion.

The others took a step back reactively. Kiru stood still, forcing himself to keep calm.

She bent down and smelled Kiru, "Your smell is . . . strange. There is a subtle heat from your chest. Your core, no doubt, but it seems wrong." She then began circling the psion, a predatory glint in her eyes, "I smell elf, and I smell human, but there's something else about you. Something different. Something *more*. Tell me, how did a Gold gain the loyalty of a Ruby, a cultivator who is his better? Not only that, how did you become the leader of a member of Imakandi's royal class? You certainly have a powerful build, but your hands and neck don't match the rest of you."

Kiru's enchanted armor covered most of his body and projected a false façade. For all appearances, his entire torso down to his wrists and lower body, looked to be rather muscular. In truth, a large majority of his musculature had atrophied away. When his spine had been broken, he was rendered a quadriplegic, only able to move his neck up on his own. As such, with continued disuse, the muscles in his body had withered. It was only through his use of mana that he was able to move at all. He was unable to truly *feel* anything, but he was able to fool most people.

Still, his armor didn't cover every part of his body. His hands were very boney, and his neck, though he was able to use it, had also become notably thin, enough for Myev to notice. It seemed the queen regent was a lot blunter than most.

"Well, it's a bit complicated," Kiru said.

"Enlighten me," she said, then gave him a large grin.

Kiru gulped and pressed on. "My friends and I were training, and we were attacked by some large hairy beast. We were able to defeat it, and it reverted into Mutt. He was so grateful that he pledged his loyalty."

She turned to her brother.

Mutt scratched the back of his head nervously. "Yeah . . . I was able to ascend to Ruby, but I didn't do it properly."

She grunted and flared her nostrils in frustration. She swore under her breath in Orcish before speaking up, "Idiot! How—"

Brunhilda stepped in front of Mutt in his defense. "What the idjit isn't telling ye is that he was unethically experimented on by a cleric without morals, turning him into a crazed beast."

"I will have words with the Kingdom of Blades. First they experiment on my brother, a royal, and then they claim he died in some 'accident,'" Myev shouted.

"Uh, your anger is justifiable, but we ask that you don't reach out to the Kingdom of Blades. Please?" Kiru asked.

Myev furrowed her brow in confusion, "Oh? Why?" she asked as her eyes flashed, and the power of her aura directly focused on the psion.

Kiru fell to his knees from the sudden pressure. He had to fight not to pass out or vomit. *She's a Sapphire? No, Emerald!* he realized. He'd felt S'Vol's intimidating Emerald power, and he hadn't even focused it directly onto the psion. *If I don't do something, this aura may kill me alone!* he thought. Kiru realized he didn't have time to play it safe. He needed to put all his cards on the table if he had any chance of coming out of this. "Because you're right. There is something more about me," he choked out.

Her aura let up slightly, giving Kiru a mild reprieve. "And that is?" she asked. "Know I will not tolerate deceit, so speak truthfully."

"My real name is Kiru Chromebane, son of the late king Ruken Chromebane," he wheezed as he managed to push himself up to his knees.

Kiru looked up to see Myev was still right in front of him, and she seemed to pause as if stuck in time. There was a heavy silence. Then she scowled. Her hair seemed to stand on edge like an angry cat, and all the sacred beasts bared their teeth at the psion in response to her anger.

"The Mad Tyrant," she said through gritted teeth.

The rooster let out a sudden loud cluck, and electricity flowed out of its feathery body and into Myev's. Blue lightning crackled around the regent queen's body, like a shroud. She displayed true power. It was awesome to witness despite the clear threat she imposed. It was a level of strength Kiru wished to attain one day.

"Choose your next words carefully. I've heard of what terrors your kind has wrought." Her body and tone were much more menacing, now promising death. "Why are you here, son of the tyrant? If I do not like your answer, none of you will leave this room alive," Myev said. She didn't exert her aura directly on him this time, but her power flooded the room in its entirety. There was no way he or anyone could escape if she didn't allow it.

"Oh, shit! Master, normally I'd tell you to fight, but this time, I won't judge you if you act like a submissive little bitch. In fact, I'd recommend it, now!"

Kiru immediately got down on his knees, bowing his head in supplication to the more powerful cultivator. He needed to find a way to convince her of the truth, but if she was already biased against him, it was not going to be easy. *I need to show her that I pose no threat, and I'm telling the truth.* He nearly touched her leg in his rush to bow down.

"Do not touch me!" she cried out and recoiled. "Also, do not try and use any techniques. If I detect any hint of such, I will kill you on the spot," the queen regent threatened.

Kiru desperately considered how he could assure her he wasn't using any mental mana techniques in order to prove his psionic heritage. That sparked an idea. "Are you familiar with trollstone, Your Highness?"

She grunted in affirmation. "It is an item meant for weaklings to suppress the strong."

"Right, it prevents anyone from using mana when in contact. To assure you of my honesty and no foul play, I will have one of my allies bind me with a pair of trollstone cuffs," Kiru proposed. "That way I cannot use any mana to influence or control anyone's minds. Not that I was intending to or am doing so now, Your Majesty," he hurriedly added.

"Go on," she grunted, not hiding her growing impatience.

"Just to let you know, without the access to mana, I can't move my body from the neck down. I have no physical sensation. You can have that wolf bite down on my foot. I won't feel it or react," Kiru said. Before Myev could respond, Zhaden pulled out the cuffs and quickly placed them on Kiru's wrists. Without access to his mana and therefore his Telekinesis technique, Kiru's body went limp like a puppet whose strings had been cut. Fortunately, the drakonid caught him.

"Hmm," Myev said as she looked at the limp psion. "Let's prove if this is true," she said, and in one swift motion, pulled out the bone dagger and stabbed Kiru in the hand, leaving the weapon embedded. She quickly took a step back, wary of any schemes. Besides blood pouring out of the wound, nothing happened—no flailing of pain or groan from Kiru at all. "It's true," she uttered. "You have bought yourself more time." She then turned to Brunhilda. "You may heal him," the queen regent said before looking back to Kiru. "Now, you will continue to explain yourself."

They did just that. Brunhilda tied a tourniquet on Kiru's limp arm, removed the bone dagger, then used her Healing Hands technique on his injury. Holy, glowing life mana emanated from her palms and into Kiru's hand. In a few moments, the wound sealed. First it was bone, then muscle and tendon, and finally, skin. It had been healed completely and was now back to its regular appearance, not even a scar present to indicate what had happened.

With that demonstration done, Kiru began telling Myev his story: his injury, discovering he was a psion, the truth about his father's death, his quest, his journey to the academy, and the Warrior Games. Kiru also had them take off one of his boots to show her his severely atrophied limb. With it being nearly just skin and bone, he used that as further evidence of his claim that there was no way he would be able to stand, let alone move his body in that armor. At least, he couldn't move it through physical force alone. The story of what had happened to Kiru and his friends that he gave Myev was more of an abbreviated summary of what happened. Mutt tried to vouch for him once, but when the queen regent used her aura on him to stay silent, neither he nor any of the others dared to speak up.

Kiru paid special mind *not* to let the orc queen know about his Subjugation technique. No need to stack the deck against him even more. He wasn't lying to the orc but that didn't mean he had to tell her *everything.* "After that, we began our journey south into Imakandi," Kiru finished.

"To find the second of these . . . artifacts?" Myev asked.

"Yes, Your Highness. We'd hoped to get your aid to help us obtain the one hidden in your homeland. We dealt with a number of dangerous creatures on our way here, including running minotaurs, a cyclops, and some two-headed crocodiles. After we ran into the Jabari on our way, though, we thought we could also provide help for you too—prove we are truly allies," Kiru replied.

At the mention of the Jabari, both Myev and every sacred beast in the room all let out a menacing growl. Even the rooster clucked angrily! "S'Vol," she spat. "So you know?" she asked Mutt.

Mutt nodded, "We accidentally wandered into Jabari Territory. We ran into S'Vol when his lackeys were hunting Nom."

"Nom?" Myev asked.

"Nom!" the little critter said excitedly as if in answer to her question as it woke up from its nap in Brunhilda's swaddle. The paladin had wrapped him up thoroughly, so he wasn't immediately visible.

"A leokin! And a male cub! Explain," she ordered.

"Well, Sis, we were going through the Jabari jungle, when out of nowhere, a full-grown leokin burst through into a clearing up ahead of us. Some of S'Vol's followers came out after it, and a spear killed the thing. They were clearly Jormuns like him." He scowled. "They all smelled of snake. Anyway, after they killed the big leokin, they tried to go after this little guy."

"Nom!"

"Brunhilda here has a big heart and couldn't let that happen. So, we intervened," Mutt said.

"I see. And S'Vol was there?" Myev asked her brother.

He nodded.

"He had a reptilian bearing to him as well," Zhaden added.

Sensing opportunity, Kiru spoke up. "I'm not 100% sure what exactly Ukufakaza entails, but I believe we can help each other."

Myev raised an eyebrow and looked down at the prone psion, still held up by Zhaden. "Go on."

"Mutt told us that the Ukufakaza is some sort of set of trials in order to determine leadership. It's clear that S'Vol is intent on winning it. I agree that the guy is bad news and shouldn't be allowed to rule."

"*He shouldn't be allowed to live in my opinion*," William added via Telepathy.

Kiru didn't acknowledge him and continued to speak. "So, we help you keep the throne, and in return, you help us get my father's item and bring Nom back to his people."

"Nom!"

Brunhilda looked visibly upset at the notion, likely due to her protective nature. Kiru also thought that the leokin's cuteness played a big factor in the paladin wanting to keep him too. Still, he knew that the beast would be best with his own kind.

"Hm, fair point, Withered One, fair point." The queen regent put a hand on her chin in contemplation, "I admit, before my father's passing, he informed me that the Chromebanes appeared to be nothing but benevolent. However, after your father's death and public condemnation by your new ruler, he grew wary. The crimes Ruken had been charged with were horrid to say the least. That is why I acted as I did earlier," she said casually as if she hadn't threatened Kiru's life multiple times in the past ten minutes. "M'Baku Otto did not want to risk Imakandi's place in the Alliance, but he did not completely trust the usurper human. Knowing that, I invite you the opportunity to prove his suspicions correct, Withered One."

She gave Kiru a warm and genuine smile for the first time. "You will help me secure my family's throne, and in return, I will help you and the leokin cub. This I swear on my core." The orc stuck her hand out to his prone body.

Kiru nodded to Zhaden. The drakonid rogue deftly unlocked the trollstone cuffs, and with them off his body, the psion was able to use his mana once more. Kiru quickly activated Telekinesis and used it to force himself up. He then reached out with his right arm and clasped wrists with Myev. "I accept your offer, M'Baku Myev. I will do all I can to help you secure your family's throne, and upon success, you will help me get my father's item and get Nom home. This I swear on my core."

The power of their words took hold as the mana inside their cores recognized their vows. There was a subtle tightening sensation around both of their cores to signify the physical representation of their agreement. Now the deal was sealed. If either of them failed to uphold their end, their cores would degenerate and revert them all the way down to a Bronze rank, or fracture, an even worse fate. Kiru knew that all too well.

Myev chuckled, "Good! I welcome this partnership." She then put an arm around both Kiru and Mutt's necks. "Now, let us feast and plan! It's not often a dead prince returns home."

At the mention of a feast, the little leokin's ears perked up. "Nom!"

CHAPTER SEVEN

Feast and Famine

Myev signaled her guards to leave. The minotaurs silently complied, and, in their stead, the large central chamber soon filled with numerous robed orc servants. As the former left, it occurred to Kiru that the sacred beasts had all heard his admittance as to his true identity. He quietly asked Myev if that would be a problem, but the queen regent waved off his concern. "They do not speak and are loyal to the M'Baku clan. You need not worry, Withered One."

Satisfied, at least for the moment, Kiru joined his friends and shifted out of the way to give the servants more room.

They quickly moved some of the multiple tables together to form one very long table, and then brought out various dishes, steaming and freshly prepared. There were numerous roasted boars, birds, and grilled fish. Bountiful vegetables and fruits as large as Kiru's head were spread about as well.

Kiru felt his mouth watering. He looked around to see his friends' mouths agape in excited anticipation as well. After eating mostly tough meat interspersed with occasional wild berries and dried rations, the psion and his companions were *really* ready for some variety in their diet. To see such a bounty of luscious fruit and juicy vegetables, he had to practically restrain himself from jumping on the table and grabbing everything in sight, and he saw that his friends were in the same boat.

Zhaden's reptilian visage appeared to be the most stoic and collected, but Kiru knew that may be more due to his anatomy rather than actual self-control.

Brunhilda's lips were pinched tight as her eyes hungrily scanned the feast before her.

Mutt was the worst of the bunch, openly drooling at the display.

Kiru realized how much they'd been deprived for the past couple of months!

Mutt's ridiculously long tongue licked his lips in anticipation, and Nom's eyes grew comically large at such display.

Before the servants were even finished with the setup, the little leokin leapt out of Brunhilda's arms and dove straight into the food with reckless abandon. There was an awkward pause at the sacred beast's lack of control before it was audibly interrupted by a loud growl from Mutt's stomach. At that, the party joined Nom. Without plates, utensils, or ceremony, they began digging into the feast before them. Kiru was in a state of bliss, consuming a variety of foods, seasonings, and flavors he'd never been exposed to before in his life. Local Imakandi river fish, large juicy fruits, and crunchy green vegetables all dazzled his tastebuds.

The psion particularly enjoyed a small bowl of grilled wildebeest stew. He asked a nearby servant what it was seasoned with; the orc told him curry and turmeric. Kiru nodded to himself, grateful for his perfect memory. It may have been silly, but made a note to himself that when he was king, he would make sure that both curry and turmeric were readily traded for and used in more dishes throughout his homeland.

"Aw! C'mon, Master! Let me out! I wanna eat some of that good lookin' food too!" William complained.

"As long as you promise to behave," Kiru sent back.

"Pfft, fine. I won't cause any trouble," William replied. Though Kiru couldn't see the imp, he imagined William rolling his eyes at the psion.

Deciding to trust his familiar, Kiru summoned William forth. The monstrous little fiend then immediately did a cannonball dive into some sort of fruit pudding bowl.

Guess no one else is going to have that dish. Kiru thought.

Once Kiru's stomach was starting to get full, he finally realized that they had dug into a royal's meal without their express permission to. He looked up to see that his friends had already come to that realization as well, both Zhaden and Brunhilda now looking embarrassed and no longer eating anything.

Mutt didn't seem to care. He was a royal and with family, so he clearly had no problem continuing to chow down, but Kiru and the others composed themselves. They all coughed in embarrassment and lowered their heads. Zhaden wiped his mouth nervously while both Brunhilda and Kiru blushed at their rashness.

Kiru reached into the pudding dish that William was swimming in and yanked him out. The imp gave an indignant cry but quickly silenced himself after a stern look from Kiru. The psion then quickly looked over to Myev, "Sorry, Your Majesty. My familiar meant no offense and neither did we. It's just been a while since we've had a proper meal, and well, I guess hunger got the best of us."

Myev gave a wry smile. "None taken, Withered One. You have proven yourselves true to your words so far. This meal is to honor that honesty. Please, continue." She gestured at the food, still observing the party, watching them like a predator.

"Don't mind if I do!" William answered right after a loud belch, not caring about the powerful orc before them. The imp then wriggled himself free from Kiru's grasp, landed back on the table, and proceeded to bite into a large fried bird leg bigger than his whole body. "So, explain to me about this Ukufuwhaza or whatever shit you've got going on," he said through a mouthful of food.

Myev gave a curious glance at the audacious William, then to Kiru as if to say, "Is he for real?"

He shrugged and nodded, answering wordlessly back that it was okay. The psion was curious too.

"Ukufakaza is the gods of the Beast Pantheon's ceremonial ritual that we orcs undergo in order to maintain the right to rule our nation," she answered.

William just rolled his eyes, losing interest and digging back into his food.

"Could you elaborate on the ritual, exactly? What happens? What do you need to do to prove yourself worthy of ruling?" Kiru asked.

"You struck me as the bookish and curious type," Myev joked and winked at Kiru.

The others let out muffled chuckles while Kiru blushed even more.

"When the ruler of Imakandi leaves Alterra, the Beast Gods speak to their guardian shamans—the leokin. They are the same as . . . what do the Vasir call them? Oh! High priests," she said.

"Nom!" the little sacred beast said excitedly.

"The leokin are beloved by the Beast Gods and are one of the few sacred beasts that have the ability to speak. They even have their own complex society. The leokin are informed of the parameters of the next proving cycle, then travel throughout the land, speaking to the chief of every clan, telling them what the pantheon requires. I assume that little Nom was being trained by an elder to do such a task," Myev explained.

The little sacred beast seemed to understand Myev's words as his ears drooped down and he stared at the table.

The queen regent reached over and used one of her fingernails to scratch his chin. Nom began to audibly purr, his mood immediately changing for the better.

"Do your people *have* to accept right to rulership this way? What's to stop them from claiming leadership not in line with your pantheon at all?" Brunhilda asked.

Myev and Mutt chuckled knowingly. "You don't know your history, Paladin. Soon after Ragnarok and the great fusing of many realms into our world today, there was great chaos. People, prey, predators, and monsters were all suddenly displaced from our homes in a sudden and violent event," Myev said. "Everyone and every clan was fighting in a desperate attempt to carve out a safe home for themselves. We all would've killed each other had not the beasts intervened: Fenrir, the wolf who slayed Odin, reincarnated with the Allfather's power; Jormungandr, the great serpent; Tanngniost and Tanngrisner, twin goats of strength and life;

Gullinkambi, the thunder rooster; Hldsvini the battle boar; Heidrun the hungry; Huginn and Munin, the wise ravens; Sleipnir the magic horse who commands the winds."

The psion's eyes shone with excitement as she continued recounting the story. It was the first time she didn't seem like a stern ruler about to have them executed or a predator watching their prey. "Together, they rallied the disparate tribes among the land to finally bring peace and balance. We descendants of those first tribes honor and readily reapply the pact our ancestors made with those who saved our people. This land is not ours; it belongs to the Beast Gods. So, anyone who wants to try and claim these wild lands, they are welcome to try."

Something Myev said jogged his memory. "But there must've been some tension at some point, right? You said Jormungandr was part of the pantheon. Based off of our recent experiences, I'd say that's no longer the case."

She gave a reactive scowl at Kiru's words. It lasted for only a moment before her composure returned. "Yes. The power our deities possessed couldn't be contained in our fragile, new world forever. So, they used their divine power to create a new plane of existence where only they and their loyal fallen can survive. Jormungandr wasn't satisfied with that. Instead, he sought to bring death and domination to the entire world. So the other beasts tricked the serpent and imprisoned him inside the realm where they now reside—the Savage Realm."

"If I may be so bold as to ask, why didn't they just kill him? Even with him being imprisoned, he clearly is still having a negative influence to this day," Kiru said.

Myev's neck visibly tensed. "It is not our job to question our gods, Withered One. So mind your tongue," she threatened.

Kiru gulped and nodded. She was clearly passionate about the Beast Gods. The psion realized he would have to tread carefully.

Myev exhaled deeply before continuing. "Still, your question isn't without merit," she admitted through bared teeth. "Despite Jormungandr's fall from grace, the Beast Gods still consider him one of them. Just because he disagreed with how the pantheon should handle the world and their followers, they did not think that warranted his death. The pantheon had a majority vote to keep him alive since he'd never acted against them directly or ever truly shown any ill will to Imakandi," she explained. "They didn't revoke his spot among the pantheon, but they did limit it with his imprisonment, hoping he would learn his lesson. Unfortunately, the World Serpent hasn't foreseen the actions his cultists would do. Jormungandr's followers have been hidden throughout the centuries, sowing chaos amidst our clans and attempting to somehow break him free from his chains. The M'Baku had done well in keeping it limited to the odd cultist up until S'Vol's betrayal. After his attempt to kill father, the cult became emboldened, bringing more death and ruin to our homeland. We cannot formally remove him from his position as chief since the Jabari still rule over their territory, but we can still suppress him."

"How, Sis?" Mutt asked.

"We prevent his ascension to rule our nation as a whole. With me as high chief, we can pressure the Jabari enough to remove S'Vol from power and eliminate his cult of extremism for good." She turned back to face Kiru, "That's where you can help. You have proven yourself in word, Withered One. Now, you can prove in deed that you are my ally."

"Name it," Kiru replied. "What do we need to do to help you secure the throne?"

Myev went on to explain what the leokin shaman who visited her had said was required. First off, they had visited her not long after her father's death. They told her that she had six weeks to meet the requirements of this iteration of Ukufakaza. That meant she had one month left now. Aside from that, there were four more things required. She needed the backing of three of Imakandi's ten founding tribes, she needed to be at least Emerald Rank, she needed to possess at least an Emerald Rank Sacred Beast Core from a dead sacred beast, and lastly, she needed to have the head of a worthy kill *or* the leader of another tribe.

A shiver went up the party's collective spines as they realized that's what S'Vol was indicating when he said that Mutt "wasn't worth the time." After one had met all the requirements, they needed to travel to the desert in the south where the main temple to the Beast Pantheon was located and where the leokin resided. There, they would present their "proof" to the shamans.

"If there is more than one contestant, another round of testing will commence at the gods' discretion," she added.

Myev had three of the four requirements. She was an Emerald and was also in possession of an Emerald Rank Sacred Beast Core. That same sacred beast—a dire spider ape—was indeed a worthy kill for Myev, so its head also worked as the third requirement. Apparently, the Beast Gods would somehow *know* if she was the one to kill it or not. Kiru knew better than to question it at this point. The only thing Myev was lacking was the backing of three out of the ten founding tribes.

"I have the backing of the M'Baku tribe, obviously, and of our loyal allies, the Tau," she said.

Mutt scratched his stubbly chin, "I get S'Vol probably has allies, but he couldn't have gotten *all* the other tribes to support him."

The queen regent shook her head, "No. That's because there is a third contender for the throne: Grimtusk, chief of the Thrar'fang."

"You serious? Phew! Good thing we avoided them when we went through their lands," Mutt said.

"Indeed," she said to her brother. "The Thrar'fangs are savages, Grimtusk especially so. Where the Jabari have used trickery and lies to acquire patronage, the Thrar'fangs have attained sponsorship through violence and the threat of it. The Jabari have garnered the support of three tribes and the Thrar'fang have intimidated the others in order to have four. Unless we find a way to get one of the others to switch allegiances, our chances will be doomed before we even start."

"Your Majesty, by my calculations, unless you mean that the Thrar'fangs have four other tribes backing them, that would still leave one tribe unaccounted for," Zhaden said.

Mutt began counting his fingers. "Hey, yeah! You're right, Stabby! Sis, why don't we just get that one to back us?"

Myev gave a look of slight annoyance. "Which tribe do you think it is that hasn't sponsored anyone this cycle?"

Mutt just gave her a blank stare.

"The one tribe who has *never* sponsored any candidate for the throne?" she asked as if it was obvious.

He shrugged. "I never paid much attention to any of that stuff, Sis. Most of the others didn't give a shit about me when I was a kid because I was blind, so I didn't give a shit about them either."

She muttered in Orcish as she rubbed her temples, clearly frustrated at her brother's ignorance. She sighed before answering. "It's the L'Khan Clan. The one and only ogre clan that is part of the ten founding tribes. I knew you were dense, but I didn't realize you'd paid so little attention to our history lessons."

She then shook off her frustration and addressed the party as a whole, "Long ago, during Jormungandr's attempted coup, Heidrun the Hungry—the sole sacred beast the L'Khans worship—was afflicted by some strange power. The L'Khan Clan reached out for help in curing whatever ailed their god. The other tribes were fighting against the Jormuns as our patron deities were fighting against the World Serpent. So, they chose not to help the L'Khan and Heidrun out of fear that, with fewer troops defending their borders, the Jormuns would seize the opportunity and overtake them. After the World Serpent was imprisoned, it was too late for the ogres. Heidrun survived but was reported to be forever changed. We know not what happened but that the Beast God was warped and had lost most of his power, keeping him tethered to our world. The L'Khans haven't forgiven the other tribes and have isolated themselves in the Wastelands ever since. Any delegation that has been sent there over the centuries has ended being refused by the ogres or killed by the creatures there."

"Wait, wait, wait," Brunhilda raised her hands. "So yer saying there be a literal god out there in the Wastelands?"

Myev nodded. "He's not much of one now if the stories passed down are to be believed, but yes, Heidrun supposedly is still alive and living here in Imakandi."

"By me grandad's corncob pipe," Brunhilda said as she pressed a hand to her forehead in shock.

Both Kiru and Zhaden were noticeably wide-eyed at the information. *Even if his power is lessened, a literal god could make a seriously powerful ally!* Kiru thought.

William was just as surprised but for a whole different reason. *"A god! Master, she said the god was really weak. This is our chance! We should kill it! Then our names will be feared throughout Alterra and beyond for eternity! Kiru the God Conqueror and William the Breaker of Divine Wills!"*

Kiru nearly choked on the water he was drinking. While there was a part of him that thought the titles themselves were pretty cool, killing a god was not on his to-do list. *"We already have a lot on our plate, William. How about we first prevent the next Draconic Campaign from happening, then we focus on killing a god, okay?"* he sent back via Telepathy.

"Harumph! Boring." William pouted.

"I promise we'll kill something big and scary, okay?" Kiru offered.

"We'd better," William sent back.

Compared to the others' astonishment, Mutt seemed to not be bothered in the slightest by the revelation that a god was living in his homeland. "Okay, so they're mad because of what happened to their god. Why don't we just fix the god, and they should be good?"

Myev rolled her eyes. "You think fixing a god is that simple, Mutt? First, we'd have to earn the trust of his followers to allow us to see Heidrun before we could even determine what's wrong with him. That's what we need, their trust."

Mutt just shrugged. "Okay, so the ogres aren't a good candidate to support you. Which of the other tribes' leaders could we get to swap support?"

"I have my spies embedded within the other tribes. Grimtusk has threatened the other leaders with violence if they didn't support him, placing some of his savage troops to 'guard' the villages. S'Vol . . . he has kidnapped the children of two chiefs, so those chiefs now support him."

"I see, he's using the little ones as leverage," Zhaden said.

"Indeed," Myev replied. "I will not risk the children's lives, so getting one of the chiefs who support S'Vol would be out of the question. So, if we had no other choice, we would have to take a full-scale assault of a neighboring tribe in order to free them of Thrar'fang influence rather than Jabari. Being just one tribe, we cannot afford to invest so many troops in such an endeavor. It could lead to Dissé being invaded in a long, costly battle."

Kiru nodded, reminded of a quote from his mother's favorite book, *The Art of War*: "There is no instance of a nation benefitting from prolonged warfare."

"Well, if you're short on troops and can't risk open war, I don't see a better option than to reach out to the ogres," Kiru said. "My party and I could even do it for you as a way to truly prove us your allies with action, not just word. What's the worst that could happen?"

"They could eat you," she said.

"Oh, well—"

"You make a good point, Withered One." She interrupted the psion. "As much as I don't like it, sending another envoy to parlay with the L'Khans is the M'Baku's best chance at getting enough sponsors for our bid to keep the throne." Myev smiled as her face grew more resolute. "Yes, I think that is a wise idea. You and your party will go to the Wastelands and entreat with the L'Khans in order to garner their support for my claim. With my brother present, they will accept it as a legitimate offer. I will gather an elite few to join and guide you on your mission. It will take the better part of a week to get them here, but we do have a month left until we to be at the main temple, so there's time."

The queen regent then took time to reexamine each member of Pandemonium, seeming to measure their capability just by sight. "As I thought, two Rubies and two Golds. Impressive. Most people never ascend past Silver. Even most dedicated cultivators never get past Gold. To be so young and so far already . . . the blood of kings must run strong through you to lead them all so far."

Kiru was a bit surprised by her words. He wasn't sure how old Myev was, but she looked to be in her early-to-mid thirties. She was already so much farther than any of them. To be at Emerald already was phenomenal! Before the psion could comment, however, she continued, "It makes sense that you all were students in the Kingdom of Blades' academy. Still, your strength is not enough."

"Your Majesty, besides S'Vol and the minotaur herd, we've been able to handle most every opponent we've come up against in Imakandi so far. Your brother has been an effective instructor. Could you elaborate as to why you think we're too weak?" Zhaden asked.

"Aye, we've been able to deal with most of the beasties here," Brunhilda added.

"Outside the Bi-Head Crocodiles and the Cyclops, what other predators have you fought?" Myev asked.

"None," Kiru answered, his perfect memory providing an accurate answer.

"Exactly. You could have fought off the minotaurs had they been fewer in number, but Mutt made sure to keep you away from likely predators. Packs of fen-wolves, gnoll scavengers, leopard boars, and blood bats are just some of the dangerous beasts that call our nation home. So, you are strong, but to make it in the wilds, especially the Wastelands, strength will not be enough. It will take a week to get the elite scouts back here from their posts throughout Imakandi. In the meantime, I offer you the palace grounds for your lodging. I recommend you use the time to train."

CHAPTER EIGHT

Capital Temple

Accepting the challenge to get stronger, Kiru and the rest of the party realized they needed a strategy for how to best train. Seeing as they literally had the queen regent of the entire country right there in front of them, they decided to ask her for help. Myev turned to Brunhilda. "I suggest you seek help from our main temple dedicated to your god, Paladin," she said.

The dwarf was already planning on going there, so Brunhilda nodded in agreement.

"Now, my brother called you 'Stabby.' Is that the name you prefer?" Myev asked Zhaden.

"It is a moniker that I did not approve of, but it's one that he insists on calling me. I request that you call me by my given name, Zhaden of Clan Ironclaw, Your Highness," the gold drakonid said in his typical hissing manner as he gave the orc a slight bow.

"I haven't seen too many from the Serpent Isles, but that doesn't mean I haven't interacted with your kind before. You gold drakonids favor fire mana, correct?" Myev asked.

"That is the case for most of my kind, Your Majesty. However, I am an anomaly. I use dream mana, which allows me to cast powerful illusions." He then performed Duplication, creating an illusory doppelganger of her to appear right beside her.

The Emerald recoiled slightly in surprise before regaining her composure. Kiru noticed that her green-skinned cheeks had grown a notably darker shade but decided not to say anything in case it caused her embarrassment. Myev then examined the duplicate. "It seems to be focused mainly on the visual." She loudly sniffed. "No odor or heat is coming off. Still, it is impressive," she admitted before looking back to Zhaden. "You've had to make do with a mana type that most with your physical form don't have. Despite that, you've done well with your illusions. I know of someone who can help make them better. Be at the front gate of the palace grounds at dawn. They will meet you there."

"My thanks, Your Majesty," Zhaden said as he bowed once more.

She waved it off as no big deal, then turned to Mutt and Kiru.

"I guess you'll be the one training me," Mutt said, obviously expecting that to be the case.

Myev shook her head. "No, Brother. I cannot train you."

The blind orc's right eyebrow raised in confusion. "Say what, now?"

"You heard me. I cannot train you. I have acquired all of my techniques solely from the sacred beasts that roam this land." Myev emphasized her point, making a downward circling gesture with her pointer finger. "You, however, smell of multiple creatures and not all of them are from Imakandi. What sacred beast cores did you ingest?"

"Umm . . . I don't know." Mutt said, his voice growing high-pitched by the end, clearly signaling his discomfort.

Her eyes went wide. "By Fenrir's howl, you don't even know which cores you took in?!"

"Well, as the Boss said, I was experimented on. Though, I guess I agreed to it . . ." He trailed off before regaining his composure. "They gave me such strong cores that I lost control of my mind. Still, I got to Ruby. So, it's all good." He chuckled nervously.

"I do not discount that, Brother, but you were the imbecile that agreed to the too-good-to-be-true deal in the first place! So, no. It's not 'all good,'" she spat out.

Mutt looked like he wanted to make a retort, but no words came out. Myev was right, and it was clear Mutt knew it. He just pursed his lips and nodded. Despite his obviously immoral treatment at the hands of both the headmaster and the school cleric, Mutt was the one who agreed to take the cores without question. Seeing as he'd made an enemy of the headmaster's son just before Niazen's 'offer,' he should have.

Seeing her brother's face, Myev's expression visibly lightened. She looked genuinely sad for Mutt. "I'm sorry, Brother. Since we have different beast cores, I do not have the knowledge on how to train you to best use them. Also—" Her look now turned from sadness to one of serious concern. "—you have to find out which beast cores you took in. If you don't, you'll never get past Ruby, let alone make it to the second tier of the rank," she said, putting a hand to Mutt's shoulder.

The usually carefree orc put both hands to his head. It was the very first time that Kiru or his friends had ever seen Mutt so upset! "You mean I won't be able to hunt stronger things or have better fights?" he asked in clear distress.

"Yes," she answered bluntly.

He gulped, "Whoa. That's . . . a lot, Sis." Mutt turned his head away from his sister and began scratching the stubble on his chin. "Hm, how can I figure out which cores I took in?" he muttered to himself.

Myev then turned to face Kiru. "It goes without saying, I do not have any of your kind here to help you on your path. You will have access to the royal grounds to cultivate and train, but I'm afraid there isn't more I can offer."

"Actually, there may be a way you can help," he said.

"Really?" she asked.

"Really?" William asked at the same time, mirroring the queen regent's skepticism.

"It's a long shot, but I had an idea when you used your blue lightning technique earlier and made that shroud around yourself. During our final battle in the Warrior Games, my opponent electrocuted my entire body continuously with some ridiculous-sounding but powerful technique. It was only thanks to my familiar protecting of my core and my previous lack of feeling that I was able to still move," Kiru said.

Myev just raised an eyebrow. "And?"

The psion pressed on. "And anyway, during that fight, I managed to push forward through the electrical technique and somehow discharged it out of my body and into my opponent when I punched him." Kiru went on to explain how he needed just one more technique to help him reach the threshold of ascending to Ruby. "I've discovered an ascension method to allow me to reach Ruby faster than the conventional method taught in my kingdom. I just need a fourth technique in order to enact it. Seeing how strong you are with your electrical technique, I think you can help me create my own. I've played around with trying to recreate the effect at night during my watch shift but have had very little success. One night, during a lightning storm, I was able to use my mana to concentrate the ambient electricity to flow down an arm. That was the only time, though."

"Master, I'm all for shocking our foes to a crisp, but I think that was just a fluke," William said via Telepathy.

Kiru just shook off the imp's negativity and focused on Myev. "Still, I think that means my mind is thinking in the right direction. So, could you teach me how to control electricity like you do?"

"Hm, what you described is not exactly what I do. I use concentrated beast mana inspired by the mana of a specific sacred beast and channel it through my body," she explained.

Kiru felt his face begin to drop at her words, and disappointment flowed through him. He quickly perked up at what she said next, though.

"Still, I find your line of thinking inspiring. It's not *exactly* what I do, but I dare say that your idea is similar enough to how I power my technique that it could work," she said, then lowered her face to be at eye level with the psion. "First, I must ask, though . . . Why?"

Kiru furrowed his brow, unsure what she meant. "Why what?"

"Why do you wish to grow in strength? Your friends are plenty strong enough. Why risk your life when it is so important that you carry on? Why not let your friends bear the burden to help you claim your throne?" she asked.

Kiru shook his head. "My life isn't more important than my friends'," he said almost immediately.

Myev raised an eyebrow in surprise.

"Your brother, Zhaden, and Brunhilda, they aren't some tools to be used and disposed of. They are people, and they are my friends. Yes, I want to get strong to reclaim my throne and live, but I also want to get strong to ensure that I can live *with* my friends. Otherwise, life won't be worth living. So, to answer your question, it's precisely because of just how important my friends are to me that I must acquire this technique and ascend."

A big grin grew on Myev's face. "Very well, Withered One, I will train you. Be right here at first light tomorrow." With their tasks assigned, Myev left the party to attend to more important royal matters and city management. Just because another round of the Proving was about to be underway, that didn't stop the people from needing leadership in the interim.

It was mid-afternoon. Since none of them would be starting their training until tomorrow and Mutt was left to his own devices for training, the party decided to go back down to the Vasir Temple. Brunhilda still had the quest that her goddess had given her, and hoped she could find some sort of trainer there too. Both Nom and William had fallen fast asleep after their meal, so they left them back in the palace grounds. Kiru knew William would do his best to boss the cub around, which meant William himself would be occupied as well. Mutt also put a cowl over his head so as to not be recognized by others. No need to draw a crowd toward the prince's return. They came up on the grandiose stone column structure. It was virtually abandoned except for an elderly orc in a toga who was sweeping the dust off the entrance.

"This temple isn't for the Beast Gods. You're looking for the other one across the pavilion," he said in a defeated tone, not even looking up at the party.

"We know, sir. We meant to come here," Brunhilda replied.

The orc sighed heavily. "If you've come to intimidate us, know that we have been granted permission to be here by the Great Alliance. To attack us is would be to incur the wrath of the multiple nations and our gods, and I assure you, they can be a wrathful bunch."

"Attack ye? No sir, I assure ye we be yer allies. I am Brunhilda Lightsworn, and I've come on an important mission from Hlin, goddess of protection."

At those words, the elderly orc finally looked up. His eyes went wide as he took in the party, namely Brunhilda. "A paladin, of the Order? By the gods, we haven't been honored with the presence of a fellow faithful warrior in oh so long. Please excuse my rudeness, madam. I am Rhodan, a cleric of Bragi." Now that he seemed to recognize who Brunhilda was, his exhausted tone was immediately replaced. Unlike any other orc they'd seen since entering Imakandi, he spoke with a rich, eloquent grace that made it sound like he wasn't from the area. "I welcome you to the main Order of Valhalla temple for the Vasir in Imakandi." He set his broom against a column and performed a sweeping bow, gesturing to the large set of ornately carved marble doors.

"My thanks, Fellow Faithful," Brunhilda replied in a ritual manner. "My company and I have traveled long and far to get here."

Rhodan rushed over to the large doors and opened the left one with a heave of effort. "Please, come in."

Pandemonium then entered the large temple with Brunhilda taking the lead. This was Kiru's first time visiting a capital temple. He'd seen the small temple in his tiny hometown and knew of the one at the academy. They were molehills compared to the mountain they now entered. It became quickly apparent that the temple was actually built into the rock pillar the capital was built around. It was nestled against the stone from the outside, but from the inside, it could be seen going back at least two hundred feet.

Numerous stone columns were spaced concentrically in two rows across the temple. Against the walls in between the columns, numerous well-carved marble statues depicting various attractive people wielding weapons and powerful magic. Each statue had a simple wooden bench in front of it as well as a few candles. People had left various coins and trinkets in front of many of them, as well. It was apparent that the statues were shrines to the various deities within the Vasir Pantheon, which the Order of Valhalla worshipped. Most of the shrines, however, had only candles set in front of them and they weren't even lit. A layer of dust and the occasional cobweb even covered some of the statues.

Kiru was able to see many of those details due to one amazing feature of the gigantic cathedral: carved into the ceiling was a massive, complex rune. Ironically, he wasn't able to see all of its features in complete detail, but strong beams of light emanated from it, illuminating the partially underground temple.

"Whoa!" they all said in unison, even Mutt. He couldn't see the light, but he could sense strong mana coming from the rune.

"I'm glad you find this temple impressive," Rhodan said, beaming like a proud parent. His pride was immediately deflated by Brunhilda's response, however.

"Well, the runework be amazing, but why are the statues in such poor care?" she asked.

The elder orc sighed and scratched his head. "I sorry, Fellow Faithful. It's not for lack of trying. Only I and Balmir, an acolyte of Odur, are left for the upkeep of this entire temple."

"Yer sayin' that the Order has thought it adequate to assign only a cleric and an acolyte to man an entire capital temple?" she asked incredulously.

"Actually, they assigned only a cleric and an acolyte for the entire country," Rhodan corrected.

Brunhilda's jaw dropped comically at the statement. "H-how?"

Rhodan sighed. "Most of the orcs here take pride in their bestial history and alliance with nature. Many are very pious, and those that are not still ascribe to the savage principles of nature. This land is irrefutably the Beast Gods'. We're not trying to usurp them, but this land's history has made it hard to spread word of our pantheon and their benefits." The cleric didn't seem to notice that an Imakandi royal prince was in their midst. *It's a good thing that royal is Mutt*, Kiru thought. If someone else had heard that, they may have taken offense. Fortunately, the orc didn't really care much of what others thought, and he was clearly off on his own train of thought, muttering to himself as to how he could better improve himself.

"I see. Is that why ye thought we were going to fight ye earlier?" Brunhilda questioned him.

Rhodan nodded.

"So this be more of a punishment than a calling. I had no idea things were so tough for those that follow the Vasir out here."

"We make do. The gods have made peace and allied with the Beast Pantheon since Ragnarok's cataclysmic end. While we have to deal with the occasional brute, the guards are quick to aid us, and we still provide valuable services to the residents of Dissé." Rhodan paused to pull out a wooden flute from inside his toga and played a quick, melodic tune. "As a follower of the god of poetry and music, I provide wonderful tales filled with music to enrich the commonfolk."

"And I aid in providing sunlight and warmth to the residents," a booming voice declared from behind them. They turned to see a muscular human man with thick brown curly hair and very tan skin, also wearing a toga, walking out from behind a column. Aside from the mop of hair on his head, there didn't appear to be a single hair on his body, not even eyebrows. "Odur's blessings of sunlight help to improve their crops' growth and their spirits." The rune on the ceiling pulsed once, then settled back down.

"Ah, Balmir, just the man I was hoping to run into. Balmir, this is Brunhilda Lightsworn, a fellow faithful within the Order of Valhalla, and her vassals," Rhodan introduced.

That last word seemed to break Mutt from his trance. "Wait, vassals?"

Kiru swiftly elbowed the orc in the gut, causing him to bow his head low. He didn't want Balmir or Rhodan to recognize who Mutt was or question what was going on. The acolyte and cleric looked back to the trio, but Kiru just waved them on. "Please, continue."

The two looked back to Brunhilda, giving her a great deal of respect. "A pleasure to meet you," Balmir said, putting an arm to his chest and bowing to the paladin.

"She's come all the way out here to Dissé on an important mission from her goddess," Rhodan explained.

"Oh, truly? Well, we are honored that the Order itself has tasked you to come to us. How may we help?" Balmir asked.

The purple-haired dwarf blushed and cleared her throat, "Er-hem, um, well, this isn't exactly an approved mission by the Order."

"If I may be so bold, Miss, which god do you serve?" Balmir asked. While Rhodan's voice was deep and dramatic, the human's voice was sharp and officious, with a tinge of overconfidence, clearly a product of his personality.

"Hlin, goddess of protection," she answered.

Balmir and Rhodan looked at each other, silently communicating as only close friends could do. It was no secret that the major deities received preferential treatment and Hlin wasn't one of them. "Well, she is in the pantheon," Rhodan said.

"But a minor deity," Balmir added, to which Rhodan shrugged and nodded in agreement. "Still, a fellow faithful is in need of help. What has your goddess tasked you with?"

She blushed a subtle shade of purple, thanks to the troll blood flowing through her body. "My goddess be the personal protector of Frigg; the major goddess has entrusted my deity with her safety. Yet despite that, the other major gods won't recognize Hlin as their equal. I humbly ask that ye allow me to create a shrine for her in yer capital temple. If I can get her shrine in all the capital temples within the Alliance, she will be recognized as a major god."

They looked at each other, then back to the dwarf. "So, you just need to make a shrine for her in this temple? Is that it?" Rhodan asked.

She blinked in surprise. "Yes. I know she be not a major deity yet, but if she has a shrine here, it will be one step closer to getting her there."

"Well, normally there's a whole process in verification and credentials, but we honestly don't really care," Balmir said. "Young lady, you are the first acolyte who we've had the pleasure of serving in years. This posting has felt like more of a punishment by our superiors since we don't follow the most popular of gods within the pantheon. Our superiors 'honored' us by giving us this posting in the middle of Beast God land, but we've received no major aid, additional acolytes, nor recognition for our efforts by the high priests in years."

"Indeed," Rhodan added. "The higher-ups have deemed our deities less worthy than theirs, despite our patrons being major gods themselves. Apparently, sunlight, poetry, and music are 'far less important' than their deities' domains.

I say, a pox on their 'important' domains. We're just as valuable, and why shouldn't protection be considered a worthy domain as well? The gods are here to protect their followers, are they not?"

"Damn right!" Brunhilda said excitedly. "So, does that mean . . ."

"We will allow you to build a shrine, but on one condition," Rhodan said.

"Name it," the dwarf said.

"Your words have reminded us of a fact that we became complacent to. This place needs some better upkeep. If you give us your word to help clean it up, maybe even help preach of our gods to the local people, you can place your shrine at one of the empty spots further down the temple," Rhodan offered.

"I swear it, on me core!" she promised instantly, without a moment's hesitation.

Both Balmir and Rhodan were visibly caught a little off-guard by her zeal, but a smile quickly grew on both their faces. It seemed refreshing to them to find someone as passionate about their faith as they were. They guided her further down the temple to a simple square podium in between two pillars. Brunhilda then pulled out a jade and gold statue the size of her head. This was the specific item she acquired from the prize room after they'd won the Warrior Games. It was a Shrine Stone, a magical item that would allow an acolyte to almost instantaneously create a holy shrine to their patron deity.

Normally, making a shrine would be both time-consuming and costly. From what Kiru had gathered, a likeness of the deity was required as well as a holy tome, candles made from special Valhallan beeswax, an area for offerings, and for it all to be imbued with holy mana. They'd seen Brunhilda create a small crude one by hand once in a tavern. It had taken her a good half-hour, and only because it was small and she had all of the materials at the ready.

With the shrine stone, all she needed to do was pray and allow her goddess's mana to flow through her. The stone would take care of the rest within minutes, eliminating the cost, time, and the sheer weight of needing to carry the required materials around. The two holy cultivators certainly looked surprised. They likely expected some simple, humble shrine carved from wood, not the ten-foot-tall jade statue that grew from the stone pedestal as if it were a tree within just five minutes. Back at the Royal Academy, Kiru had made a deal with Brunhilda to become an acolyte of Hlin as well. He wasn't as zealous as her but he was gifted with seeing the goddess's face as well as having her bless his headband with a protective enchantment. He could say from experience that this statue was almost lifelike in how well it matched Hlin's form.

Candles sprouted from the ground by the statue's pedestal and lit aflame on their own. Right at the statue's feet, a book formed. Leatherbound and with the symbol of Hlin—a spear, splintered into multiple pieces as it struck a shield—on the cover, it was clear this was a holy tome of the goddess of protection. Seeing as the statue was made of jade and not marble like the others, as well as its fresh, new appearance, it stood out.

After it was complete, Brunhilda's entire body gleamed with a subtle yellow light. "*Well done, my paladin.*" A powerful feminine voice, Hlin's voice echoed throughout the entire chamber. "*Oh, and I like the purple hair by the way,*" the goddess added. She had purple hair, so her most faithful servant having it as well clearly pleased her.

The glow faded, except in the ponytail holder that kept Brunhilda's hair tame. After a moment, it too faded. It was also blessed with a defensive enchantment. Now, that enchantment had been upgraded! The dwarf touched it and then, with a flex of will, activated it. The original enchantment had caused a temporary semi-translucent magical helmet to appear (Kiru's still did the same). Now, however, a protective dome of mana appeared over her entire body.

She beamed and looked over to her friends. "Lads, Hlin is with us. Now, let's get stronger together. We've got to get some ogres to join us, then we've got an arsehole cultist to put in his place."

The party had gone back to the royal palace for the night following that visit to the temple. Kiru had trouble sleeping, and from what he could gather, everyone but Mutt struggled as well. The next morning, they all met at the front gate at first light. As the orange light of the sun just began cresting over the horizon, it brought some surprising heat to it, quickly raising the temperature on the hilltop. Waves of heat distortion appeared as well as small clouds of fog from the various ponds.

Zhaden appeared to go on high alert. He drew a pair of daggers and took a defensive posture as he faced the fog clouds. "Identify yourself," he hissed.

From each of the fog clouds, an orc clad in a blend of sparse leathers and cloth jumped out and landed on the ground. Each of them had a hood over their heads with crisscrossed wrappings covering their mouths and noses.

"Your senses are honed, Drakonid, but they are not perfect," a harsh, creepy feminine voice said from behind the party.

Zhaden groaned and tensed as one of the heat distortions faded, revealing a female orc in the same garb, who was almost unhealthily thin. She had an animal tooth dagger pressed under his jaw. It was a weak point for many drakonids due to an artery being located there with less-tough scales covering it.

The drakonid's eyes went wide. Kiru was used to the drakonid catching people off-guard, not the other way around. "How?" Zhaden hissed.

The orc pulled away her dagger, spinning it a few times before sheathing it. "My queen tells me that you have some skill for a foreigner, but Imakandi is not as forgiving as the rest of the world. We will guide you in using what the land provides to improve your stealth. Come." The orc, who still didn't introduce herself, promptly backflipped over the gate and was quickly followed by her two compatriots.

Zhaden, seeming to be very impressed and intrigued, silently gestured bye to his friends, then jumped, grabbing the top of the gate and swinging himself over to follow his instructors.

"Well, I'm going to have the guards open the gate," Brunhilda said. "My goddess is of protection, not fancy backflips. What're ye going to do today, Mutt?"

He scratched his messy mohawk, not seeming to care to brush it before meeting up with his friends, "Well, since my sis can't train me, I'll probably go out and do some hunting. It seems I need to figure out which sacred beast cores I took in so I can advance. Hopefully, if I push myself, maybe I'll have some sort of epiphany like all those cultivators that we learned about with Niajar."

She put a hand to his arm, "I'm sorry, Mutt. It not be fair what happened to ye."

He blushed and smiled. "It's alright, Brunhilda. I'll figure it out. If there's any place to get in touch with the sacred beasts, it's my homeland. Even if the cores I ingested are from beasts not from here, this place can help me get in touch, y'know? A good hunt or fight always clears my head too." The guards began to open the front gate doors, and Mutt spoke to Kiru. "Boss, I've got one piece of advice for you. Give everything you've got when it comes to my sis." The usually carefree orc shuttered involuntarily. "She's merciless." Then, he and Brunhilda left the royal compound. Without looking back, he added. "Also, you should probably start running."

"Running?" Kiru asked. Then, he heard the familiar sound of a blue rooster followed by a crackle of electricity. On instinct, he rolled to his right, narrowly avoiding a strike of blue lightning hitting the ground. He turned and drew out his Fu Tao, seeing Myev standing twenty feet away with that same damn rooster on her shoulder, a predatory grin plastered on her face.

"Master, do you think I could sit this one out?" William asked telepathically.

"No, William. I need your help to make sure my brain and core are protected."

"Well . . . shit."

CHAPTER NINE

Training Time

For the first day of his week of training, Zhaden met up with a female orc. The gold drakonid prided himself on his stealth and ability to detect hidden opponents. His trainer humbled him almost instantly. She guided him to an isolated fountain off in a corner of one of the streets.

"Do you think yourself capable of guarding this fountain from any intruders?" the thin female orc asked, her voice harsh and abrasive.

Zhaden's eyes moved rapidly, taking in all three of the orcs who'd guided him, "Who will I be guarding this fountain from, for how long, and for what purpose?" he asked. The cautious gold drakonid was on high alert and was suspicious. Still, he would trust the queen regent's judgement for now.

The lead orc narrowed her eyes, assessing the drakonid for a moment before giving him the slightest nod of approval, "You are to guard it from me for the next hour. As for the purpose, it is to see if you are truly worthy to be trained by the Akain Tribe," she said before she and her two compatriots backed away into the busy street and disappeared into the crowd.

The drakonid growled to himself in frustration but did as bid, standing guard in front of the fountain. Being out in the open made him feel uneasy. He had trained most of his life to conceal himself and not stand out, but a gold drakonid in the orc capital was a rarity no matter how many of his scales Zhaden concealed. Even with him being in a densely populated area, many orcs stopped and stared at him. Fortunately, however, none dared to get close to him.

Zhaden's eyes frequently scanned back and forth, taking note of anyone who came near. He bounced slightly on his toes and tensed his fingers repeatedly. Growing up in Clan Ironclaw and undergoing years of roguish training had made Zhaden more than a little paranoid. At first, it had been out of necessity and now it was a difficult habit to break. There were few who he trusted implicitly. The only reason Zhaden trusted Mutt was that the blind prince was so simpleminded he wouldn't be able to hide any type of deceit. But that didn't mean the rest of the orcs were the same.

So, over the next hour, Zhaden continued to keep a sharp eye out for any spies, making sure to stay focused amidst the already rising heat that distorted the air slightly in the distance. His paranoia made him more quiet and reserved, but at least it kept him ready. He was looking forward to seeing if this so-called mentor of his could teach him anything or not. Sure, she'd gotten the drop on him once, but everyone can get lucky once. He was skeptical that she could do it again or truly teach him anything new. None could match the abilities of his clan.

It was during that moment of self-reflection that the gold drakonid learned just how wrong he was. His mentor suddenly materialized right in front of him as if out of thin air. Zhaden let out a choked cry of surprise and went to draw his stiletto, but the orc was too fast. She grabbed his wrist with one hand, gripped his throat with the other, and placed her ankle behind one of his. She pushed him back and forced him prone onto his back in a blink. "I am Akain Ebysso, lead scout for M'Baku Myev," she hissed at him. "My queen has tasked me with training you." She then leaned forward to only be inches away from Zhaden's eyes, "You do not seem to be worthy to be trained by me or my tribe."

Despite having been humiliated in front of a group of orcs, Zhaden's tail wiggled in excitement. To think that they had such skilled rogues here impressed him and made him more than a little eager to learn. "I am Zhaden of Clan Ironclaw. As to my worth, I would look down to your side."

Ebysso squinted her eyes, then looked down to her right side. There, pressed gently in between a gap in her leather armor were Zhaden's sharp claws. They hadn't broken her skin, but it was clear that the gold drakonid could wound her if he wanted to. She looked back to him and nodded. "Well done," she said before letting go of him and standing up.

Zhaden followed suit. He was a few inches taller than Ebysso, but they both had similar lanky builds, their thin forms more ideal for their fighting styles.

"Your training begins now. Follow me if you can," she said, her form distorting before Zhaden's very eyes until it had disappeared altogether.

Zhaden gave a slight chuckle, which was a bit more challenging due to his reptilian anatomy. He couldn't help but wag his tail in anticipation.

After that introduction, his training began more in earnest. Zhaden rapidly formed a kinship with Ebysso and her fellow scouts. Fighting with similar styles, he felt a connection he'd only had with his party up to this point. With his lanky body and abnormal mana type, he'd always been an outcast among most of his kind. With the scouts, however, he fit right in. He even managed to let some of his guard down among them. Strangely enough, Ebysso was even more paranoid than him, which made the gold drakonid enjoy her company even more. He felt like they understood each other on a deeper level. With that understanding, he took to his training even more enthusiastically.

The scouts began by taking him on patrols of the borders of the canyon Dissé was nestled in. Despite their relative safety being by the capital and in the heart of M'Baku Territory, the orc scouts were very strict in remaining unseen and undetected. Eventually, they made it to the entrance of a cave, tucked against the canyon's edge. "We of the Akain are a tribe loyal to the M'Baku. Though not a founding tribe, our ability for stealth remains unmatched in our homeland," Ebysso explained. "The beast mana we cultivate is inspired by the great Angler Chameleon."

"What is this Angler Chameleon? I have seen many sacred beasts during my time in Imakandi, but I am unfamiliar with that name," Zhaden said.

Ebysso kept her mouth coverings on, but the drakonid was pretty sure she was smirking based on the wrinkles around her eyes. It was harder for him to tell with those who didn't have scales or tails. She then pointed right behind him.

He turned to see a tiny pink fleshy creature hanging off a stalactite a little deeper in the cave and wriggling. It had no distinguishing features; it was basically just a pink dangling blob. Zhaden was unable to determine what was its head and what were its limbs. *If such a small, fragile thing like that can survive in these lands, its stealth abilities must be unparalleled,* he thought.

He began edging himself closer to the tiny sacred beast, hoping to glean some valuable clues to its power. He noticed that, despite going deeper into the cave, the temperature didn't cool off at all. In fact, it was a little more humid inside. Some moisture even started to accumulate on his scales. He didn't take his eyes off the creature.

Before he could make it all the way to the pink beast, a rock flew over his shoulder from behind him, landing on the ground in front of him with a *squish*. In less than a second, the air around the pink creature distorted, revealing it to be a ruse. The pink creature wasn't a creature at all. It was the fleshy end of an appendage! The stalactite was some sort of stalk, curving around and connected to the ground below. The drakonid quickly saw what was attached to the stalk just as a giant, sharp-toothed maw erupted from the ground in front of him. Like an ocean predator, the mouth surged up and snapped, scaring the abyss out of Zhaden.

A hand grabbed the back of the rogue's tunic, and Ebysso heaved him back out of the cave. He looked to the orcs around him, then back inside the cave. After the mouth had been fully exposed, two sets of limbs followed until the shape of a giant gray-and-black-striped lizard as large as the orcs could be seen in full. It had too many teeth for its disproportionately large mouth and its eyes moved independently of each other, scanning its environment. The stalk was attached to the center of its forehead, dangling out ahead of it like some kind of lure. Immediately, the drakonid realized that *this* was the sacred beast that they had been referring to! It was simultaneously fascinating and repulsive. He'd never seen such an odd creature before in his life.

The large angler chameleon hissed at the party for disturbing it. It began trudging angrily toward them. They ran back out, their speed far surpassing the beast's. Once it had followed them out of the cave itself, it stopped, realizing it couldn't possibly catch up. They were about fifty feet away from it now.

Zhaden turned to see the chameleon angrily hissing once again. The light hit its scaly hide. The direct sunlight was hot, and the heat seemed to gather rapidly around the chameleon. It snarled, then turned its back to them and moved in the opposite direction, deeper into the fjord. As it moved farther away, its body distorted and eventually disappeared amidst the heat.

"That sacred beast is what inspires your tribe? How could you even get close enough to learn from it?" he asked.

The three orcs laughed. "Trial and error," Ebysso answered and lifted a palm to Zhaden, revealing two fingers and a small part of her hand missing, obviously bitten off.

The drakonid gulped and wiggled his tail nervously. "I see." He was conflicted, unsure whether to respect the Akain for their dedication or think that they were absolute lunatics. For now, his cautious side won out, and he would do his best to gain knowledge from them. Still, he kept his eyes peeled for the easiest escape route in case he needed to get away from these crazy orcs.

"Now, what did you learn from the angler chameleon?" she asked, breaking him free of his internal musings.

"I . . ." He trailed off, thinking. "He used an obvious piece of bait to draw me closer."

"Good. And?" she pressed.

"And as he walked away, the heat distorted his presence until he disappeared," he said.

"Yes!" Ebysso said, excitedly. "While you cannot cultivate beast mana like the angler chameleon, your scaled skin should be able to use the sun's light and heat to your advantage."

The drakonid smiled as much as his reptilian anatomy allowed him to, grunting and nodding in agreement. He couldn't help it, but his tail began wagging side-to-side in excitement too.

When Brunhilda met up with Rhodan and Balmir the next day, they seemed even more delighted than before. The pair seemed to have gained some renewed vigor after seeing a powerful individual loyal to their pantheon whose faith could literally raise monuments. Brunhilda was also energized herself at finally being one step closer to helping Hlin become a major god within the Vasir Pantheon. She, Rhodan, and Balmir got to cleaning in no time. In a matter of hours, they were able to completely clean the entire capital temple.

With the rest of the week ahead of her and empowered with holy zeal, Brunhilda went out and did what she was sworn to do—protect and help others. Since Imakandi ascribed to the ways of the beast, it was a society built on both cunning and might. While that helped breed strong people, it could be merciless to those in need. Mutt was a good example of that. Despite his being a royal, his father had thought little of him and practically abandoned him due to his blindness. Mutt had explained to them previously that if it hadn't been for his mother and Myev, he most likely would have died.

With her purple hair, heavy plate armor, and disproportionately long arms, Brunhilda was, without a doubt, an oddity in Dissé. Due to that, the dwarf was met by a mixture of anger, fear, and skepticism from the locals. The merchants were nicer, but that was only because they were trying to sell various goods to her. It was at the marketplace where things took a turn for the better. From across the crowded market, there was a rush of shouting and movement. One of the fruit vendors began pointing away from his stall, yelling in Orcish.

Brunhilda had been eating a rather juicy fruit that she had bought just minutes ago from that same vendor. She set it down and gritted her teeth, frustrated that she didn't have Kiru's unnatural ability to learn language. She wanted to know what was going on. Still, the vendor had been nice to her, and it looked like the orc needed help. Trusting her instincts, she equipped her dual shields and began rushing off toward the direction that the merchant had pointed. She saw some guards heading in the same direction as well. Dissé guards either wielded wooden shields with spears or nothing at all, but that didn't mean they were helpless. No, she had seen before that they could call on either the same or a similar technique that Mutt used, Fenrir's Claws, meaning their hands *were* the weapons.

Brunhilda's size worked to her advantage as she moved, allowing her to dart in between some stalls and even under some very tall orcs. That helped her reach their destination first. There, she saw a young boy whose body was covered with dirt and wounds, clutching a couple of the same type of orange fruits she had been eating. Cornered in a dead-end alley, he uttered something and raised a hand up in surrender, a look of utter terror in his eyes.

She was confused at his expression. *What be the problem with this boy? I'm not gonna hurt him*, she thought.

A guard stormed up behind her, pointing a finger at the boy and shouting. He raised a hand high, his fingers changing into claws, and went to swipe at the child.

There was a loud clashing noise as the claws scraped against metal. Acting on instinct, the paladin had turned to defend the child and deflected the blow completely. The guard growled and shouted once again before attacking in earnest.

The paladin was used to fighting highly skilled opponents from her time at the academy, and this guard's skills and strength were far beneath those of the students she'd faced up against. The orc slashed wildly with his claws, but she expertly deflected his numerous strikes, pushing back hard against him and causing him to stumble backward. Using that opening, she slammed the edge of her right shield right in the orc's thick head, knocking him unconscious and sending him flying back.

More orc guards came into the alleyway just as the unconscious one landed at the ground by their feet, causing some dirt to rise up. Their eyes went wide, and their mouths opened with obvious incredulity. They slowly turned their shocked gazes toward Brunhilda. Seeing the paladin who'd injured their comrade, their expressions turned to anger. They bared their large teeth and growled.

Brunhilda was undeterred. She braced her twin shields together and glared right back, "Explain yourselves! Why would an orc guard attack a defenseless child?! If ye dare try and strike him again, by my goddess, I will stop ye!" she declared.

The guards halted their momentum but lowered their spears in her direction.

The child quivered in fear and hid behind the paladin.

After a few tense moments, a heavily scarred guard, taller and broader than his compatriots, made his way through. He wore a gray-brown wolf skin sash with a helmet made from the creature's head. He stepped out in front of the other guards and stared Brunhilda down.

"I am the Inkosi of this company, Inkosi Rothbart. Why have you attacked one of my subordinates, Foreigner?" he asked with a thick accent.

Brunhilda didn't know what an Inkosi was, but she could extrapolate. It appeared to be some sort of rank or designation within the Imakandi military. She gave him an exasperated look. "Are ye serious? The man tried to attack a child!"

Rothbart's nostrils flared. "You should know your place, Foreigner, for you do not know the laws of our land. That runt—" He pointed to the cowering boy behind her. "—stole food from one of the vendors." Now the dwarf understood why the boy looked so scared. Rothbart continued, "Scavengers survive off of scraps. Whenever they get greedy and take from their betters, the strong remind them of where they stand in the pecking order. That is how nature works, and that is how this city is run."

Rothbart pointed again at the boy. "He stole what was not his, and he shall pay the consequences. My guard—" He gestured to the unconscious orc below. "—was merely handing out justice. He would've simply wounded the runt or cut off his hand. That way he can learn his lesson. Now, move!"

"Cut his bloody hand off? He be a child, how is that fair?" Brunhilda asked.

"It is not for you to decide!" he shouted, his face and arms turning more wolf-like, matching the pelt he wore. It looked like scales might have been developing on his green legs as well.

Despite his intimidating visage, she didn't waiver. Though a tough and competent fighter, Brunhilda knew, however, that she would be unable to fend off both Rothbart and his guards all on her own. She needed to try and find a peaceful way to resolve this. She sighed and raised her palms out to indicate peace. "Ye know what, ye be right, Rothbart."

The Inkosi scowled as he breathed heavily through his nose. Nobody said anything for a few tense seconds. Then the orc seemed to fully register Brunhilda's words, and some of his anger visibly lessened.

"But certainly we can come to an arrangement," she said.

Rothbart started to snarl again, but Brunhilda continued before he could spiral. The people of Imakandi liked to use a lot of animal references; she could use that. "If a wolf chases a scavenger but ends up stumbling on a bigger and better kill ripe for the taking—" She pulled out five gold coins. "—wouldn't the wolf go after what be better for them overall?" Traveling through the wilderness, she hadn't needed to spend any of her coin. Another benefit to the Great Alliance was that they all used the same currency system, a convenient fact that she was taught back at the Royal Academy.

Rothbart looked back and forth from the coins to Brunhilda, assessing her offer. She pulled out one more coin. "And for the vendor's losses, of course."

The Inkosi grunted, then snatched the coins from her. "The runt can get away this time, but if it happens again, it'll be more than a hand he'll lose," he threatened, staring daggers at the dwarf. To her credit, she stared right back at the bulky orc, more than double her size. Rothbart turned and shouted a command in Orcish to his troops. The guards raised their spears and dragged their unconscious ally away, leaving the dwarf and the boy alone.

Once they were gone, Brunhilda sighed in relief and turned back to face the orc child. He had a dirty mop of thick, matted hair and a small, distinctive nose. He looked up at her in amazement, muttering in his native tongue. She put a hand on his shoulder, noticing his too-thin form. It reminded her of Kiru. "Are ye alright?"

He turned his head to the side, clearly not understanding her Common dialect. Then he smiled, grabbed her arm, and led her away from the alley. After a few minutes of navigating the busy, winding streets of Dissé, he led her to a narrow passage in between two rocky structures. The dwarf had to restrain herself from visibly recoiling as her nostrils were assaulted by the acrid smells of waste, sweat, and dirt as he led her into the dark passage. Her face slackened in horror as they came to the end.

There, laying on a bed made of straw, was a sleeping, middle-aged orc woman breathing unsteadily. She was covered in a cold sweat, and her body was riddled with scars and bruises. "By Hlin's grace!" the paladin said as she rushed over to the woman. Her body was thin like the boy's but a little more muscular. Brunhilda noticed that she had the same small, flat nose as him, marking her as a likely relative of his. It was clear that she was suffering from exhaustion as well as some sickness. The paladin was grateful to her goddess that she had found the woman.

"Healing Hands," she said as she activated her extremely potent direct healing technique. Light came from her palms, and the orc's health visibly improved. She began breathing easier. She groaned and slowly blinked her eyes open. When she processed the purple-haired dwarf kneeling over her body, she gasped and moved back in fear.

Before Brunhilda could explain, the boy rushed in between, quickly speaking in Orcish. For a few minutes, he spoke to the orc woman. The paladin didn't understand his words, but by his expressiveness as he talked and the exaggerated sound effects he made, it was easy to tell he was explaining what had happened to him and the dwarf.

Once the child was done, the orc woman looked at Brunhilda with a mixture of both concern and awe.

After a moment of silence, she spoke. "You helped my son. You helped me. Why?" Her Common wasn't the best, but it was understandable, at least.

"He be a child, and a hungry-looking one at that. Why wouldn't I help him?"

The orc mother blinked a few times, trying to comprehend Brunhilda's words. "He . . . We are not your tribe. Beast Gods have helped orcs become strong, and the strong survive."

"I don't serve the Beast Gods. I serve Hlin."

"H-Hlin? Who is Hlin?"

She smiled. "Oh, I be happy to tell you all about her, dearie."

Kiru's training was . . . different than what he'd expected. Dare he say it was torturous? At first, Myev began chasing him around the royal grounds with her lightning techniques, and she eventually caught him with one. His body spasmed and convulsed, but he didn't cry out in pain, only grunted. The queen regent gave him a nod of approval, impressed by his resistance to the technique's damage even though she didn't unleash its full power upon him. With William returned to his core, Kiru had his familiar form a protective layer over his core and brain to shield him from having his brain literally fried from electrocution.

When the blue lightning technique stopped, Kiru promptly fell to the ground. A trail of smoke came off his body, a thick strand of drool leaking from his mouth.

The smell of burned hair permeated the air, and his body was covered with a thin layer of char.

"And you said you redirected electricity through your body before?" Myev asked, scoffing.

"I . . . did." He groaned as he reactivated Telekinesis and slowly pushed his body back up.

"Pfft! It must have been a freak accident," she said dismissively.

"Please, teach me how you do it," he requested. His breath was still heavy as he hadn't made it off his knees yet. Still, he did his best to look Myev in the eyes, not backing down from his goal.

The queen regent rolled her eyes and shook her head. "Stubborn boy," she muttered in Orcish.

"It's only because of my stubbornness that I've made it this far," he retorted back in her native tongue. It was his first time conversing in Orcish, and his attempt was not the most fluent, but it was at least understandable.

Myev's eyes widened. "Did you just learn Orcish?"

Kiru shook his head. "I learned it back at the academy during my time in the library. But that was the first time I actually spoke to someone in your native tongue," he admitted.

"So, you are a fast learner. There's hope for you after all," she said in Orcish as a predatory grin grew on her face. "Fine, I'll teach you how I do it, Withered One. I was hoping that forcing the electricity through your body like before would have restimulated your control of it, but I should've known better. It is clear from your weak form that you are more of a book person, so to speak."

"*That wretched woman! Who in the abyss would learn better by getting electrocuted?!* William ranted in Kiru's mind. The psion decided not to voice his familiar's anger. It wouldn't help. She was an Emerald and could crush him like an insect if he offended her.

Best to play it safe. Kiru thought. He wiped the drool from his lips, brushed some of the soot and dirt off his body, and sat in the Lotus Pose expectantly.

"What do you know about us beast mana cultivators?" Myev asked.

"Not much, only what I've read. That and Mutt's told me a little. Your mana is the same type that exudes from sacred beasts, and you channel the mana to change your bodies into their forms, at least parts of them. An example would be Mutt's Fenrir's Claws technique," Kiru answered.

She nodded. "Correct, but there's more to it. Beast mana can—how would you say—*differentiate* into diverse types. While there is general beast mana, every single sacred beast of the Ruby rank and higher exudes their own unique mana signature. To ascend to Ruby, one must advance in insight to advance the body. Those of us who cultivate beast mana do the opposite. We have to physically ingest the crystalized mana cores of the beasts and bind them to our own, making our own unique mana."

"And that's what Mutt did? He ingested however many of those cores and bound them to his to create his own version of beast mana?" Kiru asked.

Myev looked pained at the reminder of her brother's choice. "Yes."

Noticing her change in expression, the psion couldn't help but wonder. "If I may ask, why does that bother you so much?"

"Because that means my brother isn't in sync with his mana and his core. Essentially, he doesn't know who he is. If he can't fully identify the beasts that influence his unique mana signature, he will not know how to advance himself," she explained with melancholy clearly evident in her tone.

Kiru made an "Oh" face before nodding in sympathy. "I'm sorry. I didn't know."

She waved him off and changed the subject. "Back to the lesson. Now that you know this, I want you to watch how I use the Thunder Rooster's Blue Lightning technique." The queen regent stood and made her way over to one of the blue roosters walking around and searching for insects to eat off the ground. It didn't see her as she trotted over behind it. Myev bared her thick teeth and gave a convincing predatory snarl.

The sacred beast jumped a couple of feet in the air and clucked in fear. As it did so, it reactively called upon its technique.

An orb of blue static shot out from its body and struck at Myev in a flash as the rooster fled.

Instead of the static surrounding and electrocuting the orc, however, Myev focused and forced the electricity to travel across her arm. Kiru looked on in awe at the power she wielded and the control she exerted over it. The electricity crackled as it tried to break free, but it continued to course down her arm, then up and down her right leg, then along her left leg, and up to her left arm before finally spinning in a circle around her chest at where her core rested. She bunched her fists up tight and sent the blue lightning up in the air with a thunderclap.

Kiru winced at the noise and reflexively plugged his ears. After he shook the ringing from his ears, he noticed Myev looking expectantly down at him. "What did you notice about what I did?"

"It was awesome," he admitted, his eyes trailing off as he thought about it. Ever since his injury, he didn't want to ever feel helpless again, no matter the circumstances. He'd never regained his ability to physically feel, but he'd worked hard to acquire power in a different way. Ever since, he'd admired the strength of power cultivators even more and felt an insatiable desire to continue to grow stronger as well.

"Er, hem." Myev coughed loudly, bringing Kiru's focus back to her. "And?"

"It was very loud," he answered.

She gave him an unamused look.

"Um, you also controlled it. It didn't flow wildly throughout your body," Kiru elaborated.

"Yes! Now, where did it flow?" she asked.

"Through each of your limbs and to your core."

"What are in my limbs?" Myev pressed.

He put his hand to his chin as he thought. *Bones? Muscles? Nerves?* Then, it hit him! "Your meridians!"

Myev nodded approvingly. "You see, I'm not simply guiding electricity through my body in an uncontrolled torrent. I am guiding the mana with the electrical technique. Mana is in all things, and I am directing the mana present from that technique through my meridians. And like when we take in beast cores, I eventually take in the mana from the technique and make it my own. I suspect you did the same when you took control of your rival's strangely-named electrical attack."

Kiru recoiled slightly from the revelation. He blinked a few times in surprise as he processed what Myev had said, "I . . . hadn't thought of it like that before."

She nodded sagely. Then, her savage grin returned. Blue electricity began to crackle around her palm. "Now, let's try again."

"I certainly hope we figure this out soon," William complained telepathically.

Kiru gulped and groaned a little, feeling the same as his familiar. He wondered if he should've tried to push to get his father's item *before* helping Myev. *Maybe whatever the item is will help me learn a new technique?* he thought, recalling the circlet embedded in his head which activated his mental mana core and imparted his Telekinesis technique to him. *While that hurt, it didn't take nearly as long for me to learn my technique.* More and more, he wondered how much pain he would've spared himself if he hadn't thought of the idea to re-create the electrical ability he had back in the Warrior Games. Still, Kiru believed his idea had merit and he was onto something. If pain was the price he had to pay to become stronger, he would gladly do so. He would protect his friends. He would become a Ruby, and he would get his father's second artifact.

Mutt sighed as he picked his teeth clean with a rib bone. Some of the grouse he'd hunted was still stuck in his teeth. For the past couple of days, he'd been pondering over how to figure out what sacred beasts' cores he had taken in. At first, he thought he could determine it based off of his techniques alone, but they weren't distinct enough, other than Fenrir's Claws, that is. As for the others, he had one that both thickened and elongated his already-tough teeth, one that could change his feet to talons, one that morphed his vocal chords, and lastly, one that caused his hair to grow over his entire body for an extra layer of protection.

The last one was the most perplexing. Aside from the protection the hair offered, it grew long until Mutt almost had a tail, but it didn't really do much else. The others claimed that when he was being controlled, his entire body was covered with that thick brown hair like a dense layer of fur. His memory of the time was admittedly hazy, so he couldn't fully recall how to make his body repeat that version of the technique to the degree the others had described. Unfortunately for Mutt, he quickly realized that simply analyzing his techniques didn't reveal to him which sacred beasts they came from. There were thousands of the creatures just in Imakandi alone. It was a very real possibility that all the other sacred beasts whose cores he'd ingested didn't originate from his homeland at all.

The situation frustrated the typically-carefree orc prince. All he wanted to do was hang out with his friends and enjoy hunts and fights. If his sister was right, eventually he wouldn't be able to. They would continue to get stronger while he would be left behind. Ruby wasn't a rank to scoff at, but Mutt dreamed of so much more. Plus, the Boss had a pretty epic quest. Mutt knew they couldn't afford to drag him along with them if he didn't continue to grow as well.

He sat at the top of one of his homeland's rolling hills. He had left the little leokin back in the palace grounds with his sister and was now considering his situation as a gentle breeze rolled over him. Considering . . . sucked. Mutt wasn't much of a thinker. He was a doer. All he wanted to do was just claw the problem to bits with his claws, not think about it. He grunted, then ripped off a leg from the dead grouse. Mutt was about to take a meaty mouthful of the raw bird when something suddenly attacked him from behind.

"Nom!" The tiny little leokin had somehow snuck up on him and ripped the grouse leg from his hand. Mutt was impressed that the young sacred beast already had the foresight to stalk the orc from downwind. "Oh! Hey, Little Dude, how'd you end up out here?" Mutt asked.

"Mmm, Nom!" The leokin shrugged before digging into the snack he'd taken from the orc.

Mutt smiled and began eating the rest of his kill in companionable silence. Once both of their bellies were full, Mutt and Nom both sighed contentedly. "I don't suppose you know how to figure out which sacred beast cores I took in, do you, little guy?"

The leokin cocked his head, then ran over to the grouse's skeleton. He grabbed the remains of one of its clawed feet and looked at Mutt. "Nom?"

Mutt smiled and raised one of his bare feet to Nom, activating the technique to turn it into an avian-like taloned appendage. "Same type, but I don't think it's from a grouse, little guy."

"Oooh," Nom uttered as his eyes went wide at the change, seemingly entranced by the display, before promptly biting Mutt's taloned foot.

"Ow! Ow! Ow!" Mutt cried. He shook his foot a few times, but the leokin's bite was surprisingly strong. When Nom still wouldn't let go, Mutt used his hands and forcefully dislodged Nom from his foot. "Ouch, Little Dude! That hurt!" he said, rubbing his foot.

Nom didn't seem the worse for wear. Still seemingly entranced, he wiped the orc's blood from his lips onto his furry paw. He stuck it out and approached Mutt slowly, moving as if in a daze.

Mutt leaned back instinctively, not wanting another bite. Something about the leokin cub was clearly different. He held his body much more calmly, not with the excited energy of a curious cub. Nom continued walking toward the orc, slow and steady.

While he thought the cub was behaving oddly, Mutt was still intrigued enough to go along. The blind orc walked slowly with his hand still stuck out. Unlike before, Mutt took the time to sense that Nom wasn't displaying either the predatory drive nor hunger he had been just moments before. Also, Mutt somehow *knew* what the leokin was doing. It was instinctual. Slowly, carefully, he leaned his head down to Nom. When the blood on the leokin touched his forehead, Mut's mind was transported.

Light struck his eyes. Wait, his eyes could *see*? He could see! How could he see? He looked down at his body, only to find it wasn't his body. His form was covered in feathers. Instead of arms, he had wings. Instead of his toes, he had talons—the exact same talons from his technique!

Mutt gazed around in stunned amazement, both by the experience of having sight for the first time and his fascinating surroundings. He was in a tree—an utterly massive tree taller than any other around—overlooking a large, forested island covered in conifers. Dozens of winged creatures were flying about in the sky. Letting instinct take over, Mutt unfurled his wings, jumped off the branch, and took to the sky. The rush of air surrounded him, and he allowed the warm current air to lift him up high.

He spun and twirled, flapping his wings and flying with ease as if he'd been doing it all his life. Well, technically he had . . . or at least this bestial body he'd now taken on had. Then he noticed in the sky beside him were . . . *women?* also flying joyously. To Mutt they looked like human women with wings for arms and bird legs soaring the sky with him and his kin. *His kin?*

Flying alongside the airborne women were birds just like him. They were a head shorter than the flying women but possessed a greater wingspan along with strong, thick necks, sharp beaks and claws, and a pair of majestic, curled horns on each of their heads. Realization and understanding immediately came to Mutt like someone had slapped him in the face. Those women were monsters—intelligent monsters called harpies. The birds flying with them were their companions and allies: horned harpy eagles. And that's what *he* was, meaning that was one of the sacred beast cores he'd ingested!

As soon as that struck Mutt, his mind was sent back. The orc gasped and stammered backward. It was jarring to have the ability to see one moment, then to be thrust right back to darkness the next, but Mutt didn't need to see. He'd honed his other senses enough to more than make up for it.

Once the orc had regained his composure, he smiled at Nom, who'd been sitting patiently in front of him.

The whole experience seemed to have taken something from the leokin cub because, right after Mutt's praise, he wobbled and passed out.

Mutt caught him before he hit the ground and cradled him. He grinned, as happy as could be. "Little Guy, you can hang out with me all you'd like."

Spies

The shaman quietly stalked along the back alleys and dark passages of Dissé's streets in the middle of the night. Subconsciously, he tugged at his sleeves, double-checking to make sure his arms were covered. He remembered that, before the whelp S'Vol's was even born, the Jormun Cult had grown bold once. It was during that time the shaman had been on a pilgrimage to witness the savage majesty of the beasts of the motherland. One night he had gone to sleep in the branches of a large tree, only to be awakened by the sounds of the Cult attacking a nearby village.

The townsfolk were helpless before the might of the Jormuns. The cultists massacred them in a bloody display of utter domination. It was terrible, savage, and beautiful. It was everything that the shaman believed represented the true nature of a beast: *the strong rule while the weak die.* If they couldn't protect their young, the orcs of the village and their children *should have* died. It was as nature intended.

After the Jormuns finished their slaughter, the shaman knew that witnessing them in all their glory had been a sign. He hopped out of his tree, walked right up to the cultists, and swore an oath to serve Jormungandr just like them. Since that time, the Jormuns have had to resort to hiding, quietly amassing their power before they could strike again. Though the shaman judged S'Vol a hasty orc, attempting to rule too soon, he believed the young orc was the Jormuns' best hope to acquire power and free their entrapped god.

The shaman eventually made it to a building on the lower levels, nestled right against a wooden fence bordering the city. There was a cellar built under it, with a door right beside the structure. Carefully, the cult shaman crept out from a nearby dark alley and moved toward the cellar. As he got closer, two orcs jumped up from the ground beside the cellar doors. With their backs completely covered by a layer of mud and dirt and the darkness of the night sky, the shaman hadn't seen them.

They each brandished a pair of short spears and lowered them at the surprised shaman. "State your business, trespasser," one of them barked.

The shaman quickly composed himself. He was surprised at first, but he had expected this. He grinned. "I seek for the strong to rule, as nature intends." The shaman then pulled back one of his sleeves, revealing a forearm completely covered in serpentine scales. To the untrained, it would have seemed a simple display of an armoring technique. To the wise, one would recognize the scales weren't diamond-shaped but instead squares. That was how their god's scales were. How the great World Serpent's scales were.

"As nature intends," the two guards replied in unison, activating the same technique along their arms. Mollified, they quickly scanned the area, then opened the cellar doors.

The shaman pulled down his sleeve and went down into the cellar. As he descended, the scent changed. He inhaled deeply and smiled as the smell of snake permeated his nostrils. The M'Baku and the fools that followed them thought that Dissé was impregnable. They were wrong. This wasn't a simple cellar. It was a tunnel, one that had been carefully dug right under the capital's wall to a hole hidden behind one of the vendor stalls. The tunnel was so large that it functioned as a secret base for the Jormuns.

The shaman was greeted by his fellow cultists, many of whom had at least one snake—whether it be viper or constrictor—slithering around them. There was a cluster of orcs gathered around a fighting pit, shouting and gambling on which python would kill the other first. He made it back to a large table where a group of high-ranking officers within their cult were gathered.

Namely, there was Nayla, one of S'Vol's cousins and a rather sadistic member of the Jormuns. The psychopathic orc was so thrilled to follow such a violent religion that she had butchered most of her own family, all but her twin sister, as a sign of her faith. She even disfigured her nose with a blade, cutting part of it off and slicing slits in her septa to look more snake-like. The shaman respected her violence and power, but she took it too far in his opinion by her zealous self-mutilation.

She had just finished a flagon of ale laced with viper venom, a common drink amongst the cult members, and flashed the shaman a sharp-toothed grin. "Ah, well if it isn't our pet shaman. How goes it up top with the weak cowards?"

The shaman bowed his head to Nayla, both out of respect for her rank and to hide his scowl. *I have been a loyal Jormun since before this wretch was even born. How dare she belittle me, calling me a "pet shaman,"* he thought. The shaman had been a loyal spy for decades. Sure, he hadn't been able to completely control a Jormungandr technique and therefore had had to corrupt himself with a couple of techniques from the traitors who imprisoned the World Serpent. That's why he had to keep his sleeves down and move stealthily through Dissé. He could activate Jormungandr's scales, but he couldn't control where or for how long. He was lucky that it hadn't faded by the time he'd gotten to the hideout entrance! *If only I could control one of Jormungandr's techniques. Then I would show this prideful youngling who's her better,* he thought.

Nayla seemed to sense his disdain because in just two seconds, she jumped over the table and grabbed the shaman by the throat, her nails digging into his flesh and drawing small streams of blood. "Do you have a problem, Shaman?" she asked, raising his head up to lock eyes.

He grunted in pain but didn't try to strike back. That would mean death. "No, Captain," he answered, gritting his teeth.

She gave a malicious smile. "Good." Nayla let go of the shaman's neck and licked his blood off her nails.

Her followers laughed.

"I assume you have news to report?" she asked.

Reflexively, the shaman grabbed his neck to put pressure on it and staunch the bleeding. He didn't dare keep Nayla waiting, though. "Yes." He grunted and cleared his throat. "I've received word that the queen regent is sending her brother and his allies to the Wastelands. Without any of the other tribes backing her claim besides the Tau, it seems she's going to parlay with the ogres to get their support."

Nayla seemed . . . amused at the report. "Is that all?"

"Y-yes, Captain," he replied, stammering in surprise that she didn't seem to think it that big of a deal.

"Well, then, Myev is an even bigger fool than I thought. We've already been working interference to . . . handle the locals there. Next time, give me a report worth the time of a Jabari, or you'll lose more than just a finger."

"Eh, excuse me? Gaaaah!" he cried out in pain as blood suddenly spouted from his hand.

Minutes later, Nayla was munching on one of her new favorite snacks, fried orc finger, and thinking about the shaman's words. S'Vol had indeed used his influence to cause chaos with the ogres so they would join the Jormuns. Still, the bloodthirsty Nayla was eager to acquire more power within the cult, and—let's be honest—to spill more blood. While it was fun to bite off some uppity spy's finger, there was nothing better than culling the weak from this world. Jormungandr wanted the weak to die, and Nayla was more than happy to help.

She smiled evilly as a plan formed inside her mind. With their forces spread thin, Nayla would do what the others had failed to: take Dissé. To be sure that it wasn't some ploy, she and a contingent of followers would kill the blind orc and the foreigners he hung around with, too. If the Wastelands didn't kill them, her lackeys would. Killing her cousin's biggest competition and seizing the capital, would please Jormungandr inordinately.

By the rules of this Ukufakaza, one who vied for the throne could not be responsible for the death of the families of other hopeful rulers. They were only allowed to kill their direct competitors. That's why S'Vol hadn't killed M'Toon when he had the chance. He could only be responsible for that damned Myev's death instead. That didn't mean Nayla couldn't kill the blind prince, however. By doing this and not telling her cousin, they could successfully eliminate the M'Baku bloodline for good! Nayla even considered that the World Serpent himself might choose to reward her for such a cunning and bloodthirsty plan.

"You know, Shaman, there may be a way for you to be of more use to Jormungandr, if you can handle it."

The shaman snarled angrily at Nayla, his hand pressing against the bandages covering the hole where his finger had been. Still, if he could be of use to the World Serpent, he would. "I can. What must I do to help bring the world back as he intends?" the shaman asked.

She smiled. "As you know, there are two types of serpents. One uses force, and the other uses . . . more sinister means to subdue their prey—venom and acid, for example."

He nodded. "Yes, I know. What does that have to do with me helping free our god?"

She bared her teeth in a predatory display. "While none of us have the sheer strength to eliminate Myev, that doesn't mean we can't kill her through more subtle means. Our leader has done some experiments and has been blessed with a great discovery. You, Shaman, shall be the one to use it." She then looked up to one of her guards. "Go fetch the parasite. We've found it a host."

CHAPTER TEN

Training Results

Over the course of the week, Kiru grew slightly better at controlling the flow of electricity through his body—emphasis on *slightly*. He'd repeatedly proven himself capable of asserting his will over the ambient mana within the lightning technique used against him. Kiru could force it into one of his arm meridians before losing control, the electrical technique rampaging wildly through him once again. With such an extreme training method, the psion would've been long dead had Myev not had a number of skilled healers on standby. Brunhilda was also available occasionally, happy to provide extra healing for Kiru if needed, which the psion did take advantage of more than once.

Now, many would say Kiru's progress thus far was inconsequential and unimpressive. The truth was, however, for the psion, it was productive but more in terms of information gathering.

During the respites from electrocution when Kiru would catch his breath and heal, he would ask Myev questions about Imakandi, beast mana, the people, and even about her in general. He had meant it when he said he wished to be allies, after all.

At first, she seemed wary, but Myev slowly warmed up to him, answering his queries and even showing him a detailed map of her homeland. Kiru was particularly grateful for that! It was burned perfectly into his memory.

Knowledge was power, and knowing seemingly random information had literally saved their lives in the past. During the Warrior Games back in the Kingdom of Blades, Pandemonium fought a team of shadowy cultivators who spoke a rather obscure dead language, taking advantage of their opponents' lack of understanding to openly communicate their plans to each other.

Unfortunately for them, Kiru's time in the library had helped him pick up multiple new languages, including the one they were speaking—Japanese. With his knowledge of the language, Pandemonium was able to overtake the opposing team and eventually go on to win the Warrior Games.

Through Myev, Kiru also learned that there were more benefits to ruling Imakandi besides the obvious one of being in charge. The royal palace was one of the richest areas of beast mana in all of Alterra. Growing up and cultivating in such a place naturally helped one advance much quicker than others. Also, it provided those beast mana cultivators with the most versatile and arguably most powerful path to ascension.

When he asked her to further elaborate on what she meant by "versatile," Myev told him that most tribes—at least the founding tribes—had a patron deity within the Beast God pantheon. "For example, the M'Baku follow Fenrir. The tribe only uses the wolf god's techniques. They don't deign to use any from other sacred beasts," she said.

"That doesn't make sense, though," Kiru said. "You've been using a technique from that blue rooster the whole time."

"Correct. That restriction is meant only for the lower branches of the M'Baku. We of the Royal House have the distinct benefit of ingesting cores from the most powerful and diverse sacred beasts throughout our lands, many of whom we raise here where the beast mana is more potent. I can use the Thunder Rooster's Call," she said, then a familiar aura of blue electricity crackled around her body. It quickly faded. "Fenrir's Claws." Her nails turned black and grew five inches, ending in razor-sharp tips.

"Battleboar's Armor." Her skin noticeably thickened, and a small layer of brown fur began to emerge, covering her green flesh. Her already-large canines grew even longer, curving out and away from her mouth just like a boar's tusks. "Wings of the Wise Ravens." There was a loud tearing sound as the back of her leather vest tore. Two large wings emerged from her back—one snow white, the other dark black.

"Sleipnir's Command." The queen regent's lower half morphed. She grew in height until she was at least eight feet tall, and her feet changed to hooves. Not only that, but she had eight legs now—horse legs all covered in a glittery gray coat. Kiru gave a sharp inhale of surprise before there was a *whoosh*! The wind around her immediately picked up. Her long dreads were lifted straight up as a small twister of air surrounded her body. Kiru had to grab onto one of the longhouse's supporting beams to keep from being swept away.

Once she had dismissed the wind and he was finally able to take a look at the orc again, his eyes went wide. She no longer looked like anything he'd ever seen before. She was like some monstrous centaur! With eight hooved legs covered in gray fur, an upper torso covered in thickened hide and brown fur, two differently colored feathery wings, and a remarkably porcine mouth, Myev cut an intimidating figure. If he hadn't seen her before this, he would've been sure she was some sort of monster, an alpha among the other sacred beasts.

She gave him a wry smile, before rapidly dismissing all her techniques, changing her body back to its regular form, remarkably without any unsettling noises of shifting bones or flesh. "Now you see the great power that comes from ruling this land."

He nodded.

"We must use this to protect and govern our people. Also, we must ensure that corrupt individuals do not attain such power either," she explained.

He nodded again. "Uh, this may be a dumb question, but can you fly with those wings you had earlier?"

"Yes. When my lower half is changed, I can also kick the air if my wings are ever damaged," she answered.

Kiru was impressed by Myev's power. He then noticed that her vest was hanging rather loosely off her chest. The damaged piece of clothing began to fall away in two pieces. He closed his eyes before he could see anything. "Oh! Um, it looks like you're going to need another vest," he said nervously, his face blushing a bright red nearly the same color as his jacket.

Myev chuckled and whispered in his ear, causing him to shiver slightly, "Do not worry, Withered One. I like those with a little more meat on their bones. Though, if you bulk up, maybe you could be one of my husbands one day when I'm queen." She then walked away, presumably to get some undamaged clothing. Kiru's face felt very warm, and his heart continued to race. The psion didn't dare open his eyes until a good minute after he could no longer hear Myev's footsteps.

He sighed and put his hands on his knees. Kiru's experience with the opposite sex was . . . rather minimal.

"That was pathetic, Master! You are a conqueror, and you let a pair of boobs make you look like a little child!"

"Shut up, William," he sent back. *"There's something called respectful courtesy."*

Though he couldn't see the imp inside his core, Kiru was pretty sure William was rolling his eyes. *"Well, she made you look like a respectful little bitch. One of her husbands?! She should be begging to be one of your wives."*

"You know, William, if that was any indication. I think one woman will be more than enough for me," Kiru said as he wiped some sweat from his forehead.

As promised, the scouts Zhaden trained with helped him use the natural environment to better conceal himself over the course of the week. While he couldn't use the techniques they did, he was eventually able to better grasp and understand the base principles as to how they used heat to hide themselves. It was midday during his second-to-last training session, and it was the hottest it had been during the party's time in the capital so far. Because of that, the distortions of air from the heat were much more numerous.

Zhaden had a pretty high endurance compared to his teammates, only ever being outmatched by Mutt, but so far, the orc scouts almost always outperformed him in the high heat. During sparring rounds, the scouts' abilities to use the heat to aid in their fighting style was difficult to combat. It was during a particular sparring round with Ebysso that the orc scout managed to use one of her curved kukri knives to slice off the chords keeping one of the gold drakonid's bracers on. It fell off and exposed more of his shiny golden scales to the light.

Zhaden spun and forced her back with a swing of his tail. She landed a few feet away from him and pointed her blades at him. She shook her head side to side and *tsk*ed before her form began to distort, disappearing with the heat.

The gold drakonid raised both arms up in a defensive stance. When he did so, he unintentionally reflected some of the sun's light into Ebysso's eyes.

The orc grunted and staggered back, her technique interrupted.

Zhaden let out a gasp of realization. "It's the light," he whispered. Aside from the beast mana the orcs were obviously using, it wasn't just heat that helped to conceal them. It was how that affected the light. He thought back to the angler chameleon back in the gorge and how its form disappeared when both light and heat hit its body. As Zhaden continued to spar, he quickly figured out how to utilize the sun's rays to his advantage, distorting the light and using the heat to cause a subtle mirage to conceal his form from a distance. He would never be as proficient as the orcs, especially since he required much more concentrated and direct sunlight, but even Ebysso was impressed that he acquired the ability to do so without the use of mana.

Brunhilda's time in Dissé was, without a doubt, the most impactful of any in her party to the orc society in the capital and potentially as a whole. After talking and healing the orc woman, Dalkruk, and her son, Kal, the paladin learned about some of the tenets of the beast pantheon and how orc society had revolved around them in Imakandi—sometimes too much, in her opinion. She could admit that there were definite advantages. The strong ruled and they used that strength to protect and take care of the "pack." With safety and strength, the orcs of this land had grown stronger over time.

Unfortunately, how some people interpreted the Beast Gods' will, did cause some drawbacks, however. Over time, those with higher physical strength were vaunted and began holding themselves in higher regard, thinking themselves more valuable than others. That eventually led some of the physically strongest orcs to mock the weak and sick, finding them unworthy. The kindhearted paladin couldn't stand that. Instead of doing her training, she helped the needy in the capital, including Dalkruk and Kal.

After explaining her faith, her goddess, and her intent to help, both the home-less orc mother and child swore fealty to Hlin, the great goddess whose paladin had protected Kal when he was in danger. With two new acolytes in tow, Brunhilda began evangelizing about her goddess to the people of Dissé. Most scoffed at or just ignored her. The animalistic shamans of the Beast Pantheon were downright hostile to the dwarf but wouldn't attack her outright as she was an ally of the current queen regent.

Despite the opposition, Brunhilda wasn't deterred. With Dalkruk's and Kal's aid in translating, they spread Hlin's message. *My goddess and I will protect these people, and we'll make this place a bastion so that they can protect themselves after I leave,* she thought with firm resolution emboldened by the fact she was able to convert the mother and son. Her heart also felt lighter because she was helping others aside from her team. People were listening to her and truly considering Hlin's gospel. Many poor, hungry, injured, and destitute orcs living in the large capital city praised the goddess after Brunhilda fed them or healed their wounds with her techniques. Sure enough, a large following for Hlin was established, at least two-hundred-strong by Brunhilda's count. Many of the orcs flocked to the temple, becoming loyal devotees to the Order of Valhalla. Multiple children like Kal, aspired to be a paladin like Brunhilda one day, which melted the dwarf's heart.

With so many new followers within their ranks, Rhodan and Balmir were ecstatic. They had more mouths to feed but many more able and willing people to help them as well. By week's end, the temple was being well tended and was a hub of both joy and activity. With such a large influx of orcs at the temple, some other orcs grew curious and began approaching the temple with questions about the Vasir and the Order. Over time, even Rhodan and Balmir's patron deities gained a few new faithful followers as well, though Hlin was by far the most loved amongst the three gods worshipped at the temple.

With the goddess's new popularity, Brunhilda would learn of an unforeseen consequence—namely the resistance of the shamans to help Mutt.

After Nom had helped Mutt discover that one of the sacred beast cores he'd ingested was from a horned harpy eagle, the orc had taken the little leokin back to the royal palace. It took Nom the better part of a week to come out of his stupor, and when Mutt asked for his help again, the cub cocked his head in confusion, not sure about what the blind orc was talking about. It seemed that the young sacred beast didn't remember what he'd done. When Mutt recalled that the leokin served as high shamans for the Beast Pantheon, he had the bright idea to go seek help from the shamans at the temple in Dissé.

The shamans proved very difficult to deal with. Mutt could taste the anger coming off their pores, particularly from one old orc whose right hand was missing a pinky and reeked of blood. The prince thought it must have been a fresh wound. When the prince pressed them as to why they wouldn't help with this particular task, the shaman claimed that Ukufakaza was in effect. They could not be of direct aid to anyone in the royal household during the time of the trial. Mutt didn't really care enough to pay attention to such rules, but even he knew that was a load of horse manure. The truth was they'd grown angry with Brunhilda's effective evangelizing. He could tell by how often they craned their heads in the Vasir Temple's direction.

The problem was that what the shamans had claimed was *technically* true based off the rules of Ukufakaza. He had asked Myev if that was the case, and she confirmed that the devout followers of the pantheon weren't allowed to show any distinct favoritism to any of the clans during the time of trial. While Mutt didn't believe helping him discover what sacred beast cores he'd ingested should have been considered to be any sort of favoritism, the rule was subjective. So, Mutt unfortunately wasn't able to discover any more information about himself or his techniques. Still, he had hope now. If a small cub like Nom could help bring him to a discovery about the sacred beast cores, the adult leokin definitely would be able to help him even more!

CHAPTER ELEVEN

The Wastelands

The party had each developed in their own ways over the course of the week's training. Zhaden was stronger, Brunhilda more confident, and both Kiru and Mutt were more knowledgeable. As promised, Myev had assembled a small envoy of competent orcs to guide the party on their journey. First, there were two club-wielders, one from the Tau Clan, the other founding tribe that supported the M'Baku. Neither of them spoke much. They didn't even introduce themselves. Though they looked around Kiru's age, the pair had long gray hair braided into ponytails. Kiru presumed it was because their patron deity was Sleipnir, the wind horse. Based off Myev's technique that turned her lower body into that of an eight-legged horse with gray hair, Kiru presumed the Taus' hair color had some sort of similar inspiration. The man gave off the power of a Ruby and the woman that of a Sapphire, showing they were not to be trifled with.

Next up was a bald, heavily scarred orc with a gaping hole where his left eye should have been, along with a missing right hand. Where it should have been, there was some sort of crude attachment with a long, serrated tooth at the end to function as a weapon. Myev explained that he was from one of the lower branches of the M'Baku and was actually Mutt and her great-uncle.

"I am M'Baku Mektoss," the orc introduced himself. He had a constant half-scowl on his face that only lightened up slightly when Mutt told him that he was Myev's brother. He clearly approved of finding another powerful cultivator from his own clan. That scowl immediately returned when Mutt started calling him "Mak" for short.

The other orcs joining them were two scouts from the Akain clan, one of which included Ebysso, Zhaden's instructor. All of the orcs assigned to accompany Pandemonium projected strength, even Mak, despite his only being Gold.

After everyone made their introductions and ensured they all had enough supplies for the journey, the party left Dissé and went northwest toward the

Wastelands. According to Myev, it was a day and a half day journey by foot. They left Nom with Myev in the capital. Sacred beast or not, he was just a cub and it wasn't safe where they were going. Plus, the leokin and queen regent could keep each other company and keep an eye out for each other in case of danger. More sets of eyes didn't hurt. Myev didn't protest at the idea either. Nom was still a cub and pretty adorable, so the bestial queen was nothing but thrilled to have him stay with her.

As the party and orc escorts moved out, a clear formation took place. The scouts took point, often moving far ahead to ensure of no incoming danger. Mak followed behind them. He wasn't a very talkative orc, so the party just let him be. Following him were the four members of Pandemonium with the Tau taking the rear. With such a strong group, they had little trouble on their way to the Wastelands, although at one point, a giant, hairless rat popped out of the ground to the party's right, intent on catching them off-guard and getting an easy meal.

Before the ugly creature could land on anyone, the Sapphire-ranked Tau had jumped forward and drawn her club, smashing the creature in its temple with its weighted round end. There was a loud crunch of broken bone as it was sent flying twenty or so feet away. The large rodent groaned in pain as it tried to stand, a large depression now evident on its head. Its skull had been badly fractured.

Mak was ready to capitalize on the opportunity. As soon as the beast was sent flying, he took off after it. As he ran, his legs morphed into those of a wolf, increasing his speed significantly. By the time the giant, hairless rodent had gotten to its feet, Mutt's great uncle was there. He shoved his serrated tooth weapon into the beast's injured skull, puncturing its small brain and slicing it in half. The large creature's body went limp as it died on the spot.

The party didn't face any other trouble. None of the orcs were too talkative, with one notable exception. Due to Zhaden's previous connection with Ebysso, the lead scout was willing to converse with the drakonid. Kiru noticed Zhaden's tail moving rapidly side to side like a happy dog whenever he spoke with the bandaged orc.

Kiru managed to find *some* camaraderie with the two Tau as well. When they had made camp for the night, the psion helped break the silence by stating that he'd admired their fighting prowess against the rat. He then challenged them to a spar. William cheered on the idea inside Kiru's mind, clearly hoping the psion would dominate the orcs in combat—although if Kiru were being honest, he was pretty sure William just wanted some bloodshed.

The pair of quiet Tau happily agreed to Kiru's challenge, eager to test the skill of the one who their prince had allied with. Needless to say, they kicked his ass. A Gold was capable of besting a Ruby despite the numerous advantages Ruby cultivators possessed: increased strength, speed, and more powerful versions of their techniques. In fact, Kiru had defeated more than his fair share of Rubies. More often than not, though, it required a good strategy, thorough teamwork, and more than a little cunning to defeat a foe a rank higher. Sparring with one versus two against a pair of orcs who used unfamiliar techniques and strange fighting styles, however, *did not* count as good strategy.

The psion stood at least a little chance against the Ruby Tau. Kiru figured that, with his dual swords training from his mother and Giiyam, he should be able to put up a good fight. His mother's style, Monarch's Razors, was ideal for offense while Giiyam's, The Cruel Mantis, was more defensively oriented. With the broad spectrum of sword forms, his Fu Tao, and his overall training, the psion actually was able to hold his own against the Ruby orc.

When the Sapphire Tau joined in though, it was no competition. With such a power gap, Kiru definitely got whacked a few times by a Tau club. The psion quickly grew even more grateful for his lack of pain sensation throughout most of his body because he knew he otherwise would have been hurting badly. He muttered a silent prayer that Brunhilda was there to heal any significant damage.

Over the course of their sparring sessions throughout their travels, Kiru had, in fact, started to improve against his opponents. The more times he trained with them, the more his perfect memory could grasp what they were doing. Specifically, he was able to better notice their "tells," which foot they favored and what attack they would use in doing so, etcetera. Granted, the Taus were not using mana when sparring, and when Kiru asked if they would try, their speed and strength were leagues above what he'd been dealing with. The psion also marveled at the toughness of their weapons. Whatever material they used to make their clubs was remarkably durable. His swords—even his incredibly strong Psyslime blade—had barely made a scratch on the blunt weapons.

Kiru had acquired a measure of respect from the two Tau. His continued persistence despite taking such powerful blows impressed the duo a good bit. The fact that he kept sparring despite one of his arms breaking and a few of his ribs audibly cracking made the orcs truly impressed at how tough he seemed to be. The quiet pair had even taken the time to actually speak and acknowledge him instead of silent nods of approval and praise.

"We see you and recognize you truly as a fellow warrior dedicated to the craft of combat," the female Sapphire said.

"Yes, the Tau would find you a worthy addition to our clan if desired," the Ruby added.

Kiru already respected the pair a great deal, and that acknowledgment just cemented it even more.

In the end, he decided to not officially join their clan. When he'd asked what that entailed, the Sapphire said it would require him to marry someone within their tribe. Kiru was nowhere near ready to consider that yet. He was too busy focusing on helping his friends and saving his kingdom. Also, he had nearly no experience when it came to the world of courting and romance. It honestly scared Kiru more than fighting another cultivator whenever he thought about it. *Yeah, it's probably for the best that I don't join their clan. It'll likely lead to major political ramifications once I reclaim my throne,* he thought.

Just before sunrise the next day, they all broke camp and continued their journey, making it to the Wastelands just before all the dew evaporated from the ground. The Wastelands were just that, a barren region with no remaining resources. Instead of the rolling green hills of M'Baku Territory, the ground was dusty and dry with only the sparse tumbleweed or dead tree to break up the monotony.

It reminded Kiru of a maze as there were numerous rocky caverns and twisting fjords all around. "There must've been a great river here once," he said.

"What makes ye say that, Kiru?" Brunhilda asked.

"What else could erode the rock like this?" He then pointed up to one of the stone pillars. "That stone has multiple bedrock layers exposed. It reminds me of my journey along the Tori River to get to the academy. The rocky cliff that Waketown was built against had layers exposed just like that."

She pursed her lips. "Aye. Not a bad catch there! If yer ever tired of yer quest, ye should consider becoming a miner. Yer ability to notice differences in stone be no mean feat, and that compliment be coming from a dwarf!"

"I'll keep that in mind," he replied, smiling at his friend.

In a flash, Ebysso appeared out of thin air beside Zhaden. The rest of the party recoiled in surprise, but the drakonid had seemed to have become better at detecting her presence as evidenced by his not being startled. The scout glared at Kiru and whispered in Zhaden's ear before her form disappeared in a distortion of heat. Kiru didn't like the look she gave him, but since Zhaden trusted her, he would too.

The gold drakonid then turned and moved over to the pair. "Ebysso asks that we keep the talking to a minimum as we enter the Wastelands. We do not know what we will encounter, and you two . . ."

"Yeah, yeah. We get it. We be loud." Brunhilda waved him off.

He just shrugged at her. She wasn't wrong.

They then began their trek into the Wastelands in earnest, all members being careful to be quiet. Brunhilda had taken Kiru's advice about stealth to heart all those nights ago with the cyclops. While still unarguably the loudest amongst the group, the dwarf was remarkably quieter than she'd been before. Mutt even tapped her on the shoulder once and gave her an encouraging thumbs-up in approval, which made her promptly blush a shade of purple. Kiru smiled knowingly at the two.

The Akain scouts were very skilled at leading the group, noticing signs of potential danger and navigating around them accordingly. They were also adept at finding signs of life. After a couple of hours leading the group, they'd found an old campsite tucked away behind some rocks. The scouts brought Mak over to smell it. The elder orc changed his muzzle to that of a wolf and was able to discern a subtle lingering scent of ogre. He pointed in the direction of where the scent went, and the group continued that way.

Eventually, they began to travel upward on a slope to a cluster of small mountains. With the tall rocky outcroppings on both sides, Kiru grew increasingly wary. The others matched his unease with their body language. They kept their weapons close, concerned about a possible ambush. Sure enough, after a few minutes their concerns were validated when the two Akain scouts appeared beside the party. Per usual, they manifested seemingly out of thin air. This time, though, they had their bone daggers drawn and in defensive positions.

"Ogres ahead. They've picked up our scent and have the high ground. We need to move, quick!" Ebysso said with distinct urgency, her cautious and distrustful gaze constantly scanning their surroundings.

Their warning came too late, though, as a hulking, yellow-skinned creature crested over the hilltop. Its beady eyes locked on the group and then let out a menacing roar. They turned to run, but quickly discovered the roar was not directed at them. It was meant to alert the other ogres. Some of the large boulders nestled against the rocky outcroppings were, in fact, *not* boulders, but instead sleeping ogres covered in dirt and debris. *The dirt must've masked their scent even from Mutt and his great-uncle's noses,* Kiru thought.

The group readied their weapons and braced themselves for combat. To their surprise, the ogres didn't charge at them after they awoke. Instead, they began to warily approach with their crude bone clubs at the ready. They looked much more cautious than the bloodthirsty hunters they'd expected. It was clear to Kiru they didn't want to fight but would if need be. As the ogres neared, the psion got a better look at them. They reminded Kiru of the cyclops but only around eight or nine feet in height instead of fifteen or so.

Their skin was a pale yellow, thick, and cracked in some places. Their heads were too small for their bodies, and they had protruding bulbous stomachs. Despite their swollen bellies, many of them had ribs showing, giving them a sickly, starved appearance. The ogres all looked defensive and on edge, a few of them even sporting some scabbing wounds. Their clothing consisted of various rough, poor-quality animal hides stitched together in mismatched patterns and only covering certain parts of their bodies. It was as if a child had done it. Kiru wondered if it was just that their thick fingers were not ideal for the task of stitchwork. Thankfully, their groins were one of the parts that *were* covered.

One ogre who was slightly larger than the others—standing a little over eight feet tall and wearing some kind of hide helmet with a single curved horn adorned on its top—advanced, sniffed a couple of times, and then glared at the group.

"Who are you? Why you trespass into our lands?" the ogre barked in Common, his voice rough and choppy as if unused to speaking.

Ebysso produced a small scroll and handed it to the ogre leader.

He scowled and backhanded the scroll out of her hand. "No write. Can no read. Speak."

The scout's eyes widened, seemingly unprepared for that.

"Easy there, Big Guy," Mutt casually said as he approached with his hands raised. "We come as friends."

The ogre flared his nostrils. "Hmph, friends," he said dismissively. "No orc is friend to L'Khan."

"Well . . . we're hoping to be," Mutt replied, trying to put on a winning smile. "We're looking to get your clan's support for our tribe, the M'Baku, to participate in Ukufakaza. In repayment, we will aid your tribe in return. At least, I think we will. Ow!"

Brunhilda had smacked Mutt on the back of his skull for the last part.

"I mean, of course we will help!" Mutt quickly corrected.

The helmet-wearing ogre did not look convinced. "No orc is friend to L'Khan," he repeated. "We no attack you, but you must leave Wastelands and leave all your food, too."

Mutt sighed. "Listen, Big Guy, we can't do that. We *need* your support. Is there anything we can do? Plus, we need at least *some* of the food for the journey back."

That last statement seemed to anger the ogres more than anything else. The situation became notably more tense as all the potbellied giants bared their crooked teeth and gripped their weapons tight.

"You no give food?" The ogre leader growled and lifted his bone weapon, sharpened to a point so that it resembled some crooked broadsword, onto his shoulder.

Mutt activated his Fenrir's Claws technique, bracing himself for a fight, but then snapped his head to the right and began sniffing loudly. The sound of rocks falling came from the left of the fjord they were in. Kiru looked up in that direction to discover they were not alone. The psion saw a strange creature crawling along the canyon wall like a lizard. It had dark gray fur with black spots, round ears, yellow eyes, and a flat face. When it locked eyes with Kiru, it gave a bone-chilling grin.

Kiru quickly scanned the area and, to his horror, discovered that they were all surrounded, not only by these creatures but what looked to be a separate group of very hairy ogres stalking along the clifftops. A cacophony of terrifying, high-pitched, barking laughs echoed throughout the sloped canyon they were on. It was clear that the hairy ogres and strange creatures were both aligned and enemies to the L'Khans. Goosebumps spread across Kiru's neck, and he drew his

Fu Tao from their scabbards. "Back to back! We're surrounded!" he ordered in a tone that brokered no argument from his friends. They were just a few Silvers, but most of the creatures that surrounded them gave off the aura of a Gold. Kiru had a hard time counting them all.

Though the psion wasn't the strongest nor the leader of the larger scouting party, they happily complied, sensing the danger. The yellow-skinned ogres around the party seemed to be more frightened than they were. They reminded Kiru of a bunch of disturbed cattle as they all raised their weapons and frantically scanned the area.

"Gnolls!" the ogre leader shouted. "Kill da gnolls!" At that declaration, both the spotted beasts and the hairy ogres leaped down to ambush their targets below. A couple of the panicking ogres died almost instantly, either crushed by their hairy brethren, or by having their throats clawed out by a descending gnoll.

A descending gnoll went to bite Zhaden's throat. Kiru saw the drakonid orient his scales to reflect the sun's light right into the beast's eyes.

The gnoll cried out in surprise, raising its hands to cover its eyes as it fell. Zhaden shifted to the side, moving out of the way of the gnoll's path.

As a result, the beast crashed to the rocky ground, audibly breaking both of its arms and a couple of ribs. It didn't have much time to experience pain, though, as Zhaden promptly stomped on the back of its neck and simultaneously stabbed it in the back of the skull.

Kiru nodded in approval. Zhaden had told him about using his scales to the drakonid's advantage back in Dissé, but this was the first time the psion saw it in action.

William was reveling in the bloodshed, cackling madly inside Kiru's mind. *"Hahaha! Yes! Spill their blood, Master! Show them the folly of messing with us!"* To the imp's point, Kiru was in fact slicing up some gnoll with his Fu Tao hook blades. The Cruel Mantis style he'd learned back at the academy was specifically tailored toward maiming and killing bipedal foes, and the gnolls fit that description. Kiru wrapped the hook of one blade around a beast's wrist, pulling it off-balance and slicing its throat with the other weapon.

The psion ducked under a bite from another and cut across its abdomen, eviscerating it with one swing. The gnoll cried out in pain and pressed its arm to his belly in a desperate attempt to keep its intestines from spilling out. Before it could turn back to try and kill the man who'd delivered it such a devastating blow, however, Kiru was already there. His Psyslime blade cut the gnoll's head clean off, ending its worldly concerns forever.

Kiru flicked blood off his blade. Just as he did, a large shadow obscured the sunlight from behind him. The psion turned around to see one of the hairy ogres with fists raised to smash Kiru into paste.

"Divine Shield!" Brunhilda called out.

A column of holy light surrounded Kiru. The light intercepted the impact and kept him safe from damage. The Divine Shield technique retaliated against the ogre who struck it, setting him alight in holy flame. The ogre cried out in discomfort, and while he was distracted from that pain, Kiru ran in between his legs and sliced both of the hairy ogre's ankles. The large creature fell to his knees before promptly having his skull caved in by one of the Tau with their war clubs.

Mutt and Mak charged into the fray. The prince activated his teeth technique as well as Fenrir's Claws and Harpy Eagle's Talons while his great uncle turned into what looked like a bipedal wolf. Both of the orcs began tearing through the horde of opponents in their wake. Mutt jumped and landed on a gnoll with his talons, burying the sharp claws deep into the beast's back. The gnoll coughed up blood as its lungs were pierced. Its torment didn't last long, though, as the orc stabbed his claws into its neck causing it to rapidly bleed out.

The one-eyed M'Baku charged through the crowd, heedless of the number of opponents. The wolfish orc swung both his clawed and prosthetic blade appendages wildly. The sharp points easily cut through the flesh of various gnolls and caused a fountain of blood to erupt. His charge was stopped short when a pair of gnolls bit down on each of his arms, one crushing and destroying his prosthetic blade attachment. With Mak's momentum abruptly halted, that allowed another gnoll to run up and bite the orc's neck.

Before the beast could bite too deep, Mutt re-entered the fray. The blind orc jumped off the gnoll he'd just killed and in the direction of the one behind his ally. As he descended, Mutt spun and kicked the unsuspecting gnoll, clawing multiple wounds across its face and knocking it into one of its compatriots currently biting Mak. Both the gnolls stumbled and fell to the ground as Mutt ran off to go aid some of the L'Khan ogres in need.

Despite his prosthetic blade attachment falling off, the one-eyed M'Baku used the remaining part of the artificial limb to punch the other gnoll near him square in the eye. It cried out in pain as its jaws let go of the orc's arm. Mak used the opportunity to use his now-free arm to almost completely decapitate the gnoll in one swing. Blood sprayed liberally over Mak from his enemy. The orc howled in triumph at killing his foe.

That howl brought the attention of one of the hairy ogres to the elder M'Baku. Unlike the L'Khan ogres, it didn't wield any bone weapons but used its meaty fists instead. It stomped over to the orc and raised one of its aforementioned fists in the air to smash him.

The one-eyed M'Baku gave a wolfish grin at the incoming opponent. The hairy ogre was faster than its counterparts, but based off its movements, it wasn't faster than Mak. The orc moved to dodge but was forced to stop as something halted his right leg. The orc looked down to see that the gnolls that Mutt had knocked off of him had lunged and bit down on his limb instead of getting back up off the ground, a crazed, feral look in their eyes. By the time he had clawed their faces enough to force them to dislodge, it was too late. Before he could dodge, his opponent's fist had come down. In one swing, the ogre crushed the M'Baku's body, sending blood, viscera, and bone flying in multiple directions. Mak had been reduced to a bloody pulp.

The gnolls and hairy ogres were both more numerous and more savage than the L'Khans. Even with the M'Baku envoy, the yellow-skinned ogres were outnumbered at least three to one. Thankfully, they didn't outmatch the party in skill. Surely and steadily, the attackers were being eliminated. Without the envoy's intervention, the L'Khans surely would have been slaughtered. Fortunately, Mutt and the others were there to intervene. With the party's help, they were eventually able to prevail and push the gnolls back. It also didn't hurt that one of the Tau was a Sapphire.

When Kiru noticed the tide of battle was undeniably in the L'Khan's favor, the gnolls and their hairy ogre allies retreated, only a handful getting away with their tails quite literally between their legs.

Despite Kiru's team's superior skill, the gnolls weren't without their advantages. Scores of L'Khans had been butchered, some even partially eaten. Aside from Mak, Ebysso's ally, the other Akain Clan orc was also killed in action.

The L'Khans and party cheered their victory before scanning the carnage around them. They breathed in heavily as they took in the damage. It was bloody and horrible, making Kiru sick to his stomach. He'd had his fair share of combat these recent months. The Warrior Games had been an especially dangerous event. This was the first time, however, he'd seen so much brutality all at once.

During the Warrior Games, various clerics and paladins had set up protective defensive techniques to do their best to prevent any wound from being fatal. Sure, their fights had been bloody, but there was still some degree of control. Fighting and hunting some of the animals inside Imakandi had also been gory work, but each was more isolated—just one animal killed at a time. Those hunts didn't match the carnage that he'd just witnessed. The fighting didn't last ten minutes, but the death and carnage spread about were both grotesque and gut-wrenching, particularly as the smell of spilled intestines reached the psion's nostrils.

Kiru wasn't fooling himself, though. He knew the path forward—the path to saving this world—would be paved with violence and blood. There would, no doubt, be more bloodshed and more who would oppose him. Still, if this short battle was a mere taste of what war would bring—what New Draconia promised to bring on all of Alterra—Kiru needed to stop it.

Just then, the helmeted ogre leader walked toward him. The brute sported four large gouges in his distended abdomen, but it seemed his bulbous belly fat had saved him from getting eviscerated. Still, the wound was grievous. "You small like

Metal Woman, but you fight good with your pointy sticks. Kill gnoll and hairy ogre good."

Kiru nodded in ascent. "You too. What are those gnolls exactly?" he asked.

"Sacred beasts," Jubjon answered simply. "Smart and mean. Other ogres leave tribe and join gnolls. They take our food," he said. The ogre's stomach then grumbled loudly for the psion to hear.

Noting the ogre's visible ribs and remembering his earlier demand for food, Kiru pulled out some jerky and raised it up to the brute. "Good fight. You deserve food."

The helmeted ogre's beady eyes widened, and he quickly took the food without hesitation, hungrily shoving it in his mouth. He loudly and grossly chewed in pleasure as drool and crumbs fell out of his mouth.

Kiru had to force himself not to cringe. Another thing that surprised him was that, as the ogre ate, his most serious wounds started healing before Kiru's very eyes!

"Mm, good food. You not so bad even with orcs. You fight gnolls and shared food. We will take you to Chieftain. First, we need to gather food."

Kiru looked around. "Where?"

He picked up the headless corpse of a gnoll. "Food."

CHAPTER TWELVE

Gluttony

The group soon realized that the ogres intended on eating all the dead gnolls, the hairy ogres with them, and even their own dead, which repulsed Kiru on an instinctual level. William had the exact opposite reaction. *"That is awesome!"* he exclaimed. *"Dominating your foes and taking their strength as your own. That is the act of a true conqueror. Master, you should eat our enemies too."*

"William, just . . . no." That was all Kiru sent back, nothing more was needed to convey his feelings. The psion looked back at the L'Khans. It became apparent that their prominent ribs weren't just for show. They were indeed starving.

Once they had gathered most of the dead, the L'Khans set a couple of their dead, mutilated brethren aside. Once their captain—who they learned was named Jubjon—gave his approval, the ogres tore into their dead comrades with reckless abandon. It was unsettling to watch as the ogres hungrily consumed every part of their recently deceased allies. Pandemonium all wordlessly decided to move closer to each other and keep their weapons at the ready.

Once there wasn't a single scrap left of the dead ogres aside from blood spatter, the L'Khans composed themselves, all of them giving audible sighs of relief as their various injuries began to heal. They clearly had some sort of ability to use energy from food to convert into healing mana. After their meal, the ogres continued stockpiling the dead bodies. The party didn't interrupt them, not wanting to infringe on their cultural beliefs. What did broach disagreement, however, was when the ogres tried to add the two orcs' bodies to their collection.

The two Tau stood defensively in front of the dead with their clubs. A female ogre who came to collect the bodies was completely baffled as to why the Tau were getting in her way. The air stirred up around the gray-haired Tau as they glared daggers at the ogre.

Jubjon came over after seeing his subordinate grunting in complaint. "What you doing?" he asked.

"We are protecting our dead from being violated," the male Tau answered angrily, speaking with more emotion than the psion had ever heard from him before.

"Violated?" he asked tentatively, tasting the foreign word on his tongue for the first time. "We no violate, we take dead for food."

"Ah . . . that's what he means, Big Guy," Mutt explained.

"Yes, we honor our dead with a proper funeral pyre," the male Tau affirmed.

"Me confused. We honor dead by eating them, not burning. Burning is a waste."

Kiru then huddled up the remaining members of the M'Baku envoy. "Okay, I respect wanting to do a proper burial, but there are two important factors we need to consider. One, where are we going to find enough wood here to build a pyre? Two, we are in the middle of dangerous territory with a group of ogres we just got to treat us with a measure of amicability, and that was after we fought off an ambush."

"Are you seriously considering letting these ogres *eat* our fallen comrades?" Ebysso asked vehemently.

"As much as it gives me the creeps, I agree with the Boss," Mutt said.

Zhaden grunted in agreement. "I concur. Logic dictates that we pursue the safest course of action to achieve our objective. Also, from learning about your culture, I believe these orcs would happily allow themselves to be eaten if it meant helping their chief," the gold drakonid said to his trainer.

Ebysso's mouth couldn't be seen behind her cowl, but she had the same look in her eyes as the Tau who were scowling. Fortunately, after half a minute of awkward tension, the orcs relented. "Only because we have no way to burn them," Ebysso hissed. Then, begrudgingly, the Tau moved out of the way, allowing the ogres to take their dead. The L'Khans grabbed a crude stone sled and loaded the corpses on there.

They were clearly elated. They had just won a battle against a hated foe and now had a surplus of food from their enemies and outsiders. There was something strange as well about those gnolls and hairy ogres. They had been told there was only one tribe of ogres in the Wastelands. *Why are there now two different ogre groups, and why were they fighting each other? Why were those ogres working with sacred beasts, and how come they were so hairy?* Kiru thought.

As they followed the L'Khans, Kiru decided to ask Jubjon. The captain seemed to be the most intelligent of his group, but he was still fairly simple-minded, so his answers were neither very detailed nor that informative. Still, Jubjon had *some* information, and some was far better than none.

"So, when did another ogre tribe appear in the Wastelands? I thought it was only the L'Khans who lived here," Kiru asked.

Jubjon idly scratched his chin. "Uh, was only L'Khan in Wastelands, but Chief's brother got mad. He want to be Chief. He challenged Chief to fight. Brother lost. Was exiled from Wastelands. Then—" The ogre captain bared his fangs and held his hands like claws. "—Exile come back . . . but different."

"He hairy and had lots of gnolls with him. He also seem . . ." Jubjon scratched his small head as he tried to come up with the right word. ". . . *smarter*. Exile want us to leave Chief and join him, but Chief Snout is good chief. So, Jubjon and others stay. Some scared or want hair and strength like Exile, so they leave. We fight them and gnolls since."

It was actually a simple enough story for Kiru to follow. There was, however, something he really wanted clarified. "I'm sorry. Did you say Chief Snout?" he asked, having a hard time digesting the name.

William was chuckling inside the psion's mind as well.

The ogre didn't understand what the issue was, so he just nodded in ascent.

"Okay. Well, what's his brother's name? I doubt his name is Exile," the psion pressed.

"Umm, me no remember. After so long, we forget. It no matter. He forced out of clan, so he is Exile now."

Kiru shrugged. "If you say so."

After another hour and a half going up into the mountainous craggy landscape, they finally made it to the L'Khan settlement. The air was hot and dry, and it wasn't long before Kiru and Brunhilda were covered in sweat. Both Mutt and Zhaden were not nearly as bothered; their bodies and upbringing helped them handle the heat better. Besides that, much of the earlier tension within the groups was now gone. Fighting to the death alongside people tended to help smooth over any other issues in Kiru's experience.

When they reached the settlement, the psion was impressed. Though the ogres weren't the smartest bunch he'd ever met, they seemed to possess at least *some* degree of intelligence in where they'd chosen to construct their village. It was a flat valley with tall rock surrounding it on all sides except for an entrance just wide enough for two ogres to fit through side-by-side. At the very back of the valley was a small mountain with a sizeable cave entrance at its bottom.

Thanks to the natural topography, there was only one way to safely get into the settlement, providing an effective bottleneck to protect the L'Khans. It reminded Kiru of a lesson from his Strategies I Class back at the Royal Academy with regard to large-scale tactics. One of the best ways to eliminate the advantage of superior numbers was to choose a battlefield narrow enough that the opponent had no choice but to send in their forces a small amount at a time. The ogres had clearly taken that principle to heart.

Also, with regard to defensive measures, if they were attacked or some terrible storm assaulted them, they could retreat to safety inside the cave, depending on how large it was inside. But for some reason he couldn't place, Kiru's instincts told him *not* to go into that cave. He felt some sort of primal, untamed hunger radiating from it.

Meanwhile, across the valley were various tents and other simple structures, some of them looking unstable even from a distance. Since wood was scarce, the main building materials were stone, bone, and hide. It was clear, however, that they hadn't had a skilled builder or mason amongst them.

The L'Khans in the village—seeing their allies returned with a large food haul made up of their enemies' and dead outsiders' corpses—began talking excitedly to one another. Then, they saw the outsiders with them and the excited energy died down, replaced by the sound of hushed whispers. Along with the ogres that accompanied the party, Kiru quickly estimated that the L'Khan Clan was made up of about 150 ogres. As they entered the village proper, they were able to get a better look at the others. Kiru had to hold back a grimace. These ogres were thin, even more so than the ones he'd just been traveling with. Many of them didn't even have the classic protruding guts, instead sporting sunken-in bellies with prominent ribs. They seemed to be starving. It was a wonder that some of them were even walking.

The most difficult sights to take in were the children. Their forms reminded Kiru of . . . well, himself. Ogre children varied in size, but the smallest one was still half the size of the psion, and it appeared to be a newborn. It was admittedly strange to see such tall children, but based on how tall the adults were, Kiru reasoned that that was normal for ogres. *Maybe this is how gnomes and dwarves feel compared to other races,* he thought.

All of the children stopped their play to watch the procession of ogres and the M'Baku envoy. Their gazes were equal parts awe, curiosity, hunger, and fear. Their eyes seemed haunted and their jaws protruding. One of them had worn down their teeth to blunted ends as they chewed on a rock in a vain attempt to eat it. All of the ogres were in obvious need of sustenance. As they, along with the other ogres, all noticed the pile of carcasses, their eyes widened with unrestrained longing. Long strands of thick saliva were soon hanging from the maws of many of the children and more than one adult. The sound of growling bellies reached the party's ears.

They proceeded to the cave entrance. Once they reached their destination, the ogre warriors put down the sled with loud sighs of relief. At this point, the entire L'Khan clan had surrounded the party and their food bounty.

Jubjon nodded his head meaningfully at one of two ogres standing guard at the cave's mouth. The other nodded back knowingly and went into the cave. One of the ogre villagers broke off from the group and began walking toward what he called the "meat cart" in a daze, his arms outstretched. Jubjon quickly smacked his wrist with the end of his bone club. "We present to Chief first."

The villager's tongue went back in his mouth as he came to his senses. The ogre then rubbed his pained wrist and scowled. When he didn't make a move to back down, Jubjon bared his teeth and growled at him. That made the defiant villager back away into the crowd promptly. Then, the ground began to shake. The guard Jubjon had motioned to earlier quickly jogged his way out of the cave and resumed his post. He was breathing heavily but did his best to appear unbothered.

The shaking continued for another few seconds until another ogre came out of the cave after the guard, this one undoubtedly the largest ogre that any member of Pandemonium had ever encountered! This gargantuan figure *had* to be their chief. It was clear that the rumbling had been due to his lumbering steps.

Chief Snout was three times as wide as any of the other ogres of the L'Khan Clan. His skin was also pasty-white and looked soft compared to the hardened yellow skin of the others. Aside from his sheer girth, he had a few other notable features, namely his lack of a left arm, the insectoid mandibles on both sides of his mouth, and the flat porcine snout in place of his nose. He looked like a hideous experiment gone wrong, a strange amalgamation of beast, monster, and ogre.

"Damn, that guy is the fattest person I've ever seen. He's even fatter than that pompous merchant I stole from back in Fox Hollow," William said inside Kiru's mind.

"Yeah, I'm pretty sure this guy could eat that merchant whole and still be hungry," Kiru sent back. He wondered if the chief was truly even an ogre at all given how abnormal he looked. Then again, he remembered how monstrous Myev looked when she used her techniques all at once. *Maybe he's using a technique, but I was told they worshipped a boar Beast God. So why does he look like he's part bug?* he thought.

The aptly named Chief Snout took in first his people, then the group of outsiders. "Jubjon, why have you brought these orcs and . . . others into our home?" he bellowed, his commanding voice conveying much more intelligence than Kiru had seen in any other ogres so far.

The captain took a knee and bowed his head. "Chief, we met tiny people while on patrol. We told them leave Wastelands and give us their food. Before they go, gnolls and hairy ogres attack."

The crowd gasped at the mention of their enemies, startled despite the fact that their foes' corpses were piled up before them on the sled.

Did they think we just found all these dead bodies? Kiru thought.

Chief Snout snorted and his mandibles clicked. "And these intruders helped you fight off the Exile's forces?"

"Yes, Chief! Though small, they very strong. Some died with us in fight. Even after fight, they give us food and allow us to honor their dead."

The chief just stood there, his bulbous body still, aside from his insectile mandibles clicking as he seemed to process the information. It was tense as everyone observed him for a reaction, none daring to move. Kiru held his breath. Then, suddenly, Snout nodded his head and grunted in approval before looking back at the party. "Who are you? Why have you come here? I am grateful for your help in protecting my clan, but that does not mean you are welcome to stay."

Ebysso procured a small scroll and raised it up for the chief to take.

Snout squinted his eyes. "No! No writing! Speak!"

The scout's eyes went wide and quickly looked back to the others. Though her mouth was still covered in wrappings, it was clearly agape in confusion.

Kiru was tempted to speak, but it wasn't his place to explain. The M'Baku Clan needed the L'Khan's support, and Kiru wasn't from either clan. *"Mutt, speak up!"* he sent telepathically, conveying urgency in his tone.

"You sure, Boss? My sister is much better at this stuff," Mutt whispered.

"You're a freaking prince of the M'Baku Clan. There is no better candidate. Please!"

"Alright. Er, hem." He loudly cleared his voice. "Greetings, I am M'Baku M'Toon, prince of the M'Baku Clan. You can call me Mutt, though."

Chief Snout didn't say anything. The bulbous ogre just stared at Mutt, his mandibles clicking all the while.

After ten seconds of uncomfortable silence, the blind orc continued. "We come on behalf of my sister, Myev. She is planning to participate in the Choosing Ceremony, Uh . . ." Mutt trailed off, forgetting the name at the most inopportune moment.

"Ukufakaza." Kiru sent.

"Right! Ukufakaza."

The ogre chief snorted. "Hmph, Ukufakaza. That is orc problem. The L'Khans don't associate with orc politics."

"I know, but we're hoping that we can fix that," he said, doing his best to put on a winning smile despite the situation. Mutt wasn't wrong. His sister was much better suited for this. That, coupled with his poor attention to detail and his lack of interest in little else aside from hunting and fighting, made him not ideal for this. But he had a straightforward honesty that could be very appealing.

Snout grunted in frustration. Mutt didn't seem to pay that any mind. Before the ogre chief could tell him off, he spoke up again. "You know, I'm actually wondering. Why did your tribe leave the founding tribes' alliance?"

Snout's frustration turned into a mixture of anger and confusion. "You don't know why the L'Khans left?!" His mandibles clicked wildly. "It's because you orcs abandoned us! When our god Heidrun needed help, no one came. We did our best to help. The World Serpent needed to be stopped. But when we called for aid to assist our god, none showed."

Mutt scratched his thick sideburns. "Gosh, I'm really sorry. That sucks! Obviously, I wasn't there, but it sounds real bad. What happened?"

Chief Snout clearly wasn't expecting Mutt's kind, empathetic words. The pale ogre had been about to berate the orc for his ignorance of his family's involvement in what happened to their god, but then he stopped. Other ogres flashed Mutt various looks of disapproval at his question but didn't speak up over their Chief. After a few seconds, Snout cocked his head in confusion.

After a few deep breaths, he chose to simply answer Mutt's question rather than shouting at him. "Heidrun the Hungry has the unique power of absorbing the strength of those he ingests. He took a bite out of the World Serpent during the first battle the Beast Gods fought in their attempts to subdue Jormungandr. The poison inside its flesh didn't reveal itself until it was too late. It threatened to kill Heidrun if nothing was done."

The ogre sighed. "The Beast Gods and the orc clans that followed them were so preoccupied with defeating the enemy that they refused to help their ally. So, we had to resort to a drastic measure. Instead of allowing Heidrun to die, we found a creature with the power to overcome any illness. With no other choice, our god gorged himself on a colony of glutton grubs we found, eating more and more of the creature until his body overcame Jormungandr's poison. That power, however, came with a price."

This Heidrun must've lost some of its original power in exchange for this grub's healing—

His thoughts were interrupted however, when the Chief gestured to them and said, "Come," He waved the party to follow him into the cave.

Cautiously, they did. As soon as they all entered and the cave top blocked out all of the sunlight, they were beset by some force that Kiru couldn't see. Many of them tensed and groaned as they felt some odd, overwhelming hunger. It surrounded them and then invaded their bodies. All of the party halted mid-step. Many of them visibly shook as they resisted the hungry force invading their bodies. Zhaden fell to his knees and let out a bestial hiss as he gripped his stomach. The gold drakonid bared his teeth in a savage display.

Even Kiru wasn't resistant to this force. His belly growled loudly, and his head shook. He started to look around for something—*anything*—to eat. The psion was about to start chewing on the leather of his own boot when an even-louder growl rumbled through the cave. They all looked up to see it was Chief Snout. The pale ogre's mouth was open wide, and he beat his fists against his large belly as he bellowed. Quickly, the magical force dissipated. Each of them sighed in relief, but while it had lessened, it hadn't gone away completely. Kiru wiped the drool from his mouth while he caught sight of Brunhilda focusing intently on her arms to try to keep them from shaking.

Kiru started to look around, feeling both on edge and still hungry, like he was a beast low down on the food chain, fighting for survival. The others started to scan around frantically as if a predator was watching them and about to pounce at any moment. Many gripped their weapons tightly, Ebysso and Zhaden in particular hurriedly scanning the area for any threats.

Mutt was the first to speak. "Whoa! What was that, and why do I really want a sandwich?"

Snout chuckled, snorting like a pig. "You are entering the domain of Heidrun the Hungry. He may be less than what he was originally, but he is still a god. While his core has been weakened, he is still an Onyx. His shroud affects all, even without his intent."

That gave Kiru pause for multiple reasons. Onyx was the second-highest rank in cultivation that one could achieve. *That's the rank Van Blaine is at,* he thought. It was undeniably significant. Apparently, Heidrun was affecting them all without even trying to. However, Heidrun was considered a god, worshipped by the ogres of the L'Khan Clan. *How is he only an Onyx?* he thought. From what he'd learned, to be considered a god, you had to be a Diamond, the highest rank the psion had ever heard of. Kiru reasoned that Heidrun's "healing" had weakened his core enough to reduce his rank. It was the only thing that made sense based on the limited information he had so far.

After they all adjusted to being within Heidrun's influence—albeit with Snout's aid—they continued into the cave. The tunnel was large, and not long into their trek, they saw multiple tunnels beginning to branch off the main one they were going down. They weren't just at the sides, though. Some were in the ceiling, the floor, and other odd angles. It reminded Kiru of some sort of hive, with no obvious rhyme nor reason.

In just a few minutes, they made it to the cave's central chamber. It was a large dome one hundred feet wide and a few hundred feet tall, sparsely illuminated by dim torches. The intermittent holes that they'd seen previously were everywhere in this dome, giving it the appearance of a honeycomb. Every single member of the party broke out in a sweat. Many of their bodies shook involuntarily. A few of them even took a step to run away as clicking sounds echoed throughout the chamber.

Chief Snout raised his one arm out. "Do not worry. You will not come to harm. Just stay behind me." They all happily did so. The sound got louder, and some loose rocks and dust fell from the ceiling. "Behold, Heidrun the Hungry!" Then, from one of the large holes, the divine sacred beast emerged in all its terror.

It was clear that Heidrun the Hungry was once a boar—once being the key word. The psion had reasoned that the glutton grub may have altered Heidrun's original form. He hadn't assumed it would have change him so much, though. The boar-like face had a pair of mammalian eyes but then an additional two beady black eyes over each of them. Meanwhile, his porcine tusks were surrounded by sharp insectoid teeth and mandibles. He had a large and bulbous body so long that it didn't fully leave the hole it had emerged from. Whereas the head was brown and hairy, the body was slimy and white with countless pointy limbs. Kiru knew in that instant that it was the body of a glutton grub, though on a much larger scale.

"Oh, shit! That thing is ugly!" William shouted inside Kiru's mind. The imp was pretty ugly himself, so that was saying something. Kiru heartily agreed with him too. Not only was it ugly, the massive creature was undeniably monstrous! That coupled with the fact that it was larger than a house, meant it certainly cut an imposing figure.

All of the party quickly lowered their heads, not daring to look it in the eyes. The powerful aura directly coming off the creature also took the decision to bow before him out of their hands as well.

The Beast God roared, huge globules of drool falling out of his mouth. This wasn't the first time Kiru or Brunhilda had ever encountered a deity. They both have had visions and spiritual interactions with Hlin, but this was the first time they had seen a god in the flesh, face-to-face.

The divine creature twitched as it focused on the ogre chief. "Snout! I don't have much time. Who are these outsiders, and why are they in my presence?" Heidrun snarled, then sniffed loudly. His voice projected outward, radiating power. The Beast God's eyes went distant, then gave a bone-chilling predatory smile. His mandibles clicked loudly as his sharp, buggy legs crawled him closer to the party, "Oooh, are they my next meal? They look tasty. Gah!" The Beast God opened his mouth and lunged at the orcs.

"No!" Snout shouted and shoved his arm into Heidrun's maw.

The monstrous deity bit down on his arm without hesitation, ripping it off within seconds. Heidrun pulled his head back and raised it up to chew on the limb. A spray of arterial blood shot out of Snout's wound, but he showed surprising resistance to the pain, only gritting his teeth instead of screaming and flailing. The party drew their weapons and ran in between Snout and Heidrun, ready to defend them.

"Put away your weapons, fools!" Snout barked.

The others looked back at him incredulously.

Is he serious?! William sent.

The ogre chief just stared them down. He was serious. Also, remarkably, the bleeding from such a serious wound stopped in just seconds.

The now-armless ogre walked up to be in between them and his god once more.

After Heidrun swallowed Snout's arm, the monstrous god shook his head, and the focus returned to his eyes. He looked down at the ogre. "My apologies, Snout."

"No need to apologize, Oh Hungry One. I only meant to show these outsiders your glory, and that you had survived your betrayal."

At the final word, Heidrun snapped his head at the party and snarled but quickly shook his head again. Something wasn't right with the Beast God. That was obvious. "They have seen. Now, I must go." With that, Heidrun the Hungry went into another tunnel, his long, giant grub body taking at least a good minute to fully leave one hole and enter the next due to his massive length.

"By Hlin's mercy! Are ye alright?" Brunhilda exclaimed and moved over to the chief. She, like everyone else, didn't dare to move while Heidrun's body was still visible. She activated her Rejuvenation technique, repairing the wounded flesh where the Beast God had ripped off Snout's arm.

"Hmph, we of the L'Khan are strong. Losing an arm is of no concern," the ogre chief said dismissively.

"No concern?! How is that not of concern?" she asked.

Snout's face gave a smug grin under his mandibles. "I will show you," he said and motioned with his head for the party to follow him out. The party all looked at the now-armless ogre with a mixture of trepidation and awe.

The chief had his arm bitten off by his god and doesn't look concerned in the slightest, Kiru thought. Besides showing no sign of pain, Snout evidently wasn't disturbed that the one he worshipped was clearly beset by madness. Kiru was impressed by Snout's fortitude and faith.

Once the chief led them out, he shouted, "Bring me one of our dead."

The L'Khans faithfully carried over a dead ogre from the pile of bodies that had been taken from the battle. Jubjon ripped off one of the corpse's arms with a sickening crunch and reverently raised it to his chief's mouth.

Brunhilda covered her mouth, afraid that she would otherwise have vomited.

"The outsiders have seen what has happened to our beloved Heidrun. Just like him, we have survived despite our difficulties and used our curse to our advantage," he pronounced to the crowd. "We use the glutton grub beast mana from our god, and it makes us stronger. With his power, we honor our dead by taking their strength into us. Gluttony for the good!"

"Gluttony for the good!" the ogres replied back in unison.

Then, Chief Snout bit down on the arm. With his insectoid mandibles clicking, it was even grosser than watching the other ogres eat. The show wasn't over, though. After just one bite into the arm, flesh bubbled out from Snout's stump and his bitten-off arm regrew with a surge and an audible *pop*! Within seconds, the ogre—who they now realized looked very much like their deity—had regrown his entire arm before their very eyes. It was without flaw and looked as if it had never been lost.

Snout took another bite, and the process repeated for the arm he had already been lacking when the party first met him. The ogres already had an incredible capacity to heal, as evidenced by Jubjon, but what Snout had just displayed was simply astounding. Kiru idly wondered if it could somehow help his own broken body but then thought better of it. Cannibalism was something he would never be comfortable with. Kiru had made peace with his handicaps, but that didn't mean he didn't miss moving around the normal way.

He'd heard rumors back at the academy that unless you a) reached the rank of Pearl, b) had a specific healing technique, or c) was aided by one who used one, you couldn't replace any lost body parts or fully heal any seriously grievous wounds. *Maybe once I reach high enough, I won't have to worry about how to control my body,* he thought. He then thought about Heidrun and the only other Onyx he'd ever met, Van Blaine. *If he's near the pinnacle of cultivation, why does he only have one eye?* Kiru wondered. *Whatever had damaged him must've been powerful indeed for it to not be repairable.*

The chief then looked up to the crowd and roared in triumph, raising his newly regrown limbs in the air. His clan did the same. Snout turned back to Mutt. "That is what happened to our god, and we have had to deal with the consequences. Now, you may go. Deal with your orc problems on your own. We will handle our own ogre problems," he said in a tone that was both bitter and proud.

Mutt nodded. "I understand. I am sorry for what happened. I'll be honest, I don't have a clue how to heal a god, but I think we could still help each other, Bug Guy. We could deal with your ogre problem for you, and none of your guys need to die fighting those hairy dudes."

Snout squinted his eyes in suspicion. "Why?"

He scratched the back of his head. "Well, the way I see it, we owe you. Maybe after we do that, your clan might reconsider backing us? You wouldn't have to fight or anything, no risk to your people."

Snout flared his . . . well, *snout.* "Fine. Let's talk."

CHAPTER THIRTEEN

Tactical Raid

The party followed Chief Snout over to a large stone table. There, he discussed with them in much greater detail what had been going on with Heidrun and the gnolls. "After eating hundreds of thousands of glutton grubs, Heidrun's body was able to counter the poison in Jormungandr's flesh. The cost was his body becoming more like the grub, and his mind and core being weakened by the corruption of so much of its mana. After millennia, he can only maintain sanity for mere minutes at a time before sinking again into madness. That's why he said he didn't have much time before he attacked," Snout explained.

Kiru telepathically sent Mutt questions to ask the ogre chieftain in order to help guide the conversation and help them attain more information. "So, what's the deal with the gnolls?" Mutt asked. The orc didn't use Kiru's words verbatim, but he fortunately did get the main points across.

Snout huffed in no small amount of anger before answering, "My brother grew tired of the responsibility of managing our clan and the tendencies of our god. He had wanted to abandon Heidrun and have me lead the L'Khans out of the Wastelands. I refused to leave the guardian who'd favored and protected our clan for generations. We owe our lives to him," the ogre chief said with zeal as he clenched his grubby fist.

Snout continued, "My brother and I fought for leadership of the clan to determine in what direction we should go. I was able to defeat my brother, but—" His insectoid mandibles moved erratically, conveying the mixture of emotions he felt. "—I couldn't kill him at that time. He was my brother, after all. So, instead of executing him for his rebellion as I should have, I stripped him of his name and exiled him from the Wastelands."

Kiru nodded in understanding. So that's why Jubjon only referred to the ogre as "Exile."

"I banished him, and he fled through the Skeletal Ruins, which border orc territory to the northeast."

"Skeletal Ruins?" Kiru asked.

"It is a ruined city made entirely of dirt and bones," Snout explained. "The last I saw of the Exile, he was being pursued by orcs that were hunting there. I thought him dead, but months later, he'd returned. The Exile wasn't the same as when he'd left. My brother's skin was covered in spotted hair, and he possessed a wicked staff. Furthermore, he had acquired some sort of evil power and had a new tribe—a tribe of gnolls."

Kiru learned more about the gnolls from Snout. The sacred beasts had a reputation for sadism, cruelty, and bloodlust. They were a plague on Imakandi and had been thought long extinct. Apparently, according to Snout, they had not all been wiped out as originally thought.

"The Exile had come to the village with his sacred beasts tamed behind him," Snout continued. "He offered for the L'Khans to join him. Some did. Like my brother, they were *changed*. Those were the hairy ogres you encountered," he said. "Still, most of our clan stayed loyal to Heidrun. But that didn't matter much. After all, would-be traitors joined the Exile, my brother and his pets attacked."

The party learned that this wasn't the ogre tribe's original village but instead an outpost where Heidrun stayed. The L'Khans had retreated to their present spot after their home had been overrun by the gnolls. Snout explained that the L'Khans had been fighting a losing war ever since. The Wastelands were already a hard place to survive, and with the gnolls about, it was a struggle to find anything the ogre clan could eat.

The L'Khans had only persisted this long because Snout was a Sapphire-stage glutton grub mana cultivator on the path of the Hungry Heidrun. His high rank and connection with his deity had made him extremely proficient in utilizing food to regenerate his body—much better than any other. He could eat the minimal amount of food they could find, rip off his own limbs for his tribe to have enough to eat, and then regrow them. It was the only way the tribe could accumulate enough to eat during these hard times.

On revealing that information, everyone looked at Chief Snout with a mixture of great shock and respect. Sometimes, he ripped his own body apart multiple times a day to feed his people. He quite literally gave an arm and a leg to his people. *His pain tolerance must be really remarkable,* Kiru thought. Granted, the extent to which the ogres relied on cannibalism was pretty sickening, but Snout's commitment to his tribe was still incredible.

"We L'Khans are strong, but my brother and his traitorous allies are as well. Their beast mana is influenced by the gnolls, which is better for fighting than glutton grub. We are more durable but not as skilled offensively speaking." Chief Snout let out a large, drawn-out sigh. He pursed his lips as his mandibles clicked nervously. It was clear that he was struggling with what he was about to say. "We need help. If nothing is done, we L'Khans will die. If we die, no one can tend to Heidrun, and our god will die too."

"Yeah, I've been wondering about that. Didn't all the Beast Gods go off to another realm or something after they beat the World Serpent?" Mutt asked.

"The Beast Gods harnessed their powers to open a portal and claim one of the lost realms of Yggdrasil, a place they can safely inhabit. Their amplified power was not of this world, so they risked destroying Alterra if they stayed. With Heidrun's corruption, his form and power so weakened and polluted by a being of this world, he no longer posed that risk. So, he never left. The other gods didn't look for him either. They probably assumed he died."

"Oh! That's rough, Bug—I mean, Big Guy," the orc immediately corrected himself. "I don't know why our clan didn't help yours, but it clearly was a mistake."

"Your sister told me that they didn't aid the ogres because they were recovering themselves after their gods' exertion against Jormungandr," Kiru sent telepathically to Mutt.

"I can only suppose that it was that they were so preoccupied with helping their own gods and recovering after their fight. Still, we should've helped. So, we'll help now," the blind orc added.

"You'll fix Heidrun?" Snout asked, his voice laden with hope.

"I can't promise that, Big Guy, but I *can* promise to help you with your bro."

"You will fight my brother and his army?"

"Yep. It should be a good fight." He smiled. Mutt loved a good fight. "After we take care of him, if you promise to back my sister, leader of my clan, as a candidate for Ukufakaza, I know she'll do her best to help your god."

"Prince M'Toon! You are not the leader of your clan! You cannot make such a promise," Ebysso barked out in indignation.

"Actually, I can," Mutt said with a smug look. "You said it yourself. I am a prince, after all. My sis is a good person. I know she would want to help these people."

Snout let out a smile along with a flurry of insectoid clicks from his mandibles. "Then it is agreed. We of the L'Khan Clan will back your queen after we have been freed of the gnoll threat and your clan aids us in healing our god. This I swear on my core."

"You got yourself a deal, Big Guy. I swear on my core." They both clasped hands in agreement, and the weight of their oaths settled into both of them, solidifying their bond.

Once that had been settled, Snout discussed the layout of their original village that had been overrun by the Exile and his forces. It was located at a riverbed, a small, isolated sanctuary hidden from the sun's rays most of the day.

He drew a diagram of it out on the dirt below and gave them information about how to enter, where guards would most likely be situated, and the placement of the buildings.

With his information, the party was fully armed with the knowledge for a tactical approach. It was early afternoon, but with Snout's info, they could make it there within an hour, using a few secret pathways. So they would still have some sunlight. Ready for a fight, Pandemonium, Ebysso, and the two Tau quickly made their way to the village. Apparently, the gnolls were even tougher to deal with at night, and they wanted to strike before then. All of them could tell they were getting close before they even saw the large mound where the village was based. The gnolls' foul smell was wafting over to them even from a distance!

As they neared, Kiru grew more tense and focused, feeling more on edge as they got closer to enemy territory. When they had agreed to get the ogres' help, he didn't think that they would be participating in some sort of monstrous extermination mission. It wasn't that he was scared to fight the gnolls. They were actually trying to kill their leader anyway, hoping to cut the head off the proverbial snake. Kiru just didn't like the enemy's numbers. His party was relatively small and he was unsure of just how many gnolls they would have to contend with. Given they'd displaced all of the L'Khans, those numbers had to be formidable. He was reminded of the minotaur herd and their narrow escape from them after having been nearly trampled. He was comforted by the presence of Ebysso and the two powerful Tau that he'd been training with, however. So while he was tense, he wasn't in a panic.

At one point, Mutt silently signaled for them to stop, then placed a hand on the dry earth below. He snapped his head up after a couple of seconds and wordlessly motioned for them to hide, which they did immediately while Ebysso and Zhaden stealthed and prepared to strike. Kiru watched as the scout faded away in a distortion of heat; the rogue activated his Invisibility technique, while Mutt activated Fenrir's Claws and Horned Harpy Eagle's Talons. The orc jumped onto the flat rock beside them and crawled up it with remarkable ease. Mutt then lay still against the rock, motionless, reminding Kiru of a lizard patiently waiting for prey. Everyone else hid around a big rock at a curve in their path.

After thirty seconds, half a dozen gnolls came patrolling the area. A few of them barked in a harsh tongue, and then they all stopped and went to find a spot to relieve themselves. One of them was just inches away from Zhaden.

That's when the party struck. Kiru was about to cry out to stop the gnoll but knew that the gold drakonid was *not* about to let himself get urinated on if he could help it. So the psion's aid wasn't needed. His dagger stabbed straight into a gnoll's eye, puncturing and popping it like a fruit and penetrating its brain. The sacred beast was dead before it hit the ground.

The gnolls, caught in their prone positions, were quickly eliminated, with only a couple of gurgles and bestial cries being released. Once Kiru and the rest came around the corner, the two orcs and drakonid were already cleaning their weapons.

"Aw, man!" William whined inside Kiru's core. *"Our allies look like a bunch of badasses. Master, we should've been the badasses, not them."*

"There'll be plenty of killing yet to come, William. So, don't worry," Kiru telepathically replied. He did agree with the imp's assessment, however. Killing enemies double their number with ease was badass. He didn't care about looking cool, though. He cared about surviving. To attack an entrenched foe that outnumbered them would require them to focus on being smart, not their own glory. His heart continued to race as he nervously scanned their surroundings.

"Calm down, Master. You're reminding me of Zhaden, being so nervous," William said.

The psion did give a small chuckle at that jab, some of his tension actually leaving at those words. William was right. Kiru had been getting just as paranoid as the gold drakonid's default state.

He nodded and thanked his familiar, feeling more ready but still keeping his edge in case of any more looming threats.

Mutt sniffed loudly. "All I can smell here is gnoll blood, and guts. Ugh!" Then he groaned. "Oh, no."

"What is it, Mutt?" Brunhilda asked, concern evident in her voice.

"If everything smells of gnoll, or something dead or dying, that means they'll smell us long before we get into the settlement." He put his bare foot on one of the dead beasts and stroked his goatee. "Hmm, how do we deal with that?" Mutt then snapped his fingers as an idea came. "We're gonna have to mask our scent with theirs." He pressed his bare foot into one of the gnoll's abdominal wounds, coating it in its spilled viscera.

Brunhilda and Kiru had to fight the urge to vomit from the gruesome display.

Mutt then pulled out the foot, dipped his hand in the gore like it was a washbasin and began wiping it all over his body.

Everyone recoiled at the sight—all except William. The little imp was ecstatic watching Mutt literally coat himself in "the blood of his enemies." Though disgusted, they all trusted Mutt's instincts. The blind orc knew what he was doing. Scowling and fighting the urge to vomit once more, the party began applying the blood and gore from the gnoll corpses.

Ebysso and the two Tau had had the bright idea to cut off the gnolls' hides and wear them like furs. It was still gross, but admittedly better than the alternative, in Kiru's opinion. Unfortunately, it was much too late for the other four members of Pandemonium who were already covered in the beast's lifeblood and the viscera. All four groaned in varying degrees of frustration as they realized how poor of a choice they'd made.

The cultivators still took some of the hides to cover their forms at least to some degree in an attempt to sell the part even more. Judging by the gnoll's small eyes, they didn't rely on sight as much as scent. Also, their forms were naturally hunched, so it could be hard to distinguish an obvious silhouette. So, Kiru and the others would make sure to mimic both their gait and hunched forms as they neared the village in order to not arouse suspicion.

After they adequately concealed their scents, Mutt collected a small bowl of blood for any future reapplications that might be needed, and they proceeded forward once more. They fortunately ran into no more contingents of gnolls or enemy ogres on their way and were able to quickly make it to the valley where the gnolls and their Exile leader were based. It was as Snout had described. Unlike the open area exposed to the sun's rays where the L'Khans were located, this place was situated right by a slow-moving river and nestled in between two large rocky pillars that shielded it from the worst of the day's heat.

It was clear why the L'Khans had made this place their home before it was taken. It was an oasis in this wasteland—though now no longer. Now it was littered with corpses, swarms of flies buzzed around rotten flesh, and the river was stained red with blood. Kiru took in the ruined village. His perfect memory of Snout's description helped him realize that the ogre chief's impromptu map no longer matched what could be seen. The gnolls had destroyed nearly every building, leaving only a couple of structures remaining intact.

What seemed to count as buildings for this group were organized piles of rubble reminiscent of a beaver's dam. Judging by their sparsity and immense size, those places were where the ogre traitors stayed. The gnolls seemed to stay outside and sleep around various fires, clear of the rubble piles. The two presumably intact L'Khan structures were large tents made of tanned animal hide. Based off their positions, Kiru had reasoned they were what Snout called the food storage tent and the food growing tent. The latter was no garden, however. It was where they raised glutton grubs to eat.

The party couldn't spot enough of a difference between any of the hairy ogres to distinguish one as the Exile. Kiru assumed that the leader had to be more monstrous than his subordinates. He also remembered that Snout said his brother wielded a wicked staff too. So, since they couldn't find him, the psion reasoned the Exile was likely in one of the two tents . . . but which?

The tents were placed at opposite ends of the village. There was no way they could check to see which one was which without being spotted. They needed some inside information. *If only we spoke Gnoll. Maybe we could then interrogate one for information.* Kiru smiled as an idea took hold. He didn't need to know their language; he just needed one to Subjugate.

Quickly, Kiru relayed his plan to Zhaden and Ebysso. "We need to get one of them away by themselves and knock them out without being spotted. Don't kill them, either. We need a living gnoll," he said.

Not long after, the pair were able to lure an isolated gnoll guard who had been standing by the village's border. Kiru didn't see exactly how they'd managed it, but as soon as the gnoll trudged around the corner, Zhaden snuck up behind it and struck the back of its head with the pommel of his dagger, rendering it unconscious. Ebysso crept out from behind the drakonid, making sure that none had followed. The pair then dragged the gnoll over to where the party was hiding and tied it up before it woke up.

The gnoll's beady eyes snapped open and its nostrils let out a loud inhalation as it quickly scanned its surroundings. After realizing its precarious situation, the creature began thrashing and letting out a shrill growl which was painful to hear even through its gag. Any louder and it would've alerted its allies.

Kiru then surreptitiously grabbed the gnoll by its hair—not wanting to give away his secret to those who didn't already know—pressed his free palm against its head, and activated Subjugation. His mental mana flowed out of his hand, into the gnoll's head, and quickly latched onto its brain, the psion visualizing the tendril of mana turning into a snare in his mind's eye. Kiru felt a distinct *snap* as his mana snapped tight around the gnoll's brain.

It was a sensation that the psion had felt once before when he'd freed Mutt from the psionic spirit's control back at the academy. His mana had just overridden someone or some*thing* else's control of it. *The sacred beasts are being forcibly enthralled, not doing all of their actions of their own accord*, he thought. "Not that they aren't still enemies," he uttered. Kiru could still feel the malice and bloodlust from the creature's mind. Likely, the control over them was more just keeping them coordinated and in line, like a pack of dogs with their master.

Satisfied that the gnoll was no longer a threat, Kiru undid the gag. "Where is your leader?" he asked.

The subjugated gnoll gave a manic grin and cackled lowly, gesturing with its head back in the direction of the camp.

"How many of you are there?" he pressed.

The gnoll appeared to understand his question but had trouble answering it. It chuckled and chomped its teeth up and down. *It seems this sacred beast doesn't have basic speech or counting*, Kiru thought.

Kiru grunted in frustration. This was not what he had been hoping for. He looked up past the boulder they had hidden behind to scan the camp again.

From one of the piles of rubble, a hairy ogre emerged and scratched his belly. He then saw a trio of gnolls savagely tearing at a half-eaten corpse of something now unrecognizable. The ogre scowled and lumbered over to the gnolls. As he neared, the three sacred beasts all bared their fangs, growling and moving in between the ogre and their meal.

"Move! I hungry!" he shouted at the gnolls, baring his crooked fangs right back at them.

Kiru noticed that their teeth were very similar—large and bulky. They also seemed to grow longer as the ogre bared them. *Likely some sort of technique,* he thought. He was surprised at the blatant hostility the two races showed to each other.

The gnolls just growled louder, a couple biting loudly in the ogre's direction.

The ogre roared back in challenge and charged with surprising speed. The gnolls broke off to get out of the way. One didn't move fast enough. The ogre grabbed the sacred beast with both of his hands and bit off its head with his powerful jaws. The other two gnolls turned back and attacked the ogre from both his flanks. In response, he threw the headless gnoll at one and backslapped the other. Both of the sacred beasts let out pained cries as they were knocked back, but they quickly got back to their feet.

The ogre roared. The two gnolls stopped moving mid-step, fear visibly gripping them. "I hungry!" He pointed to the rotting corpse they'd been protecting. "My food." He did the same with the headless gnoll's body. "My food! Grawwr!"

The two gnolls tensed and bowed their heads. Other nearby gnolls had seemingly been awakened from their slumber. A few of them even got to their feet to go join their brethren, but they also stopped moving when more ogres emerged.

Kiru couldn't believe it. It looked like the forces of the Exile's entire army were at a knife's edge from fighting each other. The ogres were clearly more powerful, but with the gnolls outnumbering them at least three-to-one, victory would not be a surety. A both stupid and brilliant idea sparked in Kiru's mind in the form of a quote from *The Art of War.* "In the midst of chaos, there is also opportunity."

The psion carefully laid down on his stomach so that he could still see what was going on while making himself hard to detect. Then, he dismissed Telekinesis on himself. Without constantly using it to move his own body, the range and effectiveness of Telekinesis was magnified. Kiru focused his vision on the gnoll closest to their hiding spot whose back was to him.

With a concentrated force of will, he activated Telekinesis on the sacred beast. Just as the tension began to ease between the two groups, the gnoll was sent flying, as if launched from a ballista. The force of the technique made the creature crash straight into the ogre, forcing the brute onto his back. There was a moment of stunned silence, then the traitorous ogres and gnolls struck at each other. With just one simple push, Kiru had ignited a civil war between them like a match to dry kindling.

The psion quickly reactivated Telekinesis on himself and crawled back over to the trio of orcs and his party. They were all curious as to what he was doing lying on his stomach. The orcs not privy to his psionic abilities were also glancing at the suddenly docile gnoll now without a gag sitting prone by them. They looked at Kiru questioningly. He waved them off. "We don't have time for questions now." Then he took out one of his Fu Tao and cut the bonds around the gnoll's wrists and ankles. "Can you take us to your former master?"

The subjugated gnoll nodded excitedly and began hobbling away from their hiding spot. "Follow that gnoll, and keep him alive," he said, then pulled the rough gnoll hide cloak, rubbed some of the gnoll blood and gore they'd collected earlier on his face and neck, and followed. The others were admittedly thrown off but still rolled well with the sudden change of plans. They took the fresh hides they'd skinned from the gnolls, threw them over their bodies, and followed Kiru and the gnoll guiding him.

Fittingly for his party, Kiru had succeeded in achieving pandemonium. The gnolls and orcs were attacking each other with reckless abandon. Four gnolls nearby were swarming an ogre while a different ogre picked a gnoll up in each hand and slammed them together repeatedly, turning them into jelly. The leftmost tent was apparently where the Exile was stationed, as that was the direction where the subjugated gnoll went.

They had to avoid being caught in the crossfire of fighting as they crossed the shallow river. At one point, Mutt had to save Kiru from being crushed by an ogre, but that was the worst of it up to then. As they crossed over into the village proper, however, things became trickier. There was less room to maneuver amidst the random piles of rubble and the higher volume of gnolls and ogres fighting. Rocks, blood, and gore rained down on the group as they continued toward the left tent.

Kiru realized too late that the fighting would likely alert the Exile. Fortunately, for whatever reason, he hadn't come out yet. *Maybe he's sleeping?* The gnolls didn't register the group as hostiles, instead thinking them to be fellow gnolls thanks to their disguises and masked scents. They were too busy focusing on fighting the ogres to give the party too much attention, anyway. A couple of times, one tried to incite their subjugated guide to join them in fighting the ogres. Ebysso and Zhaden swiftly took care of them and unceremoniously knocked their bodies out of the way.

A hairy ogre ripped a nearby gnoll's arms off, then saw the party trying to move about the settlement. She was genuinely fooled into thinking they were gnolls. Too bad for the party, that still made them enemies. The ogre went on all fours and sprinted toward them, closing the distance in seconds. She opened her mouth to bite down on one of them, but Brunhilda, ever the protector, was ready.

In a practiced motion, she wedged one of her round shields right into the ogre's mouth. The ogre gagged and recoiled, the momentum of her charge causing the metal to wedge deep in her maw. She glared at Brunhilda, then growled. The ogre's jaws flexed and began to bend the shield. Brunhilda's eyes widened, but before she could do anything, both the Taus struck.

The gray-haired orcs moved with impressive speed, their legs now replaced by hairy horse limbs, an aura of churning wind surrounding their bodies. Despite their clubs being blunt weapons, the power and speed at which they swung them allowed them to swiftly decapitate the ogre with a "one-two" from their consecutive swings. The ogre's mouth went limp and let go of Brunhilda's shield and arm as her head plopped to the ground.

They kept going as time was not on their side. "Hey Boss, if this keeps up, they're all gonna kill each other. Easiest battle of my life!" A gnoll's torso flew just inches over Mutt's head just seconds after he finished speaking.

"Mutt! Why would you say that?!" Kiru barked.

"Aye! By Hlin's purple hair, are ye tempting the gods?" Brunhilda said.

"What?!" Mutt shouted back amidst the chaos. That's when his question was answered. A deep, powerful roar that quickly morphed into a bloodcurdling laugh came from the tent they were heading toward. On instinct, they all hid behind a dead ogre—all except the subjugated gnoll, who kept mindlessly running toward the tent. All of the fighting immediately stopped as all the ogres and gnolls turned to face it.

As the subjugated gnoll made it to the tent's entrance, a massive, clawed hand shot out and grabbed him. The gnoll struggled as it was slowly raised in the air. Then the rest of the giant ogre emerged. Most ogres were around eight feet in height, including Chief Snout. The Exile was easily at least twelve. Though the Exile wasn't as monstrous in appearance as Chief Snout, he was no less daunting.

His fur was thicker than the other ogres around him, better matching the spotted color pattern of the gnolls. His head was still the same disproportionately small size in comparison to his body, but his mouth and nose had undeniably become that of a gnoll's. The only difference was his muzzle was massive, appearing too big for his head, with teeth that literally went from ear to ear. The Exile also had the most prodigious gut Kiru had ever laid eyes upon. Snout was bulbous, but his belly only protruded out, not down. This ogre's large, overhanging belly quite literally almost touched the ground! His bare feet had been replaced by paws, and his claws were much longer and more deadly looking than his subordinates'.

While the trapped gnoll was in one hand, in his other was a long, wicked-looking staff made of twisted dark wood with an animal skull on top, with sapphires jammed into its eye sockets. The gnoll in his grip continued to squirm. He regarded the sacred beast angrily, then opened his much-too-large maw and bit it in two. The Exile dropped the bleeding bottom half of the gnoll like it was a piece of trash, then glared at his army.

"You ungrateful fools! I give you power—a taste of *real* power—and this is how you repay me? You interrupt my meal and cultivation!" he shouted, his voice somehow barking and blubbering at the same time.

The Exile seems to have his brother's trademark level of intelligence, Kiru thought.

The Exile raised his staff, and the sapphire gems glowed with power.

All of his followers fell to their knees and cried out in pain as a wave of power flowed out from his staff. Surprisingly, Mutt did too, the orc going into the fetal position, clutching his head, and groaning until Zhaden used his Silence technique on him before he could let out a roar of pain. Brunhilda moved over to help the orc while Kiru kept focus on the Exile.

He needed to try and learn all he could in order to defeat him. Though it didn't physically affect him, Kiru *felt* that power. More accurately, he felt the *aura* of that power. The sapphire gems weren't for show. The ogre exuded the power of a Sapphire-rank cultivator. The psion reflexively touched the golden gem embedded in his forehead kept hidden under his enchanted headband.

A sadistic grin grew on the Exile's face, and he began to laugh like a hyena, a sound that seemed too high-pitched to have come from his natural vocal range. The light faded from the staff, and the pain stopped.

"Now, who started this?!"

The ogres and gnolls groaned but quickly forced themselves up and immediately turned their gazes, pointing to the ogre who had been fighting with the three gnolls at the river. The big bastard was tough and still alive despite the onslaught of combat.

"Stupid beasts try to keep food away from me. I hungry!" the ogre pleaded.

The Exile shook in anger. "You imbecile! Come here!"

The reprimanded ogre's visage turned to shock, but he walked over to the tent, his face hung in defeat. The Exile squeezed his subordinate's shoulder. "I understand. You were hungry. Well, I'm hungry now, and who's going to feed me, hm?"

"Uh, I—"

Then, a gigantic, sharp-toothed maw suddenly appeared on the Exile's fat belly. The massive mouth opened wide, and the monstrous ogre shoved his follower straight in it. The ogre gave desperate cries of pain as the large mouth bit down repeatedly again and again, tearing into its flesh and breaking bones with a series of sickening crunches until the cries were finally cut off. The belly mouth finished its meal, swallowing the last remnants of the ogre and letting out a loud belch.

Kiru involuntarily shivered at the sight.

"Okay, one, that was awesome. Two, I totally support you learning how to do that, Master," William sent.

"Not helpful, William," Kiru sent back, not sharing the imp's enthusiasm.

At the sound of the loud burp, numerous terrified shrills, cries, and bestial whines came from the tent. "Oh, now look what you've done. You've disturbed my guests," he said, and the gnolls and ogres looked back at him with obvious fear. His second mouth faded away as he scanned his followers. "If my cultivation is disturbed one more time, it'll be more than just one fool who will die. Do you understand?!"

They nodded emphatically.

"Good. Now, get ready for tomorrow. We kill the rest of those pathetic L'Khans then."

The followers all raised their arms and cheered in triumph, ready to spill the blood of their enemies.

The Exile gave a sadistic smile, then went back into his tent, and animalistic cries of terror and pain started up once more from within.

With him gone, the party began creeping over toward the tent, moving about carefully. Many of them were hobbling as if they were indeed gnolls. Mutt still seemed a little shaken from the Exile's staff for whatever reason, so he just crept along as best he could. They didn't have time to analyze that situation. Time was of the essence.

As they neared the large tent, they noticed that a couple of gnolls had scurried over to the remaining half of their ally's corpse and were eating him. Ebysso was about to move into the tent when one of the gnolls grabbed her by the arm. It was barking in their harsh language, but it was clear that it was trying to warn her from going in, clearly fooled by her gnoll disguise.

The scout quickly drew out a dagger and slashed the creature's arm. It gave a high-pitched bark and recoiled a few steps. As it pulled its arm away from Ebysso, its sharp claws drew a thin trail of blood across her flesh. The gnoll and its companion both growled but didn't make a move to attack. The party stood still and hunched over, not wanting to give away their ruse. Then, the gnoll licked the blood off its claws. Its eyes went wide as the sacred beast registered that it was not the taste of a gnoll's blood but of something else.

Before anyone else realized what had happened, the gnoll pointed at the party and let out a shrill battle cry, echoing throughout the encampment. All of the gnolls and hairy ogres turned to face their direction. The two Tau quickly bashed the two gnolls' skulls in, cutting off the one's alert, but it was too late. The remaining gnolls and ogres all charged en masse.

"Shit!" Kiru spat. They had come so close. Ebysso and the two Tau warriors stood in front of Pandemonium. Heat came from the scout's body while violent funnels of wind began to surround the Tau.

"Go kill the Exile. Save the L'Khans and get our queen her support!" Ebysso hissed as her body became distorted by the heat. Then, the trio of orcs took off and charged at the incoming forces. Kiru's eyes widened at their bravery, the three of them had to be facing at least two hundred gnolls and ogres. He knew that having a Sapphire on their side would help tremendously, but Kiru could feel the auras of at least twenty Rubies amidst the crowd. The fight could go either way.

Kiru knew none of his party liked having to leave them, Brunhilda most of all with her protective nature, but he knew what needed to be done. They steeled themselves, drew their weapons, and charged into the tent.

CHAPTER FOURTEEN

Exile

The party was already accustomed to the foul odors of the gnoll encampment, but they had to fight another wave of nausea as they were exposed to an even more concentrated force of fetid smells. That wasn't even the worst of it. Wicked-looking meat hooks were strung around the house-sized tent. On those hooks were various ogres, orcs, and sacred beasts. What was even more horrifying was that many of them were still alive! It was a scene that would haunt the cultivators' dreams for years to come.

Cages large enough to fit an orc were set around the perimeter as well. Most were empty, but there were a few terrified creatures in there—even some gnolls. The Exile was using his claws to carve into the flesh of an impaled minotaur. He smiled as it writhed in pain, its agony causing others who'd been previously tortured to scream too as if they had some sympathetic connection. The sapphires in the Exile's staff glowed in tandem with the screams.

"Yes! Give me more! More suffering!" he shouted, then licked some of the blood from the minotaur's wound. The tent floor was full of bones and viscera. A throne made of bones was visible at the back. The Exile sniffed loudly, then turned to face the party. "Oohoohoo! More things to play with. I don't have time for games today, though, so I'll need to deal with you quickly. My master gave me a strict deadline. So, be good little meat sacks and die for me."

The Exile slammed his staff down, and the gnolls in the cages began to roar in fury. Their eyes flashed blue as their bodies contorted and spasmed wildly. Mutt groaned in pain and pressed a fist to his chest.

"Ye alright, love?" Brunhilda asked as she put a hand to his shoulder.

He gritted his teeth and nodded at the dwarf. "Something about that guy just ain't right," he said.

"I believe your assessment to be correct, my friend," Zhaden replied.

The enraged gnolls then burst out of their cages—about twenty in all, every one of them giving off Gold signatures. One ripped itself off a hook and died almost instantly, demonstrating the degree of their madness.

"Deal with these pests," the Exile ordered, then went back to torturing the minotaur. The gnolls didn't look back but instead ran at the party with surprising speed.

"Pests?! Ooh, Master, kick their asses!" William said.

"Gladly," the psion responded aloud, then concentrated a portion of his mental mana into his legs. Using the focused energy, he took off and zoomed right in between two gnolls. Kiru used Demon's Inciting Strike, cutting large gashes across each of their torsos. It quickly became evident that the enraging effect of whatever the Exile had done wasn't just for increased strength, it also improved the sacred beasts' durability as well. Under normal circumstances, Kiru's strikes should've likely been fatal, but now they didn't even go past the muscle.

The psion was barely able to duck under their backhands as they swiped and turned back to face him. He cut across their bellies, making sure to use the barbed hooks to deal as much damage as possible. These bit a little deeper, scoring significant injury, but not mortal ones. To his surprise, the gnolls each dug a claw into their wounds, squeezing and injuring themselves further. Instead of crying out in pain, they cooed in pleasure and their manic grins grew even creepier as bloody drool oozed from their maws.

It seemed that they liked the pain, and when Kiru noticed that, despite their wounds, the gnolls didn't appear weakened, it clicked for him. The gnoll beast mana that the Exile was using thrived off of pain! That's why he was torturing so many and why the gnolls were so sadistic in nature too. *It's to attain more power*, the psion realized. The joy from his revelation was short-lived though as the two injured gnolls were joined by three more.

"Don't try to injure them. Just kill them!" he sent telepathically to his friends.

"Boss, whaddaya think we've been doing?!" Mutt shouted as he tripped one gnoll, then kicked another in the abdomen, slightly puncturing its tough hide with his taloned feet.

"They get stronger with pain! Only lethal blows!"

"Divine Shield!" Brunhilda shouted, as she used her technique on the psion. A crazed gnoll struck at the column of light surrounding Kiru and was set aflame. It opened its mouth and cried out in a mixture of pain and pleasure. Kiru used that opening to try out the Clean the Hoof swing he'd learned from the Cruel Mantis sword form. The hook of the blade was turned up and went straight into the gnoll's mouth. It bit into its hard palate and pierced its brain, killing it on the spot.

"Oh, yeah! Show these punks what they get when they mess with us!" William cheered.

Kiru remarked how much easier it was to kill the gnoll when he struck its mouth, how the weapon met little resistance when not going against their tough skin. *"Aim for the eyes and mouth, the parts not covered with skin!"* he sent. With that specific game plan sent out, it became much easier to fight the gnolls, despite being outnumbered.

Zhaden, already a well-trained assassin-style fighter, was very adept at targeting the vulnerable points and taking advantage of them. The gold drakonid threw his Bloodstep Stiletto at one gnoll who was about to take a bite out of Brunhilda's arm. It cut straight into its tongue and soft palate, drawing blood. The enchantment in the dagger took hold and Zhaden was teleported right on top of the gnoll's body. The sacred beast fell to its back from the sudden weight, and the rogue quickly finished it off with a few swift stabs through an eye socket.

Mutt grabbed one gnoll by the jaws and ripped its mouth in two, ending it with a loud crunch. Another one used the opportunity to pounce on the orc and bite down on his leg so deep his teeth cut all the way through the thick muscle and cracked his tibia. Mutt roared in pain. Then, Brunhilda ran up and shield-bashed the gnoll, sending it skipping across the bone-covered ground. The paladin pressed a hand onto Mutt's wound and activated Healing Hands. Life mana emanated from her gauntlet and quickly repaired the wound down to the bone.

"Thanks, Brunhilda. I almost didn't hear you coming," Mutt said.

She smiled and elbowed him good-naturedly. "I've been practicing my stealth, y'know." Meanwhile, the gnoll that she'd hit bounced so far, he ended up knocking into the Exile's leg, disrupting his focused torture of the minotaur. He took his claw out of a chest wound, and the sacred beast gave a moan of relief as it expired. Seeing his plaything dead angered the Exile, and he stomped on the gnoll's head, crushing it with a squelch.

"If you want something done right, do it yourself," he growled. The Exile, charged with impressive speed for his substantial girth, caught the party by surprise. Acting on instinct, Brunhilda pushed Mutt back and raised her shields up together to block his attack. The Exile gave off the power signature of a Sapphire. Both the ogre's increased physical strength and being two cultivation ranks higher than the paladin played to his advantage as he brought the full might of his staff down on her.

There was an audible crash as the hard wood literally shattered one of her metal shields clean in two, breaking the paladin's tough arm as well. She grunted in pain and, before she could recover, the monstrous ogre kicked her in the dead center of her unguarded chest. She went flying back.

Mutt sprinted across the ground on all fours and jumped. He grunted as he caught her with a heave of effort, keeping her from crashing into one of the cages.

Kiru wasn't shocked by the difference in power between Brunhilda and the Exile, but he was surprised at how significant it was. Based on what he knew from just sparring with the Sapphire Tau, Brunhilda likely suffered more than just a broken arm from the direct strike. She was lucky that her arm hadn't been amputated. Her armor and overall toughness were likely to thank for her fortune.

"Flank him! Brunhilda, you provide support. We need to kill him as fast as possible. Go for any exposed area. Lethal blows!" Kiru urgently ordered through Telepathy. He'd been hoping to come up with a better plan, but with Brunhilda hurt already and the power gap so great, they had no chance of winning a prolonged fight against a Sapphire, especially one that thrived off of pain.

Both Kiru and Zhaden charged, coming at the Exile from both sides. The drakonid threw a flurry of daggers at the ogre's face while Kiru ran toward the Exile's ankles, hoping to incapacitate him.

The Exile smirked as he bent back and the monstrous second mouth on his belly reappeared, swallowing all the incoming blades whole. Kiru rushed in and leaped to stab the ogre in his eyes. But the Exile was too fast. Even while dealing with Zhaden's attack, the ogre managed to intercept the psion's blades with his staff. Kiru's heart raced as he braced himself for the force of the Exile's blow. The psion hoped a broken arm would be the worst of it.

The force of the staff's strike knocked Kiru off-balance and sent him flying ten feet away. He rolled on the ground but was more than a little surprised. He couldn't feel his limbs but could tell by their fluid motions that nothing was broken at all. *How?* He was a Gold, and even though his blades had blocked the ogre's staff, the Exile was a Sapphire like his mother. Kiru should have been struck by a much stronger force like Brunhilda had been. *Maybe he couldn't swing with full force for some reason?* he thought but couldn't ponder over it in greater depth while still in the thick of battle.

The rogue leaped and grabbed onto an empty meat hook dangling off a chain, using it to fling himself at the Exile. The ogre's beady eyes widened as Zhaden activated his Duplicate technique midair, causing the brute to see two incoming rogues. Still, the Exile's speed was too great. In one swift motion, the ogre backhanded through the projection and struck the real target. The drakonid was smacked aside as if he was a child, the sheer mass and cultivation difference making themselves known. He bared his teeth as a small rivulet of blood leaked out of his mouth, but he then gave a hissing laugh.

The Exile realized too late that what the rogue had attempted wasn't meant to truly harm him but rather as a distraction. Mutt sprinted on all fours and caught the Exile by surprise as he leaped and began clawing at his face. Mutt's Fenrir's Claws technique easily bit into the flesh and drew blood on the ogre's muzzle. The others were about to charge back in when the Exile roared, "Enough!" A wave of terrifying power violently shot out in all directions from his staff.

Kiru cried out and the rest of the party did the same as their bodies were racked with pain. The impaled prisoners joined them in their moans of agony, none of them spared from the technique. Despite Kiru not being able to feel his body, he somehow *felt* pain, and it was everywhere. A mixture of drool, bile, and blood poured out of Zhaden's reptilian mouth as he fell to his knees.

A trail of blood went down Brunhilda's chin as she bit her lip. Her broken left arm was shaking violently, and she desperately clutched it to get it to stop.

Mutt had it the worst. The blind orc's body went limp and his whole body began spasming as if he was having a seizure. It could have been because he was so close to the Exile, but Kiru wasn't sure. *The Exile's power hit him hard outside earlier too,* the psion remembered as well.

The bestial ogre caught Mutt before he fell to the ground, a sadistic smile on his face as he squeezed the flailing blind orc.

Within a few seconds, the effect faded for Kiru, an unintended benefit of being quadriplegic as his nerves couldn't transmit the sensation of pain for long even with the mana flowing through them. He slowly began to stand up, and he raised his head to see the Exile and Mutt.

The Exile sniffed Mutt, who was now foaming out of the mouth, and laughed as he turned to face the psion, "You lot are even bigger fools than I thought. You dare try to attack me with the very type of beast mana that I have control over?" His fat folds shook as he mocked them. "Imbeciles," he said, then pressed the skull top of his staff against the orc's bare chest.

Mutt immediately stopped his spasming and instead screamed in pain, reacting as if his skin was being burned by the staff.

"Yes, *suffer.*" The ogre grinned.

"In Hlin's name, stop ye fiend!" Brunhilda shouted as she strained to get to her feet. "Give . . . him . . . back," she said in between heavy breaths.

The ogre looked amused. "You want him?" he asked and removed the staff from Mutt's chest. "As you wish." The Exile threw the blind orc straight at the party.

Ignoring her broken left arm, Brunhilda caught Mutt before he could fall to the ground.

"You know, it's ironic. Orcs gave me this power to build an army and kill the L'Khans. Now, an orc will help me kill you," the Exile said.

"Ooh, Master, he's monologuing! Villains love to monologue. Use this time to get him talking. It'll buy you time to recover," Willim excitedly urged Kiru.

Kiru was a little confused by William's words. He was used to the little imp sounding rather villainous himself.

"Then you can cut his fat belly open and spill his guts on the ground!"

There it was. Still, it wasn't a bad idea, and had said something Kiru had wanted clarification on.

"What are you talking about? What orcs gave you this power?" the psion asked, trying to get the ogre to continue talking.

The Exile cackled. "When Snout banished me from the Wastelands, I quickly encountered a tribe of rather . . . cunning orcs. At first, we fought and I thought I would die, but then we struck a deal. They wanted the L'Khans either dead or suppressed but didn't want to invest their own soldiers to do so. So, in exchange for power, I would do their dirty work. That way, we'd both win, and I'd get my vengeance."

"I'm confused. Why would they be interested in killing the L'Khans?" Kiru asked.

The ogre shrugged. "Don't know, and I really don't care what those blasted Jabari are interested in."

The Jabari?! They were involved? More questions came to Kiru's mind as Zhaden regained his senses and stood.

The Exile also didn't reveal what he meant by saying an orc would help him kill them, but Kiru had a sneaking suspicion. Before he could ask anything further, the ogre slammed his staff on the ground. "No more questions. I'm done playing with my food. Come, my pet! Help me kill these fools." He raised his staff and the sapphire gems glowed once more.

Brunhilda was kneeling, holding Mutt's head up and using Healing Hands on his bare chest. The dazed orc suddenly snapped to life. Kiru's heart dropped as he saw Mutt's milky blind eyes turning a glowing sapphire. Mutt snarled and tried to bite Brunhilda's face, but Zhaden's quick reflexes saved the paladin as he tackled her out of the way.

The trio backed up a few steps as Mutt jumped up from his prone position and cackled. His mohawk suddenly spread down all the way to his tail bone, the hair transforming from its regular dark brown to a spotted multicolor like that of a gnoll's. His arms grew longer, and his nails did too.

Lastly, the orc's already pronounced underbite grew even larger, and his long, sharp teeth grew even sharper and distinctly thicker.

"He could bite an anvil in two with those chompers!" William exclaimed.

"Yeah," Kiru agreed.

"It appears we have discovered at least one of the sacred beast core types our friend ingested," Zhaden observed.

"Zhaden, I like ye lad, but when ye do speak, you have a bad habit of sayin' the obvious," Brunhilda replied and lowered her one good shield.

The gold drakonid pulled his head back and appeared genuinely taken back by that statement. He then grunted in frustration. "You warmbloods have such strange social customs."

"Focus," Kiru barked, trying to get his team to concentrate on the opponents before them.

As if to reinforce that point, it was at that moment both Mutt and the Exile attacked.

CHAPTER FIFTEEN

Tasting Wrath

As soon as the bestial cultivators charged, the trio split up. Zhaden and Brunhilda went to fight the Exile while Kiru engaged with Mutt. Kiru remembered the blind orc had actually been mind-controlled once previously. *This is a bad habit, Mutt,* he thought. Previously, it had been the work of some malevolent spirit of a psion that they'd accidentally awoken. Kiru had broken Mutt of the control and gained the Subjugation technique because of it. Now he was hoping to break his friend free once more with the technique.

Unfortunately, it was hard to get close enough to safely press his palm against Mutt's temple in order to actually activate Subjugation. Kiru had always been fast, but Mutt was easily the fastest of the group—and his being a Ruby meant he could resist Telekinesis if Kiru tried to use it on him. *At least his possession is causing him to fight with less control,* Kiru thought. That made it easier for Kiru to avoid his strikes. Still, he wasn't able to avoid them all. Kiru grunted as he ducked under a bite and blocked a powerful kick with the flats of his swords. He was still sent sliding back, though, with his feet digging furrows in the ground. They needed a new plan. If he couldn't break Mutt free, the only thing to do was stop the Exile from controlling his friend.

How are we going to stop him? He's a Sapphire, Kiru thought in frustration. While the gap from Gold to Ruby was a leap, Ruby to Sapphire was an absolute canyon. That wasn't even factoring in that Kiru and Brunhilda were just Golds. He should be terrified even contemplating fighting a Sapphire. *Why aren't I?* he thought.

Then a flash of realization struck Kiru: the Exile gave off the aura of a Sapphire yet didn't seem to have the strength of one. Kiru had blocked a swing of the ogre's staff and hadn't been crushed to paste. Zhaden had taken a direct hit and was nowhere near out of the fight.

As Kiru shook off the dirt from his body, he saw Mutt charging at him on all fours. The orc's blue eyes flashed at the same time as the jewels in the staff—for a moment, it looked like Mutt's eyes were made of crystals. It was brief and could have easily been missed, but that in conjunction with Kiru's perfect recall helped him piece together exactly what was causing the orc's possession. It was the staff! He had no doubt, if they destroyed the staff, the Exile's control would stop. *"Zhaden, switch!"* he ordered telepathically.

The psion rolled under a claw strike and the rogue did a no-hands cartwheel over him to trade opponents. Using that momentum, Zhaden spun and tripped Mutt with his tail. "Be quick. I can't hold him for long," he hissed.

I don't think any of his illusions would work on Mutt, and his Nightmare technique is too risky with all these prisoners here, Kiru thought. He then joined Brunhilda in fighting the Exile. She had stabilized her left arm but still only had one shield, which wasn't in the best shape. The Exile was only mildly injured, but boy, did he look pissed off! His body was covered in various superficial cuts from Zhaden, and his face was marred by some deeper wounds, although nothing serious.

But Kiru wasn't trying to hurt the ogre. The staff was his target. So far, it was remarkably durable and resistant to their blades' strikes. It was time to mix it up. Nobody had tried blunt force against the staff yet, and Kiru aimed to fix that. "Brunhilda, time for our special attack!" he shouted.

"Aye!" she cried back. The wink she shot at him told him she knew exactly what he was talking about—they'd devised it together back at the academy.

Kiru ran and sheathed his steel Fu Tao, still keeping his Psyslime blade out. *"This time up instead of forward,"* he sent. His heart raced as he saw the ogre's staff coming down to crush the dwarf.

The paladin's efforts to be lighter on her feet seemed to have paid dividends. She instantly jumped back and dodged.

Kiru then leaped at Brunhilda, his feet landing on her raised shield, and she vaulted him up with her prodigious strength. The psion soared high, almost reaching the top of the ridiculously large tent. Kiru raised his Psyslime blade above his head and changed the malleable substance with his will. In a mere second, the Fu Tao had transformed into a massive warhammer whose head was as big as half of Kiru's body.

The Exile's beady eyes went wide as he saw the gigantic weapon suddenly manifesting in the psion's hands.

Kiru snarled in anger as he descended onto the Exile like a vengeful deity.

The ogre had no choice. He raised his staff to intercept. With a resounding crash, Kiru's large hammer slammed into it. Whatever wood the warped weapon was made of withstood the psion's blow—but not completely. Symbolic clawlike carvings in the wood flashed blue, and a cacophony of animalistic shrieks came from the weapon as a large crack appeared at the point of contact.

Despite Kiru's surprise attack from above, he still couldn't match the ogre's strength. The Exile roared and pushed forward with his swing, aiming to throw the psion wide and clear out of the tent—and he would have, had a troll-blooded dwarf not snuck up on him. Brunhilda had scurried over right in between his legs and shoved her shield upward right at his groin with all her might, catching the Exile completely unaware.

The Exile let out a distinctly high-pitched squeal and the force of his swing died midway. Kiru was still sent flying, just not as far. The psion crashed into the minotaur's hanging bloody corpse, bouncing off it and crashing to the ground with a thud. Zhaden then quickly snatched him up off the ground, promptly pushing him out of the way right before Mutt could bite down where he'd been standing.

The orc snarled, and Kiru and Zhaden raised their weapons defensively. Before Mutt could attack again, though, the ruined minotaur corpse slid off its hook, collapsing right on top of the orc with a wet squelch.

The rogue and psion stared at each other, dumbfounded. *"Well . . . that was lucky,"* William sent. *"Guess it'll work for now."*

Kiru's gaze shot back over to the ogre just in time to see the Exile's second mouth reappearing on his obese abdomen, both sets of mouths now letting out roars of fury. He quickly raised a foot up in an attempt to stomp Brunhilda into paste.

She rolled in between his legs to dodge. While it wasn't exactly graceful, it still got the job done.

"Have you discovered how best to defeat him, Kiru?" Zhaden hissed, keeping his voice low enough so the Exile didn't hear.

"We've got to destroy his staff. It's the source of his power. It has to be. I've already cracked it, but I can't use my techniques on him," Kiru replied.

"Is there a way to subdue him by still using your techniques indirectly?" Zhaden asked, his eyes still focused on Brunhilda and the ogre. Kiru noticed her wince in pain as she clutched her broken arm to her body.

Kiru thought about what Zhaden had said. He then noticed the dead minotaur laying before them and subduing Mutt. His eyes then widened as realization struck. *How could I have been so stupid?!* "Zhaden, you're a genius! I have an idea, but I need you to hold me up," Kiru said as he shifted his Psyslime back into a Fu Tao and sheathed the weapon.

"Hold you up? Why?" the drakonid asked, clearly puzzled.

Instead of answering, Kiru turned his back to the drakonid and deactivated his Telekinesis on himself, his limp body falling backward. To his relief, Zhaden caught him before he fell.

"What are you doing?" the drakonid hissed in confusion.

"Sorry. I need the extra mana," Kiru replied, then reactivated Telekinesis but not on himself. This time, he focused on the hooks hanging around.

The Exile cooed and seemed to get stronger from Brunhilda's pain. She took a step back and he gave a malicious smile as he closed the distance. The Exile looked as if he was about to body-slam the injured paladin, planning to eat her whole with his extra mouth. But before that could happen, one of the giant hooks swung at him and sunk right at the edge of the extra mouth, embedding itself like the world's largest fishing hook. A burst of dark blood shot out from the second mouth, and the hairy ogre gave a surprised grunt of pain.

Kiru pulled with his mana and sent the ogre off-balance but only by a step.

Though successful in stopping the Exile's attack, it didn't last long. After the ogre got over the initial surprise, he ground his teeth together and pulled back on the hook.

Kiru quickly realized his technique couldn't match the Exile's physical might in a direct tug-of-war.

The ogre smirked and looked like he was about to start taunting Kiru—but a second and then a third barbed hook came flying in. The weapons embedded themselves in different spots along his fatty flesh with violent force. The Exile groaned as his body was being literally torn apart in multiple different directions.

"Yes! Make him suffer! Make him bow before our might!" William cheered excitedly inside Kiru's mind.

The psion, for his part, gave a savage grin. Just because the Exile's body was too powerful to be susceptible to Telekinesis or Subjugation, it didn't mean that Kiru couldn't employ other ways to use his techniques to overcome his foe. *I may not be able to win in a direct "push versus shove" contest, but I can attack from multiple angles at once to negate that*, he thought.

"Yes, Master! Show this fool his folly!" Willima cheered.

Kiru's head shook with the effort. He had surprised his opponent, but he couldn't compete with the Exile's strength for an extended period. Kiru didn't need long, though. He just had to keep it up long enough for the monstrous cultivator to loosen his grip on his staff. Then inspiration suddenly came to him. *"Brunhilda, attack his fingers!"* he shouted via Telepathy. With a flex of will, he heaved on two chains stuck deep into the Exile's left arm where his staff was, forcing the ogre to lower the weapon down to the dwarf's height.

Seizing the opportunity, Brunhilda raised her lone shield with both hands. "Taste my goddess's wrath!" she shouted, then slammed her shield down on the ogre's fingers. Three of them were broken all at once with a loud *crunch*. She let out a battle cry as she pulled back her shield and struck his hand once again.

The Exile groaned and, for the briefest of moments, his broken fingers reflexively loosened their grip on his treasured staff.

That was the opening Kiru had been waiting for. He dismissed Telekinesis on all the hooks and focused entirely on the ogre's staff. Thanks to the Exile's now-loosened grip, it flew out of his hand and straight at his face, threatening to concuss him.

To Kiru's relief, Zhaden dropped him and grabbed the flying staff with both hands before it could hit the psion.

The gold drakonid's tail swished in excitement at getting the staff. That excitement was short-lived, however, as the still-possessed Mutt burst through the back of the minotaur corpse with an angry roar. His nostrils flared as he sniffed. A split-second later, he lunged at Zhaden, teeth first.

Zhaden let out a cry of fear, and just like the Exile had done when Kiru attacked, he raised the staff up horizontally in defense.

Mutt bit down on the staff, and the weapon let out a sickening crunch. The orc snarled and, with an explosive *crack*, split the weapon clean in two. A pained shriek came from the staff as if it were a wounded beast. The carved symbols and twin sapphire gems flashed on and off with blue light. Mutt immediately groaned in pain, and the orc fell to his knees, clutching his head, incapacitated as his body lost its gnollish features.

"Noooooo!" the ogre shouted, drawing Kiru's attention back to him. Terror was evident in his voice, echoed by countless nervous yelps and laughs coming from the gnoll horde outside the tent. Kiru turned his head and before his very eyes, the bestial, multi-mouthed ogre changed. His fatty mass diminished as his body began to shrink. In a matter of seconds, the Exile's spotted hair had regressed completely, revealing yellow, cracked skin. His claws reverted, his muscles shrunk, and notably, the aura of power that he'd radiated had lessened.

Kiru could feel the potency of mana coming from the Exile. *He's . . . just a Gold!*

Kiru reactivated Telekinesis, lifting himself up. He moved his hands to his weapons' hilts, ready to eliminate this ogre. It wasn't necessary. The paladin was on it. The Exile looked down at his shaky hands in shock and raised his head up to say something, when a large round shield was shoved into his mouth.

The ogre gagged, the metal shield too wide to fit. Brunhilda scowled as she pulled her shield back and slammed it into his mouth again. "Taste. Hlin's. Wrath!" she grunted, slamming the shield into his mouth again and again with each word. With each strike, the blunt edge of the shield bit deeper and deeper into the weakened ogre's mouth until her last strike. The shield drove deep, wedging itself between the Exile's top and bottom jaw and nearly splitting his skull.

Blood shot up in the air from the wound like a geyser, covering Brunhilda. To Kiru's horror, the Exile reached up a shaky hand to the shield, gagging from the blood, but a moment later, the top section of his head fell back only held aloft by the intact skin of his neck. His hand dropped, and his body fell limp before the dwarf.

"Damn! That was awesome! Guess Palabitch isn't as lame as I thought she was!" William mused.

The paladin turned and noticed Mutt lying prone on the ground. She gasped and immediately ran over to his side, cradling his head in her arms. "Oh, Mutt. Are ye okay?"

The blind orc gave a wry grin. "Never better, Brunhilda. Plus, you'll be happy to know that I now know *another* one of the sacred beast types I ingested," he proudly declared.

"We all figured that one out, ya idgit. Ye ate a gnoll core," she chided him with a smile on her face. Everyone had a good laugh at that, until their good mood was ruined by a chorus of pained howls coming from outside the tent.

"Shit! All the gnolls!" Kiru said.

The party sprinted to help the orcs who'd stayed back to hold off the amassed horde of sacred beasts. Upon getting outside, they found a battlefield painted red with blood. Gnoll corpses dotted the landscape, strewn about in a gory display. The Exile's followers were there too, their bodies reverted to their original forms, revealing slit throats and crushed skulls.

Both the Tau were near the tent, their corpses savaged with countless bites and slashes. One of them only had a jagged stump remaining where their head should be. It made Kiru furious. "I-I'd hoped we'd finish him off quickly enough to save them," he said as he tried to process what he saw. The psion then scowled and scanned around to find any of the gnolls to repay for what they had done. He saw the flagging remnants of the horde fleeing about a half mile out—roughly a few dozen of the hundred or so.

Kiru wanted to give chase, to eradicate every single one of those beasts, but then he spotted Ebysso, crawling weakly up a nearby pile of stone rubble.

Brunhilda gasped. "Goddess's mercy!" she exclaimed, then activated Rejuvenation as she ran over to the rogue. Healing life mana left her gauntleted hand and coated the blood-soaked Ebysso. A number of her injuries sealed themselves up, flesh and muscle knitting back together to repair damaged tissue. The scout's body visibly relaxed as she gave an audible sigh of relief.

Ebysso's body went limp and began sliding back down the rubble. She likely would have hurt herself even worse had Zhaden not caught her prone body. "I have you, mentor," he said.

"Cradle her head, and set her down," Brunhilda ordered.

The paladin then began assessing her patient, shaking her head, and clicking her tongue in concern, "Oh my, we've got a fractured skull, damage to the clavicle, and punctured rib. Not to worry, though." She cracked her fingers, then placed her hands on two of the scout's wounds. "Healing Hands," she said. More powerful, potent, and targeted healing mana left her palms and went directly into the scout's injuries.

I'm glad William "borrowed" that scroll for her. She wouldn't be able to use that ability otherwise, Kiru thought. Bone regrew, fixing Ebysso's skull. It was followed by green flesh, then hair until no evidence of her head wound remained. Brunhilda repeated the process with her clavicle and rib. She also discovered that the rib had punctured one of the orc's lungs. With another dose of Healing Hands, the damage was repaired, and the scout was as good as new.

"I am in your debt, Paladin," Ebysso said, taking a knee.

"It's by my goddess's grace that I can do what I've done. If ye be interested in hearing more about her, here's a pamphlet." The dwarf then pulled out a small piece of folded parchment and handed it to the scout.

"Does this mean there will be more people like her around now?" William asked, clearly lamenting the idea.

Ebysso seemed taken aback but took the pamphlet awkwardly and thanked her.

If he was being honest, Kiru was perplexed as to how Brunhilda found the time or resources to mass produce pamphlets. *Did the new orc acolytes do that for her?* Paper was not the most common commodity in Imakandi, so that could not have been a cheap effort . . .

After Ebysso stood, another pained groan came from the tent. *There are still survivors in there!*

CHAPTER SIXTEEN

Gnash and Grind

With Ebysso fully healed, the party sent her to go alert the L'Khans of their victory. Meanwhile, they re-entered the tent, now with their full focus on helping the numerous tortured people and creatures inside. All of the cultivators hesitated as they took in the literal torture chamber around them. The sights in the tent were horrifying—nightmare fuel, to say the least.

Blood, bones, and gore littered the space in all directions. It was difficult for Kiru to see the dirt below due to all the bones. Red splotches of blood stained the cages and tent everywhere the eye could see. More than one corpse had flies hovering around it with colonies of maggots writhing about. To see such blatant disrespect and disregard for life was more than a little unsettling. It made the psion's blood run cold. The Exile's sadism was clearly obvious by the horrible state of the near-dead and slaughtered prisoners.

They hurried to free at least two dozen poor souls from the hooks holding them up or from cages. Judging by the more-than-double that amount who were dead, as well as the even larger number of empty cages, the sheer horror the Exile wrought was more than any member of Pandemonium wanted to think about. Even the bloodthirsty William was notably silent inside Kiru's mind. Brunhilda pushed her healing ability further than she ever had before. While many of those tortured had been gnolls, those that remained were of various species. Unfortunately, not all could be saved in time. It was a hard pill for the party to swallow. All of the cultivators' faces were tear-streaked from witnessing the brutality and being unable to save all of the prisoners.

Fortunately, they were able to save more than a handful of victims. All in all, that amounted to three L'Khan ogres, five Tau orcs, two orcs from the Thrar'fang Tribe, a strange anteater creature, an even stranger giant armadillo, three orcs from various minor tribes, and to their surprise, another leokin. The Tau were easy to distinguish due to their trademark gray hair. Mutt was able to distinguish the other orcs due to their scents, each of which was different thanks to the different sacred beasts each based their techniques off of. The anteater and armadillo appeared to be normal beasts, and they bolted out of the tent as soon as their bodies recovered. Not wanting to chase the simple-minded creatures and traumatize them more, Kiru and the party let them go. The leokin definitely drew interest, though.

The intelligent sacred beast had dark brown fur with a thick, glorious, red-tinted mane. Both his left eye and arm were missing, only a bloody stump and socket remaining. It was no doubt the Exile's doing. Brunhilda sealed off the raw, exposed flesh, but regrowing the missing body parts would take hours—if not days—of concentrated healing. The only clothing the leokin had on were a leather loincloth and leather vest that was now barely more than scraps.

The leokin let out a subtle growl as he shook his head and regained consciousness. "Where am I?" he asked; his voice was deep, regal, and had feline elements. It was clear to the psion that he wasn't fully aware of what was going on.

"Easy now. Ye be safe. Ye be in the Wastelands, and our party has saved ye from the gnolls," Brunhilda said.

At mention of the gnolls, the leokin's eye snapped open. "Gnolls!?" He growled and pushed himself up to a sitting position as awareness came back to him, nearly falling over as he was clearly unused to only having one arm.

"Easy there, Cat Guy," Mutt said as he knelt down to eye level. "We took care of their boss and sent them scattering with their tails between their legs."

"A M'Baku." He sniffed Mutt. "And a royal M'Baku." The leokin's remaining eye went wide in remembrance before bowing his head to the orc. "Member of the ruling M'Baku, as a member of one of the leading clans, I must inform you, I came here to the Wastelands to find the L'Khan Clan as charged by my people. I am to bring news of the Beast Gods' decree. With the death of the last patriarch, Ukufuku—"

"Yeah, yeah, I know. Ukufuwhatever is in effect." Mutt waved him off. "That's actually why we're here."

"What?" The leokin was clearly thrown by the casual dismissal. It made Kiru smile just a little seeing how his typically carefree friend subverted expectations.

Mutt then explained why they were in the Wastelands. Kiru supplemented with some details when the leokin cocked his head in confusion. The one-eyed lion man didn't say anything for a good minute afterward, taking time to fully digest their words. "If what you say is true, then that means Imakandi is in great danger. I'm forbidden from interfering, but it's clear that the Jormuns must not be allowed to rule. Your alpha, your queen regent, must claim the mantle of High Chief. Grraah!"

The leokin groaned and clutched at his shoulder where he had been impaled.

"You alright, Cat Guy?" Mutt asked.

"My name is Zengaz, M'Baku, and I'm alright. I wasn't here nearly as long as some of the others, so I have no right to complain."

William cackled inside Kiru's brain, *"Ha! He lost his left arm, and now he's 'all right.' Get it? Hahaha!"*

"Now's really not the time, William," Kiru sent back, reprimanding his familiar.

"I mean, you can be upset, Cat Guy. What that Exile put you all through was pretty terrible," Mutt said.

"The Beast Gods have sustained me. They will continue to. It is just an eye and arm. My strength is still intact." Zengaz then groaned and forced himself up.

"Okay, Cat Guy. If you say so."

"How many of you were sent out to notify the tribe leaders?" Kiru asked.

"Seven, well, eight. Rengo took his grandcub with him to show him his future duties."

Kiru's heart sank. "I'm sorry to inform you, Rengo was killed by the Jormuns. They used the Imakandi law that, with the Jabari ruling tribe backing them, they were allowed to hunt any beast inside their territory."

The leokin snapped his head to Kiru and snarled, but it quickly faded. He wasn't angry at Kiru, just at what had happened to his friend. "I see. Thank you for telling me. What of his charge, the cub he was looking after?"

"We were able to save him before they got a hold of him," Brunhilda answered.

"Yeah, man. Nom's an awesome little guy!" Mutt added excitedly.

"Nom?" Zengaz asked, clearly confused.

"That's what we named him. We didn't know what else to call him. He liked to eat a lot and go 'Nom,' so that's what we went with," Mutt answered.

Zengaz smirked as best as his feline face could. "He hadn't been named yet by Rengo. Names for us leokin hold certain importance. It is a rite of passage. Since his grandfather couldn't give him one, his soul is no doubt pleased that his grandcub has earned one."

Kiru did his best to hide his grimace at Zengaz's words. *Technically, Nom didn't really "earn" a name. He just liked to eat, but hey, if their culture found that way of obtaining a name honorable, who am I to argue?* he thought.

The one-eyed leokin was reinvigorated by the news that forces for good were working to claim leadership in Imakandi. Seeming not at all bothered by his serious wounds, Zengaz worked with the party to help heal his fellow recently freed prisoners. The leokin was no doubt strong in both mind and body as not all had fared as well as he had, even with less serious wounds. Five of the orcs they'd rescued refused to speak, psychological trauma running deep despite their healing bodies.

Admittedly, two of the silent orcs were from the Thrar'fang Tribe whose leader was also vying to become High Chief. They were larger and more muscular than any of the other orcs. They were so muscle-bound, it was hard to even make out their necks. Their skin seemed thicker than any of the other orcs' too. Instead of the vacant look in the eyes of so many of the other orcs—the result of trauma, Kiru presumed—they just looked angry. Kiru supposed they were likely torn between being in debt to a rival clan for their freedom and their loyalty to their chief. But at least they weren't being openly hostile.

The prisoner in the worst shape was an M'Baku, his body covered in countless sores. The Exile seemed to want to give the orc a death by a thousand cuts. His eyes lacked focus and no words came from his mouth despite his looking like he wanted to speak.

"He be needing more help and time than I can give him right now. Best we get him back to the capital and let the shamans or clerics spend time with him," Brunhilda said.

Zengaz looked down at the traumatized M'Baku, a low purr coming from him. Everyone suddenly stopped in place. For some reason, the psion seemed to think the leokin and the tortured orc's hearts had begun to beat rhythmically in unison like a set of drums. The orc looked up to lock eyes with Zengaz, mouth agape. The leokin's purr grew louder. Kiru and the others watched, entranced. Zengaz knelt down to the orc and pressed his head against his. They both closed their eyes, and the sacred beast put a hand on the back of the orc's skull. "You have been wronged, my brother. Fear not, the creature has reaped what he'd sown. The Beast Gods have seen your trials, and you will no doubt come out stronger from it."

The young orc's face noticeably relaxed as Zengaz pulled his head away and they both opened their eyes. "Thank you, Shaman," he said, his voice barely a whisper.

The leokin gave a subtle nod, then went back to the party. "He will be okay. The paladin is right, though. He will need more help and a lot of time."

Both the paladin and psion just looked at him in awe, Kiru amazed at the sacred beast's ability to help with mental trauma in a way he'd seen no healer ever manage before. The pair quietly agreed with Zengaz's assessment. They continued to help the injured, kill any traitorous wounded gnolls or ogres who had previously joined the Exile who were pretending to be dead, and of course, check for loot. As suspected from a bunch of dirty, unkempt gnolls living in garbage and the remains of a razed village, it was . . . well mostly rubbish. *Most* didn't mean *all*, however.

Now that Mutt knew that he'd ingested a Ruby-rank gnoll beast mana core, Kiru saw him begin the grisly work of looting all the gnoll corpses he could to get more of their cores. The blind orc didn't know for sure exactly how, but he had told Kiru he was certain on an instinctual level they would be of use in helping him one day ascend to Sapphire.

The decapitated Exile also had some noteworthy items. First, on one of his bulbous fingers was a thick ring made of multiple concentric rings of tiny sharp teeth! It pulsed with some unknown power that made the party wary. Kiru had to rip it off the ogre's finger, the embedded teeth shearing off the flesh of the appendage. He pocketed it in his storage ring until they could determine what it actually did. Next was a necklace with what looked to be a mummified finger on it. As Kiru got closer, he felt some strange savage hunger. He removed that one with Telekinesis and placed it in his storage ring. *Didn't want to touch that thing!* William, on the other hand, cackled gleefully at the bloody trophies the psion had found.

Last was the broken staff itself. Their battle with the Exile made it abundantly clear that it was the source of his power, and hopefully, the party could use that to their advantage. Mutt gasped as they got a better look at the skull that adorned the top of the weapon.

"Boss, can you sense it?" Mutt asked.

"Yeah," Kiru replied. "Those things are giving off some real power."

"You're telling me." Mutt chuckled. He then eagerly dislodged the gems from the skull, laughingly giddily like a kid. "No way," he said as he examined the first.

Kiru could sense it more clearly now. The sapphire gem he'd just taken out was actually a Sapphire beast core. The next one Mutt pulled out was the same.

Now that they weren't in a desperate fight for their lives, Kiru could now take a better look at the carvings on the staff. He gasped as he saw them. His perfect memory helped him realize that the bestial claw mark scripts were the exact same as the technique scroll Brunhilda had taken as her prize from the Warrior Games back at the academy! But then disappointment hit the psion because even though they were the same script, it still didn't change the fact that he couldn't read them. "I'm fluent in nine languages and yet, this has to be one of the ones I don't know," he grumbled.

After taking some time to recover and cultivate, Kiru and the others were greeted by Ebysso and the Glutton Grub Clan. When Chief Snout and his tribe saw their enemy's camp laid to waste, they roared in triumph. Well, it was more a mixture of a roar and a throaty squeal, just like a boar. It was weird, but it made sense since Heidrun was still technically part-boar.

The L'Khans began rapidly piling up the dead. Kiru had to suppress a wave of nausea at the sight. The ogres' indiscriminate diet was the most disgusting thing he'd ever witnessed, and he'd seen William stuff a half-eaten rat in between his skull and brain! Kiru shuddered at that memory.

Snout quickly went over to the party. There was a skip in the ogre chief's ungraceful steps, and he seemed to be snorting happily, a crooked smile on his face.

"Incredible! You lot actually did it! It has been so long since orcs have done anything for the L'Khans."

"I told you, man, we're here to help. My sister wishes to unite this land and bring peace to Imakandi," Mutt said.

"With emissaries such as you, Young Prince, she may just achieve it." Snout then took a knee. "We of the L'Khan Clan, in seeing you've kept your word, will keep ours. Before Heidrun and all of the Beast Gods, we officially back your matriarch to be the new ruler of Imakandi. I will make a declaration to my clan tonight. With my people safe, I will follow you back to your capital to tell her myself as well, but tonight, we feast!"

The other ogres cheered at their leader's declaration. Kiru winced and suppressed a groan. Things were about to get gross.

After a couple of hours, the L'Khans had surprisingly and effectively removed every piece of flesh and bone from their reclaimed village. It was quite impressive, given the sheer amount of gore spread around the destroyed remnants of the ogres' home. They were unable to get rid of every bloodstain as some had set deep into some of the stones, but it was still a dramatic difference. Even the air smelled fresher.

During the ogres' "cleaning spree," the cultivators took more time to recover. In all the chaos of fighting and helping everyone else, they had barely had time to take care of themselves. Kiru was the only one of them who made an effort to cultivate before Ebysso and the L'Khans arrived. His need was greater since he required the mana to keep up appearances. All of them rested and braced their backs against a large boulder. Exhaustion—both physical and mental—pressed down on them.

"Oi, we sure did bring the pandemonium," Brunhilda said before taking a big gulp of water from a canteen.

"Haha, yeah. Sorry about your shield, Brunhilda. And for . . . you know, trying to kill everybody," Mutt apologized nervously.

"Ah, it be fine." She waved off his concern. "I bet I can get another shield back in Dissé. I'll just borrow one from the ogres in the meantime. As for being mind-controlled . . ." she said, then ruffled her fingers in his wild hair.

"Don't apologize, ye idgit. It not be yer fault," she said before resting her head on his shoulder.

"I concur with Brunhilda. We need not worry about what happened with the Exile, but I am concerned as to how far the Jabari's influence has spread. If they had agents all the way in the Wasteland, it makes me wonder if anywhere in Dissé is truly safe," the gold drakonid said before scanning their environment once more, his trademark paranoia back on full display.

"I have to agree with you, Zhaden. It's concerning," Kiru said.

"What's it matter?" William asked as he suddenly popped out from atop the boulder. Kiru had summoned him earlier because the imp had wanted some fresh air. Now he was standing on top of the boulder they were laying against, chewing on a gnoll toe as a snack. "If any more show up, we'll just beat them to a bloody pulp like always."

Kiru sighed. "It's not that simple, William, and you know it. These Jabari are clever. If they're willing to suppress an exiled clan of ogres on the slight chance that they might help their clan's rivals, it's fair to say they are willing to go above and beyond to interfere with others and assure their victory."

"So, what are you saying, Master?"

"That we need to get back to Dissé first thing tomorrow. We can't afford to wait here long," the psion answered.

Zhaden snapped his head in surprise. "Tomorrow? Certainly, we can't delay. We should bring their chief and travel through the night. The L'Khans don't look to be fast travelers, and we'll need all the time we can get to reach the capital if we are to bring them along."

Kiru exhaled through his nostrils at the drakonid's words. Zhaden wasn't wrong in that time was of the essence. It would also be safer to bring the small tribe into Dissé to live. However . . .

"Oh, come on, Stabby," Mutt protested. "These people just reclaimed their home. That's *really* important. We can't take that away from them. Plus, have you seen the shape some of the prisoners are in? They're not going anywhere anytime soon. You don't need to worry so much."

"I agree with Mutt here," Brunhilda said. "These people be needing time to heal not only their bodies but their minds and spirits too. A celebration of their victory, time to mourn their dead, and comfort to process their traumas are all necessary."

"But the Jabari—"

"I have to agree with them on this matter, Zhaden," Kiru added. "You're right that we don't have much time, but we have *some* time. That's why we'll help the tribe stabilize themselves here for the night before leaving at first light."

Zhaden slammed his tail down on the ground repeatedly as his nostrils flared. He was obviously not okay with the plan, but he was outvoted. "Fine," he spat out before crossing his arms, closing his eyes, and cultivating.

Following his friend's lead, Kiru closed his eyes and cultivated as well.

In the meantime, Snout and his L'Khan brethren quickly sat down around a large slab of broken stone, using it as a makeshift table. On each end of the long table, they placed a disgusting pile of dead, rotten flesh. The blend of horrendous stenches was almost too much for the party's nostrils to take. Thankfully, the cultivators—as well as all the non-ogres—were given their own smaller piece of rubble for their own table placed a good twenty feet away. Pandemonium would share their rations as there was absolutely no way they would eat what the ogres planned on consuming.

Then Snout stood up and cleared his throat. "Er, hem. L'Khans," he said, his voice echoing throughout the cavern.

All of the ogres stopped eating and turned their faces to their insect-like leader.

"Tonight, we are eating good!"

The ogres cheered in unison with their leader.

Snout continued, "It is thanks to our great god Heidrun that we've endured and made a home where others cannot. Gluttony for the good!"

"Gluttony for the good!" the ogres echoed.

"It is also thanks to our new allies that we were able to reclaim our home when it was stolen. The M'Baku Clan may not be blameless, but their young prince and his companions have proven they are willing to make amends. Heidrun will be pleased, and our tribe will be glorified. For such honor, I, Chief Snout of the L'Khans, do hereby publicly announce our tribe's support for the M'Baku Clan's claim to rule over Imakandi. May our tribes forever thrive in glorious gluttony together. Gluttony for the good!"

"Gluttony for the good!" his tribe echoed once again.

Snout wiped a bloody smear off his mouth with a pasty forearm. He then smiled and his mandibles chittered in excitement. "We've had some delicious food, but now we need something equally enjoyable," he said, then his eyes focused onto a couple guards standing at the other side of his table. "Bring out the good stuff."

The two guards each pressed a fist to his chest before trudging off behind the only remaining tent (after they'd freed all the prisoners and looted the Exile, the party had promptly burned most of the ruinous place to the ground).

All four members of Pandemonium's jaws dropped with an audible *click* of their tongues as the guards rolled out a couple of wooden barrels of liquor, each as big as Mutt. When Mutt asked the chief what it was exactly, the ogre explained it was sort of tea that they brewed using cactus juice. The blind orc couldn't tell exactly what the ogre had called it . . . Tea-Quila? Sometimes it was hard to understand what Snout was saying.

Not only that, Snout had his tribe bring out food specifically for their party. The best part, it wasn't anything that had previously been sapient or their own race! Though aligned with the L'Khans, cannibalism was still a no-go for Kiru and the others. Most notably, a couple of ogres carried out a large glutton grub—the sacred beast type that Heidrun had assimilated—and set the dead insect on the table. The glutton grub was nowhere near the size of Heidrun, but it was still large, nearly taking up the entire table.

Kiru wondered if eating the thing was considered safe, as Heidrun has been significantly changed by eating the grub, and he was a god that was once at Diamond. With Kiru being only a Gold, it made him a little worried. He then remembered it was because of Heidrun's specific ability to take in the aspects of things he'd ingested that made him change. So, he felt slightly more comfortable with the idea of eating the grub. He still thought he may have given it a pass before Jubjon began to explain that the dead insect was a delicacy to honor the party and survivors. Kiru then remembered how scarce food was here. Refusing such an honor would doubtlessly be considered an act of disrespect. So, he put on a brave face and used a crude wooden spoon to scoop out a clump of the sticky, white grub flesh.

As if that was a signal, the barrels were opened, and the festivities began in earnest. Kiru gave a moan of surprise as he chewed the mouthful. While the plump glutton grub was initially unappealing in appearance, it was actually quite satisfying to eat. It was undeniably very fatty, but it also had a distinct meaty taste to it. The best Kiru could compare it to was a very marbled steak but even more chewy. He took to focusing on his meal and conversing with his friends while the ogres ate.

As the feast commenced, the L'Khans brought out more things to honor such a momentous occasion. Small clusters of wood were placed throughout the area and set aflame. Wood was a rarity in the Wastelands, and this type in particular had a fragrant aroma that smelled just like lavender. It completely replaced any lingering scents of blood and gore that had once permeated the area. All present smiled as their nostrils were embraced by the new smells.

Next were the drums. After some of the L'Khan children had their fill of food, they brought out a few sets of large ornate drums. Each taking a set of femur bones, carved and whittled to large drumsticks, they began to play music and sing in their ancestral language. They had clearly been trained because they were quite good.

With the satisfying food, catchy music, pleasant scent, and potent liquor, everyone eventually joined the ogres in celebration. Even the paranoid Zhaden lit up. The gold drakonid's tail wagged side to side in joy, and he and Ebysso began practicing feats of acrobatics such as handstands with one hand, and so on. All the members of Pandemonium laughed heartily, and at one point, they even joined in the singing. Mutt was the best out of them all, with a smooth and deep bass; Brunhilda was a close second in vocal quality. The dwarf's voice was nowhere near as deep, though, and she preferred to sing in tenor. Kiru and Zhaden were content to be backup singers as Kiru didn't have much talent for it, and the drakonid's vocal cords and facial structure seemed to not allow for singing like his compatriots.

The psion even let William out to join in the celebration. The little imp had an idea to go "drink the blood of their enemies," but when an ogre thought him to be some rodent scavenger and tried to eat him, the demon became quickly satisfied with sharing the glutton grub. William stuffed both cheeks full of the meat until he looked like a squirrel packing acorns. While the imp liked the food, after a sip of alcohol he discovered he *loved* the booze. William challenged a few orcs to a drinking contest, and he easily won. The tea-quila was strong stuff and few could chug the potent alcohol like the demon. Kiru soon had to cut him off when he told the psion that he wanted a whole barrel for himself.

"Heeeyy, Massster," he slurred. "That ssshit is good. *Hiccup!*" He lazily reached for the cup that Kiru had taken from him.

"I think you've had enough, William," Kiru replied, wrapping his familiar around his arm.

William hiccupped again, "Aw, man!" Then, he fell asleep against Kiru's body like a baby. Kiru chuckled to himself and quickly recalled the demon before he inadvertently got himself into trouble. The psion then finished the remaining half of the cup. It burned as it went down his throat, and his face went flush as the drink warmed his body.

He felt a little disoriented, and his face tingled. "You're not wrong, William. This shit is good." He grinned and even let out a small growl involuntarily. *What was that?* he asked himself out loud, surprised at what he'd done. *Is this stuff laced with beast mana?* Kiru was about to check his core but then decided to blow it off for now. *Don't care.* He would just ask later. Because right now, he wanted some more booze! They continued the celebration, getting increasingly rowdy and louder as the night went on. The L'Khans knew how to throw a party!

At some point in the night, Snout came over to converse and check in with them. "I hope our tribe's specialties have been to your satisfaction?"

"Sssssss, yessss, I believe so," Zhaden happily answered, his tail now flopping about lazily like a worm out of the dirt.

He's almost as bad as William when it comes to holding his liquor, Kiru thought.

"Good, good! Now, there are a bit of my brother's bones left. You are welcome to have it if you'd like?" Snout offered.

"Ah, thank you, but we're good," Kiru replied, uncomfortably. Snout talking about his brother did remind Kiru of something, though. "Actually, since you're here, Chief, I'd like to show you something." He pulled out the two broken staff pieces and handed them to the monstrous ogre leader. "Your brother said he was working with the orcs of the Jabari Clan. It seemed they gave him this staff, and it was the source of his power. Can you read the script on it?"

His question caused Brunhilda to visibly perk up. After Kiru had told her it was the same script as her technique scroll, her interest in the staff had risen tremendously. Kiru had seen the paladin had been busy talking with Zengaz but was now turned to face Snout after overhearing Kiru's words. The leokin turned to look at the ogre too. The two religious cultivators were getting along smoothly despite following different pantheons. Unlike the more dog-eat-dog mentality the orcish shamans had, Zengaz explained that the leokin very much embraced the M'Baku pack mentality philosophy. This team mentality was in line with Brunhilda's mindset. "A rising tide raises all ships," as she would say.

Snout examined the broken weapon, then sniffed it. "It reeks of gnoll. I can't understand the script, unfortunately. It looks to be of the old tongue," he said before handing it back to the psion.

"It is," Zengaz said, surprising everyone. "We call it Beast Speak, a language created by the Beast Gods. Few outside us leokin can read it."

Brunhilda's eyes widened. "Ye can understand the writing?!"

"Well, yes. Of course. We leokin serve as head shamans for the Beast Gods. We are born with an innate understanding of their language."

The paladin shook with excitement and quickly pulled out the scroll she had in her pack. "Can ye help me read this too, please? It be a technique scroll, and I can't understand the script. Ye can even use it too if ye would like?" she suggested as she nearly shoved the scroll into the leokin's chest.

Zengaz was taken aback but agreed to the strange request. Kiru quickly focused even more on the conversation. He couldn't learn the holy technique, but if Zengaz could understand the writing, that meant Kiru could learn it too with his perfect memory! The leokin read aloud and taught Kiru the basics of Beast Speak as he went over the scroll's information with the pair. Apparently, the scrolls were created by a famous monk who traveled about trying to better understand the gods of Alterra.

Brunhilda gasped at that. "Sealaman the Curious," she uttered.

"Who?" Kiru asked.

"Sealaman the Curious. Ye hafta know who that be, right?"

Kiru shrugged. "Grew up in a small, secluded town, remember?"

The dwarf groaned and rolled her eyes. "He be only the most famous—or infamous, depending on your viewpoint—holy cultivator there's ever been! It's said that he wished to know about *all* the gods our world worshipped so as to bring about peace after Ragnarok. He's rumored to have been so loved that he had a patron from every pantheon."

"Is that rare?" Kiru asked again.

"By me uncle's forging hammer! Of course it be!" she said, clearly exasperated.

"She's right," Zengaz added. "Most gods are very jealous and do not wish to share followers outside of their respective orders."

"Aye. Worshippers bring power, and the gods don't like sharing." She looked back at the scroll with newfound reverence. "I can't believe we found an artifact of such magnitude. I'd bet me right shield that the only reason that the higher-ups of my order didn't burn this scroll was because no one could read the thing." She looked back at Kiru. "While some appreciate and value the monk's attempts at greater understanding and harmony, most view him as a blasphemer and a sore subject within the Order."

"What about you then, Paladin?" Zengaz asked. "This technique is clearly influenced by the Beast Gods. Do you find our ways heresy?"

She took a deep breath before answering. "I won't lie, Zengaz. Some of your followers' interpretations have led to untold cruelty and suffering. I've seen how many in the capital treat others less fortunate than them, and I dunnae like it one bit. At the same time, there have been extremists within my very own order that have used their faith as an excuse to abuse others ages ago. While I will not abandon my goddess, I also believe that understanding can lead to new allies. With new allies, we can unite to protect the innocent. As a paladin of protection, that is my sacred duty to uphold."

The leokin grinned and nodded. "Well said."

They then spent the next hour continuing to go through the scroll. Eventually, Kiru did get a basic understanding of Beast Speak, at least in written form. Brunhilda was finally able to discern the technique she'd been so hoping to learn. It was called Gnash and Grind, and it was named after Tanngniost and Tanngrisner, twin goat Beast Gods of Strength and Life.

After Kiru had learned what he could from Zengaz, he placed the staff back in his storage ring to examine it later. It was then that he heard one of the ogres giving out a loud porcine squeal after drinking some more tea-quila. It was quickly followed by a growl let out by an orc who'd just finished his own cup. Curious, Kiru called out to Snout and discovered that the time he himself had growled after drinking some of the tea-quila wasn't an accident after all. It turned out that the alcohol was, in fact, somehow laced with beast mana.

"Of course we add beast mana to our brew," Snout said. "It helps to empower us and prevents hangovers."

"What about we who don't use beast mana?" Kiru asked.

"Normally, that could cause issues, but I swear that we brew our alcohol with such a low quantity of the mana that the body would naturally filter it without any negative repercussions," Snout answered. "The high shaman here can confirm that too with his high connection to beast mana and strong sense of smell," he said, gesturing to Zengaz.

The leokin raised his eyebrows and lowered his head toward a mostly full barrel of liquor. After a couple of sniffs and a reactive sneeze, he looked over to Kiru and nodded. "It's still potent, but I can tell that what the chief said is correct. Still, whoever drinks this will contaminate the mana content in their core, albeit temporarily." Zengaz then looked directly at Brunhilda. "You should drink a lot more of this liquor, Paladin."

"Me? But ye just said it would contaminate me core. Pray tell, how would that help me better learn a life mana technique?" Brunhilda asked.

"Because this technique is inspired by the Beast Gods themselves. Drinking more of this brew will give you a stronger connection and help you learn their technique. The technique is, in fact, a life mana technique from what I've read, and Tanngrisner is the Beast God of life. How better than to establish a connection with the two types of mana than to possess them both in their system?" Zengaz answered her question with another.

Brunhilda sighed. "It seems sorta silly, but I trust ye. Plus, I've been wanting to get me hands on another technique for quite some time now. I dunnae another way to better achieve it. So, bottoms up," she said before lifting the barrel taller than her own body and chugging the potent alcohol. Both Snout and Zengaz gawked in amazement at the sheer fortitude of the dwarf. Not only was the quantity she guzzled down impressive, but the potency of the liquor could knock some of the strongest ogres on their asses.

The members of Pandemonium, however, all smirked. They'd seen Brunhilda drink before, and they all knew that her alcohol endurance was mighty. She'd told them that dwarves could outdrink most everyone, but after having her blood transmuted to troll blood, her ability to resist toxins, such as alcohol, for instance, had gone up tremendously. So, none of them were surprised at her body's— specifically her liver's—ability to handle the potent liquor. Kiru had read back at the academy that trolls have remarkable regenerative abilities. He figured that's what brought about Brunhilda's increased resistance.

Twin trails of booze spilled out of either side of her mouth as she downed the barrel. Both the life mana and latent beast mana inside her core resonated with the technique inspired by the twin Beast Gods. She sighed in contentment and slammed the empty barrel on the ground, shattering it into pieces. Brunhilda gave a wide grin to her friends, her cheeks both flushed purple.

Acting on instinct, the now-buzzed dwarf grabbed her two shields despite one being ruined beyond any effective defensive use and began to force her mana through her arms. She thrusted her left shield forward. "Gnash!" A three-foot-tall ethereal goat's head made of life mana sprang out from the large round shield. It shot forward toward the large table where the L'Khans were feasting. "And Grind!" Another ethereal goat's head made of golden life mana appeared from her other shield, also launching forward.

The left goat's head opened its mouth wide and bit down on the table right in between two ogres. Its jaw strength was impressive, literally taking a chunk out of the thick rock and quickly reducing it to rubble. The right goat's head repeated the act. The ogres at the table were startled and the ones nearby the goat heads stood up and let out audible cries of surprise. The music stopped abruptly just as the glowing golden techniques faded.

Everyone looked to Brunhilda.

The paladin, feeling on top of the world with the technique being so successfully performed and with such a good amount of alcohol in her system, looked about, then raised her shields in triumph. "Yeah!"

The ogres roared in celebration along with her, and the music began right back up, even more lively than before. Some of the people had started to drift off, presumably to find spots to sleep. After that proclamation, though, they enthusiastically came back to start all over again. It was time to *really* party!

CHAPTER SEVENTEEN

Tribal Ascension

Brunhilda was over the moon. She finally had an offensive technique! Not only that, she now had four techniques in total. That was the number of techniques required to reach Ruby via the method the party had discovered. Back at the academy, not long after the party had decided to add Mutt to the team, they encountered the spirit of a dead psion in a forgotten tomb they had accidentally stumbled upon. The spirit took over Mutt's mind and threatened to do the same to the rest. It would have, had Kiru not been present. The young psion's ability, with William forming a protective shield around his core, actually overtook the spirit. That's how Kiru gained both his Subjugation technique and learned a unique method for ascending from Gold to Ruby rank.

Ironically, the spirit transferred knowledge of a method used by an extinct group of ogres known as the Ippo Ogres. That method allowed a cultivator to ascend knowing just four techniques instead of the standard method of five taught by the Kingdom of Blades. True, you had one less technique, but the techniques were more powerful, and the Ippo Ogre method wasn't as complicated as the kingdom's. Doing it this way allowed you to take the techniques as part of your very identity versus just simply mastering them; it was ideal to only have four techniques if one wished to use this method.

Now that Brunhilda had her requisite four techniques: Rejuvenation, Divine Shield, Healing Hands, and Gnash and Grind, she could finally reach Ruby! When Kiru told Snout that their paladin was on the cusp of ascending, the ogres were more than willing to help however they could, building one of their fires into a large bonfire. The L'Khans sat in a circle around the flames, some of the adults now replacing the children on the drums. They began beating them in rhythmic unison.

"Boom! Dum dum dum dum dum dum dum boom!"

"Mak tu shak! Rollmen luff vemekdu kahn!" the ogres chanted in unison. Brunhilda stood in front of the fire, most of her armor stripped off her body, revealing her well-muscled form. Zengaz mixed wet dirt and a crushed beetle to make a green and brown tribal body, which he spread across Brunhilda's skin in a pattern that made it look like the paladin had stripes.

Brunhilda held her steel round shield in one hand. Her other shield had been too badly damaged by the Exile and broke into multiple pieces when she tried to use it once again. Fortunately, a solution had already been found. In the other was an elliptical shield made of tanned hide and wood—a gift from the two Thrar'fangs. The silent, grumpy-looking duo seemed to feel indebted to Pandemonium. So, they gifted her with one of their shields that had fortunately been found undamaged amidst the rubble as a form of payment before leaving.

Brunhilda tried to adopt a look of firm resolution on her face. She breathed heavily through her nostrils. Rivulets of sweat rolled down her muscular form from the intense heat of the fire. The trollblood transplant she had gotten back at the academy had turned her hair purple and elongated her arms more than any normal dwarf, but despite those oddities, her form was intimidating. Most of the time, she was covered in her heavy plate mail, so they often didn't see her actual body. Now, with her rippling triceps, biceps, and eight-pack abs, her strength was undeniable. Kiru thought about how heavy she had been when he had to carry her once. He then remembered reading that muscle weighed more than fat.

Kiru, Zhaden, and Mutt all stood in front of their friend. Zhaden had undergone the Ippo Ogre ascension ritual once before, and both Kiru and Mutt were there to witness it. So they were the best for the job of guiding her, especially with Kiru's memory helping him to recall every single step. Using that knowledge, he quoted the words spoken to Zhaden during his ascension ritual verbatim: "You need to accept these techniques as part of your identity. In order to attain enlightenment, these four must be part of your very being. Think of your goals, your dreams."

She closed her eyes and began to think of her desires to raise Hlin to the role of a major god. She dreamed of becoming strong, of no longer being scoffed at or pitied by her fellow holy cultivators within the Order of Valhalla. She also thought about her friends and the new dreams, desires, and aspirations she had gained since meeting them. She wanted to help them, to protect them. To help Kiru protect this world, to help Zhaden become a member of the highly vaulted Fangs, and for her and Mutt to . . .

Her eyes flashed open, the dwarf's heart racing in sync with her desires. "Brunhilda, High Paladin of Hlin, Goddess of Protection, what must you become to attain your dreams?" Zhaden hissed.

She *clang*ed her two shields together. "I must become the rejuvenator!" The large fire behind grew in intensity and a flash of golden light appeared in between the thick clouds in the night sky as a wave of power pulsed out of the dwarf, before everything reverted back to normal a second later.

"Keep it up, Brunhilda! What must you become?" Mutt asked enthusiastically.

She smiled fondly at the blind orc. "I must become the shield of the Divine." Another pulse of power emanated from her body, this time slightly more powerful. The fire and its heat responded again and the sky had that same flash of light. "I must become the hands that heal," she said, this time without anyone prompting her. And this time, in conjunction with the flare of fire, a bolt of lightning struck in the distance with a loud "BOOM!"

The ogres beat their drums with increased fervor as their voices grew louder. "Mak tu shak! Rollmen luff vemekdu kahn!"

The paladin looked deeply into the eyes of each of her friends, resolution etched on her features. "I must become the one who gnashes and grinds."

"BOOM!" Another bolt of lightning came down from the sky, this time right in the middle of the ceremony, striking the large fire behind the paladin. The music suddenly stopped as everyone was temporarily blinded by a flash of white, their ears ringing from the noise.

Kiru grimaced and lost all sense of orientation. He held his eyes shut, but the blinding white light was somehow still striking his eyes. Then, a regal, feminine voice suddenly rang out amidst the constant ringing in his ears. "Well done, my faithful paladin. Thou hast increased thy power and that of my clergy, and thou shalt be rewarded." Only Brunhilda and Kiru heard the words of Hlin, their connection with the goddess making it so. Then, as quickly as the blinding white light appeared, it left.

A final wave of power emerged from Brunhilda. All the disoriented people except Snout, Mutt, and Zhaden fell to their knees as they were struck by it. Kiru was already on his back, knocked over completely by the force from the lightning bolt no doubt brought down by Hlin. He was glad it hadn't struck anyone directly. The power from the last wave out from Brunhilda was different. It was . . . stronger. As everyone blinked their eyes clear and shook the ringing out of their ears, they finally got to get a real look at the paladin before them. The large fire was now just smoldering, pieces of the burning wood strewn about chaotically but still able to provide adequate illumination.

There she stood. Her face confident, her body enhanced, and her muscles more defined, Brunhilda had been made anew. She had taken the techniques into herself, making them part of her identity. She had ascended. Kiru also noticed something different about her tribal shield, too. It was no longer made of hide. Instead, it had transformed into that of a glistening white metal. The two-pointed tips were now sharp blades. In the center of the shield was a carving of a spear breaking off a shield—the symbol of Hlin. Carved on the flat of each blade was a goat's head, a symbol of the goddess honoring the deities whose power helped her paladin ascend.

Brunhilda looked down on the new shield. "Mithril?" she uttered in what sounded like stunned fascination. Then she gazed upon her transformed body. Externally, there wasn't too much difference aside from her increased musculature and tone. The true power from ascending to Ruby came from the potency of techniques. Through the Ippo Ogre Method, she had taken them in to be part of her identity. Thus, they were stronger and more effective. She was a paladin to be reckoned with.

Everyone slowly stood and gazed upon Brunhilda. Smiling and breathing heavily, she smiled then raised both her shields in the air and shouted triumphantly. The ogres and everyone else did so too in celebration. Brunhilda laughed and cheered, dancing and celebrating with everyone else. She was obviously tired, the ascension draining much of her mana, but she was just too damn excited *not* to celebrate.

Kiru smiled, happy for his friend. Brunhilda was the best person he knew. She had worked hard and deserved her ascension and her boon. Still, he had some internal conflict. He had worked hard too, increasing his power and martial skill, but he was still lacking in that one crucial thing final step in order to ascend to Ruby, a fourth mental mana technique.

Instead of joining in the celebrations, he snuck off to ponder his situation. He had acquired Telekinesis from a manual, Telepathy by accident while cultivating, and Subjugation from the spirit. The psion had genuinely hoped he could create his own technique with Myev's help. When he had fought Ambrose back at the academy, there was . . . something. The noble had cultivated air mana but it seemed to encompass some form of storm aspects, too. Kiru wasn't sure if they were one and the same or not. During their bout, Ambrose had used some ridiculously named technique to continuously electrocute Kiru with lightning.

Still, Kiru had resisted. He had pushed forward and punched Ambrose square in the face. In doing so, he somehow forced the lightning out from his fist and back at the noble. "I wasn't just a conduit for the lightning. I guided it. *I controlled* it. Gah, I feel like I'm just on the cusp of figuring it out," he uttered to himself in frustration. While he had made progress in guiding the lightning through his channels with Myev, Kiru had the feeling he was still lacking that . . . whatever he had before. It was the thing he needed to create a fourth technique. He was sure of it.

Kiru realized he wanted to talk to someone who could understand what was going on with him. Seeing as there was nobody who truly got it, he went with his only option. He summoned William.

The imp appeared on his shoulder and looked at Kiru, "Hey, Master, why're you so sad?" The imp's harsh voice was now a pained whisper as he began massaging his squishy brain with one hand.

Is he . . . hungover? Kiru thought. He then sighed. "I'm just frustrated, William. I mean, I'm supposed to be the leader of our group, and now I'm the weakest one. How am I supposed to lead a nation and help the whole damn world if I can't even get strong enough to reach Ruby?"

The imp seemed to be distracted as his hand was now all the way wedged in between his brain and skull. Then, to Kiru's lack of surprise and chagrin, William pulled out a glass vial from his head, uncorked it, and downed the murky liquid in one gulp. Kiru didn't know where William acquired the vial, but the familiar was known for his sticky fingers.

"Oh that? Pfft! Who cares? Yeah, they're a higher rank, so what? We've beaten up plenty of guys that were stronger than us. Besides, you have a badass transformable weapon and an even more badass familiar." William's typical gusto had returned immediately after the drink. Kiru was going to ask what liquid it was exactly, but then William belched. The distinct scent of the ogre's alcohol was undeniable on his breath.

Kiru gave a light chuckle at that, the imp never losing his high opinion of himself, "I'll keep that in mind. Thanks, William."

"Of course!" he said, then leaned in conspiratorially, "You know, if you really want to get stronger, I do have an idea," he whispered.

"What's that?"

"What every good conqueror should do—drink the blood of your enemies, or at least more of this good cactus liquor!" he pronounced, his proximity and sudden shift in volume making Kiru wince.

"How would liquor get me stronger, exactly?" Kiru asked.

"Just like how it does me. It lights a fire in the belly. It gives me confidence and newfound power, so much so that my body sometimes has a hard time keeping balance with my new strength."

"I think that's just general disorientation due to alcohol's influence on the mind," Kiru retorted.

"Master, I know you're a smart guy, but that's ridiculous. Alcohol gives me power, just like sugar! Why else would my body feel so weak after I no longer had it?" the imp asked.

"That's called withdrawal."

"No, I'm serious. The alcohol *has* to be increasing our power. Don't you remember that it worked for the freaking paladin?" William asked. "Abyss, even the leokin told her to drink more."

This gave Kiru pause. "What are you talking about?"

"Were you not paying attention? She was struggling to learn her technique, but after she had more booze, she figured it out. Ergo, my hypothesis is correct. Alcohol increases our power, and I want some more! Go get me some!"

". . . No."

"Mm, fine! I'll go get some more myself! I only have one vial left, and that's not enough." He pouted and jumped off Kiru's shoulder.

"No, you don't," Kiru retorted and began recalling his familiar. The imp needed more sobering up, not a chance to get even sloppier. William began being pulled back into Kiru's core against his will. He groaned and tried to grab the ground but couldn't reach it and was transformed back into a red orb of light before being fully brought back into Kiru's core. He grumbled for a couple of minutes inside the psion's mind but eventually settled down, comforted by the fact that he still did have another shot of the liquor stored in his head.

Now that William had been taken care of, Kiru leaned back against the rock and deactivated his mana-induced control over himself, his body going limp against the boulder. Then, he began cultivating, drawing upon the mental mana in the air. With such intense activity, the psion's impressive reserves were running low. He continued for hours into the night. The partying and festivities continued, but as they went on, more and more people began to pass out and fall asleep. This helped Kiru's cultivation tremendously.

The surplus of mana helped to provide some ease to Kiru's tired body to the point that the psion accidentally fell asleep during the process. He awoke after five hours' rest, when his body fell over to the side and his head hit something hard and metal. He snapped his eyes open to see that his head had landed against Brunhilda's new enchanted shield. Luckily, he didn't hurt himself as the enchantment from his headband protected him from actually smacking against the armor.

Kiru quickly activated Telekinesis and pulled himself upright. He blinked his eyes clear to find his friends all sleeping not far from him. Zhaden was sitting on top of a boulder in lotus position, his head down and bobbing. Kiru did notice that Zhaden's hands rested directly on the handles of two of his blades. The psion smirked. Even sleeping, the drakonid was clearly on high alert and ready for a fight.

Kiru also noticed that Zhaden's silhouette was odd-looking. He realized he must have been using his Invisibility technique while sleeping. Kiru didn't think that was the best idea for mana consumption, but he trusted that his friend knew what he was doing. Mutt was nestled in Brunhilda's muscular arms, a big grin on each of their sleeping faces. Kiru chuckled and smiled to himself. *It seems like she had the courage to finally say her feelings tonight.*

Kiru then decided to focus on what his familiar had said about her earlier. He thought about when Brunhilda was trying to learn Gnash and Grind. She had indeed taken a couple of shots of the cactus liquor then, but it was just for the sheer enjoyment of it. But then, Zengaz had specifically ordered her to imbibe a lot more, and she drank a whole barrel. "Dwarves and their alcohol," he uttered good-naturedly.

The more he thought about it, the more the psion realized that William was right. After each time she took a gulp of the tea-quilla, she was able to grasp her technique better. In fact, just seconds after finishing the barrel was when she had finally attained a full grasp of it. *Was it a coincidence, or was it purely the fact that there was beast mana in the liquor, and it was a beast-mana-inspired technique?* Kiru thought. He wasn't sure, but he felt like he may be onto something. He'd have to ask her about that after she woke up.

Still, his situation was different than the dwarf's. She had a fully developed technique. He had a technique concept in mind: some way to control electricity with his mana. Right now, he was making his up from scratch based off his experiences and understanding like the cultivators of old. *Too bad I can't talk with those ancient cultivators or know anyone that did.* he thought. *Wait, I do!* At least, he presumed he did. Hlin had been around since before Ragnarok. She had to have *some* knowledge of crafting techniques, and he was technically her acolyte. Hopefully, the goddess could help him out.

Kiru closed his eyes and attempted to commune with his patron deity, "Um, Hlin, you there?" he whispered. Despite it being pitch black out, Kiru felt a distinct warmth on his body as if the sun's rays were right on him.

"Well, well, if it isn't my paladin's ally. I cannot afford to spare thee much time, so what is it thou desires of me?" She spoke to his consciousness in a gruff manner much less tender in tone compared to how she communicated with Brunhilda.

Kiru was taken aback by her bluntness and also that she was speaking with him at all. He hadn't been sure that his prayer would work. Still, her tone toward him was concerning. *Have I angered her? Inciting the wrath of a goddess is not going to be good for my goals,* he thought.

"Apologies for any offense I may have given you, my goddess. I was just hoping you could help me in crafting my technique," he said.

"Ah, some respect. That's a good change. Still, I don't have much to tell. Much of my energy was spent with my paladin's boon. A personally blessed Mithril shield is not something easily conjured. With Brunhilda's dedicated devotion, I give her most of my strength, when called upon. I will not put my divine energy into such a simple task as crafting a technique for the likes of thee. Thou may be an ally, but a devout worshiper thou are not."

Kiru pursed his lips, disappointed but understanding where the goddess came from. He had made it clear from the beginning that he wasn't a true follower of Hlin but rather an ally. Thinking back, he did lay it on a little thick by calling her "my goddess." Kiru had only agreed to become an acolyte of Hlin because of an agreement he'd made with Brunhilda back at the academy. On the plus side, Hlin wasn't an overtly selfish goddess from what he'd experienced, and she did answer his prayer to save Brunhilda's life when she nearly died back at the academy. So, he couldn't necessarily fault the deity for not helping him. He was about to end the prayer when Hlin spoke once more.

"I will deign to divulge two things, however, since thou are aligned with me and mine paladin's cause. One, the key thing is, that it must be thine own technique." She emphasized the word "own" in particular.

What does she mean by that? Kiru wondered, but then she kept speaking.

"I've seen what thou hast been doing. Whilst thee hath made progress, thou art still just guiding things, not making them thine own," she said.

"You've been watching me?" Kiru asked, surprised.

"Of course. I keep an eye on all those bound to me," she replied.

"Oh, okay, then. And the second piece of advice?" Kiru asked.

"Thou might want to duck in three seconds," she said, and he felt her warmth and their communication abruptly cut off.

Kiru's heart raced, wondering exactly what she meant. He didn't have time to doubt her advice, though. He snapped his eyes open and ducked. *Ting!* The sound of metal on stone rang right where his head had been. The psion looked up to see a shadowy figure standing over him, a spear gripped in both hands. Before they could attempt to strike with their spear a second time, another figure suddenly zoomed up and appeared behind them.

The second figure used their dagger to cut the fingers off of the spear-wielder's right hand in one fluid motion before using their tail to wrap around their left arm and wrap the thin wire of a garrote around their throat. The first figure cried out in pain as they were subdued, their blood spraying from their amputated fingers, liberally covering Kiru's face in the warm red liquid. Kiru quickly stood up, his hands at his weapons' hilts. Both Brunhilda and Mutt, startled by the sudden noise, did the same.

After Kiru quickly shook some of the blood away from his eyes, he saw that the second figure was Zhaden, the psion looking back to where he drakonid was sleeping and seeing the figure of his friend fading away. *He even fooled me this time*, Kiru thought. The illusion the psion saw was actually Zhaden's Duplicate technique, *not* his Invisibility. Kiru once again looked back in the direction of his attacker and the real Zhaden, and his eyes widened as he took in his attacker's identity.

The spear-wielding assassin had fresh scars covering multiple parts of their body, and Kiru's perfect memory helped take notice of their placements. He'd seen an orc with injuries in those specific locations just recently. They were the same that the heavily injured orc prisoner Brunhilda had saved from near death had endured. The scars that covered the orc's skin now appeared just like scales, the same style pattern that the Jormuns used!

"What's going on?" Brunhilda asked as she and Mutt ran over to them.

"It would appear that one of the freed prisoners was a spy," Zhaden hissed, pulling his garrote against the orc's throat, drawing thin rivulets of blood.

"Hahaha! Fools, none can stop the great World Serpent. He is the strongest and the world is rightfully his," the assassin said with a manic grin. Based on the crazed look in his eyes, he looked like he was about to say something else or even make some sort of attempt to kill at least one of them, but Kiru didn't let him have the chance. The psion scowled, stepped forward, and did something the orc didn't expect. He pressed his palm to the orc's scarred temple and said, "Subjugation." Just like other cultivators, he didn't need to say the technique's name to use it, but speaking it aloud affirmed its connection to him and made it stronger.

Mental mana left his hand and went directly into the orc's brain. The mana went through, then out, and around his brain until it had formed a noose around the organ and tightened. The scarred assassin let out an involuntarily grunt as Kiru's technique took hold. The psion had his friends go alert the L'Khans of potential attacks while he interrogated his now-subjugated minion.

The traitor had confirmed that the Jormuns who had taken over the Jabari Tribe had made a deal with the Exile. They gave him a cursed gnoll staff they found in the ruins to falsely elevate his power, and in exchange, the Exile would kill off the L'Khans, preventing them from sponsoring any other tribe. The scarred assassin that Kiru had subjugated was left to monitor things from the shadows, the Exile being the only one aware of him. When Kiru's group came in, the orc quickly hid and mutilated himself, cutting his own skin deeply over his scars to hide who he was. It was all in order to kill the party when their guards were down.

The subjugated orc had also caught the scent of his fellow Jormuns not far off in the distance before he'd attacked Kiru. He informed the psion that he was surprised to find the cultists, and snuck off to communicate with them. The orc said one of the higher-ups within the cult, a cousin of S'Vol, had been leading a contingent of the cultists as they tracked Pandemonium's tracks. He had planned an ambush to kill off at least Mutt, since the blind orc was a member of a rival clan, then lead the rest of Pandemonium along with the ogres into a narrow ravine.

"How many of you Jormuns are there waiting in ambush?" Kiru asked.

"Including me, there are fifty," the orc replied, his voice still very harsh but betraying no sign that his mind had been taken over.

"There are at least two hundred ogres here. Sure, they're not all fighters, but with my team, Jubjon, and Snout, I don't think that would've been wise. What aren't you telling me?" Kiru asked with his eyes narrowed.

"You are wise to think that. The Jormuns did too. Once I informed the leader of the numbers, she said that they couldn't win a fair fight. I was to lead you to a narrow ravine where your numbers wouldn't matter. Then, we would entrap you and eliminate the ogres from a distance," the orc explained.

Kiru's grin grew predatory, similar to that of William. Now that they knew what they were up against, the hunters would become the hunted.

CHAPTER EIGHTEEN

Ambush

Kiru had ordered the scarred orc assassin to sprint forward through the narrow ravine. "They're coming!" the subjugated orc shouted to the Jormuns waiting as he ran. Once they were back in the ogre camp and had done more questioning, he had informed Kiru of where the cultists would be positioned. The cultists had moved themselves along the top of both sides of the fjord. Large rocks were placed on the edge as well, ready to be pushed over by the Jormuns to crush the incoming ogres. They would have, at least, had the ogres not already been informed as to what was going on.

After the L'Khans were made privy as to what was happening, the ogres and cultivators, including some of the former prisoners, devised a counterstrategy. The subjugated assassin would run through as bait as intended, and a few ogres would follow to keep up the ruse but at a much safer distance. Using a hidden path and the noise from the ogres chasing the assassin, Pandemonium would be accompanied by Snout, Jubjon, and a squad of ogre elites, who would outflank the would-be attackers from behind.

That was the plan they were currently executing. As Kiru and the others neared, they noticed that their strategy was working as intended. The Jormun orcs were all by the cliff's edge, staring down and standing by the large boulders assembled to crush the incoming ogres, completely oblivious to the psion and others behind them.

"They're all gathered together up top like fish in a barrel," William sent to Kiru via Telepathy.

Kiru agreed. Now, with only the elite ogres aiding them, the party was outnumbered by the Jormuns two-to-one. The party was counting on that since most of the cultivators they intended to fight gave off below-Gold signatures. Still, Kiru didn't know what other nasty surprises the cultists had in store. The scarred assassin knew *most* of what the Jormuns could do. Due to that, the party decided to play it safe.

Zhaden and Ebysso snuck ahead of the group—about fifty feet ahead, to be exact. When all of the cultists were in range, the drakonid channeled his most dangerous, powerful technique, Nightmare. Zhaden focused a majority of his mana right around his core, then released it in a violent surge. A dark shadowy form, blacker than the night sky, emerged from Zhaden's chest and surrounded his body. It eventually coalesced into a massive reptilian silhouette three times the size of the lanky rogue. The cultists were only alerted to the others' presence by the monstrous roar the shadow gave off, shaking the very ground as it echoed loudly across the Wastelands. The Jormuns let out panicked cries of fear, and they turned just in time to see the monstrous shadow fly at them, as if death incarnate was descending.

The orc cultists noticed too late the drakonid's technique. Only seconds after they saw the incoming shadow, all of them were enveloped by the Nightmare technique. Kiru and the others watched as the shadowy dragon enveloped their foes in a shroud of complete darkness. The Jormuns—with the technique obscuring their vision and invading their psyches—screamed in terror as fear tightened its grip around their hearts. Many of them went stiff, going immobile or falling to their knees on the spot.

Kiru and the rest of Pandemonium knew the Nightmare technique took a lot out of Zhaden. So, he stayed back and allowed the others to charge ahead as planned.

After the drakonid's aid, the rest of Pandemonium and the ogres easily dealt with the cultists. One by one, the Jormuns were either cut to pieces by Kiru's blades or Mutt's claws, or they were crushed into paste by giant clubs and ogre fists. They were too shaken and slow to counter. Only one orc truly put up a fight. She was by far the most difficult to deal with. She was actually able to resist Zhaden's technique and fight back with her spear, deflecting blows and stabbing with her weapon. She was the tallest and most muscular of the assembled foes. Her face was mutilated to look even more like a snake than her brethren—even more serpentine than S'Vol's, in Kiru's opinion. Her nose, in particular, was cut to make her nostrils look like slits.

She hissed as the party slowly surrounded her. Like a cornered animal, she was still dangerous, even more so, to Kiru's assessment, based off of the unease he felt by looking at her. So, he made sure to orient his blades more defensively as they closed the distance. The tall, muscular orc seemed to move faster despite her situation growing more dire. In under a second, she had jabbed her spear repeatedly, thrusting straight through an ogre's neck. Her weapons must've been coated in some sort of acid as well because the ogre's skin sizzled and bubbled from the gaping neck wound. The ogre gave a choked cough of surprise as he fell flat on the ground, dead.

Then the cultist used his corpse as a pedestal, jumped off of it to launch herself into the air, flying over the party that had been encircling her. She hissed and lowered her spear at Jubjon. At the same time, she activated one of the Jormun techniques to elongate her neck. Her mouth opened wider than seemed possible, revealing a set of snake-like teeth. Jubjon wasn't sure whether to prioritize blocking the cultist's spear or her mouth, which caused him to hesitate momentarily. Because of that, the ogre captain ended up just barely intercepting the cultist's mouth with his forearm, leaving her time to stab him in his left shoulder.

Kiru gritted his teeth in frustration as he and the others turned and ran to aid the ogre captain.

The spear didn't completely penetrate his body like the previous ogre, but the Jormun still cackled. Both Jubjon's shoulder and forearm began to sizzle and melt as acid tore away at his skin and muscle underneath. The cultist's cackling quickly turned into a grunt of surprise, however, when, instead of Jubjon crying out in pain or despair, the ogre captain just grinned. He then used his free arm to break the spear's wooden shaft before grabbing the Jormun by her elongated neck and throwing her back toward the incoming party. Her teeth tore deep gouges in his forearm, but the ogre didn't seem to care.

The cultist bounced a couple of times on the hard ground before glaring at Jubjon. Her glare turned into a gawk as she watched Jubjon ripping the spearhead out of his shoulder, his sloughed-off flesh instantly replaced by a new, unblemished layer. The regenerative abilities of the L'Khans were no joke when they had full bellies and mana to use. The cultist shifted her legs into a singular snake tail and slithered back.

Kiru's party and the ogres continued trying to surround the Jormun, slowly backing her up to the cliff's edge. Her snake-like eyes darted for an escape but to no avail.

It was clear to the psion that this large, powerful cultist must be their leader. So, before they attacked once more, Kiru's voice boomed out. He wanted to see if he could get some information out of her. "What's your purpose in attacking the ogres? What are the Jormuns planning?" he demanded. Ideally, he hoped to use Subjugation on her. He didn't think it would be likely as he didn't think he'd be able to press a palm to her head safely, so using the fear of being surrounded by a superior force would have to do the trick of intimidating the information out of her, or so he hoped.

The cultist hissed and bared her fangs at Kiru. "Infidel, you dare think to make demands of me? I am Jabari Nayla, blood relative of S'Vol," she said and looked as if she was going to lunge at the psion but thought better of it, seeing herself thoroughly outmatched. Her look of fear mixed with anger morphed into a visage of pride and contempt as she refocused on Kiru. "It matters not. I will tell you infidels if only to see the looks of despair on your faces. This world belongs to the great serpent and his master. If you do not submit, you will be laid low. We, as his subjects, work to ensure that always."

She continued, "We suppress any who would challenge S'Vol's right to rule. We did not wish to convert these fat, unworthy ogres, so we used one of their own to suppress them with a cursed artifact. Still, like Jormungandr, our influence is spread wide, and our agents are everywhere. In case you actually happen to pull off the impossible and save these miserable creatures, it won't matter. You still have already lost. We've enacted a . . . contingency to ensure that." She gave him an evil grin.

"What have you done?!" Mutt barked, concern evident in his voice.

Nayla put a hand up to her mouth and ripped out a discolored fake tooth. She popped it into the back of her mouth like a piece of candy and bit down hard on it with a loud crunch. The cultist's neck and jaw tensed, but she still answered. "Our agents have infiltrated Dissé's defenses. Though S'Vol wanted to be the one to kill your sister, he'll be more than satisfied once he hears of both of your deaths, M'BAKU!" She shouted the last word as her entire body began to glow a pale blue.

Everyone reactively took a step back as her body began to twitch and convulse. Then, it *changed*. Rapidly, the cultist leader's body transformed. Her scale-like scars hardened as they turned into actual scales. Her appendages melded into her body as her head thickened and elongated. Her skin went from green to the same pale blue glowing off of her. It was as if her body was full of molten lava that threatened to burst out from within. In just seconds, the orc had transformed into a massive serpent the size of Snout, a molten-looking, malevolent red shining from both of her pupils and in between her new scales.

The massive orc-turned-snake had a crazed, undeniably bestial look in her eyes. She hissed, then released a violent gout of acid from her maw directly at Mutt. The blind orc was caught off-guard, making him hesitate just a moment. Kiru, fortunately, was ready for his friend. The psion leapt to the side and tackled Mutt out of the way, the two narrowly avoiding the toxic liquid.

The acid continued its trajectory, striking a pair of ogres behind Mutt. The liquid liberally covered their thick bodies and immediately began eating away at them. They screamed in pain as they began to literally melt. Their voices were suddenly cut off, though, as the glowing snake cut off her acid attack and lunged at the injured ogres. The snake bit one in half and crushed the other with her bulky body, reducing him to a pile of bubbling flesh. The snake raised her head and, with a loud gulp, swallowed the upper half of the ogre she had bisected. The woman seemed to now be gone entirely. Only the beast remained.

It was fair to say that everyone else was caught off-guard by the sudden shift in the tide of battle. Yes, the Jormuns were beast mana cultivators like most orcs in Imakandi, but to *become* a beast like this was unheard of, unless you were at the highest ranks of cultivation. The cultist clearly had given off the aura of a Gold before she transformed.

"It must be the fake tooth," Kiru muttered to himself.

"*Errgh,*" William grumbled inside the psion's mind. "*What's the deal with bad guys and using items to falsely elevate their power? I mean, c'mon. Get a new schtick.*"

If William recognized the pattern, it was impossible for Kiru not to. The little imp was correct. It was clear that the Jormun had artificially advanced herself with some sort of item or pill that was in the artificial tooth she'd ingested. It was just like the staff the Exile had used. Kiru knew from firsthand experience, seeing what happened to the ogre traitor, that such shortcuts always came with a price.

There was a ripple of heat in the air beside the large snake. The air shimmered, and Ebysso appeared from it. The wrapped orc tried to slice across the scales of the snake with her daggers. Surprisingly, the blades cut against the reptile's hide with little resistance. The snake raised her head and roared in pain as blood poured out from the gash. The glowing red in between the scales flared violently at the site of the injury. Snout and Jubjon shouted and charged in, swinging large bone clubs, both hitting the large snake in unison and sending her flying back. Another ogre went in for the kill, but the cultist-turned-snake quickly got back up and bit off his head.

Kiru noticed the spots where the clubs had hit the snake. The scales were caved in, and the red glow brightened, all three spots of injury now pulsating violently. Chills went down Kiru's neck. Something wasn't right. *The hide of a large sacred beast like that shouldn't be able to be injured so easily. Was this the price? Increased offense, but at the cost of defensive ability?* Still, the pulsing didn't seem right to Kiru.

William put it together though for him, "*Oh, shit! She's gonna blow!*"

Kiru gasped. The snake was so weak because her body couldn't handle the artificial enhancement. She was burning herself out. The snake was a literal ticking time bomb! They needed to keep it away! "*Zhaden, I need to distract it! Keep it away from everyone else! She can't handle her power and will likely explode soon. We need to keep her from taking us with her!*" he urgently sent via Telepathy.

The drakonid had been keeping his distance, drained from the Nightmare technique, but had recovered enough to rejoin the fight, likely after downing a mana potion Ebysso had given him before the fight to use in a time of great need. He was now only twenty feet away from them. Glowing blood leaked out of the snake's mouth.

She pulled her head back, clearly about to strike again. Before that could happen, though, she was assaulted by an array of flying daggers, each blade penetrating her weak skin, wounding her and quickening her decay.

Nayla hissed and shot another splash of acid in Zhaden's direction. Luckily, because of his restored mana pool, the gold drakonid was able to use Invisibility and dodge the attack. Unfortunately, snakes could detect body heat, so Invisibility didn't protect him. She zoomed, slithering straight at him for a follow-up strike.

Kiru's mental mana also allowed him to see the drakonid despite the Invisibility technique too. His heart quickened as he saw the snake, her body pulsating ever faster, barreling in his friend's direction. Zhaden was ready to go down fighting, his thin, enchanted Bloodstep Stiletto at the ready.

That sparked an idea in Kiru's mind. *"Zhaden, throw your enchanted dagger at me!"* he desperately sent to his friend off in the distance.

Kiru was at least a hundred feet away now because of the drakonid's dodging. He was unsure if the rogue could hit him accurately at such a distance, but it was the best idea he could come up with on the spot. He knew Zhaden trusted him, so with the giant snake nearly on him, the gold drakonid hurled his Bloodstep Stiletto at Kiru with all his might.

Kiru stuck out his palm, and as gravity began acting on the blade and making it start to fall, he pulled it toward himself with Telekinesis. As if the weapon had taken on a life of its own, the dagger flew toward him and embedded itself in his palm. The stiletto pierced through the back of his hand, and blood shot out in multiple directions. Kiru groaned in response despite not actually experiencing any pain from the wound. At times like these, he was grateful he couldn't feel his body. Judging by the blood, that would've hurt a lot.

The giant snake raised her mouth wide, dislocating her jaw in order to swallow Zhaden whole.

With the blood touching the metal of the blade, the enchantment quickly activated, and the gold drakonid disappeared right before she bit down. Instead of a mouthful of drakonid, the snake bit off a large chunk of the stone underneath, sending up a couple of plumes of dust.

Zhaden appeared before Kiru, the weapon's pommel in his grip. The gold drakonid looked surprised to have suddenly appeared right before the psion but quickly acclimated, noticing his friend's injury. "Um, your hand."

Kiru knew better than to pull it out as that could worsen the injury. He batted the rogue's hand off of the weapon's grip. "Yeah, yeah, no time for that." He looked to see the large snake spitting out the chunk of stone in her mouth and snarling. She was furious at her prey's sudden disappearance, frantically scanning for where he'd gone to. Kiru could see she was now pulsating at least twice a second. She would blow at any moment. She noticed Zhaden once more, her eyes narrowing and a hiss coming from her mouth. With a surge of speed, she slithered with all her might in a bloody suicidal charge at the cultivators.

Snout and Jubjon stomped past the party, running at the snake as best they could. Kiru wouldn't let them die, though. They just needed to keep the snake away until she popped. "Brunhilda, Gnash and Grind," he ordered.

The dwarf was undoubtedly the slowest among them, so she was behind everyone else. "Gnash!" A large spectral goat's head surged out from her steel shield, surging forward and flying past the stomping ogres. "And Grind!" A second spectral goat head flew from her mithril shield, just behind its counterpart.

The first goat head bit down on the crazed reptile's body, almost bisecting her. Still, the serpent moved forward. The second, however, bit right behind her head, halting her dead in her tracks. The large snake writhed wildly in death throes before giving a more orcish cry of pain. Then, a red light glowed everywhere from her injured body, brighter and brighter. Everyone raised their arms defensively against the bold red light. Then, *boom!*

The snake exploded in a tidal wave of force and mana. Both Jubjon and Snout were sent flying back, nearly knocking into the two ogres in the canyon behind them. Unfortunately, some of the ogres on the cliff's edge fell to their doom from the wave of force. While everyone else had been stuck staring at the writhing snake clamped by spectral goat heads, Brunhilda seized the moment to run in front of the party before the snake exploded. She raised her twin shields to protect them. The wave of mana and force pressed hard against her but flowed over and past the shields, unable to break through.

After ten seconds, the force died down abruptly. Brunhilda lowered her shields, and the rest of the party blinked their vision clear. When that was done, they all looked to see a small, black, smoking crater where the cultist had once been.

Everyone breathed an audible sigh of relief from having survived the ordeal, but their sense of relief didn't last long.

"Boss, we've got to get back to Dissé," Mutt said, his carefree demeanor now completely gone.

"Yes," Kiru agreed. Nayla's confirmation that the Jormuns were attacking and planning on killing the M'Baku leader made him concerned as well. If she died, he wouldn't have the alliance needed to find his father's second item, and it would make trying to save this world even harder. Outside of that, Myev, despite her sadistic manner of teaching, was indeed his ally. He would not forsake her. She was also his friend's sister. *What kind of friend would I be if I just left her to die?* he thought.

"I concur," Zhaden said, walking up to them, breathing heavily. "But I'm unsure as to how we will make it there in time. It's at least a day's journey, and that's if we ran and didn't take any breaks."

Chief Snout snorted as he trudged up to the group. He had been paying attention to what the Jormun had said before her transformation and looked knowingly at the party. "We shall help our ally. As to travel, leave that to me."

"Hey, Stabby . . ." Mutt said, trailing off.

The gold drakonid cocked his head to the side. "What is it?"

"I wanna say I'm sorry. I thought you were worrying too much by always being so suspicious," Mutt said, clearly uncomfortable. "I now see why you wanted us to travel through the night."

"Aye. I must confess that I thought the same as Mutt, but I was wrong," Brunhilda said, looking at the drakonid directly in the eyes.

"We all were," Kiru added. "I still think sometimes we need time to rest and recover and even celebrate, but I should've heeded your words and kept my guard up. These Jormuns seem to have spread influence everywhere in this country, and they're damn clever. I should've suspected that they had spies and contingency plans. I'm sorry."

The gold drakonid's body went rigid, only his nostrils flaring up and down as he processed their words. Even his tail was still, not betraying his thoughts. The psion felt the tension palpably, but no one said a word, allowing Zhaden the time he needed. After half a minute of uncomfortable silence, Zhaden spoke. "I appreciate your words and hope that you will trust me next time I give what I believe to be a legitimate warning," he growled, clearly frustrated that they hadn't taken him seriously.

Then, his body visibly eased. "That being said, I may have been what you call . . . paranoid before," he admitted but then raised a clawed finger in warning. "I still think it is valid to always be prepared. We are on a mission to avert a dire fate for all the nations within the Great Alliance, and need I remind you that there are ill-intentioned forces working against our just cause? So, I maintain that a little paranoia is warranted," he said defensively.

All three of his friends looked at him and nodded reluctantly. The gold drakonid had a point, even if he was still maybe a little too suspicious.

They then took the time to recover and help their allies, taking special care to be on guard for any more potential double agents in their midst. Kiru did feel a little better after he questioned the subjugated orc about any other spies, and the assassin said he was unaware of any.

Half an hour later, Snout called Kiru and the others over to him. "It is time to get our mounts," he said, then pressed a palm to the ground.

"Um . . . what're you doing, Bug Guy?"

Snout raised a finger with his other hand, his eyes closed and his face looking focused.

Kiru and the others all shot a glance at each other but shrugged as they stood and waited in awkward silence.

After a minute or so, Snout grunted. "Ah, here one comes," he said, and a plume of dirt erupted from the ground.

Kiru and the others all jumped back and readied their weapons as the dust fell away, revealing what looked to be a huge centipede as wide as a horse and four times as long that had emerged from the stone.

Its mouth let out an angry insectile clicking.

"Easy," Snout said in as gentle a voice as the ogre could muster.

The insect snapped its head in the chief's direction, its antennae moving up and down in a steady motion. It still clicked in an aggressive manner but did seem to be more cautious versus outright hostile. He didn't specialize in insect communication, though, so that was only an educated guess.

Kiru watched Snout taking a tentative step forward with his hand out, and the centipede would repeat the gesture, albeit with multiple small steps to match the distance of the ogre's long strides. After a tense half-minute where it seemed like everyone was holding their breaths, Snout put his hand on the insect's head and sent a pulse of mana into it. The party could feel the lingering mana even from their distance. It wasn't the sensation of beast mana that made them feel better, though. It was how the demeanor of the centipede abruptly changed from cautious and aggressive to calm and unconcerned. It even began rubbing its head against Snout's belly good-naturedly, and the chief scratched under its carapace as if it were a dog.

"Master, that looked a whole lot like—"

"I know," Kiru sent back to William, interrupting the familiar's words. *"A lot like my Subjugation."* He realized that he would need to talk with Snout to see if that was indeed a technique the ogre used and to check for any overlap between their abilities. Perhaps he could learn something, maybe even a new technique? He hoped so, at least.

Snout went on to explain that the gigantic insect was called a centigrub. "Centigrubs were glutton grubs who weren't able to find enough food underground and so took on a different evolutionary path. They developed hardened carapaces and more vicious attitudes to survive above," he said. Fortunately, with Snout's control over glutton grub beast mana, the ogre chief was able to call upon the creatures with ease by putting his hand on the ground and sending a call with his mana, repeating the process until they had enough of the creatures for all of them to ride. His control over the insects was only temporary and it was conditional, somehow making a silent deal with the sacred beasts. In this instance, Snout agreed to give the creatures some of the dead cultists to eat as payment.

Kiru even added the subjugated assassin as a bonus treat, not wanting to risk the traitorous orc breaking free. He had only wished that Snout hadn't sicced the centigrubs on the orc immediately after Kiru offered him up. It was gruesome, to say the least, but thankfully, the orc's screams were cut short after only ten seconds.

After getting over such a terrifying sight, the psion wondered why the L'Khans hadn't used such formidable sacred beasts to help them fight off the Exile's forces earlier. Once he saw the sheer quantity of bodies the insects required as payment, however—roughly five orcs' worth per centigrub—he realized that the previously starving L'Khans couldn't afford such a price. They would've had to sacrifice themselves in order to sate the centigrubs' needs.

After a few minutes, the cultivators were riding the large insects, and were going at a ridiculous speed, faster than any creature Kiru or any of the party had ever ridden before. While two of them each had to share a mount, Ebysso got her own, being the odd orc out. She didn't gloat about it, however. She just clenched her body tight against the bug's carapace in a desperate attempt to not be thrown off. It was clear that any cavalry-related tasks weren't her forte. Snout required three centigrubs just for his own massive girth. Still, the terrifying, twenty-foot-long bugs were remarkably agile and dexterous. They crawled up, around, and over the various uneven, rocky structures of the Wastelands with ease. It made Kiru *very* grateful that they didn't have to fight these things! With such outright hostility and ease of movement even in such difficult terrain, the bugs would've been a menace. And that wasn't even factoring in their hard carapaces.

And once they hit the rolling hills of M'Baku Territory, the centigrubs seemed to surprise all but Snout by becoming even faster. The wind blew across the cultivators' faces even more intensely as their mounts' pace quickened. More than one tear was forced out of Kiru's wincing eyes, and he had to lower his head to fight off windburn. Despite the thrill of the ride, however, Kiru couldn't help thinking about what the cultist Nayla had said. *She specifically said "the World Serpent and his master." Why?* He couldn't have misheard her; his perfect recall wouldn't allow for that.

"William, do you have any idea why the cultist said the World Serpent had a master? I thought he was a god," he sent telepathically to his familiar inside his core.

"Hm, I don't know," William said. *"Maybe she just made a mistake and misspoke in the heat of bloodlust. It happens to me all the time."*

"Maybe," Kiru said, not convinced. *"But I can't help but feel there's something we're missing here. I just don't know what."*

William sent Kiru the mental equivalent of a shrug. *"We'll figure it out, Master. I'll say that it does make sense if their god is some sort of weak-ass servant."*

"Why?"

"Because his followers are the same. They keep needing some artificial boost in strength instead of just getting stronger on their own. It's a sign of them being too weak to fight with their own strength. Pfft! I wouldn't be surprised if we fight a couple more of those pathetic weaklings like that snake lady when we get to the capital. If they rely on items for their strength, they're the real tools," William said.

Kiru thought about William's words. Oddly enough, the imp was right. Besides S'Vol, the stronger Jormuns and their allies that the party had faced so far had all relied on some sort of item or gimmick. They were still powerful, there was no denying that. The Exile had Sapphire-level power, and the cultist they fought by the fjord turned into a monstrous serpent with insane speed and a ranged acid attack that even outperformed the regenerative capabilities of multiple ogres.

Despite those strengths, however, there were obvious weaknesses. The first was that their power was completely reliant on whatever piece of equipment they used. If the cultist hadn't swallowed the fake tooth, she would've been eliminated with much less hassle. The second thing was the drawback. Even with that transformative power, her ability to take a hit had been greatly diminished. Plus, there was the whole unstable-power-inside-her-that-exploded thing. Also, when the Exile's staff was broken, the monstrous ogre experienced terrible recoil.

The Jormuns and their allies were dangerous. The death and destruction they'd reaped was evidence enough for that. But William was right—they seemed to be more reliant on shortcuts and gimmicks than brute strength. If the party could remove those shortcuts or cheats, their foes should theoretically be much easier to defeat.

Kiru smiled at that revelation. He still didn't know if Jormungandr had a master or not, but understanding an opponent's weakness was vital in battle. He was reminded of an *Art of War* quote his mother would recite: "When you move, fall like a thunderbolt." He planned to strike back at the cultists just like that. Like a vengeful thunderbolt.

CHAPTER NINETEEN

Faithful Allies

After a heart-pounding start, Kiru had finally grown accustomed to the grub's ridiculous speed, actually enjoying the ride versus spending the entire time being afraid of falling off. It took only a couple of hours, but they finally made it to the edge of the crater in which Dissé was located. To the cultivators' surprise, the capital looked exactly the same as when they'd left it. It wasn't razed. No hordes of cultists attacking or ransacking the place were visible. Still, they knew appearances could be deceiving. To be safe, they dismissed the centigrubs as soon as they'd hopped off of them. They didn't want to send the whole city into a panic at seeing the terrifying bugs and potentially alert any Jormuns of their presence.

They soon afterward realized that Snout's monstrous appearance would stick out in the orc city as well. So, despite him being a powerful cultivator, they had him hide out at the crater's edge. It would be easier for the others to get into the city without him. They also elected to have Ebysso stay behind to guard him. Snout could clearly take care of himself, but subtle he was not. If he were discovered, it would be hard to convince any nearby orcs that he wasn't a monster or a threat. Having Ebysso vouch for him was the smart call.

With that taken care of, the party all put on hooded cowls and quickly made their way toward Dissé on foot. As they neared and entered the outer market, they spotted the customary people hawking their wares. Orcs were laughing, negotiating, and trading as if there were no threat against them at all. Everything, for all intents and purposes seemed normal—too normal for their liking.

Mutt's increased hearing capabilities picked up on more hushed conversations around them. He whispered to Kiru that, despite their disguises, the stature of a dwarf and a gold drakonid's tail would not go unnoticed. Still, no obvious words about Jormuns or a coup. "There are a number of orcs murmuring about how a section of stalls are notably empty. None of the other merchants know why, but I don't like the sound of it," he uttered just loud enough for Kiru to hear.

The party got through the open gate without any trouble, however, quickly going through crisscrossing and winding streets of the orc capital.

Suddenly, Mutt took an abrupt turn into a narrow side street, eventually stopping by a pair of small trees.

"Mutt, what are ye doing?" Brunhilda asked. "We need to be going up."

The typically carefree orc's wild hair stood on end, and he breathed heavily; he was clearly on edge.

Kiru placed his hands on his weapons and started scanning the rooftops, concerned about an ambush. He didn't see anything so far, but Mutt's unease made him *much* more wary.

"This place . . . There's a scent in the air," he said before taking three deep sniffs. "I've smelled it before, but never here. At least not as strong," Mutt said.

"What are ye smelling, Mutt?" Brunhilda asked.

The blind orc gave out a low growl. "Snake."

Suddenly, a spear thrust down toward Mutt from the branches. The orc expertly dodged the weapon by taking a step back just milliseconds before it struck. Mutt bared his teeth and wrapped his hand around the wooden shaft of the spear before the attacker could pull it back. Mutt heaved, pulling down with his impressive strength, yanking down the orc that had been hiding within the branches.

He had scars arranged in a concentric pattern going down both arms—clearly a Jormun. The cultist hissed, then snapped his head toward Mutt, neck elongating like a snake. Mutt sidestepped the attack, grabbed the Jormun by the neck, and squeezed. The cultist's cry was cut off by a loud crunch from his neck, and his body fell limp.

Kiru and the others began scanning their surroundings for any other foes lying in wait. Both the psion and drakonid had their hands at the ready against their hilts.

"We need to hurry. Come on, I know a shortcut," Mutt said as he dropped the dead cultist to the ground and waved for the others to follow. He hurriedly explained that growing up in Dissé, he was aware of some shortcuts that could cut down on some of their travel time. Those shortcuts often meant hopping from roof to roof and occasionally climbing sheer rock walls, however.

Now, that wasn't a problem for the bestial orc and dexterous rogue. For the heavily armored dwarf and thin psion, that was another story. When Brunhilda vehemently said that "nobody tosses a dwarf," they found another solution. Mutt carried her on her back. Brunhilda's face turned a bright purple from blushing, but she didn't protest. Kiru knew that was much more to the paladin's liking.

"Master, you should just levitate your body. You would look so cool, like a god as you ascend to the top of the city," William said.

Kiru raised his head up to look at their surroundings. *"I could, but that may require more mana than I'm comfortable with. There's likely a big fight ahead, and I want to make sure I have enough to go all out,"* he sent back. *"Plus, if anyone sees me floating up a sheer wall, they might start asking questions. That could expose me as a psion. I still have to be careful."*

Seeing some of the public pulley systems going up and down the different levels to carry goods, Kiru was inspired to find his own unique solution—namely, his Psyslime. Kiru forced the malleable substance to change forms, removing its sharpened edges and fashioning it into a magical rope.

He gave one end to Zhaden, and once the drakonid had made it to the top, the rogue pulled Kiru up behind him. That's how the group managed to ascend the multiple levels of the orc capital in record time and unnoticed by any more villains, as far as they could tell. The seeming normalcy of everything around them was still strangely unnerving, however. Nayla's words and the earlier ambush gave evidence that the queen regent was in danger, yet everything else going on in the capital pointed to business as usual. Either the Jormuns were extremely good at being stealthy, or they'd infiltrated the city too well. *Knowing their tendency for bribing others to do their dirty work, there may be more than just Jormuns we need to worry about*, Kiru thought.

The party's shortcut method brought them all the way to the second-to-last level, the one right before the religious district. Mutt told them they couldn't go that way. "Yeah, my ancestors placed a lot of spikes and traps up all around from here up in case of a siege. It would force any attackers to ascend along the city streets," the orc explained.

With that, the party continued their trek forward toward the religious district. Upon Zhaden's insistence, they kept to the shadows and away from the main streets. No one made any arguments about it slowing their pace. After the drakonid's paranoia being proven valid not long ago, they had no room to argue.

As the party reached the edge of the religious district, they heard a lot of animalistic noises coming from the Beast Pantheon temple. Judging by the fact that none of the townsfolk around them seemed concerned, it appeared to be a normal occurrence. What wasn't normal, however, was the blockade of orc guards standing at the district's border, preventing anyone from entering. One elderly orc was forcefully shoved to the ground by a gruff guard as the party got within a hundred feet. The elder orc gave a cry of distress and hobbled away with his cane as the guard raised a backhand in a threatening manner.

Kiru noticed that none of these guards possessed any telltale Jormun scarring nor any overt snake-like features. The psion grimaced.

"Seeing these guards here is too much of a coincidence. They've probably been bought off," he sent via Telepathy. *"Still, they don't appear to be Jormuns. So I think you should try to use your authority to make them back down, Mutt."*

Mutt gave a frustrated grunt but nodded.

The party continued forward. There were no side streets or hidden ways to get into the religious district. It was a small, open area. There weren't even any protective barriers to prevent anyone from falling to their death.

"Way's closed, scum! Go back if you know what's good for you," their leader barked. He was an orc with an imperial mustache, heavily scarred skin, and a wolf's head helmet and pelt.

Brunhilda abruptly stopped and removed her hood, "Ah, Inkosi Rothbart, I wish it was good to see ye again, but I not be surprised. Ye moved on from trying to cut off a wee child's hand to beating up the elderly, eh?"

The party stopped still at Brunhilda's provocative words. She was by far the kindest and least combative of the team, so hearing her speak with such venom was a bit of a shock. Still, the psion knew of her protective nature, which always superseded any niceties. The dwarf didn't like bullies, and he agreed.

The mustached orc scowled and took a threatening step forward. "Leave now, foreigner filth. Be gone from Dissé and Imakandi before I make it your final resting place," he growled as he activated Fenrir's Claws.

Mutt lowered his head and let out a low growl. "The smell, it's stronger behind them."

Kiru noticed it too. The smell of blood was palpable. Most of the guards had smatterings of it splashed upon their hide armor in one area or another. The hide-covered Beast Pantheon temple was liberally covered in blood, body parts strewn about it as if it were a slaughterhouse of nightmares. Fortunately, the stone temple to the Vasir Gods seemed mostly untouched; some of the pillars were chipped off but no major damage, its stone either too tough for the cultists to break, or the residents inside just weren't of great concern to the Jormuns.

Mutt removed his cowl and raised his head high. "I am M'Baku M'Toon, brother of M'Baku Myev, your queen. Lay down your weapons and surrender at once, or face the consequences." Myev's life was on the line and Mutt was clearly not in the mood for games.

Rothbart took a step back, apparently not expecting to see Mutt. He quickly regained his bearings, and his look turned into one of condescension. "Ah, so the defective prince returns. Your reign ends wit—"

"Gnash and Grind!" Brunhilda shouted, firing her offensive technique forward and tearing straight through the line of traitors. One of the spectral goat heads bit a chunk out of Rothbart's shoulder and knocked the captain back before it faded away. The orc's blood shot upward as he fell flat on his back. She was tired of this bully, so she decided to teach him a lesson.

Rothbart screamed in pain and pressed a clawed hand to his wound to staunch the bleeding.

William cheered inside Kiru's mind, *"Yeah! I'm actually glad the paladin got an offensive technique. That means more blood!"* The imp began to chant. *"More blood! More blood! More blood!"*

Rothbart then snapped himself upward from his back with just his legs, pure fury now evident on his visage, "Gah! You heathen bitch!" he spat. "Jormuns!" Then, the guards surrounding him all took off their helmets, revealing bald heads covered in ritualistic scars, their eyes and mouths instantly turning snake-like.

Kiru grimaced, frustrated at the cultists' cunning in covering their scars. The Jormuns lowered their spears at the party and hissed. Then about twenty more joined them, rapidly slithering out of the Beast Pantheon Temple, their heads, necks, or lower halves replaced with those of a serpent's.

"You will pay for this! You will die slowly! The four of you cannot hope to take us all on alone," Rothbart said. The cultists all hissed in malicious glee.

Just then, a loud boom, as if from a massive drum, came from the Vasir Temple, causing a layer of dust to fall off it. Then, its large stone doors opened wide. They could hear a lute being played from within, and out walked the orc cleric Rhodan.

"Our friends, friends-turned-traitors. What you've wrought, shall be returned," Rhodan melodically sang, then strummed his lute hard, in sharp contrast to his smooth words.

The noise coming from the cleric's instruments was harsh and made all of the cultists wince in pain. The cleric of the god of poetry had an interesting technique that Kiru had not witnessed before.

The curly-haired Balmir followed the orc. The tan human smiled and said, "They are not alone." He raised his hands up in the air and shouted, "Sun's Providence!" He stomped his foot and a beam of concentrated sunlight instantly shot down onto the grouped cultists. Many of the orcs cried out and hissed as they were temporarily blinded by the sudden, harsh sunlight. The pair's techniques were clearly more supplemental versus actually damaging in nature. They only lasted a few seconds but were still effective in subduing many of the foes' senses, whether it was sight or hearing.

Rothbart growled. He had only been annoyed. The orc captain's mouth then changed into that of a venomous serpent. *"Hsss,* is that all you've got?!" He quickly took a spear from a disoriented cultist and threw it at Balmir.

The spear flew fast, and Rothbart's aim was true. The weapon would've impaled the man straight through the chest, had a shield not intercepted it. The shield lowered, revealing Dalkruk, the orc mother who Brunhilda had told Kiru about. The paladin had fed her, and the orc had become a follower of Hlin. Her previously emaciated form was now replaced with lean muscle.

"Not today, you coward," she spat at Rothbart. "You tried to hurt my son and kill my friends. Now you will feel my goddess's wrath." She then lowered her two hide shields, "Acolytes, charge!" At her declaration, from out of the temple entrance, fifty shield-bearing orcs ran out, shouting defiantly and engaging the Jormuns in battle.

The psion's mouth dropped at the forces Brunhilda had amassed in her short time in the capital. Goosebumps ran up his neck in excitement. *We can do this!* he thought.

The cultists all got to their feet and ran forward to meet the acolytes. Spear quickly crashed against shield, and the fighting started in earnest. Shouts of anger and cries of pain rang loudly and began to echo all across Dissé.

"Ye three hafta press on to the palace! I need to stay and help the acolytes," Brunhilda shouted at her party amidst the loud battle cries.

"What? No, Brunhilda! This is the perfect distraction. We can move around them. Come with us!" Mutt protested.

The paladin shook her head. "These people aren't trained fighters. They be needing a leader. They be needing me." She took Mutt's hand in hers, then went up on her tiptoes to give him a peck on the cheek. "Be safe, 'kay?"

Mutt blushed and gave a wide grin. "You got it!"

With that, Brunhilda charged forward through the fighting, clearing a path for her friends to the palace grounds at the top of Dissé. As they ran forward and up toward the level holding the palace grounds, she turned back in the opposite direction, using her shields to prevent anyone from following. It was just in time, too, as just then, Rothbart jumped upward toward Brunhilda with claws raised. Kiru looked back to see her expertly deflecting the strike with her shield, sending sparks flying, then slamming one of the sharp ends of her other shield into his side.

Rothbart grunted in pain and jumped back reflexively. Blood was now running down his side.

Brunhilda gave a confident smile and readied her shields once more.

Kiru grinned, *"Show these damn cultists what a Ruby-ranked paladin can do."*

CHAPTER TWENTY

Venom

The three remaining members of Pandemonium ran up to the gates. They were greeted by the sight of two dead orcs on the ground. To his horror, Kiru saw that their mouths were full of foam, their green skin pale, and a set of multiple puncture marks on their necks and faces, the veins around the wounds bulging and black.

"We must hurry. They've already broken into the palace grounds," Zhaden said.

Mutt immediately went on all fours and bolted ahead of his friends past the gate, taking point.

They made their way there quickly, passing numerous dead sacred beasts along the way. They didn't have time to dwell on the horrific wounds that had killed them. From some quick glances, Kiru could see their bodies were mutilated by slashes and appeared to be partially dissolved in places. As they neared the palace proper, they could hear more of the fighting ahead. Then, there was a loud crash. A large wind tunnel burst through one of the wooden walls, sending what looked to be a large snake flying out with violent force.

It crashed into the ground twenty feet away with an audible crunch, its spine shattered. Kiru reflexively grimaced, knowing all too well about spinal injuries.

Instantly, Kiru recognized that it wasn't an actual snake that they saw. It was another Jormun, its lower half replaced with that of a snake's tail. Then they looked inside the large, newly made, comically large hole in the palace wall. Through it they caught sight of Myev with a bleeding minotaur and what looked to be a shaman at her side, or at least Kiru assumed so based on his horse skull helmet and patchwork fur robes that all shamans seemed to wear. The shaman also had a telltale Tau club and was surrounded by a slight wind.

Myev's group was surrounded by a horde of cultists on all sides. All of the scarred orcs had spears pointed at the queen and were hissing; the corpses of both minotaurs and cultists littered the ground. The scents of blood and viscera were pungent. Nom was also there, standing protectively in between Myev and the Jormuns, growling angrily at their attackers. A heavily wounded, dying minotaur lay prone on the ground right by the small leokin.

From a quick scan of their auras, Kiru could tell that, under normal circumstances, not any one of the cultists would be a match for the queen. She was an Emerald, and he knew firsthand how powerful she could be, but there were quite literally fifty of them surrounding Myev and her three allies inside the palace. Their ranks spanned mostly from Silver to Ruby, their power wildly exuding from their bodies as if they lacked any control. Still, even with those numbers, none of them had a chance of standing up against an Emerald. On quick inspection, however, Kiru realized there were two things that prevented this from being a normal fight. For one, Myev looked terrible! She was sitting on her throne, panting heavily and covered in a layer of sweat. She clutched her left forearm and held it to her chest, where bulging black veins were evident.

The other oddity was the leader of these cultists. He was a shaman, adorned in a patchwork fur robe and wearing a skull helmet like the others, but his right arm was both scary and perplexing. In fact, it technically wasn't an arm at all but rather a pale white three-headed snake, surgically grafted onto his body in a crude manner. Its power felt *wrong* to Kiru somehow. Like it was some sort of leech constantly draining its host. That sleeve of the robe was missing, displaying the monstrous appendage for all to see. It reminded Kiru of what his former headmaster had done with the heads of dead psions.

The shaman laughed. "I'm surprised you managed to stay alive so far, Queen Regent," he gloated. "None of the others have managed more than half a minute against my venom." The three snakes all hissed in unison, venom dripping off their mouths and sizzling to the floor.

"See? What did I tell you, Master? Pathetic. This guy had to go and rely on some weird enhancement instead of growing his own power. I bet he's completely dependent on it like that ogre was," William sent.

Kiru had to agree with William's assessment. For all the bravado, scheming, and childlike nature the imp displayed, he had a keen sense of observation and cunning that the psion couldn't deny. Sure, William had a *unique* way of understanding things. If you could parse things from the imp's lens, however, there was wisdom to be gained. *"I think you're right, William. Unless that is a technique, which I doubt, removing that shaman's strength will likely make him too weak to be any real threat,"* Kiru sent back before reassessing the situation as a whole.

There was a real chance Myev could die, but despite her injuries, she was strong. She was the strongest cultivator that had aligned with him to this point. Kiru knew if she had some help, the Jormuns could be divided and conquered. Luckily, Kiru the Conqueror was ready to lend his aid.

Before Kiru and his friends could jump in to help, the dying minotaur lying beside Nom groaned and reached a hand to the little leokin. Nom turned his head curiously but did the same. When his tiny paw touched the minotaur's finger, light surged from the minotaur's body, rushing into Nom's. The minotaur's arm dropped as it died, and the leokin growled as the light coalesced in his chest, inside his core.

The traitorous shaman's eyes widened in concern and sent out his snake arm like a whip, their venomous mouths open wide and ready to end Nom.

In an instant, before the snakes could reach him, however, the leokin roared and his body grew to the size of a minotaur! Then he caught the three white snakes with one meaty paw. The now-massive bipedal lion creature growled angrily at the shaman, his teeth and claws large and looking incredibly sharp. "Nom!" Nom roared as he began violently swinging the shaman around like a toy, slamming him into many of his allies as well as the walls and floor.

Within seconds, he'd killed at least ten of the Jormuns. The shaman was now a bloody mess, unrecognizable by the time the gargantuan leokin had ripped his artificial arm off, sending his limp body flying. The three parasitic snakes hissed in pain, and their bodies shriveled into dry husks without a host to feed from.

Everyone in the room gave an awkward pause at this sudden display of sheer power. Even Kiru was taken aback by it. Fortunately, he recovered his wits and called out for the other members of Pandemonium.

"Attack!" Kiru mentally ordered. The trio of cultivators jumped through the hole in the palace wall, taking advantage of the situation. Nom and the still-standing minotaur joined the fray while their shaman ally guarded Myev. The enemy shaman was one of the Rubies, and indeed just like the Exile, his rank appeared to be artificially elevated. This was confirmed when his aura of power immediately disappeared as soon as his arm had been ripped off—just as William had predicted. Kiru had to hand it to his familiar. The imp could be smart sometimes.

With two Rubies, two large, pissed-off sacred beasts, and a psion with a magic blade, the rest of the cultists didn't stand a chance. Kiru sliced throats and eviscerated abdomen while Mutt gouged furrows in their faces. Meanwhile, Nom and the minotaur crushed the smaller cultists to paste while Zhaden expertly stabbed at vulnerable areas, particularly their eyes and ears.

By the time they were done, both Mutt and Nom raised their heads up and roared in savage victory. Blood covered both the orc and sacred beast's bodies. The leokin transformed back into his smaller form during the roar, whatever power he'd borrowed from the minotaur now gone. Mutt reverted his body back to normal as well, his taloned feet, clawed fingers, and protruding jaw all morphing and shrinking back to their typical sizes and appearances. Once that had happened, Mutt snapped his head over to Myev and ran to her. "Sis! Are you okay?!" he asked with clear concern.

"I've been better, Brother," she answered weakly, then gave a wry grin, which was almost instantly cut short by a sharp grimace of pain. Her sweat-soaked body shivered slightly, her left arm most of all. The queen regent hissed and gripped her right hand around the festering wound on her left forearm. Kiru could see the black veins and necrotic tissue had already spread. A distinct ripe odor of rotting flesh came from the injury and permeated the entire main chamber of the palace.

Despite not being able to actually see the wound, Mutt gave a slight grimace as the rotten odor struck his nostrils. His lower lip quivered in clear distress.

"She may yet live, Prince M'Toon," the shaman said, then put a comforting hand on Mutt's shoulder. "Your sister is strong. Her Emerald body and core are the only reasons she's been able to resist the venom's effects so far. If we cut off her arm, we will eliminate most of it from entering her bloodstream. With the amount she's been exposed to, we'll be lucky if it only takes her a few months to recover."

"Cut off her arm?!" Mutt snarled and grabbed the Tau shaman by the throat. "You shamans are supposed to be neutral during Ukufakaza. Now you want to maim my family? You will *not* lay a hand on my sister," he growled, and claws began to regrow from his fingernails. Kiru could tell Mutt was being overly protective, and he didn't blame him. The psion knew the situation called for a calm head, however, and he wondered if he would have to forcibly stop Mutt from hurting the shaman.

Kiru saw the Tau's eyes go wide, but he didn't fight back or struggle. The shaman was in a compromised position, yes, but the orc clearly didn't feel truly threatened by Mutt, which eased some of his concern.

Myev coughed a few times and put a sweaty hand on Mutt's arm. "Brother, stop. This man is Tau Z'Goyan, leader of the Tau tribe. He just got here yesterday at my summons. He is backing my claim to the throne and is our friend and ally," she protested before coughing once more.

At his sister's words, Mutt let go of Z'Goyan's neck. The shaman took a couple steps back as he cleared his throat and rubbed his neck. "Your sister is right, Prince M'Toon. I was with my people, protecting them from both the Thrar'fangs and Jabari. I'm sorry I did not get here soon enough."

Mutt pointed a finger at the Tau. "You're a shaman, right?"

"I am."

"Then save my sister's arm!" Mutt demanded.

Z'Goyan's face bunched up in discomfort. "I can't, Prince M'Toon," he admitted sadly. "The venom has already spread too far. I've placed a tourniquet by her armpit to slow the progression, but it cannot stop it. The venom appears to be resistant to my healing techniques as well."

Mutt growled, then turned and began to leave.

"Where are you going, Prince?" Z'Goyan asked.

"To get a real damn healer up here. Guys, keep her safe. I'll be back," Mutt said to Kiru and Zhaden.

Not wanting to risk Mutt's ire, both the gold drakonid and psion complied.

Fifteen minutes later, Mutt brought Brunhilda with him. The dwarf looked tired but overall in one piece. "Is everyone there alright?" Kiru asked as she walked up.

She nodded. "By the goddess's mercy, we managed to defeat the bastards, though we lost ten good people."

"Brunhilda, my sister . . ." Mutt said, pressing her forward, and the two moved toward the throne.

The paladin rushed over to the orc queen and began inspecting her injury. She muttered to herself and began to question Z'Goyan.

"How long ago did this happen?" the dwarf asked.

"Roughly twenty minutes ago," Z'Goyan answered.

"What have ye done fer treatment so far?" she pressed him as she leaned down toward the queen regent.

"We've applied a tourniquet to prevent its spread to the rest of the body. I also had some antivenom powder which I applied directly to the site. It seemed to slow the spread but not stop it completely," the shaman said.

"And it be from a snake bite, right?"

"Not exactly. It was from some sort of weird parasitic attachment that a traitor had grafted onto his body," Z'Goyan explained.

"Is that 'attachment' thing still around?" Brunhilda asked.

Wanting to help however he could, Kiru ran over to the strange three-headed husk that had been removed from the enemy earlier and brought it back to Brunhilda.

She carefully took it with a gauntleted hand and picked up a piece of random orc flesh about three inches long from the ground nearby. The paladin then squeezed the husk right over the flesh. The dried remains started to crack and crumble, causing flakes to fall on the flesh. One other thing came from her squeezing it: a single drop of venom dripped off a fang. The droplet landed, and the chunk of flesh immediately started to blacken and sizzle. A small trail of smoke rose up from the spot.

Brunhilda wafted the smoke to her nostrils, then immediately grimaced and recoiled. "Ugh, that burns," she said, then looked back at the quickly blackening test sample. "My nose not be as good as yers, Mutt, but I can tell there be traces of both venom and acid. The flesh be degrading here due to equal parts necrosis and burnin'." She then looked to Z'Goyan. "Aside from yer healing technique, the tourniquet and medicated powder both be good ideas. If what ye say about what the venom did to others is true, it may be the only reason she's alive."

The shaman bowed in thanks at the compliment.

Brunhilda then moved back over to kneel over Myev's body directly. The powerful Emerald orc cultivator's eyes were closed, she was breathing shallow breaths, and a faint odor of decay came off her body that even Kiru could smell.

"The venom's been partially suppressed, but it still be rampaging through her arm because the powerful acidic component hasn't been gotten under control," she said before clapping and then rubbing her hands together. "Okay, this be our best shot." She then pressed her hands down hard on both sides of the wound. The queen winced, and some of her blackened skin even sloughed off from the pressure. Kiru winced at the sight, but the paladin was undeterred.

"Healing Hands." Light poured out from Brunhilda as she used her most powerful healing technique. Kiru was surprised at just how powerful it had become after she had ascended to Ruby. Everyone who saw the light winced in reaction to it. Brunhilda gritted her teeth as she focused her mana on the injury.

A voice echoed inside Brunhilda's mind loud enough that Kiru was able to hear it too. "*Verily, I've embraced our pantheon's alliance with the Beast Gods, yet I cannot salvage this one, mine noble paladin. Should her deities not deign to mend her directly from an ailment wrought by one of their traitorous gods, I shall not meddle in the affairs of their servitors, as such as this.*" It was the voice of Hlin. Kiru noticed just how much kinder she sounded when speaking to Brunhilda than to him. The goddess indeed played favorites. It seemed benevolence was not one of Hlin's tenets.

"Damn," Brunhilda muttered as she dismissed Healing Hands. "I'm sorry, Mutt. I can't heal this."

The blind orc's lip quivered, then he turned to Myev. "Sis, I'm sorry."

The black necrosis from the venom was now traveling just past the elbow. "Remember what you told me, when I teased you when we were kids, saying you couldn't get stronger than me?"

Mutt gave a slight grin. "I said, it's just eyes. I don't need them to get strong."

"Yes, and it's the same here, Brother. It's just an arm," she told him, her eyelids heavy and twitching. "Now, let's do it."

Tears ran down the blind orc's cheeks, but he nodded. He tightened the tourniquet even more.

Myev bared her large teeth in pain but didn't say anything.

Mutt then gestured for Kiru to come over. The orc used a clawed finger to just gently draw a line of blood and barely part the muscle on Myev's bicep around her entire arm. "My claws would be too slow and messy for a clean cut. Will you—"

"Of course," Kiru answered the unfinished question. He was pretty sure that the orc *could* cut the arm but just couldn't bear the idea of it. The psion didn't blame Mutt at all if that was the case. Kiru was happy to help. He drew out his Psyslime blade, changing its form to that of a straight double-edged sword, the same kind Kiru's mother used. He placed the blade right on the small line of blood Mutt had made, then pulled it back for a swing. He looked at Myev. "I'm going to count to three. One," With a swoosh, he swung his blade downward. With the limb weakened significantly, the flesh and muscle already cut into by Mutt's claw, and Myev caught by surprise, the Psyslime blade cut through the appendage in one swift motion.

To her credit, Myev only grunted slightly as her arm plopped to the ground.

Brunhilda immediately ran up to the bleeding stump, pressed her gauntlet into it, and used Healing Hands once more. As this wound wasn't due to a Beast God cult's venom, the technique cauterized the wound and brought a fresh layer of green skin over it.

Myev's face visibly eased, and she sighed in relief. Everyone else took a collective breath as well. The assassination and coup had been thwarted, and, for the moment, the queen regent was safe.

CHAPTER TWENTY-ONE

Race for a Cure

With the cultists routed out and the palace secure, Myev ordered her remaining forces to scour the rest of Dissé to ensure that all traces of the Jormun threat were gone. While that was happening, the party informed her of their journey into the Wastelands. They let her know of the L'Khans' infighting, the Exile, and the Jormuns' influence. Mutt was happy to tell his sister of their success in getting the L'Khans to support her claim to rule.

Myev put her one remaining hand to her chest and breathed easier. Still, she couldn't relax completely. "Good, Brother. That's one less thing to deal with."

"What's left, Sis? We have all the things required now. We've got the backing of three tribe leaders, that snake-armed guy's head should be part of a worthy kill, you're an Emerald-rank, and you have an Emerald-rank core. So, we're goo—"

"The shaman's venom," Myev interrupted. "Your paladin friend and the psion helped to remove . . . most of it, but it has still . . . entered . . . my bloodstream, I'm afraid." She paused to take a few heavy breaths. Though she was breathing much easier than before, it was clear her body was still under notable distress. "I won't be . . . able . . . to fully . . . recover in ti—" She trailed off as she fell into unconsciousness.

"Sis? Sis?!" Mutt shouted as he rushed over to her. "What's wrong with her?" he asked Brunhilda.

"The venom," Z'Goyan answered in her stead. "As I said before, Prince M'Toon, we'll be lucky if she recovers in a few months. Her body needs time to repair the damage done. If that traitorous shaman truly held venom inspired by Jormungandr, few things are more deadly than that. We are fortunate that the queen regent is even alive."

Mutt pursed his face in frustration. "How is it that they were even allowed to do this, huh? I thought that only she was at risk, not a full-on assault of the capital."

The shaman bowed his head slightly. "The rules state that any contenders for the throne cannot be involved in killing another contender's clan unless in defense or if attacking the other challenger directly. I suspect that S'Vol played no direct part in this, but I will consult with the Beast Gods to be sure, Prince M'Toon."

Kiru knew the shaman was right. He supposed that Mutt had just forgotten about the details. Though, they really weren't the most straightforward of rules.

"Whatever," Mutt said dismissively before turning to face Brunhilda, his blind, milky eyes directed just past her shoulder. "Is there anything else you can do?"

She opened her mouth to speak before closing it again. After a few more seconds, she shrugged. "I'm sorry, Mutt. There be . . . nothing else."

"No," he whispered in despair, pressing his head to Myev's.

"Not to sound insensitive, but have the orcs of Imakandi not experienced venom like this before?" Zhaden asked. "Back at the academy, Professor Zerkoff said during our Strategies I course, 'If you use any type of poison, make sure you know the antidote.'"

Kiru nodded his head. He had that very same course back at the academy.

Z'Goyan shook his head. "We shamans have a story that once there was a cultivator who could remove the World Serpent's venom centuries ago, but it's never been proven. If it is true, then it has been lost to time, or hidden in the records of our people inside our main temple," he said. His voice sounded both bitter and sad. "Still, we *do* know that only those of Ruby and above can survive the venom, but only with rest and aid," Z'Goyan added, seeming to be trying to find some sort of silver lining.

"That isn't good enough," Mutt muttered.

"I'm sorry, Prince M'Toon. I know of nothing else to do. The queen should be—"

"No! It is unacceptable! You swore loyalty to the M'Baku. Myev is your queen, yes?" Mutt asked, interrupting the shaman.

"Yes. Of course!" Z'Goyan answered in surprise, not sure where the blind prince was going with this.

"We don't have months! We have just over two weeks to get her better and get her to where she needs to be tested. If we don't, the Jormuns win. Your leader will be S'Vol, and I'm not letting that happen," he barked at the Tau before turning to Kiru. "Boss, I know you're really smart. Like, the smartest out of all of us. You still like to read?"

"I mean, I have a good memory. And yeah, I like to read." He shrugged, not wanting to reveal to the shaman that he had a perfect memory.

"Pfft! That's bullshit, Master! With my help, you're smarter than any of these peons! Together, we conquered the library at the academy," William pronounced proudly inside Kiru's core.

"Good, then it's settled. Z'Goyan, you'll take Boss here." He pointed at Kiru. "And bring him to the main temple." Mutt shifted his focus to Kiru. "Boss, if you're okay with it, I'll need you to use that big brain of yours to scan through all the documents you can to see if you can find any record of a cure."

"But, my prince, not only is he an outsider, he openly follows a deity from another pantheon. His headband has the same symbol as the paladin."

"The same symbol as the paladin who saved our queen's life. As for it being of a different pantheon, I don't give a shit. Our gods require that we be strong to lead. Now, I didn't pay much attention to our lessons growing up, but I do remember that we M'Baku follow Fenrir as our patron, and the Great Wolf said, 'The strength of the pack is the wolf, and the strength of the wolf is the pack.'" He pointed to his unconscious sister. "Our alpha is in need, and that man is our ally."

Mutt lifted his sister over one shoulder and pointed a sharp-nailed finger at the shaman, pressing it in slightly to draw a drop of blood. "As an ally, he is part of our alpha's pack. He is no enemy. You will help him save our queen. Got it?"

Z'Goyan's jaw tensed, as he dealt with his conflicting values. He glanced at Mutt, Myev, then Kiru multiple times before he made a decision. "You're right, my prince. Apologies. I will take him there at once." The Tau orc bowed before leaving. Kiru nodded to Mutt before following behind. Nom stayed with Kiru's friends back at the palace.

Then, they made their way back to the religious district. The main temple still stood despite suffering damage, such as a major hole in one wall where one of the twenty-foot-tall rib bones that served as support beams had been torn off.

The shamans that had been held up inside fighting against the Jormuns before were now outside, examining the extent of the damage to their temple. Many of them were sporting various injuries, many of their wounds bandaged and some rather grievous ones proudly displayed by some for all to see, like badges of honor. Kiru saw one of the shamans walking around shirtless, his right ear missing and multiple spear stab wounds on his torso. To the shaman's credit, many already appeared to be clotting and scabbing, though they would leave some large scars. *The Beast Gods must give their followers an increased healing factor,* he thought.

Some of the shamans were conversing—thankfully good-naturedly—with the members of the temple opposite them. It seemed that risking their lives to save the shamans bought some good grace, despite their following different deities. Many of the shamans looked quizzically at Kiru but, noticing one of their highest-ranked shamans leading him, they didn't ask questions. Kiru was glad he didn't have to explain.

Z'Goyan led the psion into their damaged temple. Unlike the rectangular-shaped stone temple he'd visited earlier, the massive hide tent was round. It was also poorly lit, only illuminated inside by a half dozen torches, other than the large rent torn into its side, letting in some sunlight. An assortment of various furs were arranged in a circle, some stained with fresh blood and gore from the Jormuns' attack. There were multiple other splotches of blood and bodily fluids staining the ground.

The pelts making up the walls had stitchwork sewn in them displaying the visages of various beasts. The one that Kiru presumed to be Fenrir had wolf fur patched onto the wall, as well as both teeth and claws sewn into the painting, giving it a more realistic appearance.

The most menacing thing inside this temple was the altar directly opposite the entrance. It was simple and made of stone but adorned by some monstrous feat of taxidermy made up of the body parts of various animals sewn together. It had the head of a wolf, but its lower jaw was that of a boar with various curved tusks. It had goat horns on its head, with a mohawk trailing down to a long tail made of dark blue rooster feathers. A pair of large raven wings were spread out on its back, one black and the other white.

Its rib cage was made up of various bones spread open wide, each of which ended at the top edge on each side of the rectangular altar. Under this chimera but still on the stone altar were various candles, hearts, body parts, and a bowl filled with thick red coagulated blood. Flanking each side of the altar and attached to it were three sets of skeletal horse legs, no doubt in honor of the Beast God that the Tau worshiped.

Z'Goyan turned to Kiru and gave him a serious look. "If you are truly an ally as the prince says, then you must swear to not divulge this information to our enemies."

"Of course! I swear," Kiru said.

He shook his head. "No," he said, then pulled out a serrated dagger made out of carved bone. "We swear in blood and in our gods' names." Before Kiru could stop the shaman, he cut his forearm. "By Sleipnir's name, I will help you. In so doing, you will help our people and Sleipnir in turn. If you turn into an enemy of the pantheon, may Sleipnir strike you down," he said as the blood trailed down his arm and over his hand. Z'Goyan then placed the dagger in Kiru's hand.

Kiru took a deep breath, then cut his own palm. He didn't want to expose his bony forearm and provoke any questions about his powers. Kiru wasn't sure exactly what to say, so he went with something similar to what Z'Goyan promised. "By Hlin's name, I will help you. In so doing, you will help me and Hlin in turn. If you turn into an enemy of my goddess and me, may Hlin strike you down." As they clasped hands, their cores and their gods witnessed their oaths and bound them to their words. Kiru felt some strange tether form between Z'Goyan and him. He understood that their oaths were both real and had real consequences.

The shaman nodded, then pulled out a container filled with a yellow powder and applied it to his palm before handing the container to the psion. "This will stop the bleeding."

Nodding gratefully, Kiru took the powder and poured it on his wound. Within seconds, the wound stopped bleeding and the blood coagulated. This powder was seriously impressive, even better than what the academy had to his recollection, and his recollection was perfect.

Z'Goyan nodded at Kiru. "Impressive. Most who use the powder for the first time have a much stronger reaction to its sting."

"Oh . . . I didn't feel a thing," Kiru admitted, not willing to explain *why* that was the case.

Fortunately, the shaman didn't ask for any further elaboration. He then led the psion right behind the monstrous bestial altar, revealing a wooden door on the ground. Z'Goyan opened the door, revealing a ladder and descended down it. The orc took a couple steps, then seemed to remember something, "Oh, if you start to feel anything weird, any strange urges, let me know immediately."

"Urges?" Kiru asked.

"You'll know," the shaman answered cryptically before going down and out of sight.

Kiru sighed before following. Reaching the bottom of the ladder, he found himself in a large underground chamber, only able to tell the room's dimensions thanks to his Darkvision. No torch or magical light illuminated what Kiru presumed to be the shamans' quarters, due to the various sleeping furs, piles of goods, and preserved foods scattered about.

Kiru felt another sensation—something he'd experienced recently. It was just like when they had gone into Heidrun's cave, just not as concentrated. It was beast mana. The underground bunker where the shamans stayed was full of it. The psion instantly realized this was what Z'Goyan had been warning him about.

Kiru let out an involuntary growl. Still, he was able to push off the mana's influence. There were so many different versions of beast mana competing with each other in the air that none of them outweighed any of the others in effect. Plus, after experiencing such strong and concentrated beast mana from Heidrun's influence, Kiru had somehow gotten better at resisting it.

"I see what you were warning me about," Kiru said, his tone low in the dark area. "It was a lot at first, but I already have a handle on it."

"I'm surprised. Most who do not cultivate beast mana themselves go feral for a time after being exposed to so much of the mana here. How is it that you are able to resist it almost instantly?"

Kiru trusted the Tau only due to Myev's insistence, but he was now completely out of his element. Though he couldn't see anyone, that didn't mean others weren't watching or listening in. After all of the treachery he had witnessed so far in the orcs' homeland and having been nearly assassinated last night, Kiru felt being more cautious was wise, so he decided to keep his explanation vague. "Traveling with

Mutt has afforded me the opportunity to experience some powerful beast mana. It wasn't intentional training, but it did help."

"Clearly so," Z'Goyan replied, then motioned for Kiru to continue following. "This isn't our final destination." The shaman brought him to what looked to be a closet. A warm light was glowing from under the door. When the orc opened it, it revealed a small room ornately painted with portraits of the Beast Gods: a wolf, twin goats, a pair of ravens, a muscular boar, another boar eating a dead antelope whole, an eight-legged horse, and a large blue rooster. Six brightly shining orbs of light were set in the walls, providing strong illumination. An altar, like the one Kiru had seen above, sat in the center of the room. This one was smaller, however, with an assorted pile of bones with various organs and petrified remains set before it.

Z'Goyan pressed a hand on the side of the altar. There was an audible click and a part of the stone wall shifted, revealing another door with more stairs leading down.

"A secret passage within a secret passage? What are they hiding?" William mused.

"My thoughts exactly," Kiru sent back. Whatever information Kiru would be getting access to was clearly a closely guarded secret either way. The shaman led Kiru through this final door, and the psion gasped as he began to behold the true grandeur of Imakandi's recorded history. It was a massive library within a gigantic cave, much like the one in which Pandemonium had met Heidrun. Whereas the insectoid Beast God's lair was full of tunnel holes throughout, this large cave was completely covered in carved pictures, script, and various paintings.

Kiru and the orc were standing on a platform at the very top of this underground cave. The entire cavern went downward as if it was one giant well. It was one elaborate tapestry depicting the recorded history of both the Beast Gods and the people of Imakandi. Every visible inch of stone wall was intricately carved and painted. It was unlike anything Kiru had ever seen, but when he thought about how wood, and therefore paper, was a rarer commodity within the orc homeland, it made sense that they would have to use alternate means for a majority of their records.

The stone platform descended, becoming a spiraling staircase along the cave walls that went so far down, Kiru couldn't even see the bottom. The air was also musty, evident of its lack of regular airflow. "This—" Z'Goyan gestured to the cave. "—is the entire recorded history of our country, along with that of our gods since the time of Ragnarok. The further down you go, the more recent the events. I will help you when I can, but I must help my fellow shamans and ensure that no more cultists are present within our ranks. The events of today have proven that necessity." The shaman then lit a nearby torch and handed it to the young psion.

Kiru gave the orc his thanks, then began descending the staircase, lighting all of the ensconced torches he found along his way. Going down the cave, Kiru was reminded of Dissé's infrastructure too. It was clear that the orcs liked to build in a spiral pattern. It took him about twenty minutes, but the psion eventually made it to the bottom of the library. After he lit the final torch, he looked up to take in the true beauty of this sacred room.

With the light illuminating the entirety of the space, Kiru was able to take in the fine, detailed craftsmanship of the ornate pictures and carvings. It was beautiful. No degradation was visible at all, and Kiru couldn't find a single flaw anywhere. Vibrant hues of green and brown were the two most prominent colors, but there were also lots of reds and blues.

Kiru assumed the place must have been one of the most ornate pieces of architecture on the entire continent. When he was back at the academy, he'd read about a famous pre-Ragnarok painter who had gained fame by painting the ceiling of a chapel. To the psion, this rivaled that concept. Kiru was also stunned that such a place existed where it was. First, it was in Imakandi. The orc country was known for its sacred beasts and savage bestial cultivators, not art nor craftsmanship. Most of the structures Kiru had seen in Imakandi so far were tents or crude stone buildings made with irregularly shaped blocks. The only exceptions were the wooden royal palace and the temple to the gods of Valhalla, the latter technically not counting as Imakandi architecture.

Also, the simple fact that it was located under the capital temple to the Beast Gods was surprising. The shamans appeared to revel in the simplistic, savage nature of being animalistic. The hide temple above was a testament to that. This cave demonstrated a level of refinement that seemed almost an anathema to the shaman's values.

Despite the differences in artistic approach, Kiru quickly gathered a unifying theme: loyalty and faithfulness to the Beast Gods. Pictures and Orcish words about the ascended sacred beasts were spread throughout the various levels of the cave. It made sense to Kiru that the shamans would show such care and reverence to the recorded history of their gods and people. So, it wasn't a stretch that they would invest much time and care into this place. As he descended lower and lower, the carvings became noticeably newer, as he'd been prepared for. Kiru presumed that the cave was not entirely natural. He assumed the orcs must carve out deeper and deeper as their people's history continued. *Maybe some of the rocks dug out of here were even used to help build Dissé homes?* he thought.

Kiru then began his crash course in the history of both Imakandi and the Beast Gods. A voice whined in his head: *"Oh, shit! We're gonna have to read a lot, aren't we?"*

Kiru popped some of the vertebrate in his neck to stretch. "Yep, but look on the bright side. There are a lot of pictures, and I bet they'll show a lot of bloodshed."

William seemed a little more appeased but still pouted. *"Mph, they'd better."*

CHAPTER TWENTY-TWO

Secret Remedy

U*gh! This is so boring!*" William lamented for the ninety-third time, according to Kiru's perfect memory.

"Really, William?" Kiru asked aloud in irritation. "There have been *a lot* of battles and a lot of descriptions of hunting too. There was also that scene with the horse covered in blood, remember? So, you shouldn't be complaining *again*."

"*Not enough blood*," the imp grumbled.

"Are you kidding?!" Kiru shouted, his anger spilling out. He had spent the past week and a half in the massive underground cave, carefully reading and examining the recorded history of the Beast Gods and their followers. He had first started at the bottom of the cave, which detailed the most recent events of the orc nation's history, specifically, the death of Mutt's father. Some of the paint there was even still moist. Quickly realizing that starting from the beginning would probably be the wiser choice in terms of the information he was looking for since the shaman said it was ages ago, Kiru went back up to the entrance.

Once there, he started reading this history from the beginning, starting at Ragnarok. A good half of it detailed the harsh realities of the apocalyptic event that led to the forming of Alterra. William loved the gore, while Kiru found it unpleasant. Amidst all the history, however, he still hadn't found an account of one who could counteract Jormungandr's venom.

The carved writing was written in a mix of Beast Speak and Orcish. Kiru was grateful that he'd learned the languages, but even with Z'Goyan's occasional aid and his perfect recall, the pictures and texts were quite complex, and the writing wasn't always written in a straight line as he was used to. He was progressing through the information faster than almost anyone aside from the most learned scholars, but he estimated he still had at least half a week left before he made it through it all.

He even spent most nights with the shamans to save time on his commute. Half the time he would otherwise usually have been sleeping, he used to cultivate mental mana. That replenished his stores to help him move, though it could get a bit wild in the shaman quarters. The orcs sometimes even sleepwalked, which meant they crawled around on all fours and growled like animals.

Over time, the effects of the beast mana made itself more known to the psion as well. More than once, he let out subtle growls himself. All the hair on his body had grown thicker and longer. Once, he had even gotten into a fight with a shaman over a scrap of food like a pair of hungry dogs.

The good news was that Kiru didn't need much sleep, being not only a psion but a half-elf. Still, even with that benefit, he was losing sleep. That plus the savage beast mana plus very little exposure to sunlight down there was making him very grumpy. He didn't have any visitors either, except for Mutt as he was the only one of his friends who the shamans would allow into their temple. They only had seven days left to get Myev better and off to the testing grounds. They were quickly running out of time.

"What're you getting mad at me for, Master?" William asked indignantly.

"Because you have quite literally complained almost one hundred times since we've been down here. It can be . . . grating." he answered with gritted teeth.

"C'mon, it can't be that many . . . Oh, wait. It is that many. My bad."

Kiru closed his eyes and took a deep breath through his nostrils. "It's okay, William. It has been frustrating." He sat down on the stone platform and looked up to the entrance. Fortunately, no shaman was up there. Despite his good relations with the M'Baku Clan and Z'Goyan's approval, some of the shamans would do periodic "check-ins" on Kiru. In truth, they were wary of a foreigner reading their sacred history and wanted to make sure he didn't degrade it somehow. Seeing that there was no shaman monitoring him currently, Kiru pulled out a piece of fruit for his lunch. Technically, he wasn't allowed to bring food down here, but it was a long walk to get back up, and sometimes, he just needed a quick snack.

He bit down on the small green pear with a satisfying crunch, its juices running down his chin. He thought about his situation. He hadn't found the desired information, but it hadn't been entirely for nothing. He'd learned about the history of Imakandi, the monsters and beasts that call it home, the founding tribes, their battles, and even about the Beast Gods. Kiru would bet that, aside from the shamans, he knew more about Imakandi's history and pantheon than any other person in the Alliance. He had also learned a lot about beast mana cultivation, including a rare method to help those cultivators ascend. *Given time and the right materials, namely Sapphire beast cores, I could help Mutt get to Sapphire,* he thought. *It doesn't bring up anything about Ruby's second tier, however. That's annoying.*

Feeling a little better at that, Kiru decided to skip through some of the texts, focusing only on the pictures of Jormungandr. He still had another pear if he got hungry. Hopefully, this would help save time. There was no guarantee it would have information, but it wasn't a bad idea, especially since time was against him.

He spent the next couple of hours scouring the massive cave for pictures of the World Serpent. He did learn a lot about Jormungandr. He was supposedly so big that he wrapped around the world, hence the title. Secondly, he wasn't on the continent. He had previously lived in the ocean. When the World Serpent was imprisoned, he was forcefully shrunk down, his wings ripped off of him (*Ouch!* Kiru thought when he saw the image) before he was bound in chains and imprisoned in the Savage Realm.

As he was going through and absorbing the information, Kiru thought about his mentor, the librarian Niajar J'sarko. The elf was an eccentric fellow who clearly had his own secrets and liked to gamble. Still, he was a steadfast mentor and ally to Kiru. The enigmatic librarian never said it outright, but he appeared to have been training Kiru to become his successor, and he was obsessed with the collection and preservation of knowledge. Kiru smiled, thinking about how utterly fascinated Niajar would be if he were here and how jealous he would have been if he'd learned that Kiru had access to all this hidden knowledge.

The last time Kiru had seen the elf was during the Warrior Games. Niajar was sitting in the stands, promoted to headmaster. *Likely another wager he'd made,* Kiru thought. His smile faded as he thought about how he'd handled their relationship. After all the support, Kiru had never told Niajar the truth about who and what he was. The wily elf was the closest thing he'd had to an actual father, and Kiru still kept him at a distance. Part of him regretted that. *Was it that I wanted him to not get involved? Was I just trying to keep both of us safe? Or did I just not know how to trust someone completely as a mentor besides Mom?*

Kiru shook his head out of his melancholic introspection. He resolved that when he saw the librarian again, he would tell him the truth. *That is, if he's still alive. No! Stop it!* He chastised himself. Niajar's brother had committed atrocities back at the academy, and Kiru didn't know if that meant doom for Niajar. He didn't want to think like that, though. Nothing good would come from dwelling on the negative. Besides, Niajar was a crafty one. Kiru would wager that that old gambler had countless protocols to deal with possible dangers and threats. Feeling better about that, he refocused on the wall of pictures and text before him.

Despite the fascinating information he was learning, Kiru had still not found his intended target. The young psion flared his nostrils. If they didn't get Myev to recover soon, the leadership of Imakandi would fall to another tribe, likely the Jormuns, and his chance of acquiring his father's second item would be gone!

He looked at the carving of the World Serpent being forced into a large hole by hooded shamans. Each shaman had what looked to be a spirit of one of the Beast Gods floating above them. Jormungandr fought defiantly, biting an orc in half, the dying shaman's body carved in explicit detail, the serpent's venom appearing to be melting his body. This picture angered Kiru. It seemed to goad him, mocking him with the very venom he was trying to cure.

"Gah!" Kiru shouted as he pulled out his second pear and threw it at the image in frustration. "Tell me the cure, you dumb snake!" he shouted at the carving.

"Um, Master. You know it's just a picture, right?"

Kiru snarled like a wild cat, "Shut up, William!" he shouted at his familiar.

"Is everything okay down there?" Z'Goyan asked, looking down from the top of the cave.

Noticing the pieces of fruit and juice running down the sacred text, Kiru's heart raced. "Oh, shit," he murmured before turning around and moving to make sure he was blocking the shaman's line of sight. "Sorry, just frustrated. I haven't found the information I'm looking for, and my familiar is inside my core, complaining as usual."

"Hey!" The imp said, offended.

"Not now." Kiru sent back, pointedly deciding to be more cautious about when he would speak aloud to his familiar.

Z'Goyan gave a gruff nod, then raised his head. The shaman's nostrils flared and sniffed loudly. "What is that smell? It's . . . fragrant."

The psion's heart raced. "I . . . really liked those pears up at the palace. I must've eaten about ten of them. You're probably smelling the juice that spilled on my clothes," he lied.

The orc scratched his chin, "Yes, I do smell fruit. You should be more careful about eating before coming into this chamber. We don't want any juice on your hands or clothes to contaminate our sacred history."

"Haha, of course," he chuckled nervously.

The orc nodded, then left via the secret entrance.

Once Kiru was sure he was gone, he quickly turned back to the carved picture of Jormungandr. Fortunately, he had a spare shirt in his bag of clothing, and he began frantically padding the picture dry and removing all the pieces of pear embedded in the crevices and carved words. Kiru grimaced when he'd finished. It was passable. Admittedly, his attempts to wipe the juice away did cause part of the snake's ornately painted scales to smear on most of its upper half, but hopefully no one would notice. A battle for another day.

Kiru continued, gently, until he was pretty sure he'd finished. On his last look, though, he noticed he missed a spot. A piece of pear was embedded in the snake's eye. "Shit," he spat.

"Master, you know that wasn't okay to blame me, right?"

Kiru sighed. "I know, William. I'm sorry. I panicked," he answered out loud.

"Hmph, no need to take your frustrations out on me. I was just trying to help," the imp said, impetuously. Kiru could imagine him crossing his arms and looking away from him.

"You're right, William. It was my bad. How about after we deal with all this, I see about getting you another vial of tea-quila?"

"Really? Fuck, yes!"

Kiru smiled, glad to have resolved the issue with the imp, then went to get the piece of pear out of the snake's eye. It was *really* jammed in there. As the psion reached in to pull the fruit out, the pressure from his finger actually forced the eye further into the wall. It was a complete accident, but thankfully, Kiru hadn't damaged it. No, that eye was a secret button, because before Kiru fully realized what he'd done, there was an audible *click*.

A block of stone under the Jormungandr carving popped out slightly, a small cloud of dust shooting out from it to cover Kiru's boots. Kiru's eyes widened in surprise as he comprehended what he saw. "A secret drawer," he whispered in awe. He curled his finger and finally removed the pesky piece of fruit from the carving. The psion then knelt and carefully pulled open the stone drawer. Inside was a book, an old leather-bound tome that had clearly seen better days, the corners bent and frayed and a thick layer of dust covering it. Still, it was in adequate shape to be handled.

Kiru carefully removed the tome from the drawer and blew the dust off of it. He then ran his hands over the cover. Though he couldn't directly "feel" it, his eyes noticed the leather was a familiar texture and pattern. His perfect recall helped him recognize that the leather was indeed snakeskin.

A title was carved into the cover in Beast Speak: *"Jormungandr's Imprisonment,"* Kiru translated. Due to the secretive nature of this book and the fact that the other shamans didn't tell him about it, Kiru bet that the orcs who worshipped the World Serpent had made this. He assumed they had hidden it when Jormungandr was still officially a god of their pantheon.

"Knowledge of the book's location must've been lost over time, because the traitorous weakling shaman with the weird snake arm didn't have this or any other information on the imprisoned deity on him," William surmised.

"Probably so," Kiru agreed.

He gently opened the aged tome and began frantically reading the contents inside. Sure enough, it detailed the Beast God's imprisonment. There was a lot of minutiae about strategies and positionings, but it also brought to light *when* that happened. While various accounts and stories from orc historians and shamans varied as to exactly when the Beast Gods had to leave for their own realm, they all agreed it was less than two millennia ago. This document claimed that the exact moment was only a year after the Draconic Campaign. Apparently, the World Serpent was more friendly toward his reptilian brethren and had his followers aid the drakonids that invaded the continent instead of fending them off. The other Beast Gods engaged in some minor skirmishes to force Jormungandr to join them in a new realm—the Savage Realm—with only Heidrun ever getting any serious wounds. The World Serpent's alignment with Nidhogg and the dragons was the final straw and forced his fellow gods to act more aggressively.

The Beast Gods, except Heidrun who was dealing with his corruption from his gluttony by mutating his form and damaging his cultivation, had left to inhabit their new home, the Savage Realm. Once there, they each gathered power and channeled it through either a loyal orc or leokin. Somehow, by anchoring their power to their new realm, they were able to use their servants as avatars of their will and bind the World Serpent. Despite Jormungandr's utter enormity and strength, he was unsuccessful in resisting the binds that had caught him, and he was eventually pulled into and imprisoned within the Savage Realm with his brethren.

His prison, locked by a magical seal, was secretly located somewhere in Imakandi, keeping Jormungandr isolated, away from his followers. Naturally, the orc shamans who followed the World Serpent staged a revolution. They used deception, a slew of poisons, and a venom technique inspired by the World Serpent to kill many opponents in a flash.

Despite their natural healing abilities, the shamans and citizens of Imakandi who follow the Beast Gods were severely hampered by their rapid decrease in numbers, not only due to having fewer numbers but due to mourning their dead as well.

Then, an outsider, who wasn't even a beast mana cultivator, turned the tide. He was an emissary, a knight of a small, newly formed kingdom who led the resistance against the drakonids and had now come on a diplomatic mission to Imakandi. A stern man, he had a strange set of powers that he refused to discuss. According to the tome, he was rumored to have been able to communicate with others' minds, such as forcing his opponents to drop their weapons without moving a muscle. He also had the remarkable ability to fly without wings. The most miraculous thing, though, was that he was able to cure people from the effects of any venom. From what Kiru could gather, the Jormuns who wrote this book were particularly infuriated by that.

Kiru's mind started pulling together the information. Making others drop their weapons and even flying without wings wasn't particularly specific to just one type of cultivator. If one was a high-enough-ranked cultivator, their aura could be intimidating enough to make opponents drop their weapons in fear. As for flying, Kiru remembered that Victor Constantine, the petty noble who ruled over the town of Bristelton where Kiru grew up, cultivated some kind of air mana that allowed him to fly—something that Kiru had personally witnessed.

The one unusual element, however, was his potential ability to communicate with others' minds. From his studies back at the Royal Academy and conversing with his friends, Kiru had learned of no technique that allowed for speaking directly into another's mind. Extensive research had gone into crafting an item with such an effect, but there was no official record of a successful prototype, so there was only one thing that the "mind-speaking" could have been referring to. Kiru gasped in realization. It was *Telepathy*—more specifically, the Telepathy mental mana technique. That meant that the wayward cultivator knight was a psion, and the rumored cure was not only indeed real, it was apparently carried out by that same psion, a cultivator just like him!

From recorded accounts, the knight would consume just a drop of the venom. Then, he appeared to be able to draw the venom out of a person's body. His own body would shake intensely throughout the process and then he'd promptly vomit. Kiru grimaced. It appeared that this wouldn't be a pleasant experience if he was able to figure it out. Still, he knew he'd found what he'd been looking for.

Excited, Kiru ran up the stairs in haste and grabbed Z'Goyan. "I found the cure!" he exclaimed as he all but shoved the book into the orc's face.

The shaman's jaw went slack at reading the psion's discovery. In order to cover the truth about his own powers, Kiru described the emissary as an "ancestor" of his.

"Do you have any of the venom stored up?" Kiru asked.

"Well, yes. We collected some vials after the attack in case we needed it," Z'Goyan answered.

"We definitely need it now," Kiru said.

"Are you sure about this? How can you be certain this was your ancestor? There's no mention of the human's name," the shaman asked.

"My ancestor was a decorated warrior during the founding of our kingdom's history. Trust me, this is the cure we've been looking for. Plus, if it doesn't work, Myev won't be hurt. It'll just be me," Kiru retorted, trying to convince the orc. "Besides, it's venom, not poison. So, it shouldn't be an issue if I consume it." Kiru had transcribed a book regarding the fauna within the Kingdom of Blades during his internship. From it, he learned that poison and venom were not the same thing, though people often used the words interchangeably. Poison needed to be ingested while venom needed to get into the bloodstream.

That seemed to assuage the orc's concerns. "You are correct. The queen regent shouldn't be harmed by you drinking the venom, but you are wrong about consuming it. Jormungandr's venom is both a poison *and* a venom with acidic properties. Few things are more deadly than it."

Kiru bunched his lips, "Great . . ." he trailed off. *I didn't count on that,* he thought. Kiru was worried. He would be risking his life to help Myev based on extrapolation, but he still knew it was their best chance. He wouldn't go back on his word and abandon his friend's sister and country. He had to try.

"Do you still wish to try this ancient cure? Better yet, do you even know *how* to do it? There are no specific instructions, and you could kill yourself. You are just a Gold, after all," Z'Goyan countered.

The psion sighed. His previous rush of excitement at finding this rumored cure had overridden just how grave the risk was if his assumptions were wrong.

What if he had come this far only to accidentally kill himself by intentionally drinking poison?

"Master, do not fear. You are Kiru the Conqueror. You mustn't doubt yourself. I believe you're right about this cure. Now, buck up, and kick this venom's ass! Better yet, do it even faster than that other psion. They weren't king. You are!" William said encouragingly.

Kiru smiled. *"Thanks, William. I needed that."*

"Of course! That's what I'm here for! Whenever you're acting like a hesitant little bitch, I'll always be here to set you straight!"

The psion let out a low chuckle at the crude little demon.

"I assure you this is no laughing matter, boy," Z'Goyan said, the shaman not hearing the telepathic conversation and thus assuming Kiru was laughing at his words.

"No. No, it's not. I'm sorry. I was just . . . deep in thought," Kiru replied. There was a pause and then he looked the orc directly in the eyes with firm resolution. "I can do it, and we have no other option. Get me a vial of the venom."

Half an hour later, the psion was back in the royal palace. He and his friends were standing in Myev's chambers. The queen was in a deep but troubled sleep in her fur-laden bed, her unconscious body still fighting off the venom's lingering effects. Myev's skin wasn't as unhealthy a shade of green as it had been, but it was definitely still not good. Her body was also no longer covered in a cold sweat—just her head. Some of her hair was stuck against her forehead. Myev's body was clearly fighting off the venom's effects, but still much too slowly for Kiru's liking. Every ten seconds or so, she would give a subtle shiver as well. Her pet wolf lay against her body while her rooster lay nestled on top of her head, both creatures looking intently at their master.

Kiru greeted Brunhilda and Zhaden and then told them his plan.

"You sure about this, Boss? I mean, it's kinda crazy," Mutt said.

"I hafta agree with Mutt here, Kiru. Curing someone of poison by poisoning yourself don't make sense to me. Not unless ye were transferring the poison somehow, and I don't recommend that either," Brunhilda said.

"I have to concur with our friends here, Kiru. Even with your—" the gold drakonid glanced over at Z'Goyan, "—heritage. It is a significant risk."

Kiru nodded. "I know, but we don't have the time to wait. I promised I would help, and I will not be a man who abandons his allies in their time of need."

"That's not the kind of ruler I want to be. What good is getting strong enough to save an Alliance if there's nothing left to save?" He sent that last part via Telepathy so that no one else could overhear him.

"I have to do this," he said out loud again, looking at all of them intently.

His friends didn't respond, their concerned faces clear enough. William brought up that if Kiru's plan failed, the queen's campaign would be a lost cause, and they'd have to rush to get Ruken's item before the Jormuns were able to claim power. Kiru understood his familiar's logic, but he couldn't afford to think like that. Not now.

Despite his friends' worries, they all let him proceed. He stood by Myev's large piles of sleeping furs, vial of poison in hand. It was a yellow-green liquid that bubbled and sizzled at the slightest shake. Kiru could see the cork at the top of the vial degrading from just being in contact with the venom's vapors. Kiru pursed his lips. Even though he knew this was his best chance, it didn't mean he wasn't concerned. He suddenly thought about how the psion in the book was clearly at a much higher rank than him. His hand nervously shook at the thought, but he quickly dismissed it. Like it or not, he was going to do this.

"You ready, William?" Kiru asked telepathically.

"You bet your ass, I'm ready, 'cause after this I get more of that good liquor!" the imp proudly declared inside Kiru's mind.

Kiru, feeling at least a bit better that he was in this together with his familiar, took in a deep, calming breath. Before he could talk himself out of it, he uncorked the vial of poison and downed it in one gulp. He gagged and coughed, almost vomiting the harsh, malodorous substance back up instantly. Green acidic fumes escaped his mouth and nostrils as he coughed. He could practically hear his nose hairs sizzling from the fumes. Still, the venom continued down his throat, burning some of the flesh inside his esophagus as it descended.

Kiru fell to his knees, groaning and clutching both sides of his abdomen once the venom had reached there. Brunhilda put a hand on his shoulder, but he wouldn't let her heal him for fear that it would undo his attempts to help Myev. Then, after a few seconds, the pain miraculously dissipated. Kiru snapped his head up and looked around, taking in rapid breaths. A trail of drool fell off his lower lip, and he looked around in confusion as to what had happened. Before he could say anything, the pain returned, only this time, it hit his meridians. The pathways of mana in his arms, legs, torso, and head all hurt, feeling as if they were all full of the burning acid. Kiru still couldn't feel his musculoskeletal system due to his previous spinal trauma, but he could feel *this*!

The psion's entire body shook as he lost control of his Telekinesis. After a few seconds, his body went limp. Brunhilda reached down and kept Kiru from falling flat on his face. He looked over to the paladin and nodded his thanks, unable to speak at the moment. Brunhilda's lips moved, but Kiru couldn't tell what she was saying; all he could hear were distorted murmurs. He squinted his eyes, not understanding why he couldn't hear her before recoiling at William's words reverberating in his head.

"Master? Master, it's coming. Oh, damn! Ow! That stings! Shit!" William cried out inside his mind. Being inside his core, the familiar could feel the venom's sting directly.

Kiru shut his eyes, visualizing his mental mana core. Like a drop of dye falling into a bowl of water, a small droplet of the green-yellow venom had entered into his core. It hadn't fully corrupted his cultivated mental mana, but it was spreading, albeit slowly. Kiru's core began to pulse.

The psion snapped open his eyes as the urge to vomit rose up, his body wanting to expel the toxic substance from his system. Taking a few deep breaths through his nose, he forced back the bile and looked over at the unconscious queen, noticing something he hadn't before. Somehow, he could now *feel* her body pulsating, and that pulsing was in synch with his heartbeat and with his core. "It's working," he said, shaking. Kiru continued to look at Myev, but no further inspiration came.

There were some more distorted murmurs before he could hear his friends' voices again like a sudden *pop*.

"So, are you gonna heal her, Boss?" Mutt asked.

Kiru grimaced, "I-I don't know what to do now. I can somehow resonate with the poison inside her, but I'm unsure what to do next."

"Well, in me healer training, we're told to find the exact spot of the injury," Brunhilda said.

"She's been poisoned. Her whole body's been injured," Z'Goyan retorted angrily. The orc was clearly growing more frustrated and concerned at the lack of progress. "And what's wrong with his body? Why has he gone limp?"

"He's gone limp because he's swallowed poison to try and save yer sister," the paladin snapped. "Now, in regard to her whole body bein' injured, I obviously know that, Shaman," Brunhilda replied through gritted teeth. "But like an abscess, there may be a specific spot where the infection be at its worst. Where there be the most pus, ye could say," she said, then turned to look at her friend. "Kiru, can ye tell where the venom be most concentrated?"

Kiru, now covered in a cold sweat, focused harder on Myev. He squinted his eyes as he tried to pinpoint just where he felt the strongest pulse from within her body. After a few seconds of focusing, he found it. "Her chest," he said. "The center of her chest."

"Good! Good!" Brunhilda encouraged. "That be where her core is. Now, yer book said the man drew the venom from the victims' bodies?"

Kiru nodded.

"How?" she asked.

"It didn't say, exactly. Gr—" His body suddenly convulsed uncontrollably from the pain, but he managed to compose himself after a few steadying breaths. "He didn't touch them physically. It seemed as if he just willed it out, and the poison obeyed his commands."

Brunhilda gave a light chuckle. "That be all? It be simple then."

"*Master, ow! Hurry up!*" William pleaded.

Kiru was dumbstruck. "Simple!? Well, tell me, then!"

She smiled. "If ye can't make it move with normal means, then use a *different* way," she said, then raised his limp arm and dropped it.

His eyes widened in realization. "I knew we'd make a good team," he said, then turned his head to face the unconscious orc.

"Shaman, undo her vest so that there be nothing covering the center of her chest," Brunhilda said.

"And expose her? I do not see how this will—"

"I'm not asking ye to get her naked, ye idgit, I be a woman of modesty meself," Brunhilda interrupted Z'Goyan before his rant continued. "I'm just asking ye to undo her vest to expose her sternum. Fer this, removing any barrier be vital to reducing the chance of this messing up. Ye got me? Ye can keep all the other bits covered."

The shaman mumbled something unintelligibly and his cheeks flushed a dark green as he averted his gaze. He then carefully loosened the vest just enough to expose the center of Myev's chest.

With that done, Kiru carefully refocused on her core, feeling a distinct connection to it. He realized now that the connection was the venom now in both their systems. With Brunhilda supporting him, Kiru didn't need to use Telekinesis on himself. So, he reactivated the technique again, this time completely focusing on the venom inside Myev's core.

To his surprise, it followed his command with surprising ease. Though he couldn't see into Myev's body and core, Kiru knew they were obeying his will. With a concentrated effort, he drew all of the venom out of the orc's core like a sieve. Within a minute, he had removed all of the toxic substance from her core.

The psion then began guiding it through the most-ready pathways Myev had available: her main meridians. The venom didn't resist his technique, but it did meet resistance within the queen's body. The toxic substance was still caustic and so slightly burning her meridians as they moved. At one point, the meridian constricted all around the liquid, essentially trying to entrap the venom and seal it off. Fortunately, it couldn't close off completely as that would have permanently inhibited Myev's cultivation, and the body instinctually wouldn't allow that. So Kiru was still able to move the venom. It did require a good deal more effort on his part, though, as he forced it through the more-narrow opening.

Kiru's head shook and one of his nostrils began to bleed from the exertion. The trickiest part was actually getting it out of her body. After trying to pull it out of her pores from a meridian on one of her feet to no success, the psion realized that using one of the body's natural openings would be ideal. One of the meridians by her throat was Kiru's best bet. After he had all the venom concentrated there, Kiru began the difficult job of pulling the toxic venom/poison/acid combo through the even-narrower pores of the channel and into her esophagus.

Pulling the venom from her core was like taking an item from a bowl. Pulling through the narrowed meridian was like pulling something out of a bottle.

This last bit was like pulling sticky, burning putty through the eye of a needle. It grew so intense that Myev's nose began bleeding through both nostrils as well. She grunted and her body began to spasm from Kiru's efforts.

"Um, Boss, are you sure about this? I don't want my sister to die because we took too great a risk," Mutt said, his voice growing louder in increasing concern.

Kiru couldn't spare the concentration to speak, so he just nodded as Brunhilda quickly began shoving some cotton up his nostrils to staunch the bleeding. Then, with a subtle *pop*, the last of the venom was extracted. Kiru had moved it all from the meridian and into Myev's esophagus. With a grunt of effort, he flung it out of her mouth. Everyone recoiled as a gelatinous mass of yellow-green ichor and coagulated blood shot out and slammed against a wall. There was a subtle sizzle and a trail of smoke as it scorched the wood it hit. The excised material began to drip onto the ground in a nasty, rotten splotch, and the smell of sulfur permeated the room.

Myev instantly snapped up, gasping as if she'd been underwater and in desperate need of air. The blue rooster let out a scared cry and a discharge of electricity as it was thrown off her head and into the air. Fortunately, no one was hurt. Myev didn't even seem to notice. Her eyes were distant, as her sweating instantly stopped and her color immediately returned to a healthier shade of green.

Her large wolf sat up and began to whine happily, wagging its powerful, bushy tail and incessantly licking Myev's face like an excited puppy. The queen regent chuckled as focus came back to her eyes. She placed a hand on her wolf's head to stop him, then went to pet the beast with the other before stopping abruptly as she noticed her stump of an arm. "So, it wasn't a dream," she sighed casually, as if amputation was just a common occurrence.

"Haha! Sis, you're awake!" Mutt shouted in joy as he hugged her. He sniffled and wiped a tear from his eye after he let her go. "I was worried I wasn't going to get another chance to kick your ass."

Both orc siblings grinned at each other, displaying their large, pointed teeth. "Kick my ass? I may have lost an arm, Little Brother, but I'm concerned you may have hit your head too hard if you think you've ever beaten me in combat practice," she happily retorted before pulling him in for another embrace.

That was the last thing Kiru saw, before his eyes rolled to the back of his head and he started to shake violently.

CHAPTER TWENTY-THREE

Epiphany

Shite!" Brunhilda spat as Kiru began having a full-on grand mal seizure as she held him. Quickly, she laid him down on his side, doing her best to ensure he wouldn't accidentally aspirate anything.

Z'Goyan ran over to help her. The shaman pulled down Kiru's headband in order to put a hand on his forehead. He recoiled at the sight of the jewel embedded there. "What is this? Did the venom do this to him?"

"The jewel was lodged in his head due to an . . . accident back in his homeland," Zhaden said as he ran in between the two as interference.

"Do you really expect me to believe that? What are you foreigners hiding, eh? What *is* that boy?" the shaman demanded.

"He is our ally, Z'Goyan." Myev groaned, still seeming to deal with some lingering effects from the venom. "That's all you need to know. Now, as queen regent, I order you to help him."

Z'Goyan looked back to his queen and immediately began to blush profusely as he gazed at his scantily clad leader.

Myev raised a curious eyebrow amidst the awkward silence.

At that, Z'Goyan seemed to fully process that his liege was indeed both healed and conscious, and he bowed to her. "Yes, Mye—I mean, my queen," he quickly corrected and rushed back over to Kiru. He put the back of his hand on the psion's forehead, pulling it back after a couple of seconds. "His skin is burning up." He looked over to Brunhilda. "Paladin, I believe your healing techniques would be best here."

Brunhilda nearly slapped herself for being distracted by the shaman and not thinking to do that sooner. She cradled Kiru's head with one hand and put her other on his chest. "Healing Hands." Her palms glowed, sending healing mana into the psion's body. Fortunately, since Kiru was technically a follower of Hlin, the goddess aided Brunhilda in eradicating the poison from his body.

"Mine paladin hath saved thee this time, boy. Though I shan't help thee ascend, I will ensure mine faithful have the power to heal and protect," the voice of the goddess of protection rang in Brunhilda's ears.

Instantly, Kiru's body breathed easier and his seizing stopped.

Brunhilda sighed in relief. She had been able to purify his body of most of the venom, but the dwarf couldn't get rid of it all. The portion that had tainted his core was still swirling inside him. "Kiru? Kiru?!" she said as she tried to wake him up, but he couldn't respond. He was too focused on fighting his own internal battle. The psion's vision was focused inward, his mind's eye locked onto his mental mana core.

"Master, ow! This isn't good!" William said.

Kiru agreed. With the venom inside his core, Kiru was able to connect with the venom inside Myev's core. In doing so, Kiru had unintentionally discovered a little-known fact about the venom the Jormuns used. It was laced with mana. That was how Kiru was able to move and control it. He used Telekinesis, and the mana within the venom responded. However, there was an unfortunate side effect: the caustic substance was trying to fuse itself to Kiru's core, to permanently corrupt him. Kiru visualized his core like a glass sphere full of liquid mana. The normally translucent mental mana he saw was now slowly being overtaken by the yellow-green liquid of the venom.

Both the core and Kiru's head began to shake more and more violently as he tried to resist the toxic substance's effects. He had to get it out, but *how?* The psion then remembered how he'd used Telekinesis on the venom before. Why couldn't he do it again with his own body instead? With a desperate flex of will, Kiru activated Telekinesis on the venom inside his core. He shouted with all his might as he flung the venom outward. As his unique core was in his head, he didn't have to move it far to get it out.

Kiru screamed as he forced the venom out of his body. The intensity of the action caused a set of blood vessels in his nostrils to rupture, and the venom flowed directly out of his nose and mouth. The green, acidic substance burned as it mixed with his blood being forced out in three violent streams. Though his focus was inward, Kiru could somehow tell that thankfully, Brunhilda had the smarts to turn his head to the side, so none of the vomited venom and blood spilled on anyone. After a few terrible seconds of unbearable pain, all of the venom had been forced out of the psion's system.

Though his nose was still readily bleeding, Kiru sighed in relief. He brought his focus back outward, opened his eyes, and flashed a bloody grin as its sudden removal brought sweet relief. That was when his body realized what had happened. "Gah! Crap!" he said through gritted teeth. "It burns," he moaned as the damage the acidic venom did to his sinuses made itself known. By forcing out the caustic material in the manner he'd done, Kiru had accidentally caused acid burns along his sinuses and hard palate.

Vertigo and disorientation hit him like a wave, and the pain of the acid burns made him want to vomit again.

Before that could happen, Brunhilda acted once more. The paladin used her Healing Hands technique. Light emanated from her palms as life mana poured from her body into Kiru's, restoring his damaged blood vessels and burned tissues.

After a few seconds, the vertigo left, and Kiru smiled as his body was finally, blessedly free of pain. He was still exhausted, though. Brunhilda's technique healed the body of damage but couldn't replenish energy or stamina. So, it couldn't do anything about how tired Kiru's body was after his gruesome near-death experience. "Thank you," he said to Brunhilda, exhaustion clearly evident in his voice.

"Naye." She waved off his gratitude. "It's we who should be thanking ye," she countered. "By me grandmother's famous butter muffins, ye sure do come up with some cockamamie ideas," she said.

"They work, though." He chuckled. Internally, Kiru felt a little frustrated at Brunhilda's lighthearted criticism. He knew she meant well and always erred on the side of caution, but their situation was serious. Kiru knew they had to take risks. He knew she'd meant nothing bad by her comments, but it did grate on him a little. For now, though, he wouldn't press it.

"Aye, they do most of the time." She chuckled back, conceding the point to him for now.

"Boss! Boss!" Mutt shouted as he knelt down by the psion still being cradled by Brunhilda. He wrapped his muscular arms around him and bear-hugged his limp body, lifting him up off the ground and laughing. More than one of Kiru's vertebrae audibly popped from the pressure of the orc's embrace. "You did it! You crazy son of a bitch, you did it!" he cheered. Mutt then paused, realizing what he'd said. "Oh! I'm sorry, I didn't mean to call your mother that."

"You're okay, Mutt." Kiru replied. "Could you just quit squeezing me so tight? It's hard to breathe," he winced.

"My bad, Boss." The blind orc apologized again and eased his grip. "Stabby, why don't you come over here and—"

"Got it," Zhaden answered before Mutt could even finish his request, rushing over to their side and placing one of Kiru's arms on his shoulders while Mutt did the same, holding the psion up.

"Hahaha! Yeah! You did it, Boss! Sis, can you believe it?! He cured you of the venom lingering in your system. Now, you can still compete to lead Imakandi!" Mutt exclaimed.

The queen had obviously known she'd been healed but only now fully realized that it was due to Kiru. Myev looked as if she was going to say something to the psion but then remembered the shaman near her. "Z'Goyan, thank you for doing this, my lo—my friend," she quickly corrected.

Fortunately, no one besides Kiru was paying attention to their conversation. For propriety's sake, he just raised an eyebrow and said nothing.

Both Myev and Z'Goyan blushed a dark shade of green before the shaman awkwardly rushed a reply: "Ah—of course, My Queen. I, and the rest of the Tau clan, will support the M'Baku's until the end." The middle-aged shaman bowed and kissed her hand, holding it gingerly and giving Myev a genuine smile. Kiru was by no means a relationship expert, but that little slip-up was the final clue he needed to tell there was something more than just friendship going on between them. It also explained why she relied so much on an orc from another tribe as a close advisor rather than another M'Baku. Still, the pair kept any overt displays of affection reserved in front of the others.

"Will you please fetch me my special collection of recovery pills?" Myev asked.

"Of course, My Queen," Z'Goyan said, his tattooed cheeks blushing an even darker shade of green before awkwardly excusing himself.

"That man." Myev chuckled to herself before looking back to Kiru, who was still being held up by his companions. "You have my thanks, Withered One. I would've thought removing Jormungandr's venom from someone's body impossible, but you are an impossibility yourself, Psion. The M'Baku Clan will be forever in your debt," she said and lowered her head to Kiru. She was still in her bed, but Kiru got the feeling that she would've knelt down in front of him if she could have in gratitude. Even her wolf lowered its head, and the rooster gave a quick nod as it clucked.

A little uncomfortable to have such a powerful cultivator and ruler of a nation be indebted and openly grateful to him, Kiru quickly tried to dismiss her words. "There's no need for that," he said. "As I said before, we are allies." He then remembered the M'Baku Clan's saying, "The strength of the pack is the wolf . . ."

"And the strength of the wolf is the pack." She finished with a smile. "Is there anything I can do to repay this kindness? I am in undoubtedly in your debt."

"Well, if I could get my father's second item, that wouldn't hurt," he said, scratching the back of his head nervously.

She furrowed her brow. "It is far to the south, in Tau Territory. I do not think I can lead you there and make it to the temple in time for the next round of Ukufakaza. You do not need my aid to acquire the item directly, but I can find the map to help you locate its precise location."

Kiru put his hands up, feeling slightly bad for asking such a request after Myev had just recovered from the nasty poison. "Oh, it's okay, Your Majesty. Just claim your nation and help me get my father's item afterward. Then we can call it even."

She nodded, then looked at Mutt. "Were you able to eradicate the Jormun threat from Dissé?"

"We think so, Sis. After we made sure you were safe, we scoured the entire capital. Yours truly led a contingent of scouts and shamans through every level of the city." The blind orc smiled and pointed to his nostrils. "None of them escaped my sniffer. The nose knows, you know?"

"Indeed," his sister replied with a chuckle. "And what of the L'Khans? Were you able to acquire their support?"

"We did, Sis. Not gonna lie, they have some questionable dietary preferences, but they're good people. Plus, they make some good liquor."

"*Damn right, they do!*" William agreed inside Kiru's mind. "*That reminds me. Master, you promised me more liquor.*"

"*Oh, you're right, William,*" he sent back, then summoned his familiar, wanting the imp to join him and his friends.

"Aw, yeah! We did it, bitches!" William cheered. "Hey, Mutt, go find that buggy ogre guy. I want to get some more of that good liquor. I want a whole barrel to myself. For now, I got something to tide me over." William then reached inside his brain and yoinked out a vial of the cloudy yellow alcohol that he had wedged in between a couple of his lobes. "Who knows, maybe if I drink enough of this stuff, it'll contaminate my core like the venom did to you, and I'll learn how to bend alcohol to my will."

"William, wait!" Kiru called out before the imp uncorked the small vial that still seemed too big to fit in his head.

The imp snorted. "C'mon, Master. You said I could have it, and you said you'd get me more, remember?" Then he pouted like a grumpy child.

Kiru reactivated Telekinesis on himself and grabbed William just as the little demon jumped off his shoulder in an attempt to run away and down his booze. The action was clumsy, but Kiru still managed to stop him. "I know, William. I know. You can have the booze, but you said something there. Repeat it."

The imp squirmed for a few seconds but relented. "What? I said maybe if I drink enough of this stuff, my core will get contaminated, and I can learn how to bend the booze to my will. That's what you did with the venom! Now, let me go!" he protested before he began trying to get himself out of Kiru's grip.

"That's what I thought," the psion said, his voice and his vision distant as he let go of the imp, who quickly scurried away to drink his tea-quila before anyone else could stop him. Kiru hadn't really needed William to repeat himself, but hearing it had helped him process it. Maybe it was the lack of sleep and sunlight. Maybe it was nearly killing himself by ingesting a deadly poison, or maybe it was from the euphoria of having been healed of said poison, but with William's words, the dots all connected in his mind. He had an epiphany, a moment of sweet realization that had eluded him despite his best efforts.

Everything just clicked. All those months ago back at the Warrior Games, Kiru could only control Ambrose's lightning technique *after* it touched his core. Brunhilda was only able to fully understand and convert the Gnash & Grind technique into her own *after* she had contaminated her core with the latent beast mana within the ogres' tea-quila. Hlin told him that he needed to make Myev's technique his own when he asked the goddess for advice. Finally, he thought of how he could control the venom only once it had reached his core, and how he no longer felt it after he'd expelled the toxic substance.

"I know how to create my own technique," he muttered to himself. Goosebumps ran up the back of the psion's neck and his mouth curved up into a beaming grin. "I know how to make my own technique! Hahaha!" He cheered so loud that all the other conversations going on around him died down in an instant. He jumped up and down victoriously as he turned to see Myev and his friends all looking at him in confusion. Kiru, quite frankly, did not care.

"Your Majesty, there happens to be something you can do to pay me back after all, but first, we need to drink," the psion said.

"Aw, yeah! About damn time!" William called out as he emerged from a pillar he'd been hiding behind, an empty vial in hand.

A few hours later, just before sunset, Kiru was standing in the center of a grassy patch in the palace grounds. There, standing ten feet in front of him, was Myev, the queen regent of Imakandi, already back in her tribal warrior regalia. She looked doubtfully at the psion. Standing off in the distance was Brunhilda, the healer keeping a watchful eye on the two.

"You sure about this, Withered One?" Myev asked.

Kiru unintentionally let out a belch. "Sorry! Yep. Yes, I'm sure. Just let me—" He tried to carefully set the bowl of tea-quila larger than his head that he'd drank most of on the ground. He failed. His balance was off and he spilled most of what remained. Kiru ignored the head shakes of disapproval from the two women watching. "Sorry, it's just strong stuff."

As to how Kiru had so much of the ogres' alcohol, that was easy. During the week and a half that Kiru had been looking for a cure, his allies hadn't been idle, including Snout. The ogre chieftain made his way back to the Wastelands and brought a few brutish, bone-club-wielding warriors with him, leaving the rest of his tribe under Jubjon's temporary leadership. He hadn't come back empty-handed. either. The monstrous-looking ogre brought back three barrels of their finest tea-quila as an offering to the queen regent.

Snout also brought a box with something inside for Myev, but the ogre hadn't given it to her nor revealed its contents. Now that the queen was conscious, Snout planned to give it to her at the feast tonight, but first . . .

"I fail to see how alcohol will help you," Myev said. "Last time we did this, I almost burned you to a crisp. I can't grasp how the ogres' liquor can help you improve your control. If anything, it'll make you worse. Alcohol dulls the senses, and my technique could accidentally light you aflame."

"Gosh, she just keeps talking. Hiccup! *I liked it better when she was sleeping and not electrocuting us.* Hiccup!" William slurred inside Kiru's mind. The imp was still coherent, but if Kiru hadn't forcefully recalled him, the gluttonous little demon would still be passed out and not able to help in the slightest.

"I know it seems crazy," Kiru said, before wiping some drool off his lips with his forearm, "but I promise, I know what I'm doing. So, stop being a little whiny baby, and hit me already." To his delight, his attempt to annoy Myev into using her lightning technique on him was successful. To his dismay, his attempt to annoy Myev into using her lightning technique on him was successful. To top it all off, she looked *pissed off*!

She snarled and took a deep breath. Blue lightning began to crackle around her body, traveling up to her face. "Thunder Rooster's CALL!" She shouted the last word as a beam of electricity shot out from her mouth directly at the psion, the technique and the force behind it more powerful than she had ever used on the psion before! Kiru had just enough time to think, *"Oh, shit!"* before it struck his body.

Kiru groaned as his whole body shook, the electrical beast mana unceasingly conducting along his organs and nerves. William was protecting his core from any damage, so at least he was safe in that regard. Despite the sheer power of it, though, he was ready this time. Kiru had drunk enough of the tea-quila to contaminate his mental mana core once more. Unlike the venom, the toxic effect of the alcohol was nowhere near as aggressive and was comparable to a normal amount a liver would have to filter out. Sure, it was going to suck, but it wasn't going to overtake his core, and his body would naturally rid it over time.

Right now, though, he needed that contamination because the contaminating substance in his core was beast mana. Kiru began to feel a familiar resonance to the electricity coursing through his body. He tried to direct its movement, but it wasn't enough. He growled—truly growled like a wild animal in frustration—as his body began to convulse more and more, an influence from the beast mana inside him.

Reminded of his earlier epiphany, Kiru thought about how Hlin said that he needed to make the technique his own. The psion gave a bestial grin and snarled like a wildcat at Myev, his canines seeming to grow a little longer and sharper than before. Despite the electrocution, he could feel his blood pumping faster and faster in excited anticipation. *"William! Let some of it in!"*

"But Master, grr! Are you sure about this?" the imp asked as he fought to protect Kiru's core.

Kiru growled once more, *"I'm Kiru the Conqueror! Damn right, I'm sure!"*

Though he couldn't see him right now, Kiru knew that the imp was giving a bloodthirsty grin of approval at that affirmation. *"Hahaha! Yes! Here we go!"* William declared and slightly pulled back on his shielding of Kiru's mental mana core. The electrical beast mana struck the psion's core, disrupting the Telekinesis he'd been using on himself, and Kiru's body went limp. He still stayed upright on account of the electrocution stiffening him.

Despite the pain racking his body, Kiru snapped his twitching head up to look Myev square in the eyes. Unlike previous times, he gave her a look of utter surety. He felt the electrical mana flowing inside his core. It was only a spark, but the psion could feel it starting to obey his will. *Almost,* he thought. *Just a little more.*

The queen regent gave a look of surprise before she smiled at Kiru, intrigued at his display of defiance against her technique. Eager to see what he would do, Myev dismissed her Thunder Rooster's Call.

The psion fell flat on his face, his body limp. His spiky hair was charred at the tip, and he had multiple trails of smoke coming off his body.

"Stupid boy," she said in Orcish, sounding disappointed as she began walking to Kiru. "You keep this up, and you'll put yourself in an early grave."

Kiru snapped his head up to look at her, still giving a defiant gaze. Remnants of the blue lightning still coursed through and crackled around his body.

"No," he said and slowly stood up, his body still trembling as sparks went off around him. "I keep this up, and I'll put myself in my throne."

CHAPTER TWENTY-FOUR

Lending a Hand

Kiru raised both palms up. Electricity raced from his head down his arms. The psion gave a primal shout as two bolts of lightning—not blue, but pure white—surged out of his hands and struck Myev square in the chest. The orc queen was certainly caught off-guard, and the Emerald was knocked back. The psion's power at this point was clearly considerable but still not enough to best Myev. If Myev had been at Kiru's rank, there's no doubt that it would have caused devastating damage.

"*That . . . was . . . awesome!*" William cheered inside Kiru's mind. "*Do it again!*"

Twin streaks of smoke trailed off her chest where she'd been hit, two small scorch marks apparent on her leather armor, too. Myev gave a small chuckle as she looked down before meeting his gaze with her own animalistic grin. "Turning my own technique against me. I said it before. You really are an impossibility, Psion. Do it again," she ordered, echoing what Kiru's familiar had said. Blue electricity began to crackle around her body at her final words.

Kiru matched her grin. "Gladly." he answered both William and Myev. White electricity could be seen crackling off his own body, similar to that of the queen. The psion drew mana from his core. Now understanding how to control it, he bent it to his will, making it combine and interlace the electrical nerve signals around his neck and head. The electricity sparked and grew wild, but Kiru's will would not be denied. With a mental order, he guided the crackling electricity to travel around his body via his meridians, gaining charge.

The tension between the two cultivators was palpable as they stared each other down. The hair of many of the animals in the palace grounds stood on end as they felt the presence of two predators in their midst. Many let out nervous and scared cries before bolting off to find a place to hide. Kiru could hear them all around but didn't pay much mind. He was focused on his opponent before him.

The psion knew he couldn't match her strength, but the sheer joy of his newfound power emboldened him. He wanted to try.

How can I make it stronger? This technique needs more power, he thought. Kiru focused on the queen regent. He noticed that the blue lightning was concentrating around her form. More and more, the electricity moved upward as it gathered around her upper body. That gave Kiru inspiration, his eyes widening in realization. Quickly, he forced the electricity rocketing through his arms to move back up and concentrate around his head.

Myev's eyebrows raised, seeming to understand that the psion was up to something. Instead of striking to prevent him, she waited, continuing to concentrate on the technique she was preparing. It was clear that the queen regent wanted to see what the psion was up to. She wanted to see how far her student could go.

Kiru gathered that she was waiting for him, and when he was ready, he gave her a nod.

Myev gave a slight chuckle before opening her mouth and screaming. The orc launched her Thunder Rooster's Call at Kiru while he fired his own electrical bolt right back, channeling it into a single beam that shot directly out his forehead. This method decreased the time needed for it to travel and increased the speed at which he could use it. The two techniques clashed in a loud thunderclap. Myev, Brunhilda, and Kiru were all temporarily blinded from the clash, their ears ringing. Once they had all recovered, the three cultivators found themselves surrounded by a set of concerned faces. Orc and Minotaur guards, Z'Goyan and some shamans, Snout with his L'Khans, and the other members of Pandemonium were all there, checking on what caused such a commotion.

Mutt and Zhaden helped their friends up while the Tau shaman helped the queen to her feet.

"My Queen, are we under attack?" Z'Goyan asked as he frantically scanned their surroundings.

Ebysso materialized right in front of Myev with her daggers out, joining the shaman in search of possible threats.

The queen regent shook her head and waved off his concern. "Sorry for all the trouble. I was testing the strength of my student." She gestured to Kiru before looking at him once more. "Next time, I may have to use my technique at *full* strength," she said with a grin.

"Does the queen speak true, Kiru?" Zhaden asked. "Have you uncovered a fourth technique?"

Kiru, still shaky from the alcohol coursing through his system, gave the drakonid a shit-eating grin. "Oh, yeah."

"Really, Boss?" Mutt asked as he and Brunhilda walked over to them. "What's it called?"

The psion opened his mouth to answer but stopped, realizing he hadn't given his technique a proper name. Naming a technique helped crystallize it for the cultivator. Kiru hadn't ever heard of an unnamed technique before. Also, for the Ippo Ogre Ascension Method to get to Ruby-rank, a cultivator *had* to know the names of their techniques.

"You don't have a name yet, Master? Oh, we gotta find a cool name for this one. It is too destructive not to have a cool name," William sent.

There was an awkward silence as Kiru thought of an answer, his mouth still open.

"Um, Boss? You there?" Mutt asked.

Kiru still didn't respond for a good fifteen seconds, staring off into space as he thought. Then, he remembered how the electricity from his technique always started around his head, where his core was located. He then thought about how he decided to concentrate it around his head too in order to make it more powerful. Mutt was just about to poke Kiru in the face when the psion finally answered, "I don't know." I'm not sure what to call it. Both William and I are stumped right now."

Mutt gave the psion a gentle smile and each placed a comforting hand on him.

"Do not worry, friend," Zhaden hissed. "You have at last acquired the final key to getting past Gold. Take some time to think on what to call it."

"Yeah, Boss! Names are easy! I can help you out with it if you'd like?" Mutt offered.

Brunhilda snorted. "Really, Mutt? The only one ye don't call by some nickname be me. Well, except 'Brun' sometimes."

Everyone chuckled at that, even putting a smile on Kiru's face.

"Incredible job, Withered One. It seems our business with your cultivation has concluded. We do need to discuss our next steps involving the Ukufakaza after all," Myev said.

"There is one other thing, but . . . it can wait," Kiru replied. He could get to Ruby now, but he had to keep his identity as a psion a secret. If others heard his declaration of technique names while he did the ascension ceremony, they may start to ask questions. Even though these were Myev's trusted allies, it didn't hurt to keep any information from being unintentionally leaked. With how thoroughly the Jormuns had infiltrated the capital, being cautious was the smart choice, even with the recent purging of the cultists.

The orc queen grunted and nodded at Kiru before gesturing to the crowd gathered before her. "Come, let us feast and discuss our next steps," she said, then began to walk farther into the palace grounds.

More than one of her assembled allies' stomachs loudly growled after she mentioned a feast, so it didn't take much coercion to get them moving. There was a delicious assortment of sacred beast meat, juicy fruits, and hearty tubers. Just like the ogre feast before, the L'Khans dug in with savage hunger. Unlike the last time, however, the members of Pandemonium did the same. No cannibalistic items on the menu meant the feast was fair game for everyone, and the cultivators were hungry!

Mutt was the first to talk, speaking in between mouthfuls of food. "So, what do you have to do for Ukufukwawa?" he asked, his last word getting garbled up by the food he'd stuffed into his mouth.

The queen regent ate just as much as her brother, but she had a refined grace that Mutt did not possess, eating with poise, making sure not to spill any food or beverage on herself even having only one arm. She had clearly had more etiquette training than he had or just cared a lot more than her brother did. Case in point, she was the only orc or ogre who also appeared to chew with their mouth closed.

After she swallowed a rather sizable bite out of an ostrich leg, she answered. "All that is left is to get to the first temple with both Z'Goyan and Chief Snout before the next eclipse. That gives us one week. Of course, I must bring the required offerings as well."

"Oh, yeah," Mutt nodded. "What were the required offerings again, Sis? I can't remember."

Myev rolled her eyes in mock frustration, which, of course, her blind brother couldn't see. "I swear, unless it involves fighting or hunting, you don't pay attention, do you?"

"Ye got that right, Queen!" Brunhilda asserted. Everyone at the table chortled at that.

"Well, I would pay better attention if other things weren't so boring." Mutt then cocked his head upon remembering something. "Hey, I paid enough attention to help the ogres. Isn't that right, Snorty?"

"It's Snout."

"What?"

"My name is Snout, and you did help our people, of which we are grateful, Prince M'Toon."

"See?" Mutt smugly said to his sister, completely ignoring the ogre chief's protest about their name.

"But I see why your sister is your leader," the ogre added in a low tone.

Mutt opened his mouth to protest, but after a couple of seconds, he just shrugged in agreement. "Hm, I'll give you that."

"To remind you, Brother," Myev said to get everyone back on track, "I also must present an Emerald-rank sacred beast core and the head of a worthy kill or leader of another tribe."

Both Snout and Z'Goyan visibly tensed at the last requirement.

Myev stuck her remaining arm out in a placating manner. "Not to worry. I would never do such a thing to my allies. Besides, I have the head of such a worthy kill already."

Without ceremony, Myev reached down under the table and pulled out a satchel inscribed in runes. Based on the similarity between the runes on that bag and Kiru's storage ring, he presumed it was a bag of holding of some sort. The queen then reached inside the bag and pulled out the head of the shaman—the one with the grafted parasitic snake arm who had almost killed her.

She plopped it on the table and gave a sharp-toothed grin, "I was going to use the dire spider ape, but I got a better idea. It's not S'Vol's, but the head of one of the Jormun leaders—especially the bastard that almost killed me—should do the trick." Everyone else gave a grin back, except most of the members of Pandemonium, barring Mutt and William, who was happily swimming in a bowl of liquor. While they agreed that the cultist's head should hopefully be sufficient, seeing a decapitated head so casually plopped onto the table where their food was still present still made them sick to their stomachs. The trio was glad they ate the food *before* body parts started dropping.

"As for the core," Myev said and reached back inside the bag, "I will use the spider ape's. I had hoped to use it to help my ascension to Pearl one day, but this is more important."

Before she pulled out the core, Z'Goyan gently put a hand on her arm. "If I may, My Queen," the shaman said and reached inside a pouch on the inside of his hide vest. "The Tau wish to show our support of M'Baku rule. As such, we present to you this gift." He pulled out a fist-sized orb that looked like it was made of glass. It was completely smooth, emerald-green, and without a blemish. The green came from the mana inside the orb and seemed to spiral within it as if a miniature tornado was caught inside.

"An emerald sacred beast core, taken from the finest torrent horse stallion in the Tau stables," he said as he took a knee, lowering his head, and giving it to Myev. "By using our gift, you can save the ape's core to help your ascension."

The queen regent had a look of awe and reverence on her face. Kiru couldn't blame her. To be given something of that caliber was a high honor. The power coming off the item was palpable. Each rank in cultivation one wanted to ascend to brought on more difficult requirements. To find an item all the way at Emerald rank and willingly give it up showed true dedication.

During his studies back in Dissé's temple, Kiru had found out about each of the main tribes and the specific beast god that served as their patron. For the Tau, they revered Sleipnir, the Torrent Horse. They utilized the wind-based beast mana that came from him and the sacred beast horses they kept. This information helped Kiru better understand why the Tau he'd fought with back in the Wastelands fought with such speed and why one of their techniques turned their legs into those of a horse. This also explained why the inside of the core gifted to Myev resembled a windstorm.

"Thank you. Thank you, Z'Goyan," Myev said and moved her hand under the shaman's, both orcs now cradling the core. They both looked down at it in awe, then up to each other, tenderly. They continued to stare until it got awkward for everybody around them.

"Er, hem." Brunhilda coughed loudly. "Do ye need a moment, Your Majesty?"

Both Myev and Z'Goyan's cheeks began to blush a dark green, and they almost dropped the core as they stuttered. "Oh! Um, no," Myev said. "No, that's not necessary, Brother. Thank you, honored Tau," she said more formally to Z'Goyan, bowing her head slightly.

The shaman stood up and bowed more fully. "Of course, My Queen. It is an honor for my people to serve," he replied before sitting back down, making sure his seat was a little farther from Myev than before, which wasn't fooling anyone. Still, no one wanted to call them out, and Kiru certainly didn't understand Imakandi courtship rules. *Maybe saying something like "It's obvious you two are together. Everybody knows" would be offensive to the orcs. Better play it safe*, the psion thought.

Kiru was also very grateful that William wasn't paying attention to what was going on. The brash imp was swimming in his own barrel of alcohol at the moment and couldn't be bothered to say something inappropriate. He had seemed a little grumpy when Kiru had summoned him from his core. The psion heard him grumbling about "names" and figured the imp was still trying to figure out what to call Kiru's new technique. Since he wasn't causing trouble, the psion left the imp alone.

Snout snorted a couple of times before clearing his throat. "Queen Myev, we of the L'Khans are beyond grateful for your tribe's aid us and for the promise of aiding our god."

"Of course, we M'Baku support our pack, just like the great Fenrir. You help us, and we help you."

"Yes. Well, we wanted to give you a token of our appreciation. I mean, aside from our quality liquor." The ogre then presented the box he brought to Myev. "Once I learned of your . . . injury, I knew that Heidrun could help."

Myev opened the box. Kiru couldn't see what was in it, but he could see Myev's face. Her reaction was a mixture of confusion, fear, and disgust. "Uh, is this? What is this exactly?"

The ogre chief grinned, his mandibles clicking in excitement. "A replacement for your missing arm, Queen Myev."

"Oh . . ." The orc tried to contain her concern. She failed. She opened and closed her mouth a few times, trying to get words out, but none came.

Fortunately, Snout didn't seem to notice the orc's discomfort. "Our god, Heidrun, has granted the L'Khans great healing ability that comes from his digestion. It's a skill that far excels the healing capabilities of any other Beast

God. Please, go on." The ogre gestured excitedly for her to take the item out of the box.

With a pained expression, Myev did so, revealing a large, wrinkled white prosthetic arm. The composition of the limb was similar to that of Snout's skin but, thankfully, without the slimy exterior the ogre possessed. It was bulky, nearly twice as large as her regular arm and possessed only three fingers. It was also clear that the crude contraption was crafted using dead glutton grubs.

At the very end where the limb would be attached to Myev's body was a ring of sharp, barbed fangs pointed outward. Kiru winced. One, it wasn't a pretty sight. Two, getting it on looked like it would be extremely painful!

"Whoa! Awesome, Sis! Now you'll be able to give S'Vol a smackdown, for sure!" Mutt cheered.

Myev gave a slightly defeated sigh and nodded. "Thank you, Chief Snout. I am honored by this great and useful gift. May it help in maintaining M'Baku rule and bring honor to the Beast Pantheon—Sleipnir, Fenrir, and Heidrun included," she said, nodding to each of the clan rulers respectively, a polite smile on her face. Then, before anyone else could respond or she could talk herself out of it, she jammed the attachment onto her shoulder.

Everyone gasped in surprise as blood sprayed. The prosthetic limb, empowered by the beast mana latent in Myev's blood immediately reacted. The top half of the appendage opened up and wrapped around her upper arm stump, sealing with a hiss and the wet sound of punctured flesh. The queen regent just gritted her teeth. Her nostrils flared; she was clearly uncomfortable, but she did not cry out in pain. With the upper part of the limb attached, the lower half easily slid into place, not needing to seal over anything.

Her eyes widened in fascination as she took in her new limb. It was bulky and likely didn't possess the musculature or fine control she had with her other arm, but she was able to control it as if it had been a part of her all along.

"What is it, Myev? I mean, My Queen?" Z'Goyan asked in concern.

"Can I . . . ?" She trailed off in thought, no longer seeming to notice that anyone else was around. The orc queen activated Fenrir's Claws on her right hand and cut her cheek, just enough to draw a streak of blood.

"My Queen, are you alright?" Z'Goyan asked in mounting alarm.

Still, she did not answer. Instead, she took her new limb and squeezed the ostrich leg she'd been eating earlier hard. "Heidrun's Digestion," she said. Before their very eyes, the partially eaten bird leg began to wither and dissolve, its contents sucked into the palm of the prosthetic left arm. After a few seconds, it was gone. The orc's injury had been completely healed!

Everyone, including the ogres, gasped in surprise.

Myev abruptly stood up from out of her seat, walked over to Snout and took a knee. "Forgive me. I doubted your gift. I see you not only gave me a new arm, but you've honored me with one of your sacred techniques," she said with a mixture of both awe and gratitude.

The ogre chief snorted as he chuckled. "In truth, Your Highness, I did not expect it to grant you one of Heidrun's abilities, but I'm glad that it did. There is nothing to forgive, but if you wish to make it up to us, there is one thing you can do right now."

"Name it," she said.

Snout's mandibles clicked as he smiled. "Bring out more liquor. We're almost out of tea-quila."

There was a loud burp from a nearby barrel, and William popped his head up. "Aw, yeah! More booze!"

CHAPTER TWENTY-FIVE

Brainstorm

The night continued with more revelry and celebration. Kiru attempted to join in, but he was too preoccupied by still not having a name for his technique. He didn't want to take away from everyone else's enjoyment, though, and so he grabbed William and moved away from them. The imp was unconscious, so he put up no resistance. Kiru then found a quiet spot to cultivate and meditate. With William dreaming beside him, there was plenty of mental mana for him to farm.

But still he struggled to cultivate. His head kept on running through name options for his technique. With techniques, the right name *mattered*. If it didn't "fit" absolutely perfectly, it would end up less powerful or, worse, fully ineffective. It was a subjective thing for sure, but his readings and professors back at the Royal Academy confirmed it.

"Psy-Lighting? No. Nerve Conduction?" These names were more technically accurate than some of his earlier ideas, but they still didn't seem quite right. "Ugh," he groaned and opened his eyes. "This is ridiculous."

"What troubles you, my friend?" a voice asked from the tree above him.

Kiru let out a not-so-manly cry of fear as he opened his eyes and recoiled, nearly falling over. There, sitting on a thick branch above Kiru, was Zhaden. Then he realized that Brunhilda and the other members of his team were standing nearby. Kiru had been so preoccupied with his thoughts that he hadn't heard them approach.

"Why are you no longer participating in the festivities, Kiru? Certainly this is a time for celebration?" Zhaden asked.

Kiru sighed. "Something I didn't expect, man. I worked so hard to finally get a technique, and now I can't figure out what to call it."

"You'll figure it out, Boss. Out of all of us, you're definitely the smart one," Mutt said.

"Aye. If ye'd like, we can help ye brainstorm a few options?" Brunhilda offered.

Kiru let out an audible gasp. "What was that?"

"I said we can help ye brainstorm if ye'd like?" Brunhilda cautiously repeated.

Kiru's heart raced as his mind processed what the dwarf had said. "Brainstorm" was an expression he'd heard a few times and knew what it meant, but it wasn't a common idiom in his homeland. *Could it be? No, it's too perfect. Maybe? Yeah . . . Yeah!* his thoughts rushed through his head as invisible puzzle pieces clicked into place.

"That's it! Haha!" Kiru exclaimed, jumping up and down like an excited child. He then hugged the dwarf in a tight embrace. "Brunhilda, you wonderful paladin! Praise be to Hlin! We found it!"

After he let go, the paladin raised an eyebrow in confusion. "Kiru, I'm glad ye be showing fervent praise to our goddess, but what's gotten into ye? What have we 'found?'"

Kiru gave a wide grin. "The name. We have the name."

That next morning, Pandemonium gathered in the royal palace. Myev had dismissed her guards, wanting no other witnesses for what was about to happen—other than her pet thunder rooster and wolf, that is.

"None shall bear witness to your psionic secret, Withered One. Now, show me your power."

Kiru nodded at her, then sat in the Lotus position. He was not wearing his armor at the moment. It was getting tended to before they embarked on Myev's quest. His friends were standing a few feet away and they gave him serious looks.

"I'm ready," he said.

"Kiru, Last of the Psions, you have acquired and named the four necessary techniques in order to ascend," Zhaden said. "You must accept your techniques as part of your identity, as we have." He gestured to Brunhilda and himself.

"Aye, ye must attain enlightenment and incorporate the techniques into yer very being. Think upon yer aspirations, Kiru," Brunhilda said.

The young psion closed his eyes and did just that. He thought of his father and how he had been murdered. He thought of the mission he was given, to acquire his items and become strong in order to prevent another world war. He then thought of his mother, how she died for him to save his life, in order to secure that future.

Kiru furrowed his brow as the pain of that memory gripped his heart. Having perfect memory was a double-edged sword in that way. He could recall that day in excruciating detail as if he was still there. Over time, the pain of losing his mother had dulled, his mission and friends helping him heal. Still, if he gave the thought of what had happened too much focus, he could easily begin to sob all over again from the pain of his loss.

Thinking back on it once more, sadness threatened to overcome him. In order to cope, he instinctually turned his despair into anger. Kiru was used to it ever since he'd awakened his fire mana core. It came with the territory. While his shorter temper had notably improved since Ambrose Constantine had shattered his fire mana core, it wasn't completely abated either. Fortunately, since his time back at the Royal Cultivator Academy, he had learned a way to better control his anger.

Zhaden had been kind enough to take Kiru aside and train him in a visualization method that his clan used. Despite Clan Ironclaw not using fire mana, their gold drakonid blood still made them more susceptible to fury and rage, so they had developed a method to cope with it.

Kiru took a deep breath through his nostrils and visualized his emotions, his frustration, his anger, as burning fire outside his body. Whereas previously, his mind would be kindling to the flames of anger, consuming him, he now visualized himself siphoning the flames off into his body. Kiru envisioned his body as being hollow and the fire moving as if it were liquid. The psion carefully guided it along his body, moving the flames along the paths where his meridians would be. As he did so, his anger roiled, but it didn't consume him. Instead, it empowered him.

The anger then quickly evolved into firm resolution. Kiru had lost much on his quest, but there were still others who cared for him, and he them. He would protect them, and they would protect him in return. Kiru didn't know how much time had passed by the time he finally opened his eyes, but he could see through a blur of tears that all his friends were gazing at him with both concern and a sense of hope.

"Kiru, Last of the Psions, what must you become to attain your dreams?" Zhaden hissed harshly, his voice almost a shout.

Kiru had thought about these questions all night beforehand. "I must use Telekinesis to move myself. Mana moves me. I must be the Puppet Master," he said, referring to the title he'd given to his cultivation path. In truth, he hadn't given his specific path much thought in a while, but while pondering how he would answer his questions the night before, he remembered the name and how it had so resonated with him. It was the path he clung to in order to get to Gold, and he couldn't lose sight of that.

As Kiru spoke, a translucent wave of mana pulsed out from him in all directions. At the same time, he felt something—his mana, he assumed—wrap around the core to form a new layer. It added a new weight to it as well. None of the surrounding people were forced back by the wave, but the dire wolf let out a reactive snarl. The thunder rooster squawked and hid behind Myev's leg.

"More, Boss! What must you become?" Mutt asked.

"My words and my mind must move armies. I must become the Telepath." There was another pulse of mana, and another layer wrapped around his core. His head was now heavier than ever before. Kiru reasoned it must have been a couple of pounds denser by this point.

"Yeah, Master! Yeah! Tell these fools who you are!" William cheered inside Kiru's mind.

Emboldened, Kiru stood up and shouted, "I am Kiru the Conqueror! My path has many enemies. I must make sure they either die or succumb to my Subjugation." This time, the pulse of mana was much more powerful, influenced by the Subjugation technique and powered by Kiru's will. The mana pushed the other three team members back by a few feet and forced each of them to take a knee. Even Myev visibly tensed. Kiru noticed the blood vessels along her neck bulging at her resistance.

The orc queen's wolf ran in front of her defensively and loudly snarled at Kiru, baring its teeth to protect its master. The rooster cried out in terror and reactively fired a Thunder Rooster's Call technique at the psion. Myev gasped and put a hand out to stop her pet, but it was too late. The technique's aim was true, striking the psion head-on. All who were present stood there, horrified and worried that the ascension ritual might have been ruined.

The psion didn't feel that way. While all others were stuck in surprised indecision, Kiru's focus and will just grew stronger. He let the technique strike him without attempting to dodge it. He'd been electrocuted far too frequently and his training with Myev had made him quite skilled at enduring it while keeping control of his senses. The psion groaned in pain, but despite that, he stayed focused, refusing to be stopped. After what he'd endured from the queen regent, this pain was tolerable.

Then, an idea came to him: he decided to let the technique that had been intended to harm him empower him instead. Kiru let the lightning touch his core and laced it with his own mana.

Within seconds, the blue technique crackling wildly through him turned white, now under the psion's control. Kiru moved it all up to his head, forming a sparking crown. "I must become the storm, a righteous tempest that will bring justice upon traitors, upon usurpers, upon S'Vol, and upon Van Blaine," Kiru declared, then cried out in pain and fell to his knees as a final wave of mana filled with the Brainstorm technique flew out in all directions.

Inside Kiru's mind, William chuckled in glee.

The wave of mana threatened to damage all others in the vicinity, but fortunately, Myev was present. The orc queen fired her own Thunder Rooster's Call technique and countered it, easily pushing it back and dispelling it before it could harm anyone.

The psion wasn't paying attention to that, though. His body was being reforged. After his final words, he closed his eyes and gripped his head as his core became rock-hard. It felt like he had a gemstone half the size of his fist lodged in his brain, each technique solidifying over it in multiple layers.

Once the final layer solidified, mental mana surged out of it and saturated his body, charging his very blood. The power flowed through him, permeating his flesh and bones. Sound no longer reached his ears, and he couldn't have opened his eyes had he wanted to. All sensation left him as his body evolved.

With a sudden snap, Kiru opened his eyes to find himself somehow lying on the ground, flat on his back, his body completely limp. There was a dull pain in his head, but, in terms of discomfort, that was it. He turned his head to examine his body. It had changed but hadn't dramatically shifted from how it was before. Unlike Brunhilda, who'd gained muscle and tone, his body went in the opposite direction. His once-gaunt form was now almost skeletal. It was as if his body had compressed in on itself.

After a few moments, the pain inside his head stopped. He sighed in relief and slowly forced himself to sit up. Kiru held his head low, breathing heavily. His head seemed to have doubled in weight. What helped him eventually hold it up was a new stinging sensation on his forehead. The reactive enchantment of his headband activated, forming a magic helmet around Kiru's head, but it still wasn't helping.

Kiru took off the headband but still felt a distinct stinging in the center of his forehead, like an itchy scab. He sucked in a breath through his teeth before trying to pick at the spot, only remembering after touching it that it was the jewel embedded in his forehead. Still, it stung, but just like the pain of his core, it quickly faded.

Once the pain left, Kiru fully took in his ascended body. Each of his limbs was more exaggerated than before. His already-bony hands now weren't far off from being just skin and bone, making him appear even more like a walking corpse. He moved his mouth to feel that even his face had become slightly sunken in. Still, the mana flowing through his blood moved freely through his body and, with his armor taken off, he was able to see that his blood vessels had grown in size and became more pronounced. Kiru suspected it was to help energize his body. And truly, he had never felt stronger. He still had no physical sensation below the neck, but mana flowed both stronger and more freely than ever before inside him.

He looked up to see his friends warily taking him in with caution.

"Um, Boss, did it work?" Mutt asked.

"It would appear so." Zhaden answered in Kiru's stead. He pointed to the psion's head. "You cannot see this, Mutt, but the gem embedded in Kiru's forehead has changed color. It is now a ruby."

"Oh! Aye! Ye be right, Zhaden," Brunhilda said. "Oi, Kiru. How ye feeling? Ye look . . ." She trailed off, taking in Kiru's new form.

Before she could think of what to say, a barking laugh came from the throne. "You look even worse than before! Now even your face truly matches your form, Withered One," Myev said as she descended the stairs.

"Oh, great," Kiru muttered, not too excited at what his body had become.

"*Really?*" William asked in clear disappointment. "*I was hoping we'd at least look a little more intimidating than a scrawny teenager. How come the dwarf got more muscles and we got less?*" William asked inside Kiru's mind.

"*Probably because of my path. Path of the Puppet Master isn't one that screams being super bulky,*" Kiru sent back.

When Myev came down to Kiru's level, she unceremoniously lifted up his shirt, taking in his emaciated body. "Ugh!" she said in a mixture of disgust and sadness.

"Hey! Quit it!" he said and tugged his shirt back down, blushing in embarrassment. Kiru normally would've been more formal, but the queen regent's casual nature and his own humiliation caused him to act like she was a close friend over orc royalty.

"Well, look on the bright side, Withered One. Though you may look like a walking corpse, at least you still have a good-looking face," she teased with a wink.

"Thanks . . ." he replied sarcastically, but still blushed, silently happy that she at least considered his face handsome. He then looked at his body under his shirt and had to restrain himself from reacting as Myev had. Kiru had to concur with her assessment. He *did* look like a corpse. His muscles had atrophied to the point that it looked like he was starving himself. Still, while he wasn't the most appealing to the eye, his form possessed new strength, and he could feel his techniques resonating within his soul and core. He could simply tell that all four of the techniques were now more powerful than before. His range and control were also improved.

"Awesome, Boss! Congrats!" Mutt patted one of Kiru's bony shoulders. "So, did your techniques get any cool new tricks?"

Kiru said he could tell he had increased power, range, and control but that he didn't know beyond that. He was eager to try, though.

"As for cool tricks . . ." he said, then reactivated Telekinesis. He brought out his Psyslime blade but did so in a manner that he'd previously struggled with. Kiru was controlling the blade without touching it, using only his will. As a Ruby, he now no longer needed to make physical contact with the slime in order to control it.

The psion levitated it out a couple feet from him before willing its shape to change. He converted it to a shield and drew out his steel Fu Tao, having the magic shield float and cover his blind spot. Kiru slowly made it float farther and farther away. At four feet, the slime got a little shaky. At five, notably more. Immediately past that, the slime shield fell to the ground with a clang. Fortunately, it still held its shape and strength even when Kiru's connection to it faded.

"It looks like five feet is the max range I can fully control it at, but it's still better than nothing at all, like before," Kiru said before reaching down and grabbing the slime once more.

"Good job, Boss," Mutt congratulated.

"Thanks, Mutt." Kiru replied, changing the Psyslime back into a hook blade before re-sheathing his weapons and turning to Myev. "Now, can I get my armor back? I'd prefer not everyone have a reason to call me "Withered One," he said, face aflush.

The M'Baku matriarch flashed him a wink.

CHAPTER TWENTY-SIX

Traveling to the Temple

With everyone recovered and fully prepared, Myev and company began their journey south to the ancient Beast Gods temple where her trial would occur. What they'd gathered so far was only enough for her to qualify to enter the temple. Myev would have to undergo more tests then. The queen regent was accompanied by both Snout and Z'Goyan, the respective leaders of their tribes, as well as Pandemonium. Zengaz and Nom were also with them, the two leokin happy to see a member of their race and excited to go back to their home. Also, Nom was apparently a prince, or at least what constituted as a prince according to Zengaz. When they had described to Zengaz how Nom had temporarily transformed into some monstrous version of himself, the one-eyed leokin gasped.

"That ability . . . that is something only a member with noble lineage could do."

"Noble? But I thought ye lot were shamans—a religious sect, not a people with nobility," Brunhilda said.

"We leokin are . . ." Zengaz pressed a fist to his mouth and coughed, seeming embarrassed. ". . . rather promiscuous. Oftentimes, no one knows who our fathers actually are. It is not uncommon for cubs within the same litter to have multiple sires. We raise our young communally, however, so every cub had the equivalent of multiple guardians. Still, the fact that Nom is of noble lineage is a great boon for the leokin. The nobles serve as guardians and leaders for us," the leokin explained, looking at Nom with much more respect.

Myev also had a few M'Baku royal guards with them. They were a mix of Golds and Rubies—nothing to match her or S'Vol's power, but they were loyal, each of them wearing a wolf's head helmet. Despite Ebysso being a very accomplished scout, with the recent attempt on Myev's life and traitorous guards, the orc was elected to stay back and keep the peace within the orc capital. Her skills, along with that of the Akain, would help them successfully monitor the goings-on of Dissé unseen and ensure peace was kept. Also, if the worst should happen, they would be able to spot danger and evacuate the capital. Snout had ordered his ogres to stay back for support and to follow Ebysso's commands.

The journey south was relatively uneventful. They rode in two separate carriages pulled by two pairs of torrent horses. The eight-legged equines, with their air-based affinity, were able to pull the carriages at a speed and pace impossible for most other creatures. Still, the horses weren't strong enough to pull everyone *and* Snout. The ogre chieftain was large, even for one of his people. Even if the stallions had been strong enough, none of the carriages were big enough to accommodate his bulk. Also, his monstrous insectoid appearance startled the horses. So, the ogre chieftain summoned a pair of centigrubs to carry him. It was a good thing, too, because the terrifying insects seemed to be the only animals that wanted to get close to the monstrous ogre.

The members of Pandemonium already had experienced the speed of the centigrubs, but the torrent horses were on another level. It was as if they were being carried by a hurricane. The carriages shook, and wind whooshed all around them. Out the window, the environment was hard to discern as they moved so quickly, it was all just a blur. Many inside the carriage had to brace themselves in order avoid getting thrown out by sheer force. Snout's mounts were keeping pace well enough, but they were always at least a quarter mile behind the carriages.

They were making good time. Myev had a week left to get to the temple located in the southern desert in Imakandi. The orc homeland was by far the largest nation within the Great Alliance, full of wild, vast, and beautiful country. On foot from Dissé, it would take about a month to get there if they went non-stop, and that would be thanks to a number of the travelers' high cultivation ranks giving them increased speed. With the mounts, it took only a quarter of the required time for them to reach their destination.

The only minor hiccup happened the first night they made camp. The centigrubs, being cousins of glutton grubs, used the same type of beast mana. That made the terrifying giant insects often hungry. After a day of nearly non-stop running across rolling hills, that hunger had turned into full-blown starvation. When Snout brought them close to the camp, the centigrubs immediately went wild and tried to attack one of the torrent horses.

The ogre, caught off-guard, fell on his ass as his two mounts surged forward. They would have succeeded in slaying one of the stallions too, had Z'Goyan not been taking care of the mounts. The middle-aged orc shaman surged forward with a boom of displaced air as he jumped. He wielded his staff with both hands, his body and weapon surrounded by small twisters, and slammed his weapon against the exposed underbelly of the lead centigrub.

The creature didn't stand a chance as the power of the orc's swing ripped it in two. Blood and bug guts were sent flying backward, spraying the other centigrub in its companion's gore. The lead grub cried in pain as both halves plopped to the ground and began to flail, the devastating blow bisecting it but not proving immediately fatal. Fortunately, the large centipede's sudden injury caused the other one to stop in its tracks. It was not out of fear of the shaman, however. It was due to the abrupt appearance of a smorgasbord of food.

The second centigrub raised its head up high and shrieked in delight before it began mercilessly tearing into the bottom half of its companion. To everyone's surprise, the half with the head on it was still very much alive. It flailed about in distress. However, its cries of pain began to decrease, and its spurting blood and ichor lessened by the second. After Snout got back up to his feet, he ran over and apologized for his short-sightedness and promised to prevent another episode from recurring. The ogre then asserted his will and wrangled the two centigrubs back under his control, forcing them both to share the meal of the bottom half of the one grub.

Everyone gave a look of incredulity or disgust at seeing one of the insects quite literally eating itself, but the members of Pandemonium just shook their heads. They had already witnessed the eccentricities of those who used glutton grub beast mana. This behavior was very much on brand.

One of the M'Baku guards shivered in fear as his stunned gaze locked onto the insect. Mutt put a hand on his shoulder. Startled, he turned and activated Fenrir's Claws reflexively. They would have sliced straight through Mutt's neck had the blind orc not caught the guard by the wrist. The guard gasped in surprise. "Prince M'Toon! My deepest apologies," the guard blurted out before quickly retracting his claws.

"You know, Guard Guy, those bugs are creepy, but you don't need to worry. I found it best not to dwell on it," Mutt replied before letting go of the guard's wrist.

"Not worry? But the thing—"

"Is under control now. Trust your prince," Mutt asserted before the guard could finish protesting.

"If I may be so bold, what do we do about the injured insect? Won't the ogre chieftain be delayed?" the guard asked, feeling concerned for the ramifications.

Mutt shook his head. "Nah, if that thing heals like the Bug Guy, the injured one should be ready to move by the next day. At least, I hope." Mutt uttered the last part under his breath.

The M'Baku guard was still obviously concerned but some tension notably left his body, and he grunted in confirmation.

Once that fiasco was finished, Kiru and the others practiced.

They continued this routine for the next four days. It was during the nights that most of the cultivators got to train and stretch their legs. Zhaden and Ebysso were always on high-alert and the two would instantly go out and ensure the group's perimeter was safe. Kiru used his time at night to get used to his ascended body and techniques. Ascending from Gold to Ruby didn't usually cause much change to the body aside from better blood flow and slightly better musculature for a normal cultivator. Obviously, his bodily changes were on the opposite end of the spectrum. It was his techniques and cultivation-to-movement efficiency that had shown real improvement.

When he was at Gold, Kiru calculated that one hour of cultivation using the method that William had taught him back in the Kingdom of Blades would result in roughly ninety minutes of movement. That was if there were no dreaming minds giving off extra mental mana. If there were any around, it would typically improve from ninety minutes to three hours. Kiru had found out at Ruby that one hour of cultivating would give two hours of movement with no dreaming minds and four hours with. The standard method of cultivation taught to all the commoners among the Great Alliance yielded him no improved benefits. Cultivating using that method was still an even trade: one hour equaled one hour of movement. Kiru couldn't help but assume that showed how poor the standard method truly was.

Kiru couldn't practice Brainstorm. It was too loud and bright, and they couldn't afford to bring any unwanted attention. He still could train in his other techniques, however. The motor control and mana cost for moving his body with Telekinesis were improved. He'd gotten more efficient at using the technique with his increase in rank. The range of Telekinesis was greater at the established five feet for using his psyslime and roughly fifty for controlling other items as long as they were roughly Kiru's size or more.

Kiru also worked on his Telepathy as well. It wasn't one he'd ever really practiced with before. It was again due to trying to keep his cultivation path a secret. Here, though, he couldn't afford to not discover his limits. Fortunately, he could move away from prying eyes and have Myev ensure his secrecy. The first thing Kiru tested with Telepathy was its distance. He used Mutt to run farther and farther to figure out the technique's range. Roughly, the psion estimated it to be around one-thousand feet. As for the quantity of people he could communicate with at once, Kiru couldn't adequately test while still keeping his identity as a psion a secret, but he instinctually felt it was ten. He knew for sure that it was at least five because he had been able to test it with William, Brunhilda, Mutt, Zhaden, and Myev. He wondered if he would be able to put it to a real test someday.

As for Subjugation, well, he didn't want to use it, but he knew that it would now work on Ruby-ranked people as well, and his capabilities were now up to two people or creatures at a time.

The one who made the most progress during the four evenings was Mutt. With Zengaz present, the beast mana cultivator was finally able to get some answers about the sacred beast cores he'd ingested. He now knew three of his five: Fenrir's Claws, Horned Harpy Eagle Talons, and Gnoll's Bite. There were just two left to figure out: the one that enhanced his vocal cords and throat, and the one that elongated his hair.

Having much more experience, the elder leokin was able to help Mutt discern the creatures which those techniques came from. "It's called a Beast Awakening," Zengaz said, explaining what Nom had done to help the orc learn about his techniques.

The one-eyed leokin also used the time to teach Nom about how to do a Beast Awakening without depleting himself so badly. When Nom did it the first time based off pure instinct, he had had to sleep for almost a week to fully recover. Nom still hadn't perfected it, but Zengaz said he was making progress. He was an attentive student. The little leokin still only said "Nom," but there was a definite intelligence in his eyes. He *understood*.

"It's remarkable that you performed a Beast Awakening on your own, Little One," Zengaz said.

"Nom?" the cub asked, cocking his head to the side.

"The Beast Gods must favor you to give you such strength. Still, you have much to learn. Observe." The one-eyed leokin plucked a hair from Mutt after the orc had activated his hair-elongating technique. Zengaz then plucked a hair off his own body and swallowed them both. He closed his eye, and after a few seconds, both he and Mutt began exuding beast mana from their pores.

"Whoa," the blind orc uttered in surprise. He hadn't been trying to leak mana as he was, but he seemed unable to stop it. Then, without ceremony, Zengaz placed a paw on Mutt's forehead. As before with Nom, Mutt had a vision. This time, however, he wasn't a horned harpy eagle. No, now he was a massive bear, and he was not alone. A large, saber-toothed tiger had intruded into his icy cave. Mutt flared out his thick fur and charged. His instincts told him that the fur not only kept him warm but protected him too. He clashed with the large cat, and it let out a high-pitched growl before trying to bite into one of his arms. The tiger's long fangs clamped down hard, but they couldn't puncture his flesh as Mutt's fur had become too thick to penetrate.

Mutt backhanded the tiger off of him, and it crashed into an icy wall. Mutt then raised a thick claw and advanced on it, but before his strike could land, his vision flashed white.

Just one second later, Mutt regained senses in his actual body, and he realized he was now back with the leokin. "Dweller Bear's Fur," he said in realization. "The technique is called Dweller Bear's Fur."

Zengaz gave a sharp-toothed grin and nodded. Then, exhaustion hit both Mutt and Zengaz at once. "Notice now, Little One." Zengaz yawned as he turned to Nom, who was watching attentively. "In sharing a part of yourself when you ingest the other, like I did when I swallowed both his and my hair, we both share in the exhaustion. That way, we each only sleep for a day instead of for a week."

"Oh? I see," Mutt said, yawning. In the next couple days, after Zengaz had slept fully in one of the carriages, the orc learned what his final technique was called: Bounder's Howl. It came from a strange jungle-dwelling feline that swung from branches like a monkey. The howl was used to intimidate predators and scare prey into fleeing.

On Day Four, Kiru and the others accompanying Myev made it to the desert border, leaving the rolling hills of M'Baku Territory. During their travels so far, the psion had noticed Mutt's sister to be notably quieter and more distant. She seemed to be doing her best to try and focus on what was to come. Zhaden had the bright idea that Kiru or Mutt should ask her about the second tier of Ruby. When Kiru finally asked her one night when everyone was having dinner, however, she refused to elaborate on how to help him climb higher at the moment.

"I cannot focus on teaching you right now, Withered One," she said. "I must prepare my mind and body to be ready for whatever lies ahead at the temple. The gods will challenge me. I must ponder over how to best accomplish their will." At those words, Myev excused herself from the others and went to cultivate alone.

Kiru didn't press the queen regent. He knew that she must have been going through a lot based off his tumultuous time in Imakandi so far. *She must have a better idea of what we'll encounter when we get to Nom's home. Probably best that I don't interrupt her cultivation*, he thought.

The desert wasn't officially claimed by any orc or ogre tribe but instead fell under the purview and protection of the leokin. The border also touched part of the grassy plains where the Tau lived, so it wasn't an abrupt change from rolling hills to desert. The border they crossed into was rocky and the terrain was dotted with a myriad of dry bushes and isolated patches of tall grass.

As they continued south and neared the desert proper, the air became notably both hotter and drier. Eventually, the grass turned smaller and more brittle until the landscape had been completely subsumed by rolling sand dunes.

Both of the leokin raised their heads up to the bright sun and purred in appreciation.

"Smells like home, yeah?" Mutt asked the sacred beasts.

"Indeed," Zengaz replied.

"Nom!"

"It will be good to be home. The cub and I are eager to rejoin our people," Zengaz added.

Nom gave a tight nod of agreement, but Kiru could tell from the cub's eyes that Noma was a little sad about the idea of leaving them. Despite that, the psion did think it was best for Nom to be with his own kind.

The group continued for the next few days until they finally found the ancient temple. It was still a brown speck in the distance, but both of the leokin knew instinctually that it was their home. Once Kiru and the others caught sight of the temple, the mounts began to buck and resist going closer. Both Myev and Snout fought to wrangle them in when Zengaz spoke up. "With Ukufakaza in effect, no beast other than we leokin dare to get too close to the temple. We will need to leave the mounts here and go by foot."

Trusting his advice, they all did just that and began the rest of their trek on foot. William asked Kiru to let him out to see it with his own eyes, and the psion obliged. The first thing the party noticed as they got closer were two large smoke-stacks coming from inside the temple. Next was the smell. All except the leokin wrinkled their faces in revulsion. It smelled of burning meat and . . . cat fur?

Eventually, they got close enough to behold the ancient temple with their own eyes. It was a massive, multi-level structure made of old, worn stone, cracked in many places and in various states of disrepair. Tall sand dunes covered multiple sections of wall, as well, partially burying them. Meanwhile, each corner of the temple was comprised of a multi-tiered pyramid.

One top of the walls were ten ornate beast statues spaced throughout. Most were visible and intact, the exceptions being one that was almost completely covered in sand and another that was now just a pile of rubble. *Probably for Heidrun and Jormungandr,* Kiru thought based on his recently acquired deep knowledge of the pantheon that most of Imakandi worshipped.

Soon they neared the front of the temple. There before them was a large set of yellowed bone doors at the front with the visages of ten very familiar beasts—the Beast Gods—carved and painted in the finest detail upon them to look as if they were alive and ready to leap out. Kiru knew they weren't real, but it was still an intimidating sight to behold.

Once they were only a hundred feet away, there was a loud *boom*, and the doors opened slightly, not revealing much of what was inside the temple. Myev raised her arm, and the entire group stopped. Out from the opening walked a toga-wearing leokin, this one clearly a female from her lack of mane, and she greeted the group.

"Welcome, travelers." She sniffed a couple of times. "I smell an Emerald in your group. I take it that you've come to participate in the Ukufakaza?"

Myev strode out a couple of steps ahead of everyone, proud and confident. "I am M'Baku Myev, daughter of the last high chief, M'Baku Otto. I have come to stake my claim as the next to rule Imakandi."

"Excellent." The leokin bowed. "And I see you've brought two of our own back as well. Come, Zengaz, Little One, you are home."

Both the elder and young leokin looked at the group with gratitude. Zengaz then began walking toward the female leokin. Nom's eyes welled up and his pupils seemed to get larger, making him somehow even more cute. Even Kiru had to force back a tear. "Bye, Little Guy."

To the psion's surprise, there was a loud sniffling on his shoulder. He turned to see William crying profusely, a long bead of mucus hanging off his pointed nose. "Goodbye, you miserable little cretin. I'll always treasure the time you turned into a bloodthirsty monster," he said, then loudly sucked the snot back into his nose.

Nom also wiped away some tears before joining Zengaz. The leokin cub followed his one-eyed companion into the ancient temple and out of sight. When they were gone, the large bone doors slammed shut with another boom, and the female leokin continued, "Myev of the M'Baku Clan, I welcome you to the First Temple of the Beast Gods. Since you had some of our brethren with you, I take it you know of the requirements for this proving ceremony?"

"I do," she answered.

"Good," the priestess replied. "Then, I ask for the first requirement: backing from three founding tribes. As an M'Baku, you have at least one. What other tribes back your claim?"

"I, Tau Z'Goyan, leader of the Tau tribe, give our people's backing to M'Baku Myev."

"And I, Chief Snout of the L'Khans, give our peoples' backing to M'Baku Myev."

The leokin's eyes widened. "A L'Khan? We have not been graced with a follower of Heidrun before. We revere your god, but we are curious as to why he hasn't joined his brethren in the Savage Realm and stayed in Imakandi?"

Snout snarled at that but quickly calmed down when Myev placed a hand on him. "It is not of Heidrun's doing. It is a failing of my people that the god is not with his people. It is a mistake we plan to help fix after I am declared queen."

The leokin priestess smiled at that. "It appears you have met the first requirement, but we have to ensure your words are true." She pulled out a small, serrated dagger made from an animal tooth. "I will need your blood."

Without question or protest, each of the three tribe leaders walked up to the priestess and stuck out their arms. She drew her blade on each of their forearms and collected a glass vial of each of their blood. Once that was done, she turned back to the massive set of bone doors. She raised one of the glass vials, the one filled with Z'Goyan's blood. "The Tau follow Sleipnir," she declared to the entire party, then leaped up twenty feet in the air in an impressive display of acrobatic skill. She hopped and climbed up the doors, until she reached the carving of a gray-haired horse's head at the top left of the left door.

The priestess poured the blood into the horse's mouth, and its eyes turned red. Red runes also appeared on its head.

"Um, Master, what's she doing?" William asked.

"I dunnae exactly what she be doin', but I reckon the temple doors be enchanted to ward off anyone who's not a leokin without the requirements for this ritual," Brunhilda answered before Kiru could say anything.

Both the psion and imp looked at each other. "What she said," Kiru said, thinking of no other better reason.

"I believe the paladin speaks true," Myev said. "After the doors open, I ask that you, the paladin, and the gold drakonid stay back. The Beast Gods must not take kindly to outsiders viewing our sacred ceremony."

Kiru was surprised at the last-minute dismissal. *Was this why she's been so distant? To push us away at the last second so we wouldn't protest?* he thought.

As Myev had been speaking to the psion, the leokin had repeated the process for Snout and Myev's blood, pouring them into the mouths of the carved heads of their patron deities, Heidrun and then Fenrir. Once she finished, the yellowed bone edges of the doors began to glow with red runes as well. She sat herself down on the carved head of Fenrir and gave a cheshire grin to the others below.

"The Beast Gods have found your sacrifices worthy to pass the first test, M'Baku Myev. Prepare yourself." At her words, there was a loud crash, followed by a rumbling underneath the party's feet. The whole temple began to quake as well.

"What's happening?" Myev asked. Before she could get her answer, though, the sandy ground gave way underneath. The priestess just looked down and waved as they all fell into the black.

CHAPTER TWENTY-SEVEN

Beast Gods

Shiiitt!" William screamed, squeezing desperately to Kiru's shoulder as both they and all the other cultivators fell fast through the darkness. Wind rushed across Kiru's back and his hair flew up, covering part of his face. Sand flew into his mouth, making him grimace. Kiru spit out the sand reflexively and joined in the others' cries of distress. Fortunately, his Darkvision saved him from succumbing to the complete terror of the unknown.

"Wings of the Raven!" Myev shouted in the darkness.

Kiru's eyes widened as a set of wings began to sprout from her back. Then he noticed that they were about to land and he gasped. "Look out!" he cried out just as Myev crashed into the slanted stone floor below.

The queen regent grunted on impact, her surprise from the landing disrupting her technique. Kiru didn't have time to say anything else, though, before he and the others landed beside her. They didn't stop, however, for two reasons.

First, the stone was covered in a strange, thick slime. Second, the slant of the ground was so extreme that it was effectively a massive slide which they all proceeded to slip and slide down uncontrollably in the darkness. Their course went up and down, left, then right, and even spun multiple times. The cultivators would have lost their lunch had their bodies not been previously tempered. Kiru was pretty sure that he heard William vomit once, however, but he couldn't be sure in the chaos.

Then, mercifully, light appeared, and the slide suddenly ended. One by one, they were dropped onto dry, dirty ground. Most of the cultivators, with their animalistic or just highly trained reflexes, quickly moved out of the way for the others. Most wasn't all, however, and Kiru, Brunhilda, and Snout all landed in a pile from their twenty-foot drop.

Luckily, the bulbous ogre was the first of the three to land, or he would have crushed them. Instead, both the psion and dwarf bounced off of him as if he were some sort of massive ball. Then they quickly got up and scanned their surroundings for any threat. When they saw nothing in their immediate vicinity, they returned their focus to the disgusting state they were in.

"Ugh!" William said as he stood up on Kiru's shoulder. Kiru looked to see the imp wiping a layer of slime off his body. The psion looked down to see a dirt-covered slime all over his body as well. He immediately began wiping the goo off. To his surprise, it came off easily, instantly evaporating as it hit the ground. Seeing what Kiru was doing, Brunhilda and the others did the same.

"Keep sharp. We are not alone. Do *not* draw attention to yourselves," Myev said.

Taking the hint, they paused and surveyed their surroundings further. The cultivators all gasped at the sight. They were at the very top of one of the four pyramids that formed the corners of the temple—the left front corner pyramid to be specific.

Kiru looked out and saw the desert and stone stretching far into the expanse beneath the scorching sun. He then turned to look at the temple proper.

Each of the pyramids were like imposing ancient sentinels watching the temple grounds below them. None of them had the regular tetrahedral shape; instead, the top of each had been sheared off, forming a flat plane. At the top of the north-west corner pyramid, there was a gray-haired orc, larger and covered in more muscles than Kiru had ever seen. It was hard to tell where his head ended and his neck began.

He had a large metal ring pierced through his septum and Kiru genuinely wondered if he was half-ogre due to his size and bulk. The brute was also wearing clunky plate armor adorned with various wicked-looking spikes. He was flanked by two pairs of orcs. Two were armor-clad brutes like him, and the other two had feathers growing off their bodies, one with a mullet and goatee made of blue feathers and the other with a set of black-feathered wings attached to his arms. While the former seemed nervous, the latter was the picture of calm.

Along the top of the temple walls, Kiru could more clearly see the ten majestic beast statues adorning them. Their stony gazes looked inward toward the temple with silent intensity. Crafted with meticulous detail, it was easy to recognize the deific beasts that the orcs and leokin worshipped. Their forms matched the ones on the temple doors but looked to be made of solid, unpainted limestone.

Unlike the ones on the doors, however, two of the statues weren't well-kept at all. One was extremely worn by the passage of time. Based on its curvature, Kiru reasoned it was of Jormungandr. The other was almost completely covered by a large sand dune that had partially overtaken the temple's western wall. Only a pointed stone ear stuck out. The psion deduced that it had to be Heidrun, by default.

The northeast corner pyramid held S'Vol. The cult leader had only one loyal crony with him, their scale-like scars on proud display. The other two were clearly the leaders from the other two tribes that backed the Jabaris' claim. One orc wore a helmet with long, curving, distinctly goat-like horns while the other had wraps around his head, obscuring his face. It appeared to be an archer based on the massive bow equipped on its back. S'Vol gave a sharp-toothed grin upon recognizing Myev while the armor-clad orc dismissed them completely.

Kiru ignored the cultists for the time being to examine the rest of the temple. The southwest corner was empty. Inside the temple, a stone maze twisted and turned in an almost nonsensical fashion. Besides the abundance of sand that had intruded from the western side of the temple, much of the ground below was surprisingly full of vibrant plant life. Some sections had lush green grass while others had an abundance of trees. One section of ground in between two maze walls even had tidy rows of wheat that couldn't be anything but specifically tilled farmland. Kiru was practically mindboggled to see such abundant life growing in such a harsh environment—a literal oasis in the desert.

In the center of the maze was the heart of the temple, where a fifth central pyramid stood. They hadn't seen it earlier due to its height. While it was still large, it was at least a few stories shorter than the corner pyramids. Meanwhile, the top was also flat but much larger than the other ones.

And while the other pyramids were empty, there were dozens of leokin on this one, including shamans, priestesses, and cubs. Kiru noticed a surprisingly well-maintained set of runes mixed with carvings in Beast Speak set about in concentric rows of circles carved into the top layer of the pyramid. *Some sort of ritual or ritualistic pattern?* he wondered.

At the very center of these circles was a large stone throne. A single rune was carved into its back, taking up the entirety of the exposed stone. Sitting in it was a muscular, heavily scarred shaman, most of whose fur was a solid mix of brown and gray, the exception being his majestic solid black mane, partially obscured by a feathered headdress in multiple colors. The only other attire he had on was a set of ornate pants and jewelry.

Flanked by the kneeling forms of Zengaz and the toga-wearing priestess who had tested Myev's blood earlier, this was clearly the head shaman. *How did she get up there so fast?* Kiru thought. The shaman was also holding something . . . *Nom?!* It was Nom! The head shaman was holding the cute cub in his arm like a doting father. *He has to be his father!*

The sight was breathtaking—to everyone, that is other than a certain familiar. "Why did we have to go through that whole song and dance to get inside the ruins. Those sacred beasts could've just opened the door," William complained.

Myev's eyes went wide in anger as she snapped her gaze to the imp.

Kiru winced as he felt the pressure of the Emerald's aura. *"Okay, before you say anything else that could be considered sacrilegious . . ."* Kiru quickly sent to his familiar before recalling William back to his core.

Myev immediately let up on her aura and gave Kiru a subtle nod of approval. She didn't apologize. They were in a place sacred to her people, and she wouldn't bear any insult toward it or their gods.

Kiru breathed heavily but quickly recomposed himself to stand back up proudly. His friends all gave him quick looks of concern, but he gave them a subtle nod and barely stuck his hand out to wave off their worry. *"I'm okay,"* he sent to them via Telepathy. Kiru wanted to conserve his mana for what was to come. All their gazes snapped back to the central pyramid as a voice boomed from there.

"Welcome!" the shaman declared before setting his cub down and standing up.

Nom scurried over to Zengaz, who picked up him like a doting uncle.

The head shaman then raised his arms high and addressed the assembled people. "It appears that all the candidates have assembled," he pronounced. He had the sort of smooth, grand voice that all good announcers seemed to possess. The gathered leokin roared in approval, causing everyone's hairs to stand on end.

He then gave a wide grin before cutting a gouge in his right hand with a claw from his left. Then he squeezed his right palm, making blood flow from the wound, before slamming it onto the carved rune on the back of the throne.

"With the candidates here having proven themselves worthy to compete for the throne, let the next round of Ukufakaza begin!" On his pronouncement, geysers of bloody fog erupted from the cracks and in between the bricks of all five pyramids.

Kiru coughed as the fog entered his mouth and nostrils. The overwhelming scent of blood took over until iron was all he could taste or smell. He felt his skin tingling—the parts that he could feel, that is—and his eyes stung from the fog. He didn't know what exactly it was doing, but he could tell it was trying to affect his perception.

On instinct, William wrapped himself around Kiru's core to protect his mind from any possible corruption.

Fortunately, the fog quickly faded, and Kiru felt nothing trying to control him. He did figure out what the fog's effect was pretty quickly, however. There, floating above every one of the ornately carved statues, were large floating projections of the Beast Gods. The covered and damaged ones were the only exceptions. The gods looked menacing and radiated power despite being mere avatars. Fortunately, they didn't give off auras of the true Diamonds they were as gods, but whatever the gas did to let them be perceived couldn't keep all of the Beast Gods' power from coming out.

"Sis, what happened?" Mutt asked.

"Z'Goyan?" Myev asked.

"The red gas was somehow made from the blood of the Beast Gods. I do not know how they were able to call on or create such a thing, but that must be the reason we can see their forms even though they're in another realm," the tattooed orc explained.

The eight astral projections looked down on the cultivators below with savage intensity. After Kiru's extensive studying of Dissé's Beast God temple's sacred history, he easily recognized the divine sacred beasts before them. There was Sleipnir, the eight-legged gray torrent horse, Gullinkambi, the blue thunder rooster, Huginn and Munin, the wise ravens, Hldsvini, the thick-skinned battle boar, Tanngniost and Tanngrisner, the twin goats of strength and life, and lastly, Fenrir, the great wolf, with fur black as night and eyes that demonstrated his unrivaled intelligence.

"So, the final candidate has arrived," Fenrir said. His voice was old but unmistakably wild and seemed to be just on the cusp of violence. It was also loud, booming over the entire plateau. "Good. Now, the true testing can begin," he growled and tapped his nails. The other Beast Gods all gave grunts and nods of approval. Fenrir had been their leader ever since their pantheon had formed, and the status quo hadn't changed since.

Fenrir spoke up again, looking at the gathered orcs. "You have all gotten the support of enough founding tribes and therefore have been found worthy to be brought here, to be tested by us. Here you will have your chance to prove yourselves worthy of leading our subjects on our behalf." The great wolf then turned his gaze to the armor-clad orc. "State who you are and the rest of your requirements."

The brute didn't seem deterred by the god's gaze because he scowled at Fenrir. "I am Thrar'fang Grimtusk, follower of Hldsvini." The projection of the thick-skinned boar god flared his nostrils and grunted in approval.

Grimtusk never stopped scowling but still did as bid. He reached under his breastplate and pulled out a green gemstone the size of his palm. Kiru instantly recognized it as an Emerald core from a sacred beast of that rank. "From a dire bear," Grimtusk said. Then he reached to his belt, which had a head attached to it. It was wrapped tight by its long, braided gray hair. Grimtusk took out a small dagger, cut the hair from the orc's head to free it from his belt, and raised it up to the gods, Hldsvini in particular. "This is the head of the past chief, my father, who I killed when I found he was too weak to rule."

The boar god opened his mouth and squealed in approval, revealing far more tusks than one might expect. "My follower passes. Only the strong can rule Imakandi," he cried and stomped his feet in praise despite the projection still floating in midair. Kiru was glad that they were just astral projections. They would do some major damage otherwise. This confirmed that their actual bodies were still back in the Savage Realm.

"I believe I am next," a snide voice spoke up after Hldsvini's squeals died down. All the Beast Gods turned to see it coming from S'Vol. Fenrir bared his fangs at the cultist. To S'Vol's credit, the orc didn't seem scared, for he had his own god at his side. "I am Jabari S'Vol, follower of the greatest among you, Jormungandr."

As if summoned, the severely worn and slightly curved statue glowed a dark green. Then, the entire temple quaked. "Yeeessss!" A deep, terrifying roar came out, and with a resounding boom, the green light shot up and formed into a projection of its own, that of a giant snake so large that it dwarfed the other Beast Gods. Kiru knew that the projections were at a smaller scale than their actual size because records had each of the Beast Gods being at least one-hundred-feet tall and their projections were only half that at the most. Jormungandr, however, looked to be at least two-hundred-feet tall by Kiru's estimations. The entirety of his body couldn't even be seen because the astral projection of the World Serpent was abruptly cut off, unable to encompass the World Serpent's actual size.

"How big is that thing?" William asked Kiru in amazement.

"Too big," the psion replied and gulped.

There was another distinct difference between Jormungandr and the other Beast Gods apart from size. It was the bindings. Spaced out across Jormungandr's spectral body were large manacles attached to thick chains pulled taut, preventing the World Serpent from raising himself any higher. It was clear that Jormungandr was still imprisoned against his will, but he was still plenty impressive. This was the World Serpent, the creature who took the "survival of the fittest" concept too far for even the Beast Gods.

Its massive reptilian head lowered down to the wall.

Kiru scowled as he took in the terrifying serpent. He was rightfully intimidated, but he was also . . . angered by him. Kiru couldn't rightfully say why, but the large snake just seemed *wrong*, like it was anathema to him. *Why do I want to kill it?* The psion felt an unexplainable instinctual desire to carve Jormungandr into pieces. William began to coo in approval inside his mind.

The World Serpent paid the young psion no mind, though. Jormungandr stuck out his forked tongue, as if tasting the air. Then, his slitted eyes focused on S'Vol, "About time you showed up, my disciple. I cannot stand another cycle with one of my siblings' foolish followers in charge." he hissed, giving the cultist a predatory grin. It was obvious that the repercussions would have been severe had he not come.

S'Vol didn't seem bothered by the poorly veiled threat. Instead, he put a hand to his chest and bowed his head, readily taking a knee to his god.

Before he could say anything, though, Sleipnir raised his forelegs in the air and neighed in anger at Jormungandr's words. Then he slammed his hooves on the ground, and a violent gust of air shot down from above and struck the serpent. Jormungandr was imprisoned in the Savage Realm with the other Beast

Gods, so they could still dish out actual damage to each other. *It looks like their physical bodies aren't far from each other in the Savage Realm . . .* The serpent groaned as most of his body was forced down from Sleipnir's strike.

Enraged, he hissed, trying to lash out and strike at Sleipnir, but the magic chains binding him glowed and held him back, preventing such retaliation. Once he accepted he couldn't break his bonds, Jormungandr refocused his gaze on S'Vol.

"Servant!" he roared. "Present the rest of your requirements."

The Jabari leader hastily pulled out two things from a pouch. "I have an Emerald core from a fire ant queen and—" His needle-like teeth gave an evil grin. "—the head of a truly rare and worthy kill." The cultist then raised the head of a creature that Kiru had seen before, a white leokin, Nom's guardian who had protected him from death.

The gathered leokin snarled and growled in rage at the blatant cruelty and the death of their kin. The hair on many of their backs raised, and they looked ready to attack the cultist themselves had their gods not been watching at the moment.

Aside from the World Serpent, all the other Beast Gods were visibly disturbed by the display. Fenrir was enraged. "Sacrilege!" he snapped. The air rippled around the wolf as power gathered. Every one of the cultivators, not just S'Vol, visibly quivered under the force.

"Fenrir!" Jormungandr hissed. "A rare albino sacred beast is a worthy kill, and if the fool trespassed onto my disciple's territory, they are free game. My follower passes." The snake chuckled, baring his teeth at the wolf. "Or do you wish to break your precious rules that you imprisoned me here for disregarding?"

The wolf bared his teeth right back at the World Serpent but relented after a few seconds. "Fine," he said and looked to Myev. "Disciple, present your requirements."

"Yes, honored Fenrir," she replied and bowed. "Behold, a core from an Emerald-rank torrent horse *freely given* by the Tau tribe as a sign of good faith in my rule. I had no need to force or blackmail others to sponsor me. My allies truly believe in me."

Both Grimtusk and S'Vol visibly snarled at the M'Baku.

She continued, undeterred. "As for the head of a worthy kill . . ." At that, she pulled out the head of the shaman who had nearly killed her with his venom.

"This orc was part of a coup against me and my people. He was a Jormun, a follower of the World Serpent, sent by their cowardly leader to kill me and scores of innocents in clear violation of the rules of Ukufakaza." She then threw the head in S'Vol's direction. Her Emerald strength was evident as the head soared across the temple and landed on the pyramid not far from S'Vol's feet with a wet *plop*. Blood spurted out, but the head was mostly intact, for all to see.

The Beast Gods all snorted, growled, snarled, or stomped in clear displeasure at the accusation. "Of course you'd dare to break our sacred rules again, Snake."

Fenrir growled. "Give us one good reason that we shouldn't banish you from our ranks and finally tear you to pieces."

Jormungandr let out a low hiss through gritted teeth, but after a few seconds, had a smug grin on his face. "I know the rules clearly, Fenrir. For this Ukufakaza, it clearly states the candidate cannot be directly responsible for the deaths of others aside from the leaders of other tribes, the exception being defending oneself or tribe. Now, if a member of one's tribe attacks on their own without the chief's knowing, the leader cannot be held responsible, can they?"

The monstrous snake snapped his gaze to S'Vol. "Servant, did you order an attack against any Beast God followers aside from potential rivals?" he confidently asked, his voice booming over the gathered cultivators.

The cultist gave a similar wry smile. "Of course not, Great Jormungandr. I would never dare to break the sacred rules established."

The World Serpent gave a deep, rumbling laugh. "Good." He then raised his head up high to look down on Fenrir. "You see, Wolf, my disciple has behaved within the rules. If you and your follower wish to continue with your lies and false accusations, maybe you should be the one banished and torn to pieces."

The astral wolf's mouth opened wide, looking like he was going to bite out a chunk of the serpent, but one of his compatriots interrupted.

"Enough!" Hldsvini snorted and stomped. "Fenrir, though he's taken things too far in the past, Jormungandr is still one of us. Without direct proof, we cannot prove your follower's words." The battle boar looked up to the snake. "And do not forget your place, Jormungandr. We've kept you here only because of what you did for our followers before. Try to fight us again, and we *will* let Fenrir tear you to pieces."

The two Beast Gods grunted but conceded to Hldsvini. "Fine," both of them said. Under different circumstances, Kiru might have laughed. These enormous gods were pouting like children.

Then, Jormungandr noticed Pandemonium. "For one who holds true to the rules, Wolf, it appears your candidate has blatantly broken them. She has brought outsiders with her," he hissed angrily.

The other Beast Gods all snapped their heads, their full attention now on the cultivators that Myev had brought with her. Though they were just projections, the members of Pandemonium felt the weight of the deities' direct gazes on them. Their power couldn't be denied. Just the fact of their mere attention brought Pandemonium forcibly to their knees, other than Mutt, who wasn't an "outsider."

Kiru felt as if the weight of an entire mountain was pressing down on him. Surprisingly however, there was no pain, just force. *Their auras?* Kiru thought. *No, but they're in a completely different realm. There's no way something could project their auras this far. Could they?* As he continued to think about what was happening to him, there was no other explanation that he could find. It had to be gods' auras somehow pressing down on them.

Not only was their power great, but their control. Kiru knew that the pressure he felt was carefully applied as if he were a fly delicately caught in between someone's fingers. One slight overapplication of pressure, and he would be nothing but paste.

Kiru did his best to not resist and stay still, not wanting to give the gods any reason to crush him.

"This is from them just looking at us?" William asked. *"And I thought the Flamebringer was scary . . ."*

"It is true, honored Beast Gods," Myev said, taking a quick step in front of the downed trio of Rubies. "They are not of Imakandi, but they have proven themselves to be true allies to my tribe and, by extension, to the pantheon."

"Lies!" Jormungandr hissed, his forked tongue sticking out in anger. "The dwarf is a clear follower of the Vasir. She reeks of their ilk." The snake's words angered Kiru. Though he couldn't get up, he just managed to raise his head enough to glare at the World Serpent. Jormungandr looked at Kiru, and his reptilian face flashed in a strange expression. If Kiru didn't know any better, it looked like fear, but it was there and gone in a second, replaced with an angry scowl. "And you—"

"Bwaaaah! Gwaaah!" A horrible set of high-pitched screams rang out, interrupting the snake. Everyone turned to see that they came from Tanngniost and Tanngrisner, twin goats of strength and life. "Bwaaaah! She may be an outsider—" Tanngrisner said.

"Gwaaah! But she's allied with us!" Tanngniost cried, finishing his brother's sentence.

"Bwaaaah! We've made a pact with her goddess!" Tanngrisner said.

"Gwaaaah! She and her friends are under our protection! Gwaaah!" his brother added.

"Bwaaaah!" They shrieked back and forth, screaming in the terrifying manner that only goats can do.

Jormungandr snarled. "Stupid goats. Fine, just stop your incessant screaming."

As if he'd flipped a switch, the goats instantly ceased, and it was blissfully quiet again. The gods also removed the pressure from the cultivators, and they were finally able to get up.

Eventually, Fenrir spoke up again. "My candidate didn't break our rules, Snake. Just because they are not orc or beast, doesn't mean they aren't allowed. If they are allied to us, they are permitted entry."

"Gwaaah! They are allies!" Tanngniost emphasized.

"Bwaaaah!" Tanngrisner screamed in approval.

"Allies to you two they may be, but to all others they are not," one of the ravens spoke up, their voice otherworldly and detached.

"Yes, they are unproven before most of our eyes," the other raven finished.

"Yes, Wolf," Jormungandr added with obvious glee. "We wouldn't want your champion to have an unfair advantage, would we? The foreigners must prove they are allies to the pantheon as a whole."

Fenrir visibly snarled. "You want to play that way, Snake? You'll regret it."

Both of the bestial gods stared each other down, not giving an inch. It was Fenrir who spoke up again. "The foreigners will receive their own trial before the next stage of Ukufakaza will begin."

Myev gave a small gasp of concern. "Oh no," she uttered before speaking up. "Great Fenrir, I—"

"Silence!" The wolf cut off Myev's words, his terrifying visage leaving no room for argument. He then turned to the central pyramid. "Head Shaman."

"Yes, Great Fenrir?" the leokin asked.

"Collect the Emerald cores that have been brought and place them inside my statue's mouth," Fenrir ordered, gesturing to the stone structure underneath him.

"At once." With remarkable speed and strength, the shaman quickly ran and climbed across the walls of the ruined temple and collected the dire Emerald-rank beast cores. With careful reverence, he placed them inside the wolf statue's mouth.

The lower jaw of the statue shook before raising up slowly, eventually sealing the three beast cores in its mouth and away from sight.

The eyes of Fenrir's astral projection widened some, and the wolf began to do some kind of chewing motion. "Fire ant, dire bear, and torrent horse. Grr, good," he said as if he were actually tasting the cores. He then turned to the boar god. "Hldsvini."

The battle boar grunted at the wolf.

"Rearrange the maze."

CHAPTER TWENTY-EIGHT

Maze Runners

Hldsvini squealed and slammed a hoof down at Fenrir's order. Immediately, the stone ruins began to shake violently. All the cultivators leaned against the pyramids they were on, bracing themselves. The four outer pyramids grew slightly higher, giving everyone a better view down below. The walls, dirt, and sand were being moved. They slammed together and shifted as the entire layout completely changed. The only thing that stayed the same was the central pyramid. Such was the power of a god. Even from another realm, they could massively influence what happened on Alterra.

"*Whoa!*" William said in awe.

Kiru blinked as he took in the sight, his sharp mind committing it to memory. The ruins had transformed into a new, complex maze that was even more complex than before. That wasn't all, though. The wolf statue began to glow blue, and the projection of Fenrir began speaking again: "The three outsiders must retrieve the cores placed inside my statue."

"*Pfft! That doesn't sound hard,*" William scoffed.

It didn't seem too hard to Kiru either. The statue wasn't terribly far from the pyramid they were on. He had a feeling it wouldn't be nearly as straightforward as that. His suspicions were proven correct by Fenrir's next words.

"But during their trial, they shall be pursued by sacred beasts, chimeras whose forms they have brought about themselves. They will succeed or die trying."

Kiru had just enough time to say, "Wait, what?" before Hldsvini slammed another hoof, and the section of the pyramid he, Brunhilda, and Zhaden were on became completely smooth. The trio all slid down the stone structure, crying out in surprise.

Mutt reached a hand down and shouted to them, but his sister pulled him back before he could leap down to join his friends.

"They must do this on their own, Brother," she said. "It is the will of the gods."

The three cultivators picked up speed as they descended, wind rushing over them. Zhaden used his claws and a couple of his daggers to help slow his descent, putting him farther behind the psion and paladin. While that happened, Kiru desperately flailed about, but he couldn't get a solid foothold. He thought about using his Telekinesis to stop his descent, but with so many around, that was a bad idea.

Fortunately, he had Brunhilda, who used her round, steel shield as a make-shift sled which she rode over to help Kiru. "I got ye," she said as she reached out her arm. Kiru grabbed it, and before he could figure out *how* she was going to help him, Brunhilda used her ridiculous strength to heave the psion up, wrapping her arm tight around him as if he were a child. Kiru would've protested had he not seen what was before them. Just a few feet ahead, the slope of the smooth decline turned into a sharp drop of about twenty feet.

"Don't worry, Kiru," Brunhilda said as if she were reading his thoughts. "This time, I be ready." At that, the two shot off of the slope to fly over the maze floor. Kiru squeezed Brunhilda tight, placing his full faith in her. That's when gravity took hold, and the two crashed hard on the ground, sending dust up in all directions. Kiru closed his eyes as his body suddenly lifted upward, and he winced right before impact. However, aside from a *boom* and his body shaking a bit, nothing serious happened. He opened his eyes to see that Brunhilda now held him over her right shoulder like he was a damsel in distress while her left arm with the round shield was firmly wedged into the ground. She was standing on the shield, indicating she had used the protective armor as some sort of landing pad.

That was her plan?! Just land on her shield?! Kiru thought to himself. It had worked, though, so he wasn't going to complain.

"Master, what are you doing? This is embarrassing! Make the paladin put you down now," William demanded.

Kiru's cheek went flush, now more fully taking in the position he was in. "Um, Brunhilda, you can set me down now."

"Oh, aye. Sorry, lad," she said before doing just that.

Right then, Zhaden appeared. The gold drakonid propelled himself off the ledge using his tail, gracefully flipped midair, and landed with little noise in a three-point stance before his teammates.

"See, now that was how we should've landed," the imp sent to Kiru.

Zhaden's reptilian eyes were wide, and his tail flicked up and down with concern as he looked at Kiru and Brunhilda. "Quickly, my friends. We must hurry before—"

"Screee!" A hideous, clicking cry sounded off in the distance.

"By Hlin's hardened shields, what be that?" Brunhilda asked.

"Let's not find out," Kiru replied. "This way!"

The three of them took off into the massive maze.

"Kiru, the statue is to the right. Why are you leading us to the left?" Zhaden asked.

The psion tapped a finger to his temple. "Perfect memory. I know the *exact* route out of here, and it's this—Whoa!" he shouted as the gold drakonid suddenly pulled him back and out of the path of a giant fireball. "Thanks," he said, exasperated, then looked up and to the right to see the source of the flame.

The hideous abominable creature before him was clearly one of the chimeras Fenrir had talked about—a horrifying hybrid of bear, horse, and giant ant. The sacred beast had six legs, which were perched on the side of the wall, seeming to defy gravity. The two back legs and its tail were that of a gray-haired torrent horse, the middle two were segmented black-and-red insectile limbs, and the front two were large, clawed, brown-furred bear paws. Meanwhile, the head was that of a giant red ant, its mandibles clicking in anticipation.

Giant bugs . . . why'd it have to be more giant bugs? Kiru thought, reminded of Heidrun and the bulbous glutton grubs.

The chimera chittered angrily and fired another ball of flame from its mouth. Ready this time, Brunhilda ran in front and intercepted the orb with her enchanted mithril shield. In one smooth motion, she deflected the fireball right back at the chimera. The sacred beast was caught off-guard, and its multi-faceted eyes seemed to widen before its entire body became engulfed by its own attack. It screeched in pain as it fell off the wall. It cries were suddenly cut off with a *crunch* as it landed on some large, uneven rocks that shattered its exoskeleton. There was a heavy moment of silence before more insectile cries echoed throughout the maze, as if in response to the now-deceased chimera's distress.

The cultivators all let out gasps, instinctively knowing the danger was about to get worse.

"*Run, bitches!*" William shouted inside Kiru's mind. The others had the same thought.

"Run!" Kiru said and began frantically sprinting through the maze, his blades at the ready. It wasn't long before they ran into more of the chimeras. One to Kiru's left swiped a claw at him. The psion stepped inside the chimera's guard to avoid the attack, maneuvering past it. Before it could try to attack him again, Kiru spun and used Sweep the Barn to cut off two of its legs. Blood and ichor sprayed from the wounds. Before the chimera could do anything else, Kiru cut its insectoid head off with Hammer the Board.

Just after Kiru finished the beast off, he turned back to continue running. He heard a *whoosh* of something flying past his right, followed by a screech and the sound of something crashing to the ground. He stole a glance to see another chimera, dead, with Zhaden's Bloodstep Stiletto embedded in its eye. The blood touching the blade activated its enchantment and teleported the gold drakonid to its location.

They continued their run with Kiru in the lead, Zhaden in the middle, and Brunhilda bringing up the rear. The psion was able to deal with any of the creatures in their path while he trusted his two companions to deal with any behind or on the walls. William tried to get Kiru to collect any sacred beast cores for Mutt or for them to trade for more of the ogre's booze, but the trio had no time to pause as they were being constantly pursued.

The astral projections of the Beast Gods as well as the many of the leokin and orcs present followed them intently. Fortunately for them, the deities exerted none of the pressure they had experienced before during this observation. The only noises aside from intermittent chimera cries were the cheering roars of the leokin and shouts of support from Mutt in the distance. None of the three could understand what the orc was saying, but they knew he was rooting for them, monitoring them closely by using echolocation.

Zhaden proved *really* effective in protecting the group. After their first set of encounters with the chimeras, he used his Silence technique on all three of the cultivators which helped to decrease the attention they were drawing to themselves. Just five minutes after he used it, Kiru noticed that notably smaller waves of the chimeras were finding them. He reasoned that, with the sounds of their movements gone, it was harder for the chimeras to find them amidst the winding maze. Still, that didn't mean they were safe. Zhaden threw his Bloodstep Stiletto, embedding it into a hind limb of a chimera crawling along a wall toward them.

As soon as the weapon drew blood, the enchantment kicked in once again, and Zhaden teleported right to the weapon. The chimera was caught completely by surprise and didn't react in time to prevent the gold drakonid from slitting its throat.

"Zhaden, look out!" Kiru gave a telepathic shout as the Silence was still in effect. He didn't need to worry, though; the rogue was aware.

Zhaden backflipped off the dead chimera as its limp body began to fall, deftly dodging an incoming fireball. In an amazing feat of athleticism, the drakonid began running along the side of the wall and jumped over to the other side.

Just then, however, the chimera unleashed another fireball, tracking its target in the air.

It would've hit Zhaden, too, had the drakonid not thrown his Bloodstep Stiletto once again as he leaped. Just as the orb of flame reached just a few feet in front of him, his blade struck a glancing blow on the chimera, and the enchantment activated. Zhaden disappeared in a flash and silently reappeared beside the chimera. He rolled on the creature's back and stabbed in it the back of the head, piercing straight through the exoskeleton of its skull.

Despite the obstacles set before them, Kiru believed the three cultivators were dealing with the trial impressively. Mutt continued to cheer loudly from the M'Baku pyramid, being their number-one fan.

Pandemonium was doing more and more to draw the attention of both gods and cultivators. Everyone was so focused on the display and the resultant consequences on their success or failure that no one noticed some of the Jormuns slipping away thanks to a quiet order from S'Vol.

The Jabari leader gave his command, and nine orc cultists activated a technique to turn their lower halves into that of a snake's tail. He watched them slither along the outer edge of the temple's cracked walls. Once they were at their targets, they all pulled out one of the rare, sacred scales of their deity and swallowed them. Their bodies began to morph, and red, unstable power began to rampage through them. With that borrowed power, their purpose was finally fulfilled. They would temporarily remove Jormungandr's rivals and help bring about his return.

For the next few minutes, Kiru, Zhaden, and Brunhilda were zig-zagging their way through the complicated maze, only able to make it through so quickly due to Kiru's knowledge of the mazes. They cut, deflected, and smashed their way through the monstrous sacred beasts until they eventually made it to their destination. There was a large set of stone stairs leading up to the top of the right wall, where both the Fenrir statue and head leokin shaman stood, waiting expectantly.

The trio ran up the stairs to the cheering of the leokin. Even Tanngniost and Tanngrisner let out a set of screams that Kiru was pretty sure was supposed to mean they were supporting them. He couldn't tell as they always sounded like they were in extreme distress.

Suddenly more chimeras advanced on them.

"Go on, lads. I'll hold 'em off!" Brunhilda shouted as Zhaden's Silence had recently worn off. She turned back and lowered her shields in order to be a stalwart bulwark. Her friends paused just for a moment, but on seeing how close their pursuers were, they didn't have time to argue. Kiru and Zhaden had to trust Brunhilda.

At that, the two chimeras came charging at her. The paladin slammed the edge of her enchanted shield straight at the chest of the one to her right, the bladed tip puncturing deeply and audibly cracking ribs. She raised her round shield and blocked a swipe from a bear paw from the chimera on her left. Both the sacred beasts recoiled, then immediately went to bite her at the same time.

The dwarf activated her Divine Shield technique just in time. A column of golden light surrounded her and intercepted the simultaneous strikes. Both the chimeras were immediately rebuffed and encased in holy fire. Still, more were coming.

Brunhilda gritted her teeth. "These persistent creatures," she grunted. *These gods wanted to see beasts. I'll show them a beast,* she thought.

She then punched forward with one shield. "Gnash!" An ethereal head in the shape of Tanngniost shot forward. "And Grind!" Followed by the goat's brother.

The chimeras cried in fear, then pain as they felt the fury of not one but three different deities.

Meanwhile, Kiru and Zhaden rushed forward. Two more chimeras had decided to crawl up the sides of the stairs ahead of them and crested near the top to intercept and ambush them. "Get to the statue, Kiru. I will handle these two," Zhaden hissed before sprinting past Kiru in a burst of speed.

The two chimeras charged at the gold drakonid, but they both immediately halted in panic as their one opponent multiplied into four. Zhaden had activated Duplication. As the three illusory duplicates appeared, the chimeras raised up on their two hooved hindfeet in. All four Zhadens jumped at once, and the real one successfully carved a fatal wound through the neck of one of them with a dagger.

Meanwhile, Mutt's senses helped him tell that Kiru used the space Zhaden created to rush forward. He made it to the top and over to the statue. Mutt could tell that he was so focused, so much so that he was oblivious to the fact that the head shaman was no longer standing by the statue.

"Boss, watch out!" the orc yelled, but it fell on deaf ears. Many beast mana users used smell to help them detect foes, but the scent of the new chimeras created by Fenrir was overwhelming to those with sensitive noses. The blind cultivator "saw" in a very different way, however. Mutt was able to detect things via vibration. He was the only one to sense the reptilian cultists spreading around the temple, but he was too late. As Kiru rushed forward, he slammed his palm onto the wolf statue's mouth. He then moved his fingers along the edge, trying to forcibly pull its mouth open to get the cores out. His heart sank when a giant snake emerged from behind the statue, red power pulsing in between its scales and one of the head shaman's now-bloody arms impaled on one of its teeth.

"*Master, shield yourself!*" William warned.

The young psion had just enough time to change his Psyslime blade into a shield before the snake bit deep into its body and violently ripped off a huge chunk of its own flesh.

CHAPTER TWENTY-NINE

Draconic

BOOM! The self-inflicted injury was too much for the cultivator-turned-snake's body to deal with. The mana flowing wildly inside it released in an explosion, shattering the stone statue of Fenrir, and its own body, to pieces. Kiru had originally changed the Psyslime into a shield to protect him from the snake's attack. Granted, he thought it was going to lunge at him and not blow itself up. Either way, the slime shield saved the psion's life.

Kiru was sent skipping across the top of the wall. There were audible *thunks* as his body repeatedly hit the stone. Thankfully, the enchantment on his head-band kicked in, forming a magical helmet to protect his skull from damage and his brain from a concussion. The temple shook as eight more explosions went off simultaneously along the walls. Bestial cries of shock and anger rang out before they were abruptly cut off.

For a moment, Kiru blacked out. A few seconds after his momentum had stopped and he slid to a halt, his eyes snapped wide, and he inhaled sharply. Then, he closed his eyes and shook his head. There was a high-pitched ringing in his ears and all he could see was bright light. But then an instant later, his vision and hearing came back to him.

"Ugh, what happened?" he groaned.

"*Master, there was another one of those snakes with that unstable power like back in the Wastelands,*" William answered. "*It killed itself and exploded in front of your face. Then you went flying, and I heard eight more explosions that sounded just the same as the one that echoed around the temple.*"

Kiru's heart skipped a beat as concern gripped him. Quickly, he reactivated Telekinesis and pushed himself up to see what was going on with the temple. He was greeted with a grisly sight.

Bloody chunks of snake were strewn all around him, along with mutilated pieces of the head shaman's body. A wave of nausea washed over him, and he could barely keep himself from vomiting. He didn't know if it was the concussion, the gore around him, or something else that made him feel nauseous. At the moment, Kiru didn't care. He just needed to compose himself as he knew he wasn't safe. Small fires and pockets of charred and red-hot stone were scattered around his feet. Where the statue of Fenrir had once stood was now a smoldering, black crater ten feet long.

Why didn't the leokin prevent this from happening? Weren't they supposed to be monitoring threats? Kiru then looked over the central pyramid. The leokin there were moving around wildly in the distance, like a colony of disturbed ants. *What are they doing?* Kiru then remembered his friends and looked around to find them. Fortunately, he could see Zhaden and Brunhilda back at the stairs he'd ascended to get to the Fenrir statue. Both seemed to be completely fine, and Kiru saw the forms of the chimeras around them . . . *dissolving*? Yes, their forms just seemed to be disintegrating before them and fading away into dust.

Putting together what William said about eight more explosions and what that could mean, Kiru quickly scanned along all the temple walls. His eyes widened as he got his answer as to what the other explosions were. All along the temple walls, the statues of the Beast Gods had been obliterated, all now in ruins. All except the one of Jormungandr, that is.

Even more significantly, the projections of the other gods were also gone. Now Kiru knew why the chimeras had faded away. The power that created them and held them on Alterra was no longer present in this realm. The connection with the Beast Gods had been disconnected so the chimeras had simply ceased to be.

The only Beast God remaining was the shackled World Serpent, who was flashing a cunning smile to everyone assembled in the temple below.

"This isn't good," Kiru said and changed his Psyslime back into a Fu Tao. More stone clacked to the ground by his feet as the various pieces that had been embedded in the shield were forcefully dislodged due to its new change in shape. Kiru hadn't even realized just how close to death he had come until that point.

As if to confirm what Kiru had just said, the projection of the shackled serpent let out a booming laugh, shaking the damaged temple and causing debris to scatter and fall. "Your gods cannot protect you now. It's just you and me, peons," he hissed as he looked down both figuratively and literally on the gathered cultivators before him. "I will give you one chance to make the smart decision like the Jabari have. Renounce your gods and bow to me. Join the Jormuns and release me from my imprisonment so that I may return to Imakandi once more, or choose to continue to be sheep and be slaughtered by your betters."

There was a heavy silence, everyone trying to process the damage and what exactly had just happened. From what Kiru could gather, the Jormuns had used suicide bombers to destroy the statues of the other Beast Gods, which meant the actual gods in their realm could no longer influence or directly contact their followers within the temple, leaving only the World Serpent remaining.

"We will never bow to you, Serpent. Fenrir will have your head for this!" Myev fearlessly shouted.

"Of course, the M'Baku." Jormungandr grinned. "I should've known that anyone foolish enough to follow that imbecilic wolf wouldn't see reason. I shall enjoy having my followers tear all of you limb from limb."

The massive projection turned to address both the Thrar'fangs and the leokin. "What say you? All you have to do is serve me and allow my candidate to disable the runes at the top of the central pyramid. None of you need be harmed."

The leokin were clearly terrified, many of them clustering together and shaking. Kiru couldn't blame them. Not only had the connection from the deities they served been disconnected, their head shaman was lying in pieces on one of the temple walls. Many of them were murmuring and looking at one another, clearly terrified at drawing the World Serpent's ire. They looked as if they were going to accept when a loud, high-pitched barking cut through the silence.

It was Nom. The leokin cub was shouting furiously at the World Serpent in vehement defiance. Kiru was shocked—both for his boldness, and because he was saying more than just "Nom." The other leokin slowly all turned their heads up to the young noble. Kiru couldn't make sense of what Nom was saying, but the cub's tribe seemed to understand.

"He's right!" Zengaz pronounced. "Your tribe so callously bends the rules to excuse your cruelty. You killed the prince's guardian and nearly killed him," he said, gesturing to Nom. "I've lost an arm and an eye because of your tribe's influence. You are a liar, Jormungandr, and your words are as foul as the poison in your blood."

The projection snarled as he turned from the leokin to Thrar'fang Grimtusk. "Grimtusk, leader of the Thrar'fangs, your tribe values strength. I am the strongest among my brethren. They were barely able to contain me, and that was with them all working together. Follow me, and I will grant you more power than you can even imagine."

The heavily armored orc scowled. "We of the Thrar'fang follow the strong. Despite his concerns, even Hldsvini advocated for your release, Jormungandr."

The World Serpent smiled.

The orc leader scowled. "But you have deceived yourself. You are not strong. A strong god would have prevented his opponents from imprisoning him in the first place. No, you rely on trickery and deceit to amass strength. That is not true strength. You are not strong like Hldsvini."

"Now that guy gets it," William cheered inside Kiru's mind.

The psion agreed. Although Jormungandr was a god, he relied on tricks to get his followers into places of power, not his actual strength. Kiru would've bet that the reason it was actually so hard for the Beast Gods to capture Jormungandr was due to trickery as well.

Grimtusk pointed his large, spiked mace at the projection, "You are weak and betrayed our god. We shall not follow y—"

He was cut off suddenly as a bolt of acid zoomed across the temple and struck the orc straight in the chest, knocking him off his back.

"Silence, you impudent fool!" S'Vol spat angrily, his mouth trailing twin streams of smoke.

He clearly fired the acid, Kiru thought.

Grimtusk growled, his body partially embedded in the stone pyramid beneath. He forced himself up and ripped off his rapidly dissolving chest plate with one hand, his scowl even deeper now.

Jormungandr clearly did not expect either Grimtusk's denial nor insult. His expression quickly went from shock to pure rage.

"Worthless whelp!" the Beast God roared, shaking the entire temple. "Strength is strength, it doesn't matter how one accrues it! I am no simple-minded pig! Tremble in fear of a dragon's might!" he shouted, and spectral wings suddenly grew from the snake's large body.

The worn statue under Jormungandr glowed bright with green light, and the World Serpent's decree was met by a chorus of roars.

A chill traveled up Kiru's neck. The roars came from the Jormuns on the pyramid, but there were too many for it to be coming from *just* those handful of cultists. "Oh no," he uttered.

Just then, the large doors at the front of the temple broke open, revealing an entire battalion of heavily scarred orcs. Hundreds of cultists poured out, wielding their spears and roaring proudly.

"Destroy the runes on the central pyramid, my minions! Leave none alive!" Jormungandr declared, and his astral form seemed to be absorbed into the statue. The bright light shone even brighter and then pulsed across the temple.

The Jormuns roared once again as their bodies became imbued with violent draconic power, causing them to grow in size, their muscles bulging. Scales began to form, red energy flowing in between them. Unlike the previous times, though, they didn't just turn into giant wild snakes. No, all the Jormuns' bodies quickly changed into various versions of dragon-orc hybrids. Some even sprouted wings! The red energy also didn't pulse unstably. This was the true perfected version of what they were meant to be.

Kiru felt nauseous, staggering to a knee when the pulse passed through him. While the cultists were quite literally empowered, Kiru's heart sank. In that moment, so many things clicked in his head. Why he was so repulsed by Jormungandr; why only he, a psion, could cure Myev's poisoning; why the World Serpent wanted to take over the continent. Jormungandr was a dragon, and so even though he was a god, he had a master: Nidhogg, the dragon that ruled over all others and wished to dominate the whole world. The creature that only the psion could stop, and who would no doubt want Kiru dead if he made himself known, was the true villain behind it all.

Zhaden and Brunhilda ran over to Kiru. They were speaking to him, but he heard none of it. He was gripped by fear and overcome by indecision. There was a whole fucking battalion of cultists entering the temple right now. He and his people were badly outnumbered, and the cultists were all much more powerful than before. Plus, he had a feeling he'd be risking alerting New Draconia somehow.

He could run and escape with his friends and they could do their best to find his father's second item on their own. After coming so far south, Kiru could sense the general direction it was in. He could actually do it. He then thought about his mother and how he had been too weak and helpless to save her life, and so she had to sacrifice herself. Kiru swore then to be the man who'd protect his allies, no matter the cost. He would be a king who would value the lives of his people, of his friends.

With that firm resolution, his mind snapped back to the moment, just in time to have blinding light hit his eyes as Brunhilda's Healing Hands activated as she gripped his head.

"Ah! Ow," he said and batted the dwarf's hands away.

"Oh good, ye be back." The paladin sighed in relief. "We were jabbering away but yer eyes went distant. It seems I be right, ye must've suffered a concussion."

Zhaden wasn't looking at Kiru. The rogue was keeping his sharp eyes peeled for any enemies. Just then, a loud crash echoed out from within the temple. They snapped their heads toward the noise. There, atop the central pyramid, S'Vol was duking it out with Grimtusk and Myev, who were working together to finish off the Jabari. The three Emeralds fought with greater power and speed than any others in the temple. Kiru was barely able to keep track of their movements!

Meanwhile, the Jormuns were storming the temple. The structure was still in the form of a maze, but the empowered cultists were literally flying or crawling over the walls to get toward the central pyramid, ignoring the winding pathways of the maze entirely. It was slowing their charge, but it wouldn't help for long. Z'Goyan, Snout, and the other forces Myev had gathered were doing the same, rushing along the top of the maze walls but to the leokin's defense. The ogre was notably slower, so he was much farther behind. Grimtusk's forces were also running to aid the leokin from their pyramid.

Kiru spared a glance to look over at the pyramid where the Jabari were originally and noticed the allies they had brought with them were now just bloody corpses splayed about. Apparently, their usefulness had run out for the cultists. There was a loud thump behind them, and they all raised their weapons instinctively until they saw it was Mutt. The blind orc was distressed, his wild mohawk even more unkempt than usual.

"Boss, what do we do?"

Kiru took a deep breath, his face firming with resolve. "We protect the innocent. We help our friends. We fight."

William cheered inside Kiru's mind, "*Yeah!*"

"Let's go," Kiru said and began running across the top edge of the temple's wall. His friends followed close behind. Copying what the Jormuns did, Kiru jumped over to a nearby maze wall and began sprinting across the top, using it as a shortcut to get to the central pyramid. Zhaden was right by the psion. Mutt ran on all fours and carried Brunhilda on his back. The paladin blushed in embarrassment, as, even though she was powerful, she did not possess the dexterity the others did to perform such maneuvers. Her heavy armor didn't help either. So, she held on.

Quickly, just half a minute before the Jormuns, Pandemonium made it to the central pyramid. The leokin civilians were evacuating to the safety of the stone structure, Zengaz and Nom at an entrance at the bottom of the structure waving all their people in. While they did that, the pyramid continued to shake as the three Emeralds clashed on top, the sounds of their weapons and techniques resonating loudly. Kiru and the others landed and ran over in front of the pyramid.

"Should you be sending them in there?" Kiru asked. "It seems like it could collapse at any moment."

"There are tunnels under the temple that span its entirety," Zengaz said. "None of our people are staying under the temple but moving away to safety. This entrance is the nearest one, and I fear no one would make it to another before the Jormuns got them."

"Indeed," the female priestess said.

"Nom!" the little leokin added in confirmation.

"I can feel the tunnels underneath, Boss. They're right," Mutt said, tapping one of his bare feet on the dirt for emphasis.

"Very well then. This is where we make our stand," Kiru said with grim determination.

Kiru had learned that the runes were on the top of the pyramid that kept Jormungandr bound. He also knew that was where the Emeralds were fighting, and he and his friends would be crushed to paste if they got too close. He couldn't do anything up at the top, but he knew he and his team could help in keeping the other Jormuns away from the building. Hopefully that would give Myev enough time to end S'Vol.

The members of Pandemonium joined up with the assembled forces of both the Thrar'fangs and the M'Baku with their backers from the other tribe leaders present as well. Most were Gold with two Rubies. The most powerful were Z'Goyan and Snout at Sapphire. As such, the Tau shaman took charge.

"Hold the line for as long as possible! Keep them away from the pyramid and our leaders! Give your life if needed to save our country and our gods! Fight!" he shouted, then slammed his staff on the ground, activating a technique at the same time which turned his feet into gray horse legs as a small gust of wind continuously spun around him.

"Boon of Sleipnir," Z'Goyan said. At those words, the wind spread out wide until it surrounded the legs of all the surrounding cultivators, who looked down at their legs in awe. Despite not having physical sensation in his legs, even Kiru could detect less mana drain on them than usual. *I should be able to move with greater ease. It will take me less mana to shift my legs, so I can use more of it on my techniques,* the psion thought.

"Raaaaaa!" The assembled defenders let out a battle cry, emboldened by their new boon. Kiru examined their faces. Some were eager like Mutt and Snout, some had looks of firm resolve like Zhaden, and others had a mixture of the two like Brunhilda and Z'Goyan. Kiru noticed they were breathing rapidly, seeming to be trying to stave off panic attacks. Kiru couldn't blame any of them for what they were feeling. All in all, they numbered just twenty-two. Though they had two Sapphires with them, as the cultists crawled over the top of the nearest wall like they were one giant entity, the aura of power exuding from *all* of them were that of Ruby. It didn't take a genius to figure out that they weren't likely going to defeat the force of at least three hundred. Still, even if the odds were slim, there was at least a small chance of victory.

The beast mana cultivators among them snarled and growled as their bodies morphed into various animal hybrids. One of the Thrar'fangs changed so much they looked like a bipedal boar with sharp fur and tusks that could be mistaken for sharpened short swords.

Kiru forcibly steadied his breathing. He'd been in life and death situations before, but not like this. If he'd ever been up against a foe with superior numbers, he either ran away from them, such as during the first round of the Warrior Games or with the minotaurs, or he just avoided them entirely, such as the gnolls who had taken over the L'Khan's village. Kiru had never before been on the frontlines of open war. He was resolved to fight these incoming foes, but that didn't make him *comfortable* with it. Both his blades shook slightly in his grip, betraying his internal conflict.

Oddly enough, it was the bloodthirsty imp in his mind who brought Kiru solace. *"Master, I know you're worried. Don't be."*

"Pretty fucking hard not to be right now, William," Kiru replied.

"Listen, whatever happens, you're acting in spite of your fear. You're doing what is right, not cowering like a little baby. Even if you fail, you will have died in glorious

battle, having lived your truth without regrets. That is something to be proud of," the imp said, sounding profoundly wise, to Kiru's astonishment.

"Wow, William. You're right. Thanks!"

"Of course, Master. Now, let's show them who we are: Kiru the Conqueror and William the Breaker of Wills! Generations will revel in the tale of the blood we shed here! We shall use all our skills and training to make these fools piss their pants as we end their lives!"

"And we're back to normal," Kiru uttered aloud with a smile, comforted by hearing the little demon's familiar bloodthirsty rambling. William had a weird way of viewing things, but the psion couldn't deny he had a way of helping him overcome his own self-doubt. His grip firmed, and he readied his Fu Tao to prepare for combat. A loud rumbling filled the ears of the cultivators as they waited, the sounds of the horde closing in. The ground underneath shook more and more as the Jormuns neared. Those noises, mixed with the thunderclap-level sounds of conflict from above, brought everything to a feeling of such chaos, it was like it was literally pressing on the cultivators' nerves. The thought of running ran through most of their minds, but fortunately, none succumbed. There wasn't anywhere to run to, anyway, as the leokin closed the doorway under the pyramid.

After a few tense seconds, the Jormuns were within sight. There were a couple of hundred feet between the cultivators and the maze wall, and the Jormuns just began to fly or crest over the stone structure. As soon as they were within sight, some of the cultivators started using their long-range techniques to attack the cultists from afar. The orc with a blue-feathered goatee screeched and fired a technique Kiru was intimately familiar with, Thunder Rooster's Cry. The black-feathered orc, on the other hand, started slinging thin slashes of mana from his wings. Z'Goyan notably fired gusts of wind from his staff with the force of a ballista bolt, swinging the weapon with practiced ease.

Many of the draconic orcs were killed—either scorched to a crisp, cut to pieces, or crushed by the various techniques–but that still didn't stop the oncoming horde. If anything, it seemed to only anger them as their roars grew even more savage. The three orcs continued their volleys of long-range techniques, but as they got closer, Kiru noticed that the attacks against the cultists weren't as devastating as he'd initially thought. With Jormungandr's power coursing through them, their scales were able to resist much of the damage. Plus, some of them began their own long-range assault, spewing bolts of acidic venom at the defenders below.

Z'Goyan stopped firing wind attacks in favor of spinning his staff to form a defensive barrier of wind. It didn't stop all the acid, but much was blown back. After only a few seconds, many of the Jormuns had made it over the wall and began swooping down and charging the defenders. Not one of the Jormuns were the exact same—some just had reptilian muzzles and scaled hides, while others still had serpentine tails instead of legs, and others looked like a dragon upper-half had been smashed into an orc lower-half. One thing was for sure, though: they were all powerful.

"To me!" Z'Goyan shouted. He dismissed his wind barrier and took off in a burst of speed, the wind forcing him forward in a gale. The orc shaman tore a path through the oncoming cultists, sending many of them flying as he swung his staff. Using that as the ignition, the rest charged forward to join him. The battle had begun.

CHAPTER THIRTY

Heat of Battle

Kiru and the others charged headlong into the swarm of Jormuns as the three Emeralds battled above them. As the psion got closer, he focused his mental mana and fired a blast of Brainstorm at the cultists. It wasn't as impressive as Z'Goyan's dash, but it definitely threw some Jormuns back from the sheer force while causing others to stagger as white electricity visibly coursed around their bodies. Sections of their scales blackened and scorched as small trails of smoke puffed out of their wounds. All of this gave Kiru an opening.

He ducked under a jerky spear thrust from one cultist and deflected another's with Hammer the Boards. He closed the distance with his dodging and used Trim the Grass to slice straight through a scaled abdomen, eviscerating his enemy with his Psyslime blade. Then he spun and quickly continued with Sweep the Barn, cutting through the left ankle of another cultist and following up with a sharp slash to their throat with his steel blade.

The psion was caught by surprise when his Fu Tao didn't cut as deeply into their scaled hide as he'd expected. Normally, his blade would have carved a deep gouge, but this time it only left a minor wound. The cultist snarled as blood trailed down their neck. Kiru had been confident that he was going to be dealing them a killing blow. Because of that, he had allowed himself to get close to his target . . . too close.

The angry cultist opened their toothy maw and, before Kiru could get away, bit down on his shoulder. Though he couldn't feel, he still reflexively groaned as the metal of his Bronzium armor bent and gave way to the draconic teeth. Before the cultist could strike again, the psion took his Psyslime blade and crammed the hooked tip right into his opponent's left eye. With a scream, he heaved and tore the Fu Tao through the eye socket and out of the cultist's skull. Kiru didn't have time to celebrate, though, as more of the draconic orcs came toward him.

"Gnash and Grind!" Brunhilda's voice boomed from behind and two spectral goat heads flew past Kiru. They rammed through a few incoming cultists, then bit down on a pair, grotesquely crushing the draconic orcs in half with their blunt teeth. She then rested her hand on Kiru's injured shoulder. "Restoration." Life mana flowed from her, glowing slightly and healing the multiple punctures in his shoulder. She knew he couldn't actually feel the injury, nor could she repair the armor, but he could have still died from blood loss.

Both Kiru and Brunhilda nodded to each other before reengaging their foes en masse. A pair of cultists spat large globs of acid at them. Brunhilda, speed-enhanced from Sleipnir's Boon, rushed in front of Kiru and quickly raised her shields to intercept. To their surprise, however, Mutt jumped down in front of them and crossed his arms in front of himself.

"Dweller Bear's Fur," the orc said. Thick brown fur rapidly grew out from every bit of exposed skin, making him unrecognizable. The acid splashed against his fur and immediately began to sizzle, the smell of burned hair blending with that of blood and dirt.

"Mutt!" Brunhilda cried out in distress, but she didn't need to.

The affected fur sizzled as it was eaten away. The orc's body visibly reacted as needed and ejected the affected hairs from his body, landing on the ground in thick plops and keeping him free from harm.

The two acid-spitting Jormuns slithered quickly toward the blind orc. One heaved their spear at him, thinking him to be an easy target.

To their surprise, he uncrossed his arms, caught the spear, and in the blink of an eye, threw it at their companion, impaling them straight threw their mouth and killing them instantly.

The remaining Jormun's eyes widened, and they tried to halt their charge, but it was too late.

Mutt leaped in the air, shouting, "Harpy Eagle's Talons!" His feet morphed from wide and green to large, yellow, three-taloned bird feet. The momentum of his leap and the sharpness of the talons pierced straight through the cultist's hide, stabbing their heart and crushing their sternum in one devastating blow. Fueled by the beast mana coursing through him and flowing in abundance in the battle-field, Mutt raised his head and let out a savage roar of triumph.

For all of Mutt's advantages of enhanced senses aside from vision, not having classic sight did have its drawbacks. Mutt often "saw" through sensing things via the vibrations in the ground through his feet. Because of that, he could have dif-ficulty detecting things in the air, just like the incoming flying draconic orc. The cultist swooped down and shoved their spear into him and picked Mutt up in the air. His Dweller Bear's Fur was still active, so it prevented too much damage from occurring, but it went a couple of inches into his muscular chest, and he flailed about desperately in the air trying to get at his foe.

Kiru turned, wanting to activate Brainstorm.

Brunhilda clearly wanted to do the same with Gnash and Grind, but neither of them used their techniques. They couldn't risk hitting Mutt.

Before the orc prince was carried too high, however, a thin stiletto expertly arced through the air and hit the Jormun right in one of its nostrils. The narrow blade struck true, avoiding the tough scales and hitting the vulnerable flesh below. The cultist cried out in pain just before Zhaden teleported to appear right at their face with his hand gripped on the blade. With the sudden addition of weight, the flying Jormun dropped and crashed hard. Kiru and Brunhilda wanted to run over to their friends, but they quickly found themselves surrounded by five Jormuns all at Gold, the savage looks in their eyes promising death. The psion knew they had to trust that the others would be okay.

For the next ten minutes, Pandemonium and their orc allies, along with the Thrar'fang subordinates, fought against the horde of cultists charging at them. At first, Kiru was surprised by just how strong some of his opponents were. More than once, he thought he was going to overpower them, only for a cultist to push back against one of his blades. Still, they didn't match Kiru and Pandemonium's skill, despite the latter's significant number disadvantage.

That changed about halfway through the battle.

The epic clash of three Emeralds fighting atop the pyramid resounded all around them. The three cultivators were soaring and zooming across the sky. From what Kiru had glimpsed, S'Vol and Myev had grown wings, and Grimtusk had a technique or leg power to propel himself for at least a temporary time. Since they weren't restricted to just the pyramid, they were actually fighting throughout the entire temple grounds, destroying much in their wake and giving everyone at least a fleeting glimpse of their battle.

Being the cunning and cruel fighter that he was, S'Vol repeatedly tried to kill the members fighting against his horde of cultists. He was even successful a couple of times, melting some unfortunate orcs with a stream of acid. Kiru thought to retaliate and use Brainstorm on the cult leader, but S'Vol was too fast and Kiru didn't want to risk accidentally striking Myev or Grimtusk. Out of Kiru's twenty-two fighters, there were now only twelve left. In order to protect the gathered force remaining, both Z'Goyan and Snout had to back off from fighting directly in order to focus on protecting the other ten from any strikes directed toward them. The two Sapphires had the best chance of combating any technique or strike that S'Vol might send their way. There was still a power gap, but it was the best they could come up with at the moment. Without the shaman or ogre leading the charge, Pandemonium and their allies were slowly losing. The empowered Jormuns were too numerous and too fierce. Both Mutt and Zhaden survived their crash landing from earlier in the battle and were doing their best to overcome their enemies. Now, having complete knowledge of all his techniques, Mutt had activated them all at once, transforming into the large hairy beast form he had when he first encountered the party. This time, however, he had complete control of his body *and* mind.

The blind orc swiped his claws across a cultist, just managing to slice off some of the scales covering their left clavicle. The Jormun had a draconic muzzle, small horns, and a large tail. They had lost their spear in the fight, so they growled in pain, then lunged at Mutt with their claws. The orc met their attack head-on, and the two bared their teeth in a clash of wills.

"Give up, insect," the cultist snarled. "Our bodies are protected by our god's scales. You cannot win."

"So, where there are no scales, they aren't protected?" Mutt asked but didn't wait for an answer. With his empowered teeth and jaws, he used Gnoll's Bite and bit down on the soft flesh that had been exposed when the scales were removed.

Mutt's jaws flexed and his teeth not only tore through muscle but shattered the cultist's clavicle. The cultist let out a cry of pain, and their grip weakened. Mutt seized the opportunity and forced their arms down, bending their wrists at a painful angle. The cultist was forced to give a little ground and slither back. Meanwhile, the blind orc kicked both of his feet into their chest. Given his feet were currently those of a horned harpy eagle, the sharp talons penetrated the scales.

The cultist was forced on their back with Mutt atop them. Mutt was relentless, and just as his opponent opened their mouth to let out an angry roar of pain, he grabbed the inside of each of their jaws with both hands. The cultist's cry was abruptly cut short as Mutt began to forcefully pry their mouth open wider and wider. Their serpentine body began to flail wildly as muscle and bone snapped as Mutt ripped the bottom jaw and part of their throat away from their body.

Mutt stood on the fresh corpse and let out a roar of triumph. This time, he used the Bounder's Howl technique, which caused many slithering spear-wielders coming at him to stagger in fear and trepidation, allowing an invisible Zhaden to appear and deal them fatal blows. Whereas Mutt dealt with his opponents by brute force, the rogue dream mana user fought with precision. Instead of having to fight through the thickened scales of his draconic foes to create weak points, Zhaden directly targeted already-vulnerable areas.

His daggers swiftly stabbed into the cultists' eyes and ear canals, two places not reinforced by the hardened scales. The assassin killed the four terrified cultists in a matter of moments. An orb of acid was sent flying toward him, but through the use of Duplication, he managed to dodge the technique as it passed through an illusion.

Kiru flanked the one who tried to melt his friend. He blocked their spear thrust with Sweep the Barn with his steel blade, then used Hammer the Board with his Psyslime weapon to cut straight through the cultist's neck, decapitating them in one fell blow.

In the midst of the fighting, Kiru had discovered a surprising thing. While the Jormuns' scales were resistant to bladed weapons such as his steel Fu Tao, they were notably susceptible to his Psyslime weapon. The slime was able to simply ignore much of the durability the scales provided and slice through them as if they were just thick animal hide, making the cultists much easier to deal with. During a brief lull in the combat, he had asked William if he knew why, but the imp only replied that it was a "psion's weapon" and because of that, it was superior. Kiru didn't have time to argue with the imp's reasoning. For whatever reason, it worked better and he would capitalize on that.

"*Three-Sixty Formation!*" he telepathically shouted to his teammates. Having trained to fight in different formations back at the academy, the four cultivators all moved together and pressed their backs to each other. They each scanned in one of four directions, effectively removing their blind spots.

"I don't get it. How're these guys so much stronger than before?" Mutt asked, then grabbed a cultist by the wrist and threw them into the midst of the fighting, making them crash into their own allies. "I mean, in the past, when they powered themselves up, they turned into those snake things that would blow up when they got too damaged. What's changed?"

"Well, love," Brunhilda answered as she broke a spear thrust with her mithril shield, then used that shield to bash in a draconic muzzle, "it appears their god be giving them a boost in a different way this time."

"Your assessment appears correct, Brunhilda," Zhaden said. "They are obviously much more like drakonids as opposed to the mere serpentine nature they displayed previously." The rogue then blocked a spear thrust with his daggers, spun, and tripped the cultist with his tail. Just a second after the Jormun landed on their back, Zhaden ended their life with a precise stab from one of his daggers. "Though they're clearly more like strange hybrids versus full dragon-blooded like my kin. It would seem all we need to do is remove the source of their empowerment. I must confess—" He paused to parry another spear attack. "—I am unfamiliar with how to remove one's connection with their deity."

Kiru pondered on those words as he continued to fight. He quickly thought about what they said in conjunction with remembering how exactly Jormungandr bestowed his powers to the others. As Mutt had said, they'd first turned into unstable ticking bombs. That was when they would ingest one of their banished god's scales.

"How have these cultists gathered so many of the serpent's scales anyway? Hasn't it been centuries? Shouldn't they have run out by now?" William asked.

Kiru agreed that the sheer number of scales the World Serpent had scattered about seemed almost comical, but he'd figured out the likely reason that there were still so many left. *"If Jormungandr is a being that supposedly spanned the entirety of Midgard, I bet he would've shed quite a few scales over the course of centuries. I also bet he made sure his followers had a large supply as well,"* he sent back. He didn't know how to remove the scales from any of the Jormuns once they had ingested them. Maybe he could cut open their stomachs?

"Whatever, but it doesn't seem like his stupid scales are what's powering up these guys this time," William countered.

He was right. This time, it seemed that the projection of the imprisoned Beast God who revealed that he was both beast *and* dragon, had dissipated and suffused his followers with a portion of his power. *How exactly had he done that?* Kiru thought back to exactly what had happened. Jormungandr's form sank into the warped, worn stone that remained of his statue before spreading out like a wave. *The statue . . .*

Kiru ducked under an incoming bite from a low-flying Jormun, then stole a glance up to the curved rocky structure. It was still glowing. The light was dull, but the green color coming off it was unmistakable. There was also something distinct about the stone. It was guarded. A contingent of Jormuns stood in front of the structure with their spears at the ready. Why would these bloodthirsty cultists *not* try to kill them to destroy the pyramid? In the psion's experiences with the Jormuns so far, they did everything they could to further their sinister plots. Kiru knew that their presence by the statue had to be for a similar reason. *So, why are they up there and not in the fight?*

It has to be the statue, he thought. There was no other explanation. At least, no other one that they could do anything about. It must be serving as a conduit for the Jormuns.

"Kiru," Brunhilda said before blocking a cultist's tail strike, "ye got that look on yer face."

"What look?" he asked.

"The look that says ye be coming up with one of your rushed cockamamie plans."

"Hey!" the psion protested, almost getting skewered due to the distraction.

"Did she just insult you? Oh, Master, if I weren't in your core, I'd show that pal-abitch who's boss," William said.

"Brunhilda is right," Zhaden said through gritted teeth as he was forcing a spearhead back with his daggers crossed. "You do have the tendency to make a certain face when you're planning." The gold drakonid tripped his opponent with his tail which allowed Mutt to stomp on them with his taloned feet, swiftly stabbing straight through their eyes to their brain.

"I don't know what 'cockamamie' means, but I like the Boss's plans," Mutt said, reveling in the heat of battle.

"Well, a crazy plan be better than no plan. So, just hurry up and tell us what we got to do to get out of this shite, Kiru," Brunhilda retorted as she traded a blow with an opponent. She jabbed them in the throat, damaging their trachea, but they managed a glancing stab in between the plates of her armor. Fortunately, a use of Healing Hands quickly repaired the damage.

Kiru was a little insulted that his plans were called "cockamamie" once again. He would need to have a serious discussion with Brunhilda about always jabbing at him if they survived this. His plans had gotten them this far, hadn't they? Then again, they were surrounded by a horde of bloodthirsty cultists who wanted them dead. So . . . maybe she had a point? *No time to deal with that,* he thought. The point is, he *did* have a plan, and it would save them.

"Master, your plans are way better than the paladin's. After this works, we should rub it in her face," William said.

Kiru switched to telepathic communication to speak with the others of Pandemonium, *"Okay, so the statue is the key. Zhaden asked how to remove a connection with one's deity. It looks like all we need to do is what the Jormuns did to the other Beast God statues."*

"The logic is sound, but how are you going to destroy it?" Zhaden asked.

"Trust me. I have a cockamamie plan," he said, then flashed Brunhilda a grin.

CHAPTER THIRTY-ONE

Enemy Shrine

N ow!" Kiru shouted telepathically to Z'Goyan, which surprised the shaman at first, but once Kiru explained they didn't have enough time, and they needed his assistance to help Myev, the orc quickly came to terms with the situation. On the psion's command, the shaman broke off from protecting his allies from damage from the battle above and turned to face the battle in full once more.

The aura of wind around the orc quickly picked up until he was almost surrounded by a small tornado. This technique took a lot of mana, but if it would save his queen, Kiru knew he'd risk it. Z'Goyan slammed his staff on the ground, and the churning gust of wind surged forth.

Just before the technique made it to Kiru, he looked over to the shaman. He was just in time to see the orc being stabbed by the spears of two opportunistic cultists who had waited for an opening. Kiru's eyes widened, and he was about to turn back to help when—

"GO!" Z'Goyan shouted as he backhanded one of his attackers, blood trailing from his mouth. The shaman wouldn't let this opportunity go to waste simply because he'd been severely injured.

The psion joined his friends, all now letting the wind technique take them. Guilt gripped at him. Because of his plan, Z'Goyan was vulnerable. The orc was a Sapphire, but the spear wounds were deep. Kiru desperately hoped he would be all right. The wind picked up all four cultivators and carved a trail through the gathered Jormuns. All the members of Pandemonium let out cries of panic as they were flung about like rag dolls, flying forth at a ridiculous speed. In that moment, Kiru could see why Brunhilda called his plan crazy.

They flew so fast the psion was scared they would crash into the maze wall ahead of them, when the wind blessedly took a sudden surge upward. The members of Pandemonium crested over the top of the maze wall . . . and continued to fly both up and forward. They made it a good third of the way to their goal before gravity reasserted itself, and they began to descend. Zhaden's adept skills helped the assassin land with barely a sound. Brunhilda had grabbed on tight to Mutt as they were picked up by the wind technique and didn't let go. The extra weight was hard on the blind orc, but with Brunhilda being his eyes, he managed to grab tight onto a ledge with the use of Fenrir's Claws.

Kiru was trying to use Telekinesis to control his momentum, but what he'd just seen happen to the shaman in conjunction with the speed and power of Z'Goyan's technique, had rattled him. Fortunately, Zhaden was *just* able to catch him with his tail. Kiru knew the gold drakonid was a lankier specimen of his species, so he wasn't surprised when he heard Zhaden falling as the rogue was nearly pulled off the wall too. The only thing that kept that from happening was his quick reaction speed at grabbing the other side of the wall they'd landed on to brace himself. Mutt and Brunhilda quickly scurried over and helped Zhaden get Kiru up to join them on top of the maze wall. As Kiru's feet landed firm on the stone underneath, his heart was racing. He didn't have time to catch his breath. They had not gone unnoticed.

The tornado-like technique was not subtle, and the small squad of cultivators that were flung across the air by it had garnered the attention of the Jormuns guarding the statue. Kiru looked at them and estimated there there were around thirty, many hurling spears or orbs of acid down on them, while others were actually beginning to slither down to engage them directly.

"Don't try to engage all of them. Just find a way to push through while avoiding their attacks," Kiru ordered via Telepathy. Pandemonium then began charging forward along the top of the maze walls. The walls were thick but only allowed one person at a time across comfortably, which forced the cultivators to charge single file. That was until Zhaden and Mutt used their dexterous skills to spread out their claws, helping them run on the sides of the wall instead of on top. Brunhilda was doing a good job of deflecting both spears and acidic projectiles while Kiru fought any Jormun that got too close.

Still, fighting on top of a maze wall while being fired upon from above was far from an ideal fighting situation. More than once, all the members of the squad were hit by either a weapon or technique during their advance. They had just pushed through the Jormuns that had moved to engage them, and had made it most of the way to the statue. The orbs of acid and spears began raining down on them with reckless abandon, some of the attacks even hitting fellow cultists.

Brunhilda raised both her shields, and Kiru knelt down under their protective cover. Zhaden and Mutt began dodging the attacks, but after Mutt got hit with two more acid orbs, they both ran over to hide under Brunhilda's shields. Kiru turned back to see that, despite the raining orbs of acid, the Jormuns they had run past had turned back and were coming toward them.

"Kiru, ye and the others need to leave me behind. I'm too slow," Brunhilda pleaded.

"She's right," Mutt said. "But I'm not leaving you, Brun." He turned back to Zhaden and Kiru, putting a hand on each of their shoulders. "So, you guys need to take out that statue. Now, go!" he said as he hurled the two, sending them flying once more. The two of them were nearly impaled by spears being thrown at them before they crash-landed on the temple wall, the impact knocking a couple of Jormuns off the wall and sending them falling to their deaths.

Kiru and Zhaden quickly righted themselves and took in their situation. They were about two hundred feet away from the statue, and ten Jormuns stood in their way. Then, to their utter horror, a slithering mass of about thirty more crawled up over the wall to join their compatriots. Both the psion and gold drakonid gripped their weapons, gritting their teeth. They were strong, but they knew they couldn't take on forty opponents of the same rank all by themselves. They needed something big to even the playing field.

Electricity crackled and sparked around Kiru's head. "Zhaden, hold them off while I gather mana."

The rogue twirled his two daggers and charged the incoming cultists. For the next few seconds, Zhaden expertly fought off his opponents, dodging and deflecting their blows. Still, he couldn't avoid a thrust from an acid-laced spearhead, at least not completely. Zhaden turned his head too slow and received a nasty gash under his left eye. He repaid that attack by stabbing that Jormun directly in their left eye.

Still, Kiru could see the acid had taken its toll. The gold scales on Zhaden's face began to sizzle and melt, and he fell to one knee, grabbing his face in pain. Three more Jormuns raised their spears to kill the rogue, but they were too late. Zhaden had bought Kiru enough time.

"Brainstorm!" Kiru shouted. White electricity shot out from around his head and struck the three cultists. The technique surged through them and connected to seven more Jormuns, forming a chain. Their flesh and scales sizzled and blackened. The electricity coursed throughout their bodies, empowered by Kiru's mana. All of them grumbled unintelligibly as their bodies convulsed. Then they fell limp, dead by electrocution.

Despite the devastating power of Kiru's technique, there were still thirty more cultists on their way. Kiru ran over and helped Zhaden up.

The gold drakonid hissed as he took his hand from his face, the scales underneath his left eye now gone and exposing pink flesh. "That was an impressive technique, my friend. Now, allow me to do the same," he hissed and walked in front of Kiru. "Just make sure you destroy the statue, as I will be vulnerable." Then, the gold drakonid used his most dangerous technique, Nightmare.

Dark shadows oozed out of Zhaden's body, eventually coalescing to form the silhouette of a giant shadowy dragon above the rogue. The Jormuns hesitated for a moment, both in fear and in reverence at the massive draconic form they were witnessing, unsure what it was. Then, the shadow roared and surged forward. The Nightmare technique enveloped all of the cultists, invading their minds with illusions of great and terrible horrors. Most of them screamed and fell unconscious, overcome by the terrors.

Only a few were able to withstand it, and only *just*. Zhaden fell to a knee, exhausted by the technique.

Kiru charged forward, intending to cut through his foes and get to the statue so he could destroy it.

"Spill their blood, Master! Show them what happens when they oppose a conqueror!" William cheered.

"Gladly," he replied, ready to dish out the pain. He reversed the grip of his Psyslime blade and punched the first cultist with his bladed guard, both crushing their neck and slicing their jugular vein in one swift motion. He spun his blade back around and deflected the next cultist's spear thrust with Sweep the Barn. He followed up with Thief's Punishment, slicing off their hand at the wrist.

Kiru rolled out of the way of an orb of acid from the final standing Jormun. This one kept her spear out and was focused on keeping Kiru at a distance using her longer weapon, her eyes occasionally darting to the right back inside the temple grounds. *Why is she . . . ?* Kiru thought before a shadow suddenly covered him. A sudden pang of fear gripped his heart as he turned to see the winged S'Vol flying directly at him from the central pyramid, his toothy maw opened wide.

The cultist was too fast for Kiru to do anything, but not too fast for Myev. One of the queen regent's wings was visibly broken, preventing her from flying, but in her centaur form, she could kick the air hard enough to allow her to temporarily soar. Before S'Vol could take a bite out of Kiru, Myev appeared right under the draconic orc and wrapped a clawed hand onto his leg, dragging him down and crashing into the wall just under Kiru's feet.

The ground under the psion's feet began to shake, forcing both him and a nearby cultist to stumble for a couple of moments. Kiru had dropped his Psyslime blade, and the cultist gave a reptilian grin. She slithered forward with her spear raised to gore the psion when the blade flew up seemingly on its own, carving a deep furrow from her belly to neck. The Jormun dropped her spear and just stood in shock, blood and viscera spilling out rapidly from her body.

"My mom told me to keep my strengths hidden. You didn't know I could control my weapon without holding it, and that's why you lost," he said, then threw her body off the wall behind him.

"Master, that was fucking sweet! Hahaha! Yeah! Kiss our asses, you punk!" William laughed. Kiru wasn't focused on that, though. S'Vol showing up to hurt him meant that his assumption was right—the statue was the key. He needed to hurry and destroy the thing. Quickly, he sheathed his steel Fu Tao and gripped the Psyslime weapon with both hands. With his will, he forced it back into the giant hammer form he used to fight the exiled ogre. There was more crashing in the back, from the fighting, but he couldn't afford to distract himself. With all his might, Kiru pulled back the hammer and swung it into the stone. There was a crack, and then it shattered.

CHAPTER THIRTY-TWO

Down but Not Out

BOOM! A new wave of energy rushed out from the shattered statue in all directions, washing over all in the temple vicinity. "Noooo!" a voice echoed out with the wave, the deep voice of Jormungandr, full of unrestrained fury. Just like with the Exile's staff when it was broken, the cultivators empowered by the structure immediately began to weaken. They didn't become lethargic like the ogre had, but their bodies morphed back into their pure orcish forms, and their falsely elevated power regressed from Ruby to Gold with most going down to Silver. Even S'Vol was affected, his bulk noticeably lessened. A moment later, Grimtusk's mace struck the scarred cultist directly in the chest, and he crashed atop the pyramid.

Both Myev and Grimtusk stood atop the Jormun, both covered in blood, Myev looking like a monstrous chimera with multiple techniques active at once, while Grimtusk looked like a terrifying bipedal boar.

"It is over, S'Vol. Surrender now, and we will grant you a swift death," Myev said.

S'Vol scowled and wheezed from his broken ribs. He saw one of the runes he was meant to destroy. It was on the back of the throne at the very center of the pyramid, but he was too far away to reach it. But he refused to let these weaklings win. He would set his master free, and he would rule beside him, just as the strong were meant to. S'Vol didn't relish what he had to do, but he was certain Jormungandr would protect him once the god was free. The cult leader turned back to the two cultivators standing over him. He grabbed his necklace.

"A dragon does not bow to lesser beings, and neither will I," he said, then shoved the scale that was hanging on his necklace into his mouth.

Both Grimtusk and Myev moved to strike, but it was too late. Only S'Vol knew this, but he had ingested the last of Jormungandr's scales left in Imakandi. The Beast God's power coursed through the cultist, filling him with his deity's power once more. But unlike with the statue, he knew the power from the scale was unstable and more volatile. Still, he knew it was worth the risk to take it in. Draconic beast mana surged out from the cultist in all directions, pushing both Grimtusk and Myev back by pure force.

S'Vol's body morphed once more, but this time it was something new. His body shifted, elongated, and contorted until he was unrecognizable. He wasn't a large snake like the others who'd ingested a scale, nor was he a half-dragon hybrid like before. This time, he turned into a pure dragon. His body was long like a snake's, reaching at least fifty feet into the air. He had two large wings and four three-clawed feet with emerald scales that reflected the sun's light. The red, unstable energy of Jormungandr flowed throughout his body, the glow pulsing rhythmically in between his scales. His reptilian snout had two long whiskers, and he somehow possessed a mane of the unstable red energy, flowing wildly as if a strong breeze was constantly on him.

S'Vol's eyes were yellow and betrayed intelligence just for a moment before the violent shade of red completely overtook his pupils, and he succumbed to Jormungandr's power, becoming a genuine beast. The dragon took to the air, blocking out the sun in the sky.

"I WILL DESTROY YOU!" he boomed.

All but Grimtusk and Myev were forced to their knees by the power. He then fired a gout of acid down onto the pyramid. Myev quickly recovered and zoomed back to the top of the pyramid to intercept. She raised her artificial limb and activated Heidrun's Digestion. The arm rapidly absorbed the acid stream that descended, protecting the pyramid and the runes that kept Jormungandr imprisoned from destruction. Some of Myev's wounds healed from that technique but JUST barely. Even with Heidrun's technique, acid wasn't the best substance to convert for healing.

The crazed orc-turned-dragon flew down with reckless abandon, his mouth open to bite down on Myev, but he was struck in the jaw by Grimtusk's mace. The armor-clad orc had leaped to the top of the pyramid in a single bound and swung his weapon, sending S'Vol crashing down to the back part of the temple. Many of the southern maze walls were crushed by the force of his momentum, sending birds flying in the air amidst large clouds of dust. The dragon wasn't done, though, as S'Vol's long tail whipped out as he fell, striking Grimtusk square in the chest, sending the orc himself flying and crashing into a wall on the western side of the temple.

Myev watched S'Vol quickly getting up and roaring in defiance, drool mixing with the acid readily flowing from his mouth like he was a rabid dog, his red pupilless eyes indicating that he was running on crazed instinct alone. She noted that, unlike others who'd ingested a Jormungandr scale, his skin was notably stronger, instead of being fragile like a snake's. Even after taking a direct blow from an Emerald-rank cultivator, there was just a slight scratch on his jaw oozing the bright red power. *It seems that the instability of the power he ingested manifested more mentally than physically,* she thought. Myev took in a deep breath to steady her resolve. S'Vol might be hurt. Killing him, though, was going to take a lot more.

For a few moments, Kiru stood on the northern wall and watched the titanic battle before him in awe and horror. Two Emeralds were fighting a literal dragon at a similar level, empowered by a god no less. He had hoped to help, but it seemed he made things worse. S'Vol had been strong before, but both the cultist's size and the scale of power he exuded made the idea of attacking him seem absolutely insane. Kiru felt utterly defeated.

That was when he heard many of the Jormuns nearby who had been knocked unconscious by Zhaden's Nightmare technique before suddenly hissing in anger. He turned to see them awakening and glaring angrily at the gold drakonid. They seemed to be emboldened by their leader's new form. Zhaden gripped his Bloodstep Stiletto and faced them. The Nightmare technique had drained the rogue. It would take both time and a number of mana potions to replenish his energy. Sensing his weakness, the cultists all bared their teeth in excitement.

Kiru squeezed his weapons. He may not be able to do anything about the fighting with the colossus, but he could still protect his friends. Speaking about his mother earlier reminded him of the sword form she taught him before she died. She hadn't been able to instruct him fully, but Kiru had a firm grasp of the basics of her style, the Monarch's Razors. He had been primarily using the semi-defensive forms of the Cruel Mantis style, because it was made using the Fu Tao in mind rather than any simple short sword. Unlike the more defensive and disabling forms of the Cruel Mantis, however, Monarch's Razors was a highly aggressive style that used overwhelming speed to defeat an opponent. And seeing the distance he had to cross to get to Zhaden, speed was what he needed.

Kiru bent his knees and focused his mana into his legs. He crossed both his swords over his body in an X. Then, in an instant, he used the mana in his legs to propel himself forward in a flash. Kiru literally flew, his speed still boosted by Sleipnir's Boon, slashing dozens of cultists with Demon's Inciting Strike before they could even register it. The placement of his blades, coupled with the speed, allowed him to eliminate multiple opponents at once. He finished by spinning and slicing an orc from groin to neck using Dragon Ascends the Sky. The Jormuns looked confused, as they at first seemed to have been unharmed. Two seconds later, they all gasped as blood spilled out of grievous wounds from their torsos or necks as if the wounds had appeared out of thin air.

Kiru didn't have time to spare them any more attention. They were already dead. He turned back to help Zhaden deal with the rest of the lower-rank opponents. Orc cultists surrounded the drakonid and were in between him and Kiru. Before the psion could go back on the offensive, however, he heard a roar. But it wasn't draconic. It was more like an angry bear.

Mutt then leaped over onto the wall and tackled one of the cultists in between Kiru and Zhaden, stabbing his opponent with his Horned Harpy Eagle Talons. In a matter of seconds, he eviscerated another two with Fenrir's Claws and quite literally crushed the skull of another with Gnoll's Bite. The cultists' morale may have been boosted by S'Vol's new form, but they were still notably weaker after losing their divine empowerment.

A pair of large spectral goat heads flew upward from the maze and overtook the cultists behind Zhaden, either biting down on them or bucking them off the wall with their horns. Both the drakonid and psion turned to see Brunhilda down below on one of the maze walls, spectral lights fading from her shields and a confident smirk on her face.

"Well, what're ye idgits waiting up there for? We got a dragon to slay."

The three of them hopped down and ran over to the paladin, all embracing each other and glad to still be alive. They then were almost knocked off back into the maze by a gust of wind from the battle around the pyramid. Each clash of strikes sent sound and wind bursting through the temple, which Kiru figured would become a pile of rubble if something wasn't done to prevent it. Both Myev and Grimtusk were doing their best to fight their bigger, stronger foes, but it was clear to the psion that they were losing. They had already been visibly injured and exhausted from fighting S'Vol earlier, and now the cult leader was powered back up to an even greater level. Kiru reckoned that the only reason they were in the fight was due to the madness of the newly formed dragon—the power of Jormungandr too much for his mind to handle.

Kiru sighed, breathing heavily from his recent exertions. "I don't know what else we can do now, Brunhilda. I think the best we can hope for is to not die. In case you hadn't realized, we almost got taken out by an errant gust not even directed at us. I don't think another one of my 'cockamamie' plans is going to work," he said, resigning himself to the inevitable. He could protect his friends, but he the main battle seemed lost. They'd dealt with the followers; there was nothing more they could do.

Another gust of wind came toward the party, but Brunhilda raised her dual shields to intercept it, protecting them all.

"I can't believe this! Master, let me out!"

Surprised, Kiru asked, "William?"

"Now!" the imp demanded. Kiru did as asked, and the ugly imp appeared on his shoulder and proceeded to slap Kiru across the face.

"Ow! What was that for?" Kiru asked.

"Because you're acting like a little bitch! You are a conqueror, not some sub-servient peasant! It is your destiny to rule or die in glorious battle fighting for what you believe in, not cowering in fear. You are a freakin' psion, the one best suited to killing dragons, and that looks like a dragon to me! Besides, your plans always result in violence, so they're great, no matter what Palabitch says," he said, gesturing to Brunhilda.

Kiru just stood there in stunned silence. Everyone did. Well, everyone except Brunhilda who was holding back the gust of wind. Once it had subsided, she gasped from the effort, then spoke. "As much as I dislike the little bugger, he be right," she said.

"He is?!" Kiru asked.

"I am?!" William echoed, even more surprised than Kiru.

"Not about me being a . . . *bitch*." She said the last word through gritted teeth while glaring at William. "You be a psion. I literally cannae think of a better per-son to fight a dragon." She sighed. "Plus, yer plans aren't *so* bad. They just involve more risk than I be likin'. Lookin' at this, however—" She indicated the battle before them. "—there's no such thing as a low-risk plan."

"See?" William said to Kiru, indicating the paladin and obviously feeling *very* vindicated. "Even she agrees!" the little fiend's face was now grinning manically.

"I got to agree too, Boss. We gotta do something. I don't think S'Vol's gonna let us live if he wins," Mutt added.

"I concur with their assessments. We trust you, Kiru. What do you surmise is the best course of action?" Zhaden asked, his tail happily wagging.

Kiru felt overwhelmed with sentiment. These four people—all very differ-ent, with unique backgrounds, goals, and dreams—trusted him. They looked to him as their leader. They were putting their very lives in his hands. He would honor that.

Plus, they made some valid points. If they just let things proceed as is, S'Vol would likely win, and he would *definitely* make sure all of Pandemonium was dead as well. If there was anyone best suited to slaying dragons, it was a psion. Him. But how?

How could I use my psionic abilities to help kill the dragon? What dragon-slaying knowledge do I have that I can actually use right now against an Emerald? he wondered.

Unfortunately, he knew very little about dragon anatomy. What he did know was from fighting the draconic abominations the cultists became earlier, but that wouldn't necessarily help him against a pure one. He did know a good bit about fighting drakonids, however, from his time with Zhaden. Back at the academy, Kiru had read up about drakonids and the rogue had taught him more about how to fight others of his kind.

"Zhaden, is it fair to say that dragons share a pretty similar anatomy to drakonids?"

"There are variations, for certain, but my kind and the dragons do share a common ancestry. So, that would not be an unfair assumption," Zhaden replied.

Kiru grinned.

"Ye got that look on yer face again," Brunhilda teased.

"I do, indeed. It's a long shot, but I've got a plan. Who wants to kill a dragon?" he asked.

William gave a bloodthirsty grin. "Die in a blaze of glory or kill a mother-fucking dragon? Let's do it!"

CHAPTER THIRTY-THREE

To Kill a Dragon

BOOM! CRACK! WHOOSH! The sounds of battle echoed throughout the temple as the newly created dragon fought the two orcs. As Kiru watched them and their techniques flying around the temple maze, he could sense that their impressive power could easily level whole cities. So much was reduced to rubble in their wake. If it wasn't due to S'Vol crashing through stone, it was from the sheer power of their impacts striking each other. The fighting would've been easier for Myev and Grimtusk had they not had to focus on keeping the central pyramid intact as well. Jormungandr had made it glaringly apparent that destroying the runes atop the pyramid was important to his release and thus made keeping it intact vital to those opposed to the World Serpent. That forced both Myev and Grimtusk to fight more defensively, making sure to take careful aim with their attacks as well as taking extra defensive measures they otherwise normally wouldn't have. S'Vol had no such issues, and the near-feral dragon fought with ceaseless recklessness.

The members of Pandemonium finally made it back to the central pyramid after a few minutes of running across the top of the maze walls. The ground below was littered with corpses. When Kiru had destroyed the statue, it did weaken the cultists significantly. Even a hundred Silver-ranked cultivators couldn't hope to defeat twenty Golds and Rubies. By the time Kiru had actually done that, though, it was too late. The horde of Jormuns had wrought a significant toll on those who had opposed them.

Before they had been forcefully regressed to their lower cultivation levels, the orc cultists had killed all but four of their opponents. Z'Goyan, Snout, and two Thrar'fang subordinates of Grimtusk were all that remained. The latter two were covered in armor that barely seemed to be hanging on, both sporting more than a few significant wounds across their thick skin. Still, they had held on and brought retribution to their opponents after the tides had turned.

None of them were without injury. The powerful followers of Gullinkambi and Hugin and Munin that were now mangled, feathered corpses strewn amidst the piles of bodies were a testament to that. Seeing the carnage and how their side had just barely held on, Kiru was glad the Thrar'fangs hadn't joined the Jormuns. He held no illusions that they would have won had Grimtusk's tribe switched allegiances.

The survivors of those that Pandemonium had left were now on top of the pyramid, each standing over a rune they found in order to protect it. The exception was Snout. The ogre looked horrible, undoubtedly the most injured of the four that had stayed back. He was missing his right arm, right leg, and his left arm up to the elbow. His white slimy skin was covered in gashes and a particularly grievous wound on his belly where the skin seemed to have melted away by an acid orb.

The party didn't give him much notice, though. They didn't need to. The ogre was crawling around the battlefield and eating the dead bodies in order to accelerate his remarkable healing ability.

So, Pandemonium continued forward toward the pyramid, and then ascended its stairs, boosted by the speed their tempered bodies afforded them, soon joining their allies at the top. The three gave them cursory glances before looking out to check for any other threats. Z'Goyan's eyes lingered on Kiru for longer than any of the others, but he then seemed to tamp down his distrust for the time being.

"Hey, Myev's boyfriend, how goes my sister's fight? It's hard to tell with them moving so fast," Mutt said.

The shaman's eyes widened in surprise. While the two had not been the best at concealing their relationship, it was clear that they were *trying* to keep information about it under wraps.

Meanwhile, Mutt couldn't see Z'Goyan's look, but Kiru knew his other senses helped him realize how taken aback and frustrated the shaman was. Mutt just shrugged. "Man, we all know. It's not the time to worry about it."

Z'Goyan huffed but did eventually answer Mutt. "There is little I and the Thrar'fangs here can do besides putting all our power and lives on the line to protect the runes. The power that S'Vol has . . ." He trailed off before looking back to the fighting off in the distance at the edge of the temple. He didn't say anything else. He didn't need to. The message was clear. The dragon intimidated them.

The members of Pandemonium glanced at each other in concern before looking out and assessing their situation from their new vantage point. S'Vol had previously managed to destroy the lower half of one of the pyramid walls with his tail, but thankfully, the flat, rune-covered top remained intact. The foundations also seemed to be in good shape despite the obvious age of the temple and the damage. The dragon had a few injuries, but most were pretty superficial. The worst was the oozing wound from where he had been cracked on the jaw by Grimtusk's mace.

Grimtusk and Myev were much worse. From the brief moments when the orcs stopped moving, Kiru could see that both of them were covered in gashes, bruises, and dirt. Myev's left arm hung limp while Grimtusk was so covered in injuries, he was more red and blue than his normal green. The situation was growing dire. If the three Emeralds continued to fight, S'Vol would certainly win. Unless, that was, a new variable came into play.

"Are we ready?" Kiru sent telepathically to his friends.

They all gave him a nod of confirmation. On their sprint to get back to the central pyramid, the psion had relayed his plan. It was reckless, untested, and a huge gamble, but it was their best chance. The others moved off as Kiru enacted Stage One of their strategy.

With all his might, Kiru sent out a telepathic message to Myev, making sure to keep all others out. Even with his ascension to Ruby increasing his range for Telepathy to a thousand feet, he still had to push himself to ensure his message reached her. The challenge was also making sure that he could direct his mana to reach the moving target that was the queen regent.

"Myev, this is Kiru. We're not going to win if we keep fighting as we are. Listen close, I have a plan."

The queen regent's form stiffened as she clearly had received his message. Kiru wanted to get some sort of nod of confirmation as he finished relaying his plan, but couldn't as Myev had to move, avoiding a downward slam of S'Vol's tail. All Kiru could do was trust that she would follow through on her end, because his gambit depended on it.

For another half-minute, the three Emeralds continued their battle, getting closer and closer to the central pyramid. Eventually, they reached a point where Myev and Grimtusk were on the ground standing defensively in front of the base of the pyramid at the ruined wall, the dragon zooming above them. The forces of their fight sent powerful gusts of wind in all directions, forcing the cultivators up on the top of the central pyramid to cling onto the carved throne in the center. Myev and Grimtusk were breathing heavily, clutching at their wounds, looking up to the dragon, who was hurt but undeniably in better shape.

S'Vol's claws rested on the top of a maze wall underneath him and he lowered his head down, slightly reminiscent of a predator who had finally cornered its prey. The dragon growled and bared his teeth before licking them with his forked tongue.

Myev saw the blood-covered Grimtusk scowling. He was hurt but did not give up. He bared his teeth right back at the dragon and readied his mace to attack when something he clearly did not expect happened. Myev quickly moved over to his side and clenched his shoulder with her glutton grub hand, piercing through already exposed cuts and into his muscle. Grimtusk groaned and fell to a knee. He looked up at Myev in utter contempt.

"Traitor," he spat, unbridled fury in his gaze.

"Heidrun's Digestion," she said in reply, activating her technique. The artificial limb greedily drew in both Grimtusk's blood and remaining mana, weakening him rapidly and healing many of Myev's injuries. Before the Thrar'fang leader could actually strike back with the last of his strength, Myev spun and hurled Grimtusk like a kid's toy. In an amazing feat of strength, she sent the muscle-bound, heavily armored orc chief flying, clearing past the temple completely and landing in a large sand dune.

The dragon closed his mouth and pulled his head back, clearly not at all expecting what had just happened. He seemed to have regained a bit of intelligence as well, as a small pupil appeared in each eye where there had just been solid red before.

Grimtusk's subordinates cried out in anger and ran off to the pyramid to attack Myev, but they were quickly dealt with via a shield bash to the face and a rabbit punch delivered by Brunhilda and Mutt respectively, rendering the pair unconscious. Z'Goyan and Snout, who had finally regenerated enough to be able to reach the top of the pyramid with the others, looked dumbfounded at what just happened, but no one was more surprised look than the dragon itself. If this wasn't such a life-and-death situation, Kiru would've laughed.

Suppressing a scowl, Myev turned to face S'Vol and took a knee before him. "I surrender, S'Vol. Please, spare my people."

"My queen, what are you doing?!" Z'Goyan cried from atop the pyramid. His face looked lost in despair.

"Saving my people, Shaman. Now, shut your mouth!" Myev angrily spat, keeping her head down, her true intentions hidden.

The dragon's look of surprise quickly turned into one of pure malicious glee. "Hahahaha!" His laughter boomed, and then he lowered his head down to the ground to reach Myev's level. "At last, you see reason, Myev. None can compete against Jormungandr's might. Against that of the draconic Beast God. I accept your offer."

Myev sighed.

"But on one condition," the dragon added.

She raised her head to look at his large eyes gleaming like a predator's.

"You must become *my* queen and bear *my* children."

Those words set Z'Goyan over the edge. "No . . . Noooo!" he screamed. Then, before he could be stopped by Mutt or Brunhilda, the shaman flew down in an explosion of wind, the power of his technique and rank making him a blur. Z'Goyan zoomed through the air like a missile and raised his staff to crack on the dragon's massive head.

While he was a Sapphire and his wind-based techniques undeniably fast, Myev's Emerald status made her faster. The M'Baku chief activated her Thunder

Rooster's Call. She shouted and blue electricity struck the shaman and sent him flying back, crashing into a small cluster of trees on the ground. Z'Goyan groaned as smoke trailed off his scorched body. Myev barely contained a grimace on her face.

"Hahaha! Good, it seems you were honest about becoming my servant," S'Vol said, then turned his head over to where Z'Goyan lay unconscious. "First—" He licked his lips with his forked tongue. "—I need to teach that despicable shaman a final lesson."

"*Keep him close, just for a little longer!*" Myev heard Kiru's plea inside her mind.

"My lord!" she called out to S'Vol, who had just opened his mouth and begun to advance on the downed shaman. Myev managed to capture his attention by playing on his blatant attraction to her. She did her best to walk slowly and seductively toward the dragon. It seemed she was doing well, especially since she partially healed some of her wounds. Her non-prosthetic arm was still limp, but fortunately, the dragon didn't seem to mind. She leaned up against the dragon's face. "He is nothing, not even worth your time. Come, let us destroy the rune on the Leokin Throne. Isn't that what you came for in the first place, hmm?"

S'Vol cooed in approval. "Thinking like a true Jormun queen. Jormungandr will be pleased that I have convinced you to join our side," he said, then turned and casually moved his head up to the top of the pyramid.

"Myev . . . Wha—What have you done?" Snout uttered in horror as he looked down at the M'Baku chief. His face then contorted in anger. "All orcs are oath breakers. I should've known." He growled in a mixture of fury and despair. He clinched his grubby fists and snapped his head toward Pandemonium. "And you . . . their allies. Before I perish, I will make you feel the wrath of the L'Khans." He paused then, noticing just Brunhilda and Mutt present. "Where are the others?"

Mutt clicked his tongue a couple of times before pointing toward the massive dragon. "They're right over there, Bug Guy."

Just as S'Vol was raising his head up from the ground and nearing the level of the maze wall he'd rested his body against, two figures suddenly appeared as if out of thin air. Zhaden materialized as the drakonid descended from jumping off the maze wall above, his body becoming fully visible when he plunged his two daggers in S'Vol's left eye. The dragon roared in pain and flung his head upward. Zhaden heaved back with all his might, pulling the dragon's head just to the right before his daggers dislodged and he fell off. While the strength of a Ruby drakonid couldn't compete with a dragon at Emerald, S'Vol's acute pain gave Zhaden a temporary advantage in helping guide his movements. While it may not have looked like it, the direction the rogue was heading was intentional. It had left S'Vol's jaw injury more exposed.

Kiru was standing atop the maze wall just feet from S'Vol's head. With a flex of his will, he shifted his Psyslime weapon into a barbed spear and stabbed it right on the inside of S'Vol's left jaw, at the exact point where his scales had been damaged from Grimtusk's mace strike. The weapon easily bit deep into the exposed injury as if it were butter. The weapon shook, and there was a sharp click as it tore something. Despite the pain from his left eye, the dragon went rigid as if frozen before a deluge of blood began spilling out from the spear wound at an alarming rate. Kiru was covered by the sudden downpour.

"Hahahahaha! Yes! Drenched in our enemy's blood! Give me more!" William cheered inside the psion's mind.

It had been a gamble for Kiru, a desperate plan based on extrapolation, but it appeared to have paid off. While back at the Royal Academy, among the numerous books he'd read, there was one pertaining to drakonid anatomy. A key piece of information was that drakonids have a *very* important artery toward the inside of their left jaws, adequately protected by hardened scales. That information had been useful when Kiru fought against Zhaden back when the rogue had first ambushed them.

When it came to the anatomy of *actual* dragons, the psion's knowledge was lacking, making his plan a risky one. A risky plan with small chance of success was better than a certain loss though. Zhaden told Kiru that it wouldn't be an unfair assumption that drakonids and dragons shared similar vasculature anatomy, and so Kiru formulated a strategy based on that. Knowing that there was a possible chink in its armor, and that his Psyslime weapon was super-effective against dragons, Kiru knew they had a chance to deal a devastating blow. The only problem was they had to get close to the dragon and ensure that he was moving slowly enough that they could catch him.

That's where his allies came into play. In order to get close, he had Zhaden use both his Invisibility and Silence techniques on them. They still had to move carefully back to a maze wall, then up and along it so as not to disturb any debris. Kiru also knew from Grimtusk's defiant words to Jormungandr that the Thrar'fang leader clearly would not approve of this plan.

Kiru had a stark difference of opinion with him as to what strength was. Unlike the orc, Kiru didn't believe that strength was mere simplistic brute force. He could testify from personal experience as to the power of planning. Knowledge is power, and Kiru could argue that it was the main power that had gotten him this far.

So, to avoid Thrar'fang interference, both Mutt and Brunhilda stayed back to deal with them. Fortunately, everyone on top of the central pyramid was so focused on the fighting between the three Emeralds that no one noticed the psion and gold drakonid slipping away. It was a risk, and Myev visibly gawked at the idea of forcefully subduing such a strong ally who had been the only reason she had been alive thus far. Still, given the direness of the situation, she silently agreed the risk Kiru's plan encompassed was worth it.

S'Vol let out a hideous cry, high-pitched and shrieking. The dragon raised his head and began to shake back and forth, desperately trying to get the weapon out. Kiru clung onto it with all his might as he was being thrown about, his body repeatedly slamming into stone and trees. William was cackling madly in joy as if he were taming the dragon. Being the one who was being thrown about, Kiru was decidedly not. He was much more focused on staying alive.

S'Vol began to claw at the wound, frenziedly trying to remove the embedded weapon, raking his claws over his own flesh and Kiru's dangling body repeatedly. Kiru kept his head lowered and his eyes closed as the blood pouring down was relentless. The psion urgently focused his Telekinesis technique solely on his hands in order to best ensure that he would be able to keep hanging on. Kiru even morphed the spear's handle to wrap tightly around both his wrists to aid him in that as well. Still, based off the vigor the dragon was still showing, the psion knew it wouldn't be enough. Despite not feeling anything from the neck down, Kiru's body was getting slammed, crushed, and clawed repeatedly from the dragon's flailing. The enchanted headband was thankfully still protecting his head, the blessed item forming a near-translucent helmet to absorb damage. Even with that, his ears were racked with the sound of bones breaking and his mother's enchanted armor getting more and more damaged.

Kiru moved his face to look up from the spear and saw both his legs bending at unnatural angles. One boot had been ripped off entirely, leaving a bloody hunk of flesh that was his foot. The psion managed to avoid any head trauma, but his chest piece was badly damaged, large furrows gauged out of it and three trails of blood flowing from his chest. Kiru wasn't sure how much of the blood was his or S'Vol's. Seeing that the dragon wasn't notably weakening or relenting despite the grievous wound, Kiru realized he had just seconds before S'Vol managed to remove his spear. In the midst of the chaotic flailing about the temple, the psion had no idea if he'd done enough damage to render a fatal blow yet. He still had one crazy idea left, the absolute last shot, one so dumb he intentionally didn't tell Brunhilda about it.

"Myev, use Thunder Rooster's Call on me, full blast!" he sent out via Telepathy. He didn't have the time to focus the message directly to the queen regent, so he just projected it out to the entire temple a thousand feet in all directions, not caring about revealing his psion status. Even S'Vol got the message.

"You speak in my mind? Telepathy? Wait . . . You're a psion?! *No!*" The dragon made it clear he quickly understood what hearing a telepathic message meant and became even more worried for his life. So, he began flying upward in a desperate attempt to get away.

Kiru gritted his teeth. *"Myev, do it now!"*

The queen regent had initially hesitated. She was an Emerald, and Kiru knew she could easily kill him. He supposed that was the reason for her delay, but he knew she trusted him. He had faith she would honor his request. That faith was rewarded as she looked up at the bleeding dragon ascending into the sky and gathered all her mana for one last attack. Blue electricity crackled all around her body, and she shouted with all her might, firing off a Thunder Rooster's Call directly at the small figure dangling like a limp doll off S'Vol.

Kiru heard the thunderclap from below. *"William, it looks like we're going to die in a blaze of glory just like you hoped for."*

The imp wasn't deterred at all. *"Hahaha! I wouldn't have it any other way! Time to kill a dragon!"*

Then, Kiru was struck by Myev's technique. He thought she'd given him a full-power attack before, but from the pain he was now experiencing in his head, the way his body was flailing about from full-on convulsions, and how he could barely breathe or keep conscious, this was truly the most powerful technique he'd *ever* been hit by. His vision went white as an electrical current raged, coursing and crashing wildly through his body like he'd never experienced before—and he'd been electrocuted *a lot* more times than was healthy, even for a cultivator. The psion gritted his teeth in pain, breaking a few from the sheer pressure. The only thing keeping him alive was that William was inside him, the imp actively doing his best to protect his core and brain. Even with the familiar's protection, he lost consciousness within seconds. Kiru would have let go of his Psyslime weapon had he not previously locked it around his wrists. The metallic slime spear worked as a conductor, electrifying the dragon right in his vital wound.

After a few more seconds, Kiru came back to consciousness. His body was still convulsing as the technique was still flowing. Through the loud sparking around his body, Kiru could still hear the pained roars of the dragon being fried as well. The freaking lizard still wasn't dead yet! *Come on. Die already!* Kiru thought angrily.

"William, let the technique into the core," he sent to his familiar.

"Grrah!" the imp cried out in pain. *"Here goes nothing, bitches!"* William removed his protection of both Kiru's mental core and brain. The psion's body convulsed even worse, and he began to foam uncontrollably at the mouth. The bestial mana flooded his core. It surged though his body and out, but strangely, Kiru focused on keeping some of it inside with his will.

The technique raged against his constraints, causing hairline cracks to form within both his core and meridians, threatening to break him, overloading his body just like Ambrose had done back in Bristleton. This near-suicidal attempt at control was not without purpose, nor was it without results. Utilizing the same method that he had used to learn Brainstorm back in Dissé, Kiru converted the Emerald power into his own technique.

The blue electricity flowing through him bleached into a bright white, and the psion fired his technique with more power than he had ever before. It was more power than he could use, either—at least safely. The overcharged mental mana technique surged through the psion, up his weapon, and into S'Vol with violent purpose. Whereas the dragon had earlier roared in pain, this time it was the pained choking cry of a dying animal. That sad noise was only met with Kiru's foamy screams and the crackles of his technique.

The last thing Kiru heard was William shouting in his mind before he felt his Brainstorm forcefully cut off. A sharp *crack* resounded in his head and a sharp headache struck him. It was joined with a feeling of disorientation and a nosebleed. When his technique stopped, S'Vol's body was just a charred husk. Smoke flowed out from his body, and the scent of burned meat filled Kiru's nostrils. He was pretty sure it was coming from his own body too. Then, the rigid body of the dragon went limp, and S'Vol began free-falling to the grounds of the temple.

CHAPTER THIRTY-FOUR

The Pack

Kiru's vision faded to black. He was too hurt, too drained from the overflowing power that had rushed through his body. It was a good thing for his psyche, though. If he had still been conscious, he would've heard William's shrill cries inside his mind as they descended toward their likely deaths: *"Shit, shit, shit, shiiiiitt!"*

Myev and everyone else watched in a mixture of awe and horror as the dragon and the smoking psion attached to him fell, the gargantuan creature's body blotting out the sun. All of the cultivators had been significantly drained by the conflict, even Myev, so, their hearts dropped as the plummeting dragon corpse threatened to crush both them and the pyramid they had fought so hard to protect. Even after all their hard work, they had failed. They stopped S'Vol, but the cult leader was going to destroy the pyramid and the runes on it that imprisoned Jormungandr.

Then, something happened that none of the cultivators in the temple expected. They heard a roar. A deep and strong roar bellowed out from the bottom of the pyramid, distinctly cat-like and familiar.

"NOOOOM!"

Myev saw a gigantic leokin bounding up the pyramid. The massive cub's Bloodline technique suffused his bones and muscles with an overabundance of beast mana. Technically, all leokin could do it if they were trained, but few survived their first transformation. Nom, however, could use it on instinct, as Zengaz had explained during their journey to the temple. In three large strides, the noble leokin made it to the top of the structure where Brunhilda, Mutt, Snout, and now Myev stood.

The queen regent would've been scared to see such a creature, but since she'd witnessed Nom's transformation once before, she was only mildly startled. With her defenses down, she was still caught completely by surprise when the massive cub wrapped his paws around her, pinning her arms tight to her body. In addition to her disbelief, she was too drained of mana to resist Nom biting down on her shoulder. He could've gone deep into her muscle, but his sharp fangs just nicked her skin enough to draw blood.

Myev let out a sharp inhale through her nostrils as her eyes went wide. Power surged into her body as the overabundance of beast mana flowing through Nom rushed out from his teeth and began infusing her body, replenishing her. In a matter of seconds, Myev let out a roar and she activated nearly all her techniques at once. Her broken arm snapped back into place, and her body grew and morphed until she again appeared like a massive chimera herself.

Then, in unison, both Nom and Myev jumped from the top of the pyramid, their control just enough to prevent the stone cracking from the force of their leap. The bestial cultivators crashed into S'Vol. They couldn't completely catch the gigantic dragon, but they still were able to intercept it.

Both Myev and Nom transferred their upward momentum to knock the corpse away from them and the central pyramid. Myev was also able to remove the charred Kiru with one of her arms as well, by pulling out his Psyslime weapon. S'Vol's corpse landed with a boom, reducing a couple of sections of the ancient temple's southern outer wall to rubble, exposing the sandy desert outside while she and Nom gracefully landed back atop the pyramid, Kiru still in her arms.

"By Fenrir's fangs!" Myev cursed as she took in her friend's ruined, unconscious body. The enchanted armor that covered him was so scorched and cracked from the abuse that it crumbled in her arms, leaving his broken, bruised, and emaciated body exposed and bleeding. "How is he still alive?" She then looked down toward her brother. "Mutt, bring your woman up here! This man needs her help, now!"

Before she could get a response from her brother, the entire temple shook. Her skin—and likely the skin of every beast mana cultivator present—prickled as a discordant chorus of animal cries came from everywhere all at once, putting them on edge. The piles of rubble that were once the Beast God statues all began to glow. Lights flickered above the stones until familiar projections appeared. The astral projections of the Beast Gods had returned, and they were not as reserved as they had originally been.

The projections showed the shackled Jormungandr fighting off his eight brethren. The World Serpent had made his play, revealing his careful plan to distract the other gods' servants in order to return back to Alterra. He had openly defied and tried to weaken the other deities within the pantheon. Nothing he could say would save his life. Despite the World Serpent's gargantuan size, the manacles and chains binding him as well as his being outnumbered were proving to be fatal handicaps.

Jormungandr hissed, flailed, and spat acid at his fellow Beast Gods within the Savage Realm, but it was to no avail. In a continuous, vicious cycle, the serpent was being bitten, crushed, gored, then clawed by the other Beast Gods in a tortuous pattern. He let out a desperate howl of pain, which shook the entire temple once more. Within the multi-tonal cry, there was a strained high pitch, but it had no effect on the orcs and leokin other than a momentarily wincing.

The World Serpent's cry and life were cut short when Fenrir leaped up and gouged deep furrows through his throat with his razor-sharp claws. Just like S'Vol, the draconic Beast God abruptly went limp, and the projection began to fall. Fenrir bared his teeth, then howled in triumph. His fellow Beast Gods let out cries of victory as well, which overwhelmed everyone within the temple, forcing all but Brunhilda to roar as well. Myev did spy that the paladin wasn't 100% resistant, however, still letting out some snarls.

Despite such evident power on display, the paladin visibly did her best to focus on Kiru. She quickly rushed over after Myev asked Mutt for her help. Kiru reeked of blood and burnt flesh that permeated the nostrils of all the cultivators nearby. Before she even got a hand on him, Brunhilda started using Restore. The distance healing technique wasn't the most powerful, but *some* healing was better than none.

The glow that radiated off her life mana technique empowered by her Vasir patron resonated outward. Even though they were in a different realm, the Beast Gods' connection with their temple allowed them to sense power coming from another divine source. They all stopped their cries of dominance and looked over to the top of the central pyramid. The astral projections watched as the dwarf moved toward her friend and began using Healing Hands on him. Myev wagered that Brunhilda had used a lot of mana and was likely pushing herself to the max to try and heal Kiru.

She and Nom then both instantly kneeled before the staring gods. "Oh, Great Beasts of the Divine, we your humble servants ask that you please heal this man," Myev said, gesturing to Kiru. "He is an ally to me and was instrumental in bringing down Jormungandr's top servant."

Hldsvini squealed angrily. "Only the strong survive, and besides, Ukufakaza is not finished."

"Come now, Hldsvini," Fenrir said. "Your candidate is clearly bested."

The boar snorted and stomped. "Hmph, death or submission are the only ways to defeat our enemies. My servant has done neither before the M'Baku's power."

"Graaaah! That may be your way, Boar!"

"Bwaaaah! Indeed, but it is not the pantheon's way!" the twin goats retorted in between their screams.

Myev had to force her face to remain neutral when she saw Fenrir give the battle boar a predatory grin. "Yes, the rules of Ukufakaza state that the opponents must be rendered unable to battle. Since your candidate is unconscious, he clearly falls under that category."

Hldsvini was clearly not pleased. "Hmph! Rules can be changed, if necessary!"

"Indeed, but only if the council agrees. Unless you wish to go rogue like Jormungandr? You saw how well it went for him, but please try. It's been ages since I've had pork," Fenrir said giving a sharp-toothed grin.

Myev felt great pride at her patron's display. He was the clear alpha of the pantheon, and she would be for her nation. It made her hopeful that Kiru might be helped.

The battle boar gave a quick, scared squeal and reluctantly bowed his head in submission to the wolf.

Satisfied, Fenrir turned his gaze back to Myev, then to Brunhilda and Kiru. The wolf's eyes flashed as he analyzed the psion fully before addressing the orc. "The boy is an acolyte of a Vasir. We cannot directly heal the damage his body's sustained, let alone what has happened to his cultivation."

Myev's grew disheartened. She wasn't surprised at all to see that her god was able to examine what had happened to the psion's core as well. The orc looked over to see a tear running down Brunhilda's face. While the dwarf focused her technique, she uttered a quiet prayer to Hlin.

Zhaden had made it back up the pyramid. Both he and Mutt joined the dwarf, looking at Kiru in concern and comforting the paladin.

Fenrir continued on, unperturbed. "You keep interesting company, Young Queen. We of the Beast Pantheon recognize your victory over all other rivals in this Ukufakaza. You are the new alpha of Imakandi, and as such, we decree that Imakandi's isolation is now over," Fenrir said, then lifted his head up and howled.

The rest of the projections followed suit, giving a mix of squawks, squeals, and screams to join the wolf in a display of solidarity. Their unified cries shook the temple, and as they did so, the purple barrier surrounding the orc nation began to dissolve for all within to see. The mana quickly dissipated, all evidence of the barrier's presence gone within seconds. Fenrir was the first to stop his cries, and his counterparts immediately followed suit.

The projection of the divine wolf lowered his head and locked eyes with Myev. "And to you, my faithful servant, I bestow upon you a boon."

The rune carved on the stone throne glowed red, and a trickle of thick blood poured out from it, collecting in a small bowl underneath that had suddenly appeared when a section of stone shifted.

"I bestow upon you my blood. My divine power can work wonders, even bringing those back from the brink of death. If used by the right hands, it can help any beast mana user who ingests it ascend up to the rank of Onyx Many would consider it a waste for any *other* cultivator to imbibe it."

Fenrir gave a casual shrug before continuing back in a more formal tone. "We recognize you, Alpha. We recognize you, High Chief. We recognize you, Queen. May you continue to keep our lands wild. May the hunt continue forever." He then let out a howl that was joined one by one by the calls of his fellow gods. Then each one of the projections began to fade until only the wolf remained.

Fenrir stopped howling, and his projection slowly began to dissipate itself. "Remember, Young Queen, the strength of the pack is the wolf, and the strength of the wolf . . ." He trailed off as his form fully faded.

"Is the pack," she finished the phrase in a whispering gasp of recognition as all the dots fully clicked in her head. The newly minted queen then ran over to the bowl and quickly brought it over to Kiru.

Mutt put a hand on Myev's shoulder, "Sis, you sure about this? I mean, you'll never get something like this again."

Myev smiled, confident in her decision. "He is my ally, part of my pack. What kind of Alpha would I be if I didn't take care of him?" She then kneeled down and put a gentle hand on Brunhilda. Then she leaned over to Kiru's face, put her hand under his head, and poured the bowl of blood in the unconscious cultivator's mouth. He coughed when the blood first hit his tongue but then easily drank the rest down. There was a heavy silence as all of them watched in worried anticipation, unsure of what exactly would happen.

Just seconds after Kiru finished, his eyes snapped open. He took in a deep breath as if he'd been held underwater. His eyes weren't his typical blue though. No, they were yellow and bestial. His body shook and snapped repeatedly as his broken and displaced bones were all forcefully repaired in a gruesome display, as if he were possessed. The bruises covering his body rapidly faded before their very eyes. His body had been healed a bit already thanks to Brunhilda, but the rate at which his body was regenerating now far surpassed the dwarf's capabilities. One of his feet had been barely hanging on, only a few tendons keeping it connected. Before their eyes, bone, tendon, muscle, and flesh grew to fill in the space, reconnecting the appendage fully. They all stared in wonder at his miraculous healing.

Then something happened they didn't expect: Kiru's body *improved.*

His broken spine audibly fixed with a sickening streak of cracks. Muscles grew on his bony form in layers until the psion rivaled Mutt in build.

Thick, black hair grew all over his body. Claws grew from his nails, and his teeth elongated and sharpened. In seconds, his entire form had shifted into a large bipedal wolf. Kiru's wolf eyes were distant and unfocused. He just stood there, breathing heavily.

"Kiru, are ye there?" Brunhilda asked tentatively.

He snapped his head and snarled at the paladin before letting out a proud, primal howl as the beast mana from Fenrir's blood permeated his system.

Realizing that the psion wasn't in control, Myev watched her brother and his friends dogpile on top of him to subdue him. The three Rubies were not enough, however. The bipedal wolf pushed them off and hopped to his feet.

Kiru growled and locked eyes with Myev. The beast in him recognized her as a rival and instantly went to challenge her.

Though he had been given newfound strength, Kiru was still no match for Myev's power. She caught him in glutton grub arm, stopping his leap midair. It wrapped tight around his torso, and she activated Heidrun's Digestion. She instantly began draining the beast mana inside Kiru and using it to heal her own body fully. He struggled, but his resistance became weaker and weaker as the technique continued.

After ten seconds, he stopped resisting altogether. That was when his body began shifting back to his half-elven form. Myev let go of him when that happened, the overflowing abundance of beast mana from Kiru somehow providing enough energy to heal her back to 100%. Kiru stood panting, staring at the assembled cultivators like they were complete strangers. The air distorted all around him as beast mana leaked out of all his pores. Rapidly, his canine features reverted. His fur disappeared, and his bones began to shift back.

Fenrir's healing ability was clearly remarkable, bringing the psion back from the brink of a very painful death. Still, Kiru was officially an acolyte of a different deity now. Myev quickly discovered the wolf Beast God was restricted from fully reversing Kiru's previous injuries even if he wanted to.

Kiru's body continued to revert back to the point that, even after all bestial features on his body were gone, his muscular physique began fading. His spine acutely shifted as it returned to its disjointed form, held together by scar tissue, and Kiru's body went limp once more. In a matter of moments, the psion was back to how he was before. He was pain-free, but he didn't realize the fleeting hope his friends had held that he may no longer require mana to move.

There were two permanent changes, however. His red-tinged hair was now fully black and a good bit longer than before, reaching down to his shoulders. The other thing was his face. Elves weren't known to be too skilled at growing facial hair. It was possible but very uncommon. Given Kiru's heritage, he'd never had to shave once in his life even though he was now nearly twenty. However, now he had a thick black beard reaching down to his bare chest that could rival that of many dwarves.

His friends ran over to him.

"Boss?! Boss?! You alright?" Mutt asked.

The psion's eyes cleared and focused, taking in his body's pink, undamaged skin. He was still terrifyingly skinny, but he'd grown accustomed to that. What he wasn't accustomed to being, though, was being naked in front of a bunch of people. "Uh, yeah, Mutt. I'm okay, but how did I get here?"

"Oh! Well, you see . . ." The party then began excitedly filling in Kiru on what happened. He did try to rise and get some clothes on during the explanation, but when he activated Telekinesis, it gave him a sharp headache, probably just from strain and overuse from the day's battle. So, reluctantly, he had his friends clothe him like he was a child. He blushed in embarrassment but didn't complain. William was notably silent too, but Kiru was too tired to question his familiar at the moment.

Once that was done and he thanked Myev profusely for her sacrifice to save him, he, his friends, and all of the leokin exited the safety of the pyramid to go look for any injured survivors who might have been in need.

CHAPTER THIRTY-FIVE

Recovery

Kiru fell into a deep, dreamless sleep that night. Just half a minute after his body had reverted back to its regular state and his friends explained what had happened, he promptly passed out. Having your body get damaged, then healed, then quite literally shattered by a dragon, then miraculously healed again all in one day was very exhausting. He slept for four days straight. No one could wake him. On the fourth day, he finally stirred, but he was still in a state of semi-consciousness. He was floating in a dark space, unable to feel or see anything. That was, until light entered his vision.

At first, it was red-orange, glowing from what seemed to be about a hundred feet in the distance. The light was warm, and as Kiru's eyes adjusted, he saw it was a conglomeration of small, uneven lights spaced out to form a rough circle. The warmth was soothing but also invigorating to Kiru, and he felt it deep in his chest. He pressed a fist there, and another light appeared. This one was higher than the first one.

This light glowed a bright white, as if it were a large moon. It gave no sensation of warmth but somehow did of peace, bringing calm and serenity to Kiru's heart. As its glow began to fade, he was able to see that the light's source was indeed an actual orb. There was, however, a large, deep crack running across it center, nearly dividing it into two separate halves. While the white light was now less intense, it still pulsed out from the crack rhythmically, similar to blood leaking from a wound. Kiru quickly realized that the pulsing light inside was somehow holding the two pieces together.

A small spark of white electricity crackled off of it, and the psion gasped. He recognized what he was seeing. *They are my cores!* Kiru instantly realized that he was somehow in his own mind's eye. On the one hand, actually seeing them was incredible. On the other, the state of his mental mana core was more than a little concerning. *My mental mana core looks like an egg about to hatch.*

"What happened?" he asked no one in particular. He was answered by a groan of relief.

"Ugh! Good, you're finally awake," a familiar, almost villainous voice replied. The light glowing from the crack in between the mental mana core pulsed in unison with the words.

"W-William?" Kiru asked.

"Well, duh, Master," the imp replied. It was clear that he was indeed the light within the core.

"What's going on? How did I get here, and what happened to my mental mana core? Did you do something?"

"Hmph, did I do something?!" William shouted, another spark of electricity shooting out from the crack. "Yes, I did do something! I! Saved! Us!" he said, emphasizing each of the last three words. "You kept letting that orc's technique ravage our core so much that it was breaking apart. I shouted at you to stop, but you wouldn't listen."

Kiru vaguely recalled this but couldn't tell exactly what William had been saying at the time due to the electricity coursing loudly through his body.

"So, I stopped you from being an idiot and saved your core," the imp continued. "I likely saved your life too. You're welcome, by the way."

"Oh! Well, thank you, William," Kiru said. "I'm a little taken aback, though. Didn't you want us to go out in a blaze of glory?"

"Well, yeah, but . . . the dragon died, and I realized we didn't have to!"

"Aw, well thanks, William. It's nice to know you care."

"Pfft! It's not because of 'feelings' or that 'I care'," the imp said, trying to conceal how he actually felt but not fooling Kiru. "It's just because I am awesome, and if you die, we won't be able to spill more of our enemies' blood. We're gonna make that winged king beg for mercy before our might!"

Kiru smiled, instantly seeing through his familiar's lies. William cared. He just didn't want to show him. Kiru wouldn't bring it up again for now. "Okay, okay, William." He chuckled. "Still, I'm grateful for what you did."

"Damn right, you are! I'm the only thing that's keeping this team together. Literally," the imp replied.

The psion winced at that. "Yeah . . . that doesn't look good." He *tsk*ed. "I've got a *really* bad habit of trying to get my cores broken." Ambrose did so to his fire mana core, and Kiru nearly repeated that on himself. Based on how his mental mana core appeared to be only held together by the equivalent of bandages, he was still at risk of letting that happen.

"No shit, Master! If you summon me, I'm pretty sure this core is gonna split in two," William explained.

"Ah, crap." Kiru sighed. He sure was an idiot when it came to plans, sometimes. Brunhilda was right. "Do you know how to fix this?"

"Well, yeah. You just need to drink the blood of another mental mana cultivator."

Kiru recoiled at the thought. "First off, that's disgusting. Second, I don't think that's going to work anyway, William. Remember? Kind of the last of my people here," Kiru said.

"Well, it doesn't have to be another psion. It can be anyone who uses mana from the same realm as where mental mana comes from," the imp retorted.

"Um, do you know what realm mental mana comes from originally? Because I don't," Kiru said.

"Ugh! Fine, we can do it the boring way," William let out an exaggerated sigh before continuing. "Despite how it looks, if you cultivate enough mana over time and don't overtax the core, it will heal on its own."

"Well, that's a relief," Kiru said, smiling at the information.

"Drinking blood would be cooler though . . ." William said.

Kiru rolled his eyes. "Maybe so, but I don't think that's going to be a possibility any time soon."

William just muttered in response, then said, "Whatever, why don't you just wake up now? Hurry up and cultivate so I can get out of here."

As if on cue, Kiru was flung out of his mind's eye and awakened from his deep slumber. He let out a loud gasp as he took in the room he was in—simple, square, and stone. Light came in from a solitary window up high, illuminating the space. He moved his head from side to side, noting that he was alone. He was lying on his back on a flattened pile of straw, made to be a makeshift bed for him. The room was spartan in its adornments, a simple wooden table with two chairs the only other pieces of furniture in there.

Kiru activated Telekinesis and was instantly struck by a sharp pain in his head. He stopped his technique and dropped his head like dead weight.

"Ow, that sucked."

After a couple of minutes, he activated his technique again, bracing himself for the pain. Kiru grunted, but after a few moments, he adjusted, slowly forcing himself up on shaky limbs. He felt . . . weaker, his movements jerky like a puppet's, just like when he was still at Silver-rank.

There was a large bowl of water on top of the table. Kiru leaned over it and took a good look at his reflection. He recoiled slightly at what he saw. His face was slightly more gaunt, and he looked older. He also looked as if he were a beggar who hadn't had a good meal or been groomed in years. Oh, and he had a beard! It wasn't just a patchy thing either. No, it was thick and wild, as was the hair on his head.

Kiru also noticed that he no longer had the red tints at the tips of his hair; it had gone almost a solid black now. His father's circlet was still embedded, as evidenced by the jewel visible in the center of his forehead. The stone was still a

Ruby too. The young half-elf looked like he was some kind of hermit who lived out in the woods.

Kiru then looked down at his body. That . . . was still uncomfortable to digest. His skin was tight against his bones. And now his body was also riddled with scars. The largest was on his right shoulder. It was almost completely covered with the new tissue. Kiru recognized that was where one of the cultists had bitten into his shoulder and destroyed that section of his mother's armor.

Wondering what had happened to the equipment, he scanned the room again. "Nope, no clothing in there." He himself was just wearing a pair of simple rough spun wool trousers. Kiru then moved to open the door and explore just where in the world he was. Before he could, however, he heard talking coming from the other side, and then someone else opened it.

"I'm telling you, I heard footsteps coming from in here," Mutt said as Brunhilda led the rest of Pandemonium inside.

The paladin's eyes went wide as she saw her friend standing there. "Kiru . . . Kiru!" She exclaimed and ran up to hug him. "Bless ye. Ye be awake. How're ye feeling?"

"Well, for being electrocuted by an Emerald-rank technique and thrown about by a giant dragon, I'm doing alright." He smiled weakly, but it quickly faded.

"What aren't ye telling us, lad?" she asked, putting a gentle hand on his bony arm.

"I was pretty sure I was going to die, but now that I know I'm not . . . I almost regret how I went about the plan. I almost broke my core again," he confessed.

"But you didn't though, right, Boss? Else you wouldn't be able to walk?" Mutt asked.

Kiru nodded to Mutt. "I didn't, but it's a near thing. The only thing keeping my core together is William. He's essentially serving as a bandage, and that's not the worst of it." He rubbed the back of his head nervously. "It . . . hurts to use my mana. It's like I'm drawing from a leaky faucet and every time I need mana, my core leaks. With each leak, I feel a pain in my head."

"So, are you feeling pain now, Kiru?" Zhaden asked.

Kiru nodded. "Whenever I activate Telekinesis, I get a sharp sensation. Afterward, it's a dull throb in my head. It's tolerable, but still not fun," Kiru said, then moved over to the straw bed. He noticed everyone raise an eyebrow as they observed his less-than-graceful movements, truly looking like a marionette being operated by an amateur puppeteer.

"Is there not any way to heal such an injury?" Zhaden asked.

Kiru sighed. "It should heal over time. I just don't know how much. Other than that, no," he said, shaking his head.

"Don't forget about drinking the blood of a mental mana user," William added.

"Or drinking the blood of a mental mana user should heal the damage, William tells me. Seeing as I'm likely the last psion in all of Alterra, though, and I know of no other that can use mental mana—"

"That solution is unlikely," Zhaden finished Kiru's words.

There was a heavy silence after that, everyone processing what was said. Even William didn't say anything.

Maybe it was his temper breaking through his restraint. Maybe it was all the near-death experiences he'd survived, or maybe it was just the fact that he was damn tired of feeling sorry for himself, but Kiru clenched his fists. Time and time again, he was placed under what many would claim as insurmountable odds. Time and time again, he'd overcome them. Just like William had said, he was a conqueror. He would conquer this obstacle as well.

The psion stood up. "I'm sorry, everyone. I'm being such a downer. We'll find a way through this." He smiled at his friends. "We always do. I mean, shit! We helped kill a freaking dragon! A cracked core? Pfft! We can handle that."

Everyone chuckled lightly at his words.

"Seriously, though, we kicked ass! I mean, wow! We helped stop not one but two attempted coups and killed an Emerald-rank dragon!"

"The coups, yes, but Boss, let's be honest. *You* killed the dragon," Mutt said.

"Indeed," Zhaden agreed.

"*Damn right!*" William cheered inside his mind.

"Aye," Brunhilda laughed. "Hlin knows ye be the only one crazy enough to be a living lightning rod."

Everyone laughed at that, even Kiru. The psion then looked around at his teammates, his eyes getting teary. "Either way, I couldn't have gotten this far without your help. I would've been long dead. Thank you, my friends, all of you."

"*You too, William,*" he sent.

Brunhilda smiled.

Zhaden happily wagged his tail.

As for Mutt, well, the blind orc was crying large rivulets of tears and beginning to loudly snuffle. "Oh, Boss," he said and then wrapped everyone up in a group hug. "We make a great team! You guys . . . You guys are the best."

A bit later, Kiru told them exactly what he remembered from his fight with S'Vol. He vaguely recalled being able to walk again and having a tail? Kiru thought it a dream until they told him that's exactly what happened. Now Kiru understood why he'd gotten so hairy.

Brunhilda also pointed out that his hair wasn't the only thing that had changed. She took the large bowl of water over to him and told him to smile.

Kiru visibly startled at his reflection. Eight of his teeth had elongated slightly and were sharpened to a fine point. If he hadn't known any better, Kiru would've thought himself a monster. *Or some kind of beast,* he thought. Understanding what was done to save him and what was given up in order to achieve that, Kiru was extremely grateful. He would have to thank Myev for her sacrifice when he saw her next.

In addition to his body, Kiru also learned what had happened to his gear. Indeed, the Bronzium armor his mother had left him as well as his Fist House jacket had been utterly destroyed by S'Vol, which explained his current garb. Kiru was surprised to realize that he even missed the Fist House jacket that had been bedazzled by his school patron, Niajar, just as much as his mother's armor. The garish item was burnt to a crisp from Myev's technique. Fortunately, his mother's enchanted storage ring and his blessed headband had survived along with his Fu Tao.

Then the party informed him that they were inside the pyramid they had fought so hard to protect, in a room on the western side, the section of wall that had sustained the least damage. They told him that many had died but even more survived the ordeal due to their efforts.

"That shaman got understandably mad when my sister told him what we'd planned and that we hadn't involved him," Mutt said. "He got over it, though, after learning that Myev won."

"I imagine that the public display of affection she gave him afterward also helped in convincing him. I hadn't realized orcs kiss so loudly," Zhaden added.

"Well . . . yeah," Mutt said, clearly uncomfortable thinking about his sister smooching someone.

Kiru chuckled.

"*How do orcs kiss?*" William asked inside the psion's mind. "*Their teeth are so big and stuck out. How do they not just cut each other's lips all the time?*"

Kiru decided not to take the bait and just left William to wonder. The psion was informed that Myev and her compatriots, Z'Goyan and Snout, had gone back to Dissé. They went both to inform the people in person of their tribe's victory and to have a celebration, which was custom. The shamans throughout Imakandi were already informed of the M'Baku Clan's official leadership via their gods, but it was important to be at the capital in person, per tradition.

Kiru then asked what happened to the dead and the Thrar'fangs, and his friends gave him a quick summary. For those that died, to prevent disease from festering, a large pyre was constructed. As for the Thrar'fangs, after Grimtusk regained consciousness, he and his subordinates were irate at what had happened, almost attacking Myev on the spot for her deception, but upon seeing the still-empowered Nom and the other cultivators backing her, he relented. That still didn't mean he was happy about it, and he immediately took his followers and stormed out of the ruined temple, unwilling to help in the recovery efforts.

"My sis told me that, even though she's the new high chief, she believes that Grimtusk will challenge her authority one day. Man, that will be a *good* fight," Mutt said.

With everything currently settled and since there wasn't a need to rush back to the capital, the members of Pandemonium stayed for a while in the ancient temple with the leokin. They spent time with Nom and Zengaz, comforted those mourning the deaths of their tribemates, and healed from their wounds.

Without a doubt, the biggest hurdle for the feline caretakers of the ancient temple was repairing the extreme damage and removing the remains of the dead dragon from their home. Zengaz told Kiru that, not long after the psion's miraculous healing and Myev's blessing of authority, Kiru had been rushed into the central pyramid. It was while he was in there that the lingering power of Jormungandr burned out inside S'Vol's body. The scorched skin, muscles, and tissue of the corpse rapidly decayed, fading away into floating tufts of ash until only the orc-turned-dragon's bones remained.

While that meant a huge amount of the corpse no longer needed to be dealt with, there was still a two-hundred-foot-long by twenty-foot-tall skeleton of heavy dragon bone to be moved. While some would consider the task daunting, the leokin were not deterred at all. They quickly and efficiently went to work using the gargantuan remains as substitute material to rebuild their damaged temple. The first thing they did was replace the caved-in ornate doors that the Jormuns had burst through. It had been made of bone as well, so it proved a worthy replica.

Aside from aiding in the construction efforts, Kiru specifically took the time to practice his various sword forms. He also worked to get accustomed to simply moving about by siphoning mana from his newly injured core, trying to make his movements as smooth and precise as possible. It certainly took some getting used to. Every time he activated a technique, Kiru was met with an acute sharp pain in his head. If he kept it up, the pain quickly morphed into a dull throb, like with his Telekinesis.

Kiru's year and a half of near-constant use of mana to move made his mana efficiency extremely impressive among those who were Ruby-rank. He had surmised while he was back in Dissé that he was even more efficient than many in Sapphire too. His injury, though, had effectively reversed his progress. He was still better than a lot of other cultivators at his rank, but even with pushing himself to the limit, the most he could move in a row now was about six hours. That wasn't even using any other techniques either.

Essentially, his cultivation efficiency had been reduced nearly fourfold. Instead of one hour of cultivating resulting in four hours of movement, it only yielded ninety minutes' worth when there were dreaming minds present. When none were around, it was an even trade at a one-to-one ratio. It wasn't that William's method was now insufficient; it was that Kiru constantly leaked mana out of his core like a sieve.

As for other techniques, Kiru did place a limitation on himself. To be *really* safe, he decided to not use Brainstorm until his core recovered. The technique was easily his most devastating, and with how wild it was, the psion didn't feel comfortable generating such raging power inside his core again, short of a life-and-death situation. He hoped that maybe his father's second item could help him with the damage.

He pondered on that while taking some time to cultivate. The day after he'd woken up, Kiru had been able to acquire a shirt, but it was quite literally a burlap sack with holes cut out for sleeves. Most of the leokin preferred togas, and if not that, very minimal clothing with tribal adornments. With Kiru's emaciated form, he preferred something to cover his torso more effectively than a mere sack. His bare arms and feet were exposed as well. The psion was grateful for the warm climate of Imakandi, but if he wasn't careful, he would get a bad sunburn.

Myev wasn't the only M'Baku orc who'd received a boon. In gratitude for all that he'd done to help, the leokin also granted Mutt secret knowledge about how to ascend to Tier Two of Ruby. To Mutt's shock, it turned out to be surprisingly easy for him. That was only because he was a beast mana cultivator and hadn't reached Gold in the way that most do. All he'd done was eat enough hearts of powerful sacred beasts, intentionally avoiding their cores. The heart contained an abundance of beast mana, and by eating enough of them, Mutt flooded his meridians to open.

Most cultivators instead cultivated and spent a specific amount of time in an area dense with the mana type they used. That allowed the mana to swarm around them and eventually seep into their bodies and forcefully overflow them for a temporary time until their meridians opened. Since Mutt hadn't ascended to Gold this way before, he could use that way now. To reach Ruby Tier One, one needed to incorporate their techniques or master them on such a level with their minds and souls that they had complete control. While that tier required mastering of the mental and spiritual aspects, Tier Two was utterly physical. The mana needed to lace and flood every part of Mutt's body: muscle, bone, connective tissue, nerves, organs, and even the entire bloodstream.

So, being in one of the most beast-mana-dense areas on the whole continent, Mutt was able to spend the next few days in a mix of cultivation and meditation on the very top of the central pyramid, overloading his body with the magical energy. He nearly passed out from the efforts. Fortunately, Nom came to his rescue, and the cub compelled some of his leokin brethren to forcefully insert beast mana directly into Mutt's bloodstream, helping suffuse the blind orc with enough the first member of Pandemonium to reach Tier Two.

The party was fortunately present for the last part. They heard Mutt let out a roar as the orc desperately tried to draw in more and more mana to permeate his bodily tissues. When he stopped, the orc visibly relaxed and sighed in relief.

Despite his wounds, he gave a genuine smile as the leokin released their jaws. As soon as he was free, Mutt turned and hugged Nom and laughed in joy. All of the other leokin surrounding Nom and Mutt would've moved to intervene but they were all too lethargic from having given the orc most of their mana.

"Hahaha! Thanks so much, you little furry thing," Mutt said, completely ignoring that he was rubbing his blood all over Nom. The party ran up, and they all paused as they felt the new level of power coming off their friend. All of them stood in slack-jawed amazement and a bit of jealousy. To be able to surpass them all once again and with only a few days' dedicated efforts lit a competitive fire in each of the three, most notably Zhaden. Out of the entire party, he was the only member of Pandemonium to have not advanced since their time in Imakandi. Regardless, all of them felt a renewed drive to advance even higher.

Mutt turned to them and gave a wide grin, "All of you are good fighters, but you still have a long way to go to catch up to the best," he proudly declared as he pointed at himself with his thumb before setting Nom down on his throne.

The others all grinned back, both proud of Mut and eager to rise to the challenge he'd just set.

William huffed in annoyance inside Kiru's mind.

Kiru knew that he was about to make the challenge more difficult, but he knew that it was for the good of the party to tell Mutt what he'd discovered. "Mutt, that's amazing! Congrats! Do you know what this means?" he asked.

"That I'm still the best fighter of us all?"

Kiru shook his head. "No, that means you're ready to work to get to Sapphire."

"Well, duh, Boss. That's the obvious next step," Mutt replied.

Brunhilda rolled her eyes. "Yes, ye idgit. Sapphire be the next step, but I dunnae suppose ye can tell me *how* ye get to Sapphire, hm?"

Mutt opened his mouth to answer but then stopped. Eventually, he said, "Uh, I don't know."

"That's what I'm getting at, Mutt," Kiru said. "When I was back at the Beast Gods Temple in Dissé, I read some carved texts about a method to help beast mana users get to Sapphire. I don't understand what it all exactly means, but hopefully with your innate understanding, we can help you ascend even higher."

"Really, Boss?"

"Yeah," Kiru replied.

Before Kiru could say anything else, the orc rushed over and wrapped him up in a big bear hug, and as with Nom, rubbed a fair amount of blood on him in the process. "Oh my gods, Boss! Thank you so much! Haha! We'll have to start working on that after we head back to Dissé," he said. "Oh, I almost forgot!" Mutt then dropped Kiru before turning back to Nom who was sitting on his throne, licking the blood off his fur like a housecat. "Would you mind getting the stuff we talked about, Little Guy?"

Nom's ears perked up at Mutt's request, and the little leokin went quickly scurrying down the pyramid, his entourage following close behind.

"Where's he going?" Kiru asked.

"Well . . ." Mutt trailed off, scratching the back of his head.

"Many of the leokin were extremely grateful to the 'berserker' who bravely went on a suicide charge to kill the dragon. That is what they've been calling you. After things settled down again, the leokin approached us about finding some way to compensate you for all you'd done," Zhaden explained.

"Aye, after hearing ye talking 'bout wanting some better clothing and armor, we came up with an idea," Brunhilda added.

Kiru thought he knew where this was going but wasn't 100% sure. When he asked his friends to elaborate, they refused. They just told him to wait for the leokin to return as it was a surprise. Kiru was indeed very surprised when twenty minutes later the group of the leokin led by Nom ascended the pyramid and approached him.

"What's going on?" he asked, noticing that a few leokin priestesses were holding some wrapped-up items. Zengaz walked beside them too.

Nom was now wearing a small, well-fitting headdress reminiscent of what the previous head shaman had worn, as well as a cute cub-sized toga. It was clear that this was some sort of formal tribal custom.

"Nom," the small sacred beast said as he puffed out his chest proudly and slammed one of his fists onto it.

"Our newly appointed head shaman wishes to present you with a token of our gratitude, oh Great Berserker," Zengaz explained.

William loved the nickname the leokin had given Kiru.

The psion, on the other hand, grimaced a little at the title.

"No reward is necessary," he said.

He was, in truth, more eager to get his father's second item. He also had a feeling that whatever they were going to offer him was likely going to be fairly crude. Kiru had witnessed the sacred beasts to be impressive in feats of construction, Beast God knowledge, and control of beast mana, but aside from that, everything else they'd produced seemed rather simplistic. He'd assumed the only reason that most of them wore togas was because it was something that didn't require much skill to make.

Nom shook his head vehemently, pursing his furry lips.

"No! Kiru!" the little creature bellowed.

Kiru's eyes widened at hearing Nom say something other than his name in his own language. Kiru had seen him barking something fiercely at the projection of Jormungandr, but it was in a language he couldn't understand.

Nom glared intently at Kiru, pointing a small, clawed finger at him, then not blinking as he moved his finger to point back at the wrapped items the priestesses carried. "Nom!"

"I don't think refusal is an option," Zengaz said.

"I gathered that," Kiru replied, then walked over to the priestesses.

They laid their items on the ground and unwrapped them.

Kiru audibly gasped at what he saw.

"Whoa! I knew I liked that little critter. This is awesome!" William cheered.

The leokin had created a set of armor with tanned hide and bone. The psion quickly recognized that it wasn't just any bone, either. It was from the skeletal remains of S'Vol.

"My time with the L'Khans didn't only allow me to teach them Beast Speech. It was a learning opportunity for me as well. Though not skilled with tanning, they were quite adept at working with bones. They taught me a few things about crafting weapons and armor using them for material," Zengaz explained.

At a glance, most of it looked to be well crafted. It seemed to provide a similar level of protection as his mother's gear, yet there were some stark contrasts aside from the obvious differences in materials. The hide under the pauldrons ended halfway between the elbow and shoulder, leaving much of his arms still exposed. And instead of high-quality boots made of metal, these were just simple leather cut crookedly but seeming to be adequate and sturdy enough to suit his current needs.

The cuirass looked both imposing and impressive. The bones were well apposed, giving great coverage to most of his torso, his shoulders, and thighs, with flexible tassets. There were even some bits of bone that had been sharpened and attached to the armor. Most notably, there were outward-pointing spikes sewn into the knee padding of both legs of the brown hide pants, along with two particularly nasty pieces of curved bone on each shoulder pauldron. Zengaz informed Kiru that those specific pieces were actually cut from some of the dragon's fangs, though they didn't seem to possess any venomous properties anymore either.

Kiru was admittedly taken aback by the armor. On the one hand, it was *very* barbaric—a poor choice for someone who didn't want to draw attention to himself. On the other, it was *very* cool, reigniting Kiru's memories of childhood dreams of being a warrior of unrefuted strength. Wearing armor crafted from literal dragon bone went a long way toward at least looking the part. William was all but drooling.

After Nom's proud declaration that Kiru *would* take their gift, the psion didn't argue. He quickly realized that he'd be dumb to do so. He had no other suitable replacement for his mother's gear. Though savage-looking and crude, this armor would be a whole lot more effective at shielding him than a literal sack with holes in it. Seeing as beggars couldn't be choosers and he didn't want to appear rude, Kiru smiled and graciously accepted the proffered gift.

When he had made it back to his room, he put it on. The dragon bone armor was, without a doubt, too bulky and large for him, making him look a bit ridiculous in it, given his thin frame. Still, it performed its main function—protection—well. The bones were thick, and moving his body with Telekinesis in the armor wasn't too much of a strain. Admittedly, with his too-thin body and bony gear, he looked like a half-dead necromancer, but he still cut an imposing figure. While not the muscle-bound berserker the leokin imagined him to be, the psion had an intimidating look all to his own.

At least to anyone other than his friends. When they saw him in his new equipment, they all burst into laughter. Knowing he meant them no harm, he couldn't frighten them, so they felt very comfortable poking fun at his outfit. William was irate, but Kiru calmed him down. The psion blushed at first but eventually laughed good-naturedly too.

"That's what friends are for, to laugh with and call you out on your bullshit . . . or when you look ridiculous," he sent to William. And he wouldn't have had it any other way.

CHAPTER THIRTY-SIX

Sins of the Past

After a couple of weeks recovering, the members of Pandemonium began their trek back north to Dissé. With the threat to the orc homeland gone, it was time for Myev to escort Kiru to his father's item. Kiru knew the artifact was in the southeastern part of the orc homeland, but that's as far as his knowledge went. So, that was why, even though they were going in the opposite direction, they needed to rejoin the new orc queen. Only she had access to the information, and it was sealed within a vault in the royal palace.

The group had to stop more than once along the way to allow Kiru to rest and cultivate more mana. The bone-and-hide armor wasn't enchanted like his Bronzium armor and school jacket had been, so it was more difficult to move. Plus, the jacket had been enhanced to magically regulate temperature, keeping Kiru pretty comfortable no matter what the environment. Now without it, the psion had to deal with much more heat and humidity on his thin body, which decreased his stamina.

Despite the stops, they were doing all right in terms of progress. Mutt took the lead, using his enhanced senses to keep them out of trouble, while Zhaden's inherent paranoia allowed him to keep a watchful eye from the group's rear. It was as they neared the border of the desert toward the rocky, rolling hills of M'Baku Territory that things changed.

They had just reached a small gorge with rolling rocky hills about a hundred feet ahead when Mutt groaned and wiped some sweat from his forehead. "Phew! Gosh, you'd think it'd be less hot given we're now *leaving* the desert," he said.

Zhaden walked up beside Mutt. "Hmm, I concur with your assessment," he hissed, thumbing the pommel of one of his sheathed blades. "Wait here." Then he began to walk forward. After about ten feet, the heat distorted the air as well as

Zhaden's form. His shaky silhouette looked semitranslucent, then it appeared to split in two before fading away completely.

The party's hearts raced as the sound of blades clashing suddenly filled the air.

"Scorpion's Stance," Kiru ordered, and the three cultivators went into a defensive formation they'd learned back at the academy. All three of them frantically scanned their surroundings, looking for signs of the battle they were hearing. Then, someone flew toward them, seemingly out of thin air. Brunhilda battered the person—a female orc—away with one of her shields as if she was a projectile. She bounced once on the sand, then used the momentum to gracefully get back to her feet. From behind the orc, a form materialized. Zhaden appeared with a dagger to her throat and his tail wrapped around one of her legs.

"I see you've made good use of my training." The female orc gave a light cackle. "Using your Duplication technique and disguising it with the heat waves was clever."

"Of course, Ebysso," the drakonid hissed. "And, by my account, I've learned all the tricks of your art, and I've bested you."

The orc *tsk*ed. "Tut, tut, tut. Not *all* the tricks, my apprentice," she said and motioned her head down to her left hand. The gold drakonid's eyes moved down to see the orc scout holding a small blade in a reverse grip, the point of the weapon pointed directly at him. He was confused, though. It was a good six inches away from his body. Then, the air around the blade distorted until the weapon changed, revealing the blade to be much longer than it appeared. It was practically touching him.

"A stalemate, then," he hissed, then retracted his blade and unfurled his tail.

"It's your best performance to date." Ebysso did the same and turned to face the entire party.

"So, I'm confused. Why'd you attack us?" Mutt asked.

"It was merely a test for my pupil here, My Prince," the scout answered with a bow.

"Oh, um, okay," Mutt replied, confused.

"Still, why are you out here? Shouldn't you be back at the capital?" Kiru asked.

"I was, but things have changed since Myev returned," Ebysso answered, revealing more than a little discomfort.

"Changed how?" The psion kept his hand on his weapon's hilt. Something didn't feel right.

The scout's mouth was covered in wrappings, but her eyes weren't. It was clear that she was glaring pointedly at Kiru.

"It seems you're a person of great interest to your homeland. As soon as the barrier surrounding our nation was dismissed, the Kingdom of Blades sent their

Inquisition along with their delegation to meet with our newly selected queen. Queen M'Baku Myev knew they were sent to find you, Kiru."

Kiru turned pale. He'd heard of the Inquisition back home. None of the stories were good. They often contained a gruesome mix of violence and more than a couple of references to torture. Unlike the standard royal guards, members of the Inquisition were a mysterious bunch, said to be a mix of assassins and enforcers who carried out the king's will through less-than-noble means. The militaristic division was established after Van Blaine had been officially appointed as the new king. There was even a rumor that a large majority of inquisitors were violent criminals, too unstable to be in regular society, so they were used as collared attack dogs for the kingdom.

No matter how the stories varied, there were always three things that stayed the same: they were violent, they were zealously loyal to Van Blaine, and they would stop at nothing to get the answers they sought. Basically, they were lunatics who the king somehow had under his control. They were also known as "Bladeheads," but Kiru didn't know why. Parents would tell stories of them to scare their children into going to bed—even his own mother had done that to him. Now that Kiru thought about it, she was more than a little scared when she had told him about them. Now knowing what he did, it made the psion even more concerned.

"Is the Inquisition here?" he asked.

Ebysso nodded. "They came a day after Queen Myev arrived back at the capital. We were 'visited' by the strong arm of your kingdom as soon as our barrier went down. How *convenient*. Normally, we don't tolerate any other nation meddling in our affairs, but we were not in a position to oppose the Inquisition with Myev's rule being so new. Plus, news of your team's presence in the city was well-known. A purple-haired dwarf paladin preaching her goddess to the masses is not easily forgotten in Dissé."

Brunhilda blushed at the admonishment but did not apologize for her faith.

"There were also rumors that the blind prince had come charging through the front gate like a wildebeest, and that he saved many guards and shamans in the religious district along with said dwarf and a half-elf wielding dual blades. It seems that Zhaden is the only one who knows the definition of stealth, as there was no mention of him," the bandage-wrapped orc said, gesturing to the gold drakonid with a thumb.

This time, both Mutt and Kiru lowered their heads. Admittedly, time was of the essence, so hiding their identities was of lower priority in their mad dash to the top of the orc capital.

Ebysso continued, "With her position so low among leaders of the Great Alliance along with the confirmed sightings of you three, the queen had no choice but to allow them into Dissé and aid them in their pursuit of you. She sent me to get to you before the rest of her forces and the Inquisition could." Ebysso then squinted her eyes at Kiru. "I must ask. Who exactly are you, Half-Elf?"

Unease gripped Kiru. The cautious scout was getting curious. That could be dangerous.

"*Master, I don't like this. We should kill her before she ousts us,*" William said, showing the same concern the psion did.

Kiru resisted the urge to grip his blades' handles. He had learned from Zhaden that Ebysso was like him—paranoid but loyal. Zhaden would speak about her with a fond familiarity that Kiru rarely saw from him in regard to anyone else. So, the psion reasoned that it wasn't shocking for her to ask him those questions. However, despite having proven herself to be a stalwart ally, the fewer people to know who—or, more accurately, *what* he was—the better. "Let's just say, the leadership in the Kingdom of Blades and I don't see eye to eye. I'm afraid if I tell you more, it could put your life in danger," he answered, trying to be both vague and honest.

The scout raised her eyebrows. "So, a fugitive, then? Curious . . . Well, if my queen trusts you, I do too. And if you're anything close to as dedicated as my pupil here, then you have a good heart as well. Here," she said as she tossed a small scroll over to Kiru.

He nearly dropped it but managed to catch it by the edge.

"What is it?" he asked.

"It's the location of—"

"Hey," Mutt interrupted Ebysso before raising his head up and sniffing loudly. The blind orc then spread his legs and arms out wide, his bare feet sensing vibrations. A shiver went down his back, and his wild hair stood up like a cat's hackles.

"What is it?" Zhaden asked as he walked up beside Mutt, the rogue thumbing the pommel of one of his blades.

"The ground . . . it's shaking." Mutt then gasped as a boom echoed and, quick as a shot, he tackled Kiru to the ground. A sudden *whoosh* passed through the air over them a moment later, and a pair of daggers that looked to be made completely from carved stone struck the ground ahead of them, one coated in blood. Mutt turned his head and growled. "It seems you were followed, Ebysso."

The scout groaned and gripped her upper arm. Blood ran down it, solving the mystery of whom the dagger had cut. Her eyes widened and began frantically scanning their surroundings. "No, impossible! I left just as the Inquisition entered the capital," she barked as she and Pandemonium scanned their surroundings.

"You did," a snide voice called out as if in answer. Another blade struck Ebysso in her left shoulder blade seemingly out of nowhere, and right after, the dirt around them erupted up in a set of cacophonous booms. When it settled, there were ten armored soldiers surrounding the group. They were a mix of humans, elves, and one dwarf. They all wore armor made of steel and leathers, the former somehow glistening in the sunlight despite just coming out of the dirt. A chill went down Kiru's neck as he took them in. They were all completely bald and clean-shaven with deep, dark rings around their eyes that indicated barely contained madness.

The most terrifying part were their heads. Along each of their bald scalps were blades. Four upward-pointing daggers were embedded in their flesh at the handles, forming some sort of hideous crown. It was reminiscent of Kiru's circlet, but instead of being magically absorbed, the Inquisitors appeared to have each one of the weapons physically seared into their flesh. The term "Bladeheads" instantly now made sense.

An older human male with a nasty scar across his mouth took a step forward—the clear leader of the group.

"But the Inquisition was already monitoring Dissé from afar. You aren't the first criminals we've hunted, nor will you be the last," the man said, his scowl matching his tone. He wielded a great sword in one arm and a dagger in the other, clearly ready for a fight. "Kiru the commoner, you and your compatriots are under arrest for the murder of the headmaster of the Royal Academy, for disobeying the direct order of our illustrious King van Blaine, and for desertion of your duty to serve in the army of the Kingdom of Blades. You will surrender now both willingly and quietly, or you will face the judgement of the Inquisition," the man said in a snobby and authoritative tone.

"Oh, please fight back. It's been so long since I've gotten to carve someone up," the inquisitor dwarf said and cackled maniacally.

Kiru looked over to see him licking one of two short swords he held, drawing a line of blood on his tongue, both weapons entirely made of sharpened stone. The psion took a moment to fully look at the inquisitors. In fact, each one of them wielded two blades of varying forms. Some of their blades glowed with the different lights of their mana.

It seems that they took the "Kingdom of Blades" theme to heart. The aura of power each of them was giving off was that of Ruby.

Kiru was quiet, but it wasn't because he was scared. He'd fought a fucking dragon and survived—a dragon much stronger and scarier than these inquisitors. He'd helped defeat a whole battalion of violent draconic cultists; ten zealots off their rockers was a drop in the bucket compared to that. Still, cockiness could get him killed. So, yes, he held his tongue, but it was because he was strategizing.

Kiru also fought to contain a smile as he fully took in the situation. He noted that they hadn't called him a psion or accused him of mental mana use at all. *That means they don't know yet, or at least they don't know for sure,* he thought. Kiru apparently took too long to say anything in response. That was all the excuse the bloodthirsty Inquisitors needed.

"If you would rather scheme, then you have chosen death," the lead inquisitor said before the swordsmen charged.

"*Mutt, roar!*" Kiru sent via Telepathy, fighting back the sharp pain on activating a technique.

The blind orc smirked before raising his head up high and bellowing out his Bounder's Howl technique. It was much like Zhaden's Nightmare technique, only not as devastating or costly. The mana-laced noise washed over the inquisitors, causing them to falter only a half-step as they charged. A half-step of hesitation may not sound significant, but in a battle—especially one between cultivators—it can make all the difference between life and death. Brunhilda fired out a Gnash and Grind. One of the inquisitors who had hesitated had tried to leap over the technique, but to his misfortune, was caught midair by the mouth of a spectral goat head. Another inquisitor closed the distance and swung his blades at the paladin, both weapons' edges glowing orange. She blocked them with her round steel shield, but the inquisitor just pressed harder against the metal, the fire mana surrounding the blades quickly heating it up.

She gritted her teeth as her arm began to burn and the metal started to bend. The zealot gave a mad grin, but it was quickly cut short as a blade embedded itself in his neck. The Bloodstep Stiletto's enchantment kicked it once it tasted blood, and Zhaden appeared right there. The drakonid put a hand under the man's chin, pulling his head back, and ripped his dagger out in the opposite direction, killing the inquisitor. The dwarf Bladehead stuck one of his stone blades into the ground and dragged his weapon forward and up. The ground in front of him rose, and a wave of jagged spikes surged forth in a straight line toward the pair.

The Trollblooded paladin met the technique with her enchanted mithril shield and stopped the wave of stone spikes with just her pure force of will.

The inquisitor gave another crazed laugh. "This one's got some fight in her," he said before jumping on top of the stone spikes and charging toward Brunhilda.

Mutt activated Dweller Bear's Fur and began running on all fours at some oncoming inquisitors whose weapons all glowed blue with either water or ice mana.

He ducked under a pair of blades from one zealot and kicked out the legs of another. Then Mutt grabbed the armor of the first inquisitor and threw him into the way of the third, who had raised his twin kukuri blades, made of solid ice, to strike and was already swinging by the time his compatriot was thrown into his way.

In one swift motion, the inquisitor sliced straight through his ally's armor, his blades biting deep into his chest. The ice weapons cut into the lungs and heart, and a gout of blood sprayed from the fatal wound, the red liquid freezing midair from the wound due to the ice mana.

Mutt gave an animalistic grin. "I love a good fight."

Kiru charged toward the leader of the inquisitors, the scarred middle-aged human with a great sword. The inquisitor just scowled as three of his subordinates ran to intercept. Two had blades dripping with what looked to be green venom, while the other held ones made of pure shadow. One fired an orb of acid. Kiru dodged the projectile, then intercepted a green-tinged blade with Sweep the Barn. The inquisitor growled and lowered his head, attempting to gore Kiru with the blades grafted on top.

Caught off guard, Kiru fell onto his back and used the momentum to kick the Inquisitor over him with his legs. He got back on his feet just in time to intercept the shadow-blade wielder. Kiru raised his blades up in an "X" crossguard. To the psion's surprise, the blades of shadow passed through his steel blade as if it wasn't there, somehow making contact against the Psyslime blade, the weight of the two far too much for him to handle. His arm shook as he fought, and it eventually gave way, allowing the shadow blades through, where they attempted to make two vertical slices along Kiru's face. Only, before they could strike, his headband's enchantment mercifully kicked in to form a magic helmet, intercepting the strikes. Before the inquisitor could swing at Kiru again, the psion shoved him back using Telekinesis. The Bladehead's eyes went wide as he realized what had just happened. The leader's did too.

The shadow inquisitor pointed a blade at Kiru and began to shout something when the air behind him began to distort. Ebysso's body appeared, her right arm limp and bleeding. She stabbed a blade in the exposed part of the inquisitor's armor in between the shoulder and neck. The man's shout of alarm was cut short, turning into one of pain as the skin by the blade began to bubble and sizzle. It seemed that the inquisitors weren't the only cultivators who could use a technique on a weapon.

The two acidic inquisitors fired another two orbs of acid at Ebysso and Kiru, both of them being so close that each technique should have hit. Acting on instinct, Kiru used Telekinesis on the dying shadow inquisitor once more. With his mind, he pulled the inquisitor free of Ebysso's blade and moved him to shield them from the acid orbs. The Bladehead screamed as the techniques struck him, melting his flesh and armor. Wanting to kill two birds with one stone, Kiru telekinetically threw the shadow inquisitor at his compatriots, knocking them all to the ground.

"Heretic!" the lead inquisitor shouted in fury. The king and head inquisitor had informed them of their suspicions that the Mad Tyrant's followers may still be skulking about to control the populace. When he had seen the Defunct boy somehow force one of his men back, the inquisitor was concerned. After seeing him levitate and hurl the man without a word, however, his fear was realized. That boy was a damn psion! He must stop at nothing to eliminate this threat to his king—this threat to the world.

Kiru snapped his eyes to the shouting inquisitor and almost lost his head as the man flew forward at him. He barely deflected the man's long sword but was thrown back by the force of the blow. Kiru's body struck Ebysso and both were flung back into the sand. They rolled back to their feet to see the man effortlessly splitting his blade into two equal halves, a technique of one who cultivates metal mana. The two acidic inquisitors stood back up to flank him.

"Psion, the plague of your existence ends here," the scarred inquisitor said, his eyes shining with fanatical focus.

The two acidic Bladeheads bared their teeth at the psion.

"You handle the pretty one," Kiru said to Ebysso about the lead inquisitor, his voice dripping with sarcasm. "I'll deal with the other two." They charged forward.

Ebysso pressed her fists together and said, "Angler's Heat!" Mana rapidly circulated throughout her body causing heat to surge out from her pores, covering her skin in a thick layer of sweat, which glistened in the sunlight. Then her entire body distorted and became hazy to the naked eye.

Kiru easily got the trio of Bladeheads to focus on him. *Apparently, psions are popular guys among the Inquisition.* He deflected one's blade with Sweep the Barn, guiding his opponent's weapon and body in front of the other inquisitor. The other acidic Bladehead hesitated, not wanting to strike his ally, which allowed Kiru to kick the first opponent into him.

Kiru would've forced the lead inquisitor to join his compatriots, but after running a couple of steps forward, the Bladehead was attacked by Ebysso. Her speed was superior to the psion's and quickly closed the distance to fight her foe. Her form was blurry from the technique she was using, making it difficult for the inquisitor to get a clean hit.

He blocked her daggers with his own pair of swords and gritted his teeth at his hazy opponent. At the sound of one of his allies being kicked, he glanced over to see them stumbling back from Kiru's move. The inquisitor's face creased in frustration. The metal-mana user pulled a surprise technique of his own, however. "Blades of Fury," he said. After his words, the heads of the two acidic inquisitors exploded with a wet squelch, sending the blades embedded in their heads flying outward like shrapnel.

Kiru reflexively curled and turned his body away. The blades struck him but, fortunately, bounced harmlessly against his bone armor cuirass and shoulder pauldron.

Unfortunately, the blades didn't just fly out toward the psion. They flew out in multiple directions—specifically toward Ebysso.

The scout winced and her blurry form solidified after she was hit, revealing a blade embedded in her belly and leg. The scarred inquisitor, now able to fully visualize his opponent, used that to his advantage. With a shout, he forced her daggers back and shoved one of his long swords forward, impaling Ebysso straight through the gut.

"Noooo!" A pained hiss came from Kiru's side. The psion turned his head to see it was from Zhaden. He'd told Kiru that he'd grown close to Ebysso, and seeing his friend get stabbed seemed to send a similar pain through his gut.

The drakonid hurled eight daggers at the inquisitor at once in a display of reckless anger, but it was pure folly. The scarred man used metal mana.

Before the flying blades could strike, he let go of the blade in Ebysso and raised a hand. With his mana, he took control of the airborne blades, and in one smooth motion, redirected them toward Kiru.

The psion didn't have time to think. Acting on instinct, he gritted his teeth and took a page out of the inquisitor's playbook, furrowing his brow and flaring his mana outward. A sharp pain shot through his head as he did it. He stopped the redirected blades right in their tracks with Telekinesis.

The inquisitor's eyes widened at the power before him.

"The plague of *your* existence ends here, asshole." Kiru spat, a heavy nosebleed coming from his left nostril, then mentally shot the daggers back at him.

The scarred lead inquisitor, desperate, raised his hand and attempted to take control of the blades once more. They halted in their tracks midair, being held aloft by two opposing forces: one Kiru, the other being the inquisitor. Both Bladehead and the psion glared.

"*Master, you're staring daggers at him. Get it?*" William asked, chuckling at his ill-timed pun.

Kiru didn't reply. He couldn't afford to. Opposing the inquisitor's technique with his Telekinesis whilst still using it on himself was almost too taxing on his injured core.

While the two were competing for control of the airborne blades, the inquisitor also failed to give enough credence to the fact that the psion wasn't alone. Before the inquisitor could fully take control of the blades once more, a very angry gold drakonid descended from the sky.

During the time Kiru stopped the eight daggers, Zhaden had jumped on top of Brunhilda's shields and the strong dwarf had flung him upward. The inquisitor was too focused to even notice, and because of that, Zhaden fell upon him and cut the man's hand off at the wrist, disrupting his technique. The inquisitor only had time to gasp before his body was struck by the eight daggers. Like Kiru, most of them deflected off his armor, but a few struck at some joints where the armor was weaker in a series of simultaneous thuds.

None of the dagger wounds were immediately fatal, but that was okay. Kiru followed up with his Fu Tao right after. In a blaze of anger, the psion executed Thief's Punishment, amputating the inquisitor's other hand and then jammed the sharp pommel of one of his blades directly into his right eye. There was a wet *pop*, and the scarred inquisitor went still before slinking off the blade, dead.

With their leader killed, the other inquisitors visibly deflated, losing hope of victory—all except the laughing dwarf. Despite his obvious madness, he was also deceptively clever. "This victory is only momentary. The Inquisition will not stop until you are purged, heretics! Grah!" He cackled, then grunted as he pushed Mutt's claws away with his stone blades. Before anyone else could say anything, the earth-mana cultivator slammed both his blades into the ground and activated some sort of tunneling technique.

He and his three surviving allies immediately disappeared deep underground and out of sight, kicking up a large cloud of sand that completely engulfed those above. The force of it also sent Brunhilda and Mutt back. The dwarf wanted to taste more of their blood, but when their leader discovered the boy was a psion, priorities changed. The boss had failed, and they needed to let the High Inquisitor know what they had discovered. Plus, she'd probably promote him and let him taste their blood once more after he updated her.

As the dust began to settle, Kiru and Zhaden noticed the other inquisitors were gone. They also noticed a barely breathing Ebysso a few feet away. They ran over to her prone form. She lay on her back, clutching at her belly. When she had fallen on her back, the sword embedded in her had been forcefully dislodged. That made the injury worse, and she was now lying in a rapidly growing pool of blood.

"Shit! Zhaden, grab Brunhilda," Kiru said.

The assassin hesitated, his body stuck in fear.

"Now!" Kiru shouted.

That broke Zhaden out of his sudden stupor, and the drakonid wordlessly took off to grab the paladin. Kiru put pressure on the wound, both blood and viscera coating his hands.

Ebysso groaned and coughed, breathing rapidly. Her cowl was down, revealing a blood-covered mouth. "Do you still have the scroll?" she managed to wheeze.

Kiru nodded, suddenly remembering that he'd hidden it as soon as he'd seen the Inquisition. He tapped one of his pockets. "Put it here before the bastards decide to attack in earnest."

"Good . . . It has the location of the item that my queen promised you." She then gripped his right arm as tight as she could, a desperate final burst of strength.

"I don't know what you are, but you are strong. Please, continue to help her and Imakandi. And tell Zhaden I'm glad I found someone as cautious as me. Tell him, I'm sorry I couldn't join . . ." She trailed off as her eyes went dull. The scout's grip on his arm lessened as her body went limp.

"I will," Kiru said, feeling both the pain and frustration of another ally dying to keep him safe. He would honor her wish. He would hold true to the alliance and promise he'd made to Myev.

Ten seconds later, Zhaden brought a limping Brunhilda over. The rogue went quiet, his tail going completely still as he saw Ebysso's lifeless eyes. They were too late. The drakonid kneeled toward his teacher and clutched her body to his. He pressed his forehead to hers, feeling true loss for the first time in his life. Then, Zhaden wept, lifting his head up to the sky and bellowing a primal cry of mourning and despair.

Tears ran down Kiru and Brunhilda's faces at seeing their friend in such pain.

Mutt had been using his senses to scan for any of the Inquisition. When he couldn't find any traces of them, he went to the group.

"I'm sorry, Stabby," Mutt said to Zhaden once he'd returned from scanning for any more signs of the Inquisition about and found none.

Zhaden didn't say anything, just clutched Ebysso's body a little tighter.

Mutt then turned to Kiru. "Boss, it seems that the laughing dwarf and the others ran off. I can't feel any vibrations in the ground, so I think they've already left the immediate area. Still, I can't be sure. We can't stay here."

"We need to bury her," Zhaden hissed through his tears.

Kiru opened his mouth, then closed it again, uncomfortable with what he was about to say. "Zhaden, we can't. We have to keep moving."

"She died to save you, and in repayment, you're going to let her body become food for the flies?!" he snarled at Kiru, angrier with him than he'd ever been before.

Brunhilda knelt down and gently placed a hand on Zhaden's shoulder, looking him directly in the eyes, "It ain't ideal, Zhaden, but Kiru be right. We gotta get goin'. The sheer scale and wildness of the land had aided our ability to move unnoticed, but that's changed. It's clear that the Kingdom of Blades be hot on our heels, and now that they know Kiru's a psion, I doubt getting from place to place will be easy from this point on." She gave his shoulder a gentle squeeze. "We can't let Ebysso's sacrifice be in vain."

"She's right, Stabby," Mutt added. "The scout's now with the Beast Gods. Her soul has joined them in the Savage Realm to revel in the eternal hunt. Trust me, she's doing much better now."

"It is comforting to know that her soul will not suffer in the next life. Thank you, Mutt," Zhaden said, giving a small nod. "I confess that I never knew you to be so knowledgeable about religion."

The blind orc gave a wide grin. "Eh, I normally wouldn't be, but I love a good hunt. So, it definitely piqued my interest when they started talking about hunting during my religion lessons growing up. I mean, you get to hunt forever! How awesome is that?!" Some of the tension eased with Mutt's childlike enthusiasm.

"At least she died in a blaze of glory, dying in battle. A warrior's death," William said inside Kiru's mind. The psion cocked his head as the imp's words pulled slightly at his memory until . . . *it clicked.*

Kiru looked over at the drakonid. "Zhaden, we may not be able to give her a proper burial, but we should be able to let her go out like a warrior."

CHAPTER THIRTY-SEVEN

Riddles

Back at the academy, Kiru had read about an ancient group of warriors who had worshipped the Aesir pre-Ragnarok. They would either bury their dead in mausoleums of crude stone or send their bodies on a boat and set it aflame. It had reminded him of his mother, who had literally died in a blaze of glory. This had given him comfort and made that tidbit of knowledge stick out in his head. Inspired by that idea, Kiru quickly gathered some branches from some spare bushes, set them around Ebysso's corpse, and used his sword and flint to set it on fire.

The fire was burning, but it would be a long process. The flame was also very weak, looking like a mild gust of wind could extinguish it. Upon noticing this, Brunhilda demonstrated a clever, little-known use of her Divine Shield technique. Apparently, when the cylindrical column of light and mana came into contact with a set of flames, it had the ability to strengthen them with its holy power. After she maneuvered the Divine Shield over Ebysso's body and the small flames underneath her, the orc's body became engulfed in holy fire.

They didn't have the time to give her a proper burial, but they could honor her and her bravery. While the smoke could alert more inquisitors, it would hopefully signal any leokin or Imakandi orcs to come and investigate as well. Hopefully, that would stop or at least delay the Inquisition's plans. The scroll Ebysso had handed Kiru was indeed a map to the location of his father's second item. It was very detailed, showing numerous minor landmarks and containing intricate design. With the latent knowledge he already had of the item's general location, it was now easy to know where they were going without getting lost.

They moved quickly, Brunhilda hopping on Mutt's back and the orc moving on all fours to help improve their pace. In only a few hours, they had crossed southeast out of the southern desert into Tau Territory. The sand slowly transitioned into verdant green grassland as far as the eye could see. Mutt informed Kiru that Tau Territory was much wider than it was long, so their journey shouldn't take them nearly as much time as their journey from the capital to the temple. Kiru knew that was significant as they had taken nearly a week before, and that was with their fast mounts. Aside from the green grassland, there were two main features of this part of Imakandi: the land was dotted with a number of round lakes as the land was once beset by meteors long ago, and it was windy. Very windy . . .

The gusts of wind never stopped. Sure, they would change direction, but the party was constantly beset by them. Whatever wasn't securely fastened to their person would undoubtedly get blown off. Kiru had to cinch his enchanted headband on even more securely as one particularly strong gust almost flung right off him. He also had to look at his map very infrequently so as not to have the parchment ripped out of his grip. Nearly everyone was also getting some degree of windburn—all except Mutt, who had activated his Dweller Bear's Fur technique, the long hair growing off his body now protecting him from the wind. Brunhilda buried her head in his fur to protect herself as well.

After only a day's travel, they made it to the location of Ruken's next item. There was a stone building, reminiscent of a temple to the Vasir, on a small island in the middle of a lake formed by a crater. The biggest difference between this lake and the others, though, was the size. The crater that had formed this lake was massive, at least ten-to-twenty times larger than any of the others, making a large bowl shape in the ground. The lake didn't fill the entirety of the crater, allowing for thick trees to take root along the sloping ground around, stopping not far from the water's edge.

Kiru could feel the item's presence coming from the island. It was calling to him, beckoning him to enter the stone structure. The party descended into the crater. They all visibly relaxed as the dip below the ground level and the trees growing around the edge of the lake effectively blocked the strong wind that had been constantly assaulting them. None of them had ever been so bothered by wind before. The Tau who lived here must have been strong, indeed, to have made their home in this area.

The party had gotten so excited to finally make it to this destination that they hadn't realized there was another problem: the lake itself. A few hundred feet of open water separated them from their island destination.

"There be another problem," Brunhilda added. "My heavy armor will make me sink if I get in the water."

"That shouldn't be a problem, Brunhilda," Mutt said. "Just take off that heavy armor of yours. That should take at least a hundred pounds off of you."

The paladin shook her head as her face began to blush a strong shade of purple. "There . . . also be one more thing. I can't swim."

Fortunately, being the local, Mutt had a solution. "No need to worry, Brun. We won't need to swim," he said. The orc then clicked his tongue, using echolocation to sense his surroundings. After a few seconds, he smiled and pointed to the water, and the party saw numerous large shells starting to emerge from the water, followed by large reptilian heads with mouths containing too many sharp teeth for Kiru's liking.

Mutt called them "turtle crocs." "Hahaha! I haven't been croc-hopping since I was a kid!" he laughed.

"Croc . . . hopping?" Zhaden asked in clear confusion. The drakonid had been even quieter than usual since Ebysso's death.

The blind orc grinned, his face still facing the water, "Oh, yeah. You see, turtle crocs are vicious bastards. Real fast and mean too. During the daytime, they make for a fun and challenging hunt."

"Mutt, dearie, that would be great and all, but how does that help us?" Brunhilda asked.

He wrapped his arm around her neck. "Because, Brun, that's only in the daytime. At night, they're slower than a pregnant cyclops giving birth to twins." Mutt went on to explain the specifics of croc-hopping. It was just as the name suggested. One would literally jump from croc to croc, leaping off their bulbous shells protruding out of the water.

Kiru looked up to the sky. The sun was getting low. In just an hour or two, it would be nighttime. "I don't like waiting to give anyone following us a chance to catch up, but this is our best bet. Let's rest and cultivate, but still keep an eye out. As soon as the sun goes down, we go toward the island."

For the next couple of hours, the party did just that. Despite the delay and risk, Kiru was especially grateful to get the time to cultivate since he no longer had the efficiency he once possessed. Mutt did take some time to fight off some of the hungrier turtle crocs who thought the members of Pandemonium would make an easy meal. Even after all the combat they'd gone through recently, Mutt still loved a good fight.

Aside from cultivating, Kiru got a chance to grab Zhaden and speak with him privately. "How're you feeling?" he asked him.

Zhaden's tail went stiff at the question. He breathed heavily as he looked at Kiru, his reptilian face betraying none of his emotions. After half a minute of tense silence, he finally spoke. "I wish vengeance for what has been done to Ebysso. I want to kill every single one of those inquisitors. Why did we not pursue them, Kiru? Their leader was dead, and they were on the run."

Kiru shook his head. "You know as well as I that we couldn't go after them. They could've led us to another ambush, and we have to get this item."

"*We* have to get it?!" Zhaden spat. "No, Kiru. *You* have to get it while *we* get dragged around and lose those close to us." The gold drakonid was now baring his fangs at the psion.

Kiru just stood there, stunned. Zhaden was always so stalwart and the most stoic of the party, unquestioningly loyal ever since he'd joined. But the venom he was now showing Kiru was something the psion had never experienced from him before.

Kiru wanted to ask why his friend was so angry when the dots connected in his mind. He knew that Ebysso's death was weighing heavily on the rogue. That made sense. Ebysso had been an ally to them and Zhaden's trainer. Zhaden had told Kiru that they'd grown close from their time together—that, again, made sense. Kiru didn't pay attention as to *how close* though. Based on the vehemence his friend was now displaying, however, Kiru was gaining a better idea as to how close they *really* were.

"Zhaden, what was Ebysso to you?" Kiru asked.

The gold drakonid inhaled sharply at the question but didn't speak. He just stared at the psion.

Kiru, for his part, waited and didn't press his friend despite William's whining inside his mind.

Eventually, Zhaden answered. "She was more than a friend. Nothing happened physically, unlike Mutt's sister and the shaman. Unlike you warmbloods, we who possess dragon blood do not choose a partner for physical attraction or compatibility, but on how our minds and spirits resonate."

Kiru raised an eyebrow. "Your partner?" he asked.

"Indeed," Zhaden answered.

Thinking back on something, a burning question popped up in Kiru's head. It wasn't the ideal time to ask, but he had to know. "Does that mean *all* who have dragon blood think like that? Because I'm pretty sure S'Vol wasn't thinking that way when he said Myev would bear his children back at the temple. That is a scene I do not want to think about."

Zhaden let out a low growl before giving a small laugh. "I must confess that not all share that mindset," he admitted before quickly raising a clawed finger. "But most do."

Kiru raised both hands up in surrender. "I get it," he said. His question may have been ill-timed, but it did succeed in defusing some of the tension between them. Kiru could tell because his friend's tail was now relaxed and lying on the ground. Kiru looked down and gave out a small sigh before gazing back at his friend. "I'm sorry, Zhaden. I never meant for you to lose someone so important to you, and I never meant to devalue the bond you two shared by making us leave so quickly. There's been so much fighting and death recently that I've gotten too callous in how I've processed our losses. In truth, it really is the only way I know how," he admitted, dropping his head down.

Upon speaking those words, Kiru was reminded of his mother. Kiru's heart raced as he thought about her. It had been a year and a half since that had occurred, and yet the pain was still there. He reckoned it would never go away—not completely. But he didn't want it to. It helped him remember her in some strange way.

Kiru remembered that he was utterly distraught. Despite the danger that was around him at the time of her death. He would've likely succumbed to despair had not William been there for him. The imp was rude and brash, but he was Kiru's friend. William had honestly saved the psion's life that day. When Kiru had lost the most important woman in his life, he needed a friend. Twisting the enchanted storage ring she'd left him, he realized that Zhaden needed the same.

Kiru lifted his head and looked at his friend once again. "Even though that's the case, that doesn't excuse how I handled the situation, my friend. I am sorry for the loss of your partner. I know it is hard to lose someone you love. If you need time to grieve, I understand. If you can no longer stay with us, I also understand."

Zhaden shook as he fought with his emotions. Kiru didn't know if he was going to cry or punch him. After a minute or so, the gold drakonid let out a pained exhale. "She was the only one who understood me. Never did I think that I would find one who would best me in stealth and preparation," he said as tears flowed down from his reptilian eyes.

Kiru placed a comforting hand on his friend's shoulder. "I hadn't gotten to say this yet, but before she passed, she said that she was glad to have found someone as cautious as her."

"Truly?" the drakonid asked.

"Yeah," Kiru answered. "She also said to tell you that she was sorry she couldn't join . . . something. What couldn't she join?"

At that, Zhaden gave a slightly uncomfortable look. He glanced away from Kiru before saying, "She was going to join Pandemonium." He then looked back up to Kiru nervously. "I hadn't revealed the truth about your identity, but she already suspected something. I know I hadn't asked the team for permission yet, but I couldn't leave without her."

"She was important to you," Kiru said knowingly.

"She was important to me," Zhaden echoed.

After that candid discussion, the two friends felt a lot better. Zhaden wanted to take some time to be alone, and Kiru respectfully left him alone and went off to cultivate.

When night fell, the party readied themselves to attempt croc-hopping. The lake glistened in the light of the twin moons, revealing just how many of the predatory reptiles were in the water. The lake was riddled with them. Kiru bet the sheer number of them raised the elevation of the water by quite a few feet. He also wondered if this number of creatures surrounding his father's item was just pure coincidence.

"Probably another protective measure to ensure no one gets to the item," he whispered to himself.

Pandemonium walked up to the water's edge, Mutt nonchalantly picking some croc meat out of his teeth. "Yep, alright everyone. It's pretty simple. Just jump from shell to shell to get to the end. There are three rules. Make sure you land on the top and center of their shells, don't follow the same path as anyone else, and since it's night, you have roughly about five seconds before the crocs react. Aside from that, it's easy peasy," he said, then promptly picked up Brunhilda and leaped into the water.

The dwarf let out a high-pitched cry of surprise and began to protest, but it was too late. Mutt had already jumped toward the lake and began expertly hopping from shell to shell as if they were just simple rocks. They even looked like rocks, too, until five seconds past and a large, angry predator snapped its toothy maw upward. Mutt was too practiced and skilled, though, for that to deter him, and by the time any of the crocs reacted, he was already on another one. Now, the rule about not following anyone else's path made sense. Any turtle croc who had just been jumped on was primed to react.

Not wanting to waste any time, Zhaden followed suit. The assassin had no trouble at all navigating a path across the water.

Kiru was about to follow when William spoke up in his mind. *"Are you sure we have to do this, Master?"*

Kiru turned his head up as if the imp was actually on his shoulder. "What? Yeah, my father's item is in there. We have to go."

"What if those three just got the item for us instead?"

"Wha? Why are you? Oh!" Kiru said, now understanding the imp's hesitation. Ever since William was almost eaten by a large koi fish sacred beast, back when Kiru was training to get into the Royal Academy, the imp had been absolutely terrified of bodies of water. The little demon's phobia was significant enough that a bathtub's amount of water was too much for him. Funnily enough, Kiru could tell he wasn't even scared of the turtle crocs. William was scared of there being a fish underneath that would eat him. "You know that you're inside my core, right? There's physically no way any fish could get you."

"Oh, yeah. Okay then, Master. Let's go already. Wait! What if a fish eats you?!"

Shaking his head and deciding not to answer that question, Kiru ran forward and leaped onto the nearest shell. Kiru was not as skilled as Zhaden, but he did okay despite such fresh damage to his body's cultivation and therefore his movements. He only faltered twice. The first time was due to not landing exactly on the top of one shell. The hard surface was very smooth, allowing no traction for his footing. He managed to narrowly avoid falling into the water. The second time was due to difficulty finding a path forward. He was scanning to see which shell to jump to next and accidentally took too much time. The turtle croc under his feet began to rumble, and Kiru had to throw himself forward a good twenty feet with Telekinesis to not get his leg bitten off. Doing that also caused a sharp spike of pain in his head from his injured core.

Even though Kiru had some close calls, he and the other cultivators made it to the central island safely. They all stood in front of the columned structure made of white stone. Kiru felt something almost quite literally tugging at his armor to get him in there.

"Let's go," he said excitedly and practically ran into the building.

Inside the building was a simple ten-by-ten-foot room made of stone and marble. In the center was a sphinx that looked to be made of hardened sand sitting on a pedestal at the end. It was the size of a large dog, and its face wasn't what Kiru would've expected. As chance would have it, he'd read about sphinxes. They were intelligent creatures that preferred intellectual challenges over physical combat. That didn't mean they weren't above it, however. Sphinxes were ferocious and used their sharp minds in conjunction with their bodies to enact horrible damage.

They had the face of a human but the body of a lion and were reported to be at least twenty feet tall. What was interesting to the psion was that they weren't considered to be sacred beasts. Sphinxes were categorized as monsters, and it was from a Monster Manual at school that he had acquired his knowledge about them. So, with the orc nation being all about sacred beasts and cultivating beast mana, why was a monster statue here? Sure, monsters lived in every nation, but it didn't fit the typical Imakandi aesthetic. Kiru also idly wondered why sphinxes were considered to be monsters while the leokin—a different type of humanoid lion—weren't.

"*What's going on with its face?*" William asked.

By all accounts, sphinxes had human heads. *So, why does this one have the mouth of a canine?* Kiru wondered as he stared.

As he took another step forward, he staggered as he abruptly no longer felt the incessant pulling. Concerned about a possible trap, he turned to get his friends out, but it was too late.

As soon as the last of them crossed the threshold, a large marble door slammed down from the top of the open doorway, sealing all of them inside and blocking out the moonlight that had been coming in from the doorway.

Ensconced torches along the columns consecutively lit in flame on their own moments later. The room was now adequately illuminated, but long shadows sprang up, giving everyone a sense of unease. The four walls and columns began to glow subtly, and the room began to shift. Specifically, it began to grow. The columns became thicker and taller. The walls spread, shifting back and growing taller.

"Back to back," Kiru ordered via Telepathy, his face wincing as the backlash from using the technique struck him.

In only thirty seconds, the entire chamber had tripled in size.

Per Kiru's order, the party had gone into a defensive formation, putting their backs to each other to try and avoid getting struck from any blind spot. Only once the temple had settled down around them, the party relaxed, no imminent danger apparent. Kiru looked around. He noted that everything other than the strange sphinx statue had altered. The only way that had changed was that it was now occupying the center of the chamber due to the room's rapid expansion. Kiru knew it had to be important. Acting on instinct, the psion began walking toward it. Before he could touch it, though, the stone structure turned to sand and collapsed to the ground, mixing with the sand below.

"Uh . . . Did you guys just see that?" Kiru asked.

"Well, I can't see anything, Boss, but yeah. That was weird," Mutt replied.

The sand below Kiru's feet began to churn on its own. The psion gasped and jumped back to rejoin his friends, everyone with their weapons at the ready. The sand throughout the chamber moved toward the center of the large room, shifting and coalescing until before their very eyes was a living sphinx made of sand. Like the small statue earlier, it also had the mouth of a wolf.

The sand sphinx snapped its eyes down at the four travelers and immediately locked eyes with Kiru. "One worthy to be king has entered my lair, but, Young One, you must beware. To receive your boon from me, you must answer my riddles three." The rhyming creature had a drawn out, gravelly voice that sounded otherworldly in nature.

The party just stood there, observing the intelligent elemental monster.

"Um, okay," Kiru tentatively answered, taking a small step forward. Both he and Brunhilda actually enjoyed puzzles but preferred doing them when *not* being faced down by a creature that could conceivably kill them.

Without preamble, the sphinx began. "A girl has the same number of brothers and sisters, but the brother has half as many brothers as sisters. How can this be?"

Kiru tapped his chin as he mulled over the question. "So, she has the same number of brothers and sisters, but the brother doesn't," he muttered to himself.

"This is so boring! Why can't we have a trial where we get to kill some stuff?" William whined.

"Not now, William," Kiru reprimanded, his eyes closing from the sudden backlash of acute head pain.

In the midst of this internal conversation, Mutt—whether due to impatience or not having paid full attention—decided to answer, "Uhhh, is it because one of the brothers is a lot shorter than the other?" Brunhilda slapped him on the back of the head.

Kiru's heart sank as the sphinx growled. "Wrong answer," it said before attacking the psion.

"Shit!" Kiru shouted before rolling out of the way of its bite and moving behind a column. His three friends charged in to attack the sphinx. Mutt clawed one of its legs and two of Zhaden's daggers hit it in the eyes. The sphinx showed no signs of pain as its leg easily regenerated and the blades simply slid out and fell to the ground. It growled, then took a swipe at Mutt but was blocked by Brunhilda's shields.

"Kiru, hurry up and give this thing its bloody answer!" the dwarf said through gritted teeth.

"*Haha! This is my kind of challenge!*" William laughed.

"William, if you don't shut up or be helpful, so help me, when I get my core fixed, I am going to throw you in the deepest body of water full of angry fish I can find!" the psion threatened out loud to avoid another flare of sharp head pain.

"*You wouldn't!*" William protested.

"*Do not test me right now, William!*"

"*Mmph, fine! There are four girls and three boys.*"

"What?" Kiru asked.

"*The answer. It's because there are four girls and three boys. I . . . also like riddles,*" the imp admitted in embarrassment.

Not having time to process what he said, Kiru moved out from behind the pillar to look at the sphinx and simply shouted, "The answer is because there are four girls and three boys!"

The sphinx was on both its hindlimbs, poised to slam its front paws into Kiru's friends, but then it froze. Then, turning its half-human, half-wolf face to Kiru, it said, "You are correct," before gently backing up and lowering its front paws so as not to land his friends.

"*Don't answer its questions. Let me do it,*" Kiru telepathically sent to his friends.

"Next riddle," it growled as it prowled over to Kiru. "A man shares the same father and mother as his king, but to call them siblings would cause a lie to spring. How can this be?" it asked with its sandy maw just inches away from the psion's face.

Kiru gave a small smile despite his proximity to the sand monster's teeth. He actually knew this one from his childhood. "They are the same person," he answered.

The sphinx moved its head back in surprise at how quickly Kiru responded. "You are correct again." The monster then lowered itself to lock eyes with the psion. "Final riddle," it said before it started circling around him, its bulky form surrounding and blocking him from his allies. "To receive your quaesitum—the ruler's Imakandi item—give the answer that explains the following."

It raised its head to recite its final test. "To some a source of trust and love, to others, ball and chain; for me, some go beyond, above, while others but complain. For I'm a thing you cannot choose, you're stuck with what you've got, but I'm a thing that one can lose. For granted, take me not. The leaves, the branch, the roots, the seed, the living crimson flow, as each of them their lives they lead, forever shall I grow. What am I?"

"Oooh! I know," Mutt said before the loud sound of a metal shield clanging against the orc's face echoed in the chamber.

The sphinx snapped its head in the others' direction.

Brunhilda laughed nervously to the sphinx as she stepped in front of the orc, now groaning, clutching his head, and lying on his back. "Sorry, um, Mister Sphinx. We defer to our leader to make all answers from now on."

The sphinx just growled before looking back to Kiru. It thumped its front two feet down hard on the ground as it glared at the psion. "Your answer. What am I?"

Kiru heart thumped rapidly as he thought. He needed more time to think. "Give me a minute, please. You gave me no time limit!" He glared right back at the sand monster.

The sphinx pulled its head back, visibly thrown-off by Kiru's sudden snark. Secretly, the psion was just playing for time. Technically, he was right. No time limit had been given. Hoping that acting like he wasn't bothered and calling the creature out on that technicality would help him. To his fortune, it did.

"Grr. You are correct, but I shall not ask thrice. I'll give you one minute. That shall suffice," it said.

Kiru nodded, acting like this was not bothersome at all. In his head, he chastised himself for only asking for a minute. *How was I to know that the sphinx would take me so literally?* he thought. Kiru began pacing back and forth. He closed his eyes and braced himself for the pain of what he was about to do.

"*William, you got any ideas?*" he sent to his familiar.

"*I got two things, Master: Jack and Squat,*" the imp replied.

Kiru pursed his lips and continued to mull over the riddle. He had to focus. He'd heard of the phrase "the ol' ball and chain" referring to someone's spouse. That didn't exactly fit, though. Yes, some people didn't choose their spouses, but there were plenty that did. There was one thing that was tugging at Kiru's head in particular, though. It was what the sphinx said before the riddle. Aside from it being only the second time he'd heard the word "quaesitum" ever in his life, the sphinx calling it the "Ruler's Imakandi Item" stuck out to him.

Why did it call it that in particular? he thought. It was obvious that the item was in Imakandi, but it seemed to have placed more gravity in that description than mere location. Kiru figured that he could glean an answer from it. *Maybe whatever item it was had been previously influenced by the orcs?*

Kiru thought once more about the riddle, his perfect recall bringing up all the words in his mind precisely. This time, he thought about it whilst also thinking about the orcs of this land, trying to draw any connection between the two. Since he was in Imakandi, he reasoned that to attain this item, the riddle may be related to the orc nation somehow. The M'Baku mantra kept repeating in his head.

"Is it a pack?" he asked hopefully.

The sphinx made of sand looked at Kiru with a puzzled expression. Its face twitched as it thought about Kiru's answer.

Am I partially right? he thought.

"I have judged your answer insufficient," it said.

Oh, shit! I was partially right! Kiru thought, noticing the sphinx hadn't said he was incorrect.

The sphinx opened its toothy maw and reared its head back to snap at Kiru.

If a pack is almost *the right answer, think! What's a broader definition for a pack?!* Then, it clicked.

"A family!" he shouted as the monster began to descend.

The sphinx's head stopped mid-lunge. "You are correct. Mmm—" It trailed off as its body destabilized and dissolved once more into formless sand. It did leave something behind, however: a mask floating in midair and pulsing with power.

CHAPTER THIRTY-EIGHT

The King

The mask appeared to be made from wood. It was mostly dark red and black, ornately carved, and would cover just the lower half of one's face. The mask represented the muzzle of a wolf and was the exact shape as the strange sphinx's, just smaller. Kiru could feel the tugging connection once more. This was it. This was his father's second item.

"Well, go on! Take it, Master!" William exclaimed.

Without hesitation, Kiru quickly walked over and placed a hand on the wolf mask. It glowed on contact, and right after, Kiru's forehead began to itch. Knowing something was going on, he lowered his headband with his other hand. With the ruby gem in his forehead revealed, an image suddenly projected from it. Kiru sharply inhaled. It was King Ruken Chromebane, Kiru's father! The psion had seen his father appear like this only twice before, each time from the items he had left behind. Kiru was unsure exactly how these holograms came to be, but honestly, he didn't care. He was just happy to see his father once more.

"So you've come to Imakandi," Ruken said. The projection then turned to face Kiru directly. "The orcs of this land are strong warriors and even stronger friends. To rule the Kingdom of Blades, you must learn from their leaders, the M'Baku. The reason that their tribe continues to rule, despite so many strong cultivators in this land, is that they recognize that their strength comes from their people—their family as a whole—rather than an individual."

Ruken gave a slight smile. "To have come this far, it is a lesson you have no doubt already grasped. Well done, my son." The projection then put his hand under the floating mask. "This is the mask of Fenrir, a gift bestowed on the founder of our nation by Imakandi's high chief at the time. While equipped, the enchantment inside the mask shall enhance your senses to that of an ancient dire wolf, one of the first descendants of Fenrir himself."

"Whoa," Mutt said, truly impressed. "And I thought the Psyslime was impressive."

Brunhilda shushed the orc as the three continued to observe Kiru's interaction with the projection.

The king continued, "However, it does not come without cost. The mask siphons mana while worn, so you can run dangerously low on your stores if you're not careful. Many a cultivator has lost their life due to careless management of their mana supplies." He then removed his hand from under the mask and took a step back, resting his arms behind his back.

"Thank you, Father," Kiru said. The psion knew it was just a projection, but he couldn't help but state his gratitude. When he then placed both of his hands on the mask, something seemed to snap into place. It was imperceptible, but he felt more whole with the item in his grasp.

The projection of Ruken also seemed more alive, despite his form beginning to fade.

"*You're welcome, my son,*" Kiru heard in his head. Goosebumps traveled down his neck, and his eyes widened as the fading projection of his father nodded both knowingly and urgently at him. "*Quick! Is there any information that I can bestow upon you? What knowledge can I give?*" Ruken asked.

Kiru just stood there with his mouth open, dumbfounded at what he was hearing in his head. He didn't know why the projection was only speaking telepathically or how it seemed to be suddenly self-aware, but it was fair to say that Kiru was completely thrown.

"*Master! Ask the guy something, like how do we fix your core?*" William urged.

"Uh . . . My mental mana core is damaged. It's cracked and it causes physical pain to use my techniques. I don't have the time to let it heal on its own. How can I repair it?" he asked out loud, too shocked to think to ask via Telepathy.

The king's eyes flashed in concern. "*I see you've inherited my recklessness, a trait I wish I hadn't passed on to you. Either the blood of those who use mental mana or ingesting enough mental mana condensed into a liquid should repair the damage, depending on what type of injury. Seeing as you are likely the last psion and I know not of any other being that can utilize our gifts, getting the liquid mana is your only option.*"

Kiru gulped. "Where can I get liquid mental mana?"

Ruken's form was now almost completely gone, only the neck up remaining and fading fast. His face was concerned but still conveyed trust in his son. "*You have two choices: head north to the human Kingdom of Rowe and go deep in its mines, or venture south into the Torn Empire right at its center. You'll know when you're close. Good luck, my so—*"

Kiru just stood there in silence as the room began to shrink down to its original size, and the door opened. He had no idea as to how exactly he'd just had a conversation with his dead father, but it stirred up a flurry of emotions.

Without even realizing it, Kiru started both crying and laughing at the same time. He'd felt uncontrolled joy at speaking with Ruken but also sadness. Despite the latter, he smiled. *He'd talked with his dad!* In addition, he now knew that he could fix his core too.

"You okay, Boss?" Mutt asked.

Kiru sniffled and wiped his face. "Yeah, Mutt. Just happy I got to chat with my dad."

"That be a right fierce-looking mask ye got there, Kiru," Brunhilda said.

"And by you saying 'having a conversation,' do you mean your sire could hear you speak?" Zhaden asked. "We observed you asking the projection questions, but I could not hear it answer."

Kiru put a hand to the gold drakonid's shoulder. "Come on, I'll explain as we get out of here." The psion then told them about his telepathic conversation with his father. He figured it had to do with having more of the dead king's items in his possession, but exactly how that worked, he didn't know. Kiru decided to hold off on trying the mask on for now. He also told them about what Ruken had said about how to fix his core.

The party discussed their options: either the Torn Empire or the Kingdom of Rowe.

"Ugh, Rowe," the dwarf spat out.

"You are familiar with the human kingdom?" Zhaden asked.

"Oh, aye. It be to the far north and shares a border with my homeland. It be a dangerous place where it can blizzard any time of the year. Don't get me wrong, there be plenty of nice people there. They're a hearty folk that can make a delicious yak stew."

Mutt's stomach growled audibly, interrupting their conversation. "Uh, sorry," he apologized.

The paladin smiled and shook her head before tossing Mutt a piece of jerky and continuing, "But from my experiences, there are just as many nasty folk in Rowe as there be kind. While that bitter land brought many a folk together as warm communities, me grandpappy said that even more grew just as cold and cruel as the winds that blow across that place."

"According to my research back at the academy, Van Blaine has many kin from Rowe. His family came from a duchy bordering the two kingdoms," Zhaden said.

Kiru nodded. That made sense to him as well. He remembered a few of his fellow students from Rowe back at the academy. There were two distinguishing factors about them. They were pale, and they all used some form of ice mana. *Guess that place had a favored mana type like Imakandi does.* That also fell in line with how Brunhilda said the place was a cold land and with the one-eyed usurper's cultivation path. Kiru tensed his jaw, thinking about the man that killed his father.

"Well, how far is this place?" Mutt asked through a mouthful of jerky.

"Far," Kiru answered. "It's on the other side of the continent."

"Aye," Brunhild added. "To get there, I see three options. One, we go back through the whole of this massive nation once again and then through the Kingdom of Blades. Two, we go east through the elves' territory, then north through my country, and use a mountain pass to get to Rowe. The final option would be to go to the West Coast and hire a ship." Despite being so far north, Rowe shared a coastline with Imakandi and the Kingdom of Blades that bordered the Justinean Ocean to the west.

"*No! No boats!*" William shouted inside Kiru's mind. "*Boats mean water. Water means fish. Ugh! I hate fish!*"

Kiru smiled at his familiar's words.

"Well, any one of those options could work to go north, but it would take a long time, I bet. What about the other place? The Empire," Mutt asked.

"The Torn Empire?! Pfft, good luck with that!" Brunhilda replied.

"I must admit, I don't know much about it," Kiru said. Growing up in an isolated mining village, then learning of his quest to find his father's items within the countries of the Great Alliance, there wasn't much need to think about an unallied territory to the south. In terms of concrete information, Kiru knew very little. Most of his knowledge about the place was from secondhand rumors from the various bar patrons his mother had served. What the psion did know was that the Torn Empire was a mysterious and dangerous place. Its waters were erratic, never staying the same and containing numerous unknown monstrous creatures in its depths. Almost all who ventured there never returned. That was why many resorted to rivers and land travel for trade instead of traveling around the continent.

Brunhilda nodded at Kiru's words. "I'm not surprised. Unless one travels through there, few have any idea about it."

The dwarf's friends all shared a puzzled look at her words. The dwarf nation where she came from was very far north—almost as north as Rowe. Why would she be familiar with a coastal southern area?

The paladin took a deep breath before explaining. "I've got an uncle who be a merchant specializing in rare gems. Growing up, aside from taxes, Uncle Jayson only ever got mad 'bout one thing: the Torn Empire. It be made up of the coastline to the south, separated from Imakandi by a massive gorge. Aside from that, the only other spots of land are the nearby islands below. The Empire be mostly water, honestly."

"*Another place full of water?! Oh, come on,*" William whined.

"The weather there be volatile. Ye could have clear skies one moment, then acid rain the next. Me uncle told me that even the locations of the islands seem to change," Brunhilda said.

"That does sound unwelcoming," Zhaden said.

"Oh, aye. It wouldn't be so bad, though, if not for the inhabitants," Brunhilda added.

"The inhabitants?" Kiru asked.

"Ye got three nasty types of beings that call the Torn Empire home." She raised three fingers. She bent one. "First, be pirates. Those no-good marauders will take whatever they can and destroy whatever they can't, including people. Almost killed my uncle a few times, too." She bent the second finger. "Next, ye got the monsters. Uncle Jayson told me that horrendous creatures call the waters of the Empire home." She shivered a little. "One of his stories still gives me the creeps to this day."

Brunhilda lowered her third and final finger. "The final inhabitants are known as the Crazed, local islanders who've lived on those islands since before Ragnarok. They don't speak any known tongue and are a bunch of warmongering cannibals."

"Wow! That is bad," Kiru said. It made him wonder exactly *why* liquid mental mana could be found in such a strange place.

"By the information you've presented to us, Brunhilda, it seems that if we wish to adequately repair our friend's core, we are stuck between two equally dangerous locations. Still, heading south toward the Torn Empire appears to be our only viable option," Zhaden said.

"Did you just not hear what I just said, Zhaden?" Brunhilda retorted. The two then began to argue over what they should do. Brunhilda tried to get Mutt to agree with her, but her orc boyfriend had stopped paying attention to the details. He didn't care which way they went as long as there were some good fights on their way.

"What is your opinion on this matter, Kiru?" Zhaden asked.

Kiru stroked his chin in thought.

"There are pros and cons to both sides," he said.

The Torn Empire was much closer. With it not being part of the Great Alliance and having both erratic weather and plenty of enemy cultivators around, it should make it more difficult for anyone in the Inquisition to follow them. However, the pirate-infested shores were uncharted, they had no boat nor obvious way to get one, and many of the dangers that could help them were just as likely to hinder or even kill them.

Going north to Rowe would obviously take more time to get to, not to mention the increased risk of being caught by the Inquisition. Whether by boat or by land, they would almost *have* to travel through the Kingdom of Blades' territory, which would inevitably increase their chances of being found by those hunting them. Now with Kiru's identity as a psion about to become known to Van Blaine, there was no doubt he would be redoubling his efforts to capture him.

Still, Rowe's lands and people were well-known, reducing the risks of surprises. Plus, besides being a place where he could fix his mental mana core, another one of Ruken's items was located there. Kiru knew that because each nation in the Great Alliance had one. So, going there would knock out two birds with one stone.

"Both options aren't great," Kiru admitted. "But I think going north to Rowe is our best bet. We should hopefully be able to pay for passage in a fast-enough merchant vessel. With Mutt being the queen's brother, finding a ship shouldn't be too hard. Plus, another one of my father's items is there."

"Master, how about we go east through the Elves' territory? One of your dad's items is there too, right? I mean, I'm glad we don't have to go to that Empire place that's mostly water, but do we really have to take a boat to go north? Why don't we just go by land?" William pleaded.

"This is our best chance right now, William. I'll make it up to you by feeding you some fish, how about that?" Kiru offered.

The imp didn't say anything, but Kiru took that as silent agreement.

Brunhilda smiled at the tiebreaker decision while Zhaden gave a begrudging nod in acquiescence. After another bout of croc-hopping, the party made it to the forested edge of the crater lake. Despite wanting to gain even more distance from anyone pursuing them, they made camp at the water's edge. Night in Imakandi was in full swing, and they were exhausted from the day's events. They needed to rest and recover. Also, according to Mutt, there were even more dangerous nocturnal predators around, and no one wanted another fight on their hands. Well, all except for Mutt and William, but the nays outvoted the yeas, even if you counted Kiru's familiar.

Kiru was interested in trying on the mask, but he was honestly too drained to do it. At this late hour, the psion didn't want to deal with any unforeseen side effects the magic mask might have. After a few minutes, Kiru was out cold under his bedroll. He didn't even take the time to stay awake and cultivate any mental mana from his friends' dreams.

CHAPTER THIRTY-NINE

Change of Plans

Everyone fell asleep not long after Kiru, but it wasn't a restful sleep for anyone. Kiru woke up a couple of times in the night due to nightmares.

The first time Kiru woke, he noticed all his friends tossing and turning as well, seeming to be having nightmares themselves. The second time Kiru snapped up in bed, he saw Zhaden sitting up and staring into the fire, a haunted look in his eyes. Seeing that and feeling his friend's pain, Kiru decided he would just stay up too. Plus, based on the moons' locations and the growing pink hue in the sky, it wouldn't be long until dawn would be upon them. Though his friends were all having troubled sleep, their bad dreams were still dreams, meaning more mental mana for him to intake.

He spent the next hour or so cultivating the overflow. Just as when he activated a technique lately, his core hurt when he took in the magical energy. Fortunately, the pain of withdrawing mana was mild compared to expending it. The best way Kiru could describe the sensation was like having to use sore muscles the day after an intense workout.

It was still worth it for him to cultivate, though. Like it or not, he needed mana to move, so he had no choice. There was the extra benefit that his cultivation seemed to help his sleeping friends relax, their uncomfortable expressions visibly easing. The more mana he cultivated, the calmer their faces grew. Their breathing eased as well. It looked like their nightmares had passed. *I can cure night terrors?! Huh, you learn something new every day,* he thought.

After he replenished his stores, he got up to relieve himself and then to refill their canteens from the nearby lake, which was a large source of fresh water. If they were going to take a boat out on the ocean to get to Rowe, fresh water would be more valuable than gold. Kiru wanted to get moving soon, but his friends had earned at least a few minutes of good sleep. On kneeling down and refilling the party's third canteen, something fell off his belt and thudded against a piece of driftwood.

Kiru looked down to see his Mask of Fenrir. His heart skipped a beat at the thought of losing it, and he quickly picked it up. Through all the craziness of his trial with the sphinx, he never took the time to fully appreciate the item. It was made mostly of wood and ornately carved to look like the toothy maw of a wolf. It was painted a dark red with pearlescent teeth.

"*That looks so cool,*" William said, chipping in for the first time for the day.

Kiru had to agree. It was intimidating and cool. While examining the wolf-ish oni mask, Kiru could swear he heard the howling of wolves off in the distance. *Did that noise actually come from the mask?* he thought.

As if in answer, the Mask of Fenrir vibrated in his hand, sending a pulse of beast mana up his arm. The howls returned but louder this time. Kiru also felt something. It wasn't physical, but somehow, the mask conveyed . . . *emotions* to Kiru? *Is it alive?* From what Kiru gathered, the mask was scared, frustrated, and hungry. It was a predator, and its position as an alpha was being challenged. *How can I understand it?*

Kiru recoiled as he processed the signals the mask was sending him. Was the mask scared of him? Was it challenging him?

"*Ooohoohoo! Master, put it on!*" William nagged inside Kiru's mind. "*I think it wants to try to assert its dominance over us. Put on the mask and show this paltry thing who the real conquerors are.*"

Kiru shrugged. He wanted to try the mask on in the first place, and this crater was likely the safest place they'd be in for a while. Ignoring the reservations he had, Kiru put the Mask of Fenrir on. Once he'd securely fastened it to his head, the magic of the item activated.

Fine, nearly invisible needles made from hardened spider hairs jutted out along the edge of the mask and pierced Kiru's skin. The needles were incredibly thin and so barely stung Kiru, not drawing any blood. It still startled him, though, and he took a reflexive step back. Nothing else happened for the first second. Then, the needles piercing his skin began sending concentrated beast mana into his body. The mask's enchantments were strong and well-made, so it sent beast mana only to certain parts of Kiru's body, the mana extending out as threads from each needle and never losing its connection.

In milliseconds, a complicated web of beast mana threads had interwoven throughout Kiru's head, carefully avoiding both his mental mana core and meridians and not bringing them any changes or effects. Where the threads touched, however, became drastically altered. Kiru looked at his reflection in the water and watched as his ears grew longer and more pointed, black fur suddenly growing out of them in thick clumps. Though it was hidden under the mask, he could also feel his nose had elongated slightly and turned into a snout. Lastly were his eyes, which had turned from blue to bright yellow, with smaller pupils and a feral intensity.

"Gaaah!" he groaned through the sudden pain. Metamorphosis was painful, at least for him. Kiru hoped Mutt didn't go through this pain each time he used a technique. He took a few deep breaths, his body shaky from the mask's influence. The influx of sensations nearly disrupted Kiru's Telekinesis, which would've resulted in him falling to the ground like a limp noodle.

After he got a few lungfuls of air, however, he realized he could sense so much more. His half-elf eyes were already sharp, but he could see so much more clearly than before, noticing faint movements even from great distances. His nostrils took in more types and variations of scents than he thought possible. He could smell small rodents scurrying across treetops in search of food and the distinct scents of each of his three friends.

The psion laughed in elation at the mask's power, his hairy right ear twitching as sound came to him. A songbird sang on a tree branch all the way on the other side of the large body of water. Mutt's heavy breathing was so loud to Kiru that he could easily locate him in the dark, and he could hear the faint rumbling of a herd of torrent horses moving west, away from their location. He snarled at the scent, the desire to hunt causing him to take a couple of steps out of the crater.

Kiru gasped as he realized that wasn't his desire. It was the *mask*'s. "No, I'm in control. You will do as I command, not the other way around," he said.

In response, the beast mana that had threaded along his head began churning violently. Kiru snarled and snapped his head back and forth. His teeth sharpened even more until they matched the mask's silhouette. It would've been too much for him had he not spent so much time around beast mana. Just as a seasoned drunkard could tolerate a much higher level of alcohol than someone who'd never tried booze, Kiru had become quite accustomed to the influence of beast mana. The months spent in Imakandi, the days spent in the depths of Dissé's temple, allowing some of Myev's mana inside his core to help him figure out how to create Brainstorm, and ingesting Fenrir's blood had all hardened him to the influences of beast mana.

The mask resisted, but Kiru would not be denied. It hurt, but he focused his will on the mana laced around his head. His core pulsed once, and the wildly churning strings of beast mana instantly settled, like a dog who'd been given a command.

"Without me, you are just a mask. Under my command, you will taste the blood of our enemies—our prey," he said, sending out his intent into the threads of mana and directly back into the mask.

William practically purred in excitement at Kiru's words.

The Mask of Fenrir shook for a moment before quickly settling. It then sent another set of emotions into the psion: respect and begrudging submission. It recognized Kiru's authority, and no longer tried to force its will upon him.

"Hahahahaha! Yes!" Kiru laughed as he raised his fists up high and shouted in triumph. The dull pain that came from using Telekinesis heightened some with the mask equipped, but it wasn't unbearable for now. Still, he knew that he couldn't keep it on forever. He could feel the pain slightly increasing as time went on. It would eventually build up to become too much for him.

Another pulse flowed from the mask to Kiru. This time there was one primary feeling it conveyed: worry. It was warning him of something. Startled by this, Kiru ran up a large boulder at the lake's edge and desperately began using his enhanced senses to scan his surroundings, just as the sun crested high enough to provide some direct illumination into the crater. His sharpened wolf eyes detected what the mask was trying to warn him about.

Two pairs of orange reptilian creatures under the surface of the lake glistened in the sunlight. They were large and moving quickly toward him. Kiru had just enough time to draw his Fu Tao before a large, dark, two-headed turtle crocodile surged up from the water. He jumped to the right, narrowly avoiding one of its jaws snapping at him.

Kiru rolled to his knees, his back turned to the croc. His right ear twitched as the sound of moving scales came toward him. Instinctively, he jumped to the left, then swung his blade upward. The blade made contact and cut out a large chunk out of the left lower jaw of one of the heads. The turtle croc recoiled, allowing Kiru to take in the sacred beast fully for the first time. As he had noted before, it had two heads. Its body was dark green and brown, perfectly blending in with the sediment and vegetation under the water. It was also quite large compared to the others Kiru had seen, the top of its spiked shell rising high above the psion's head.

The right head shook and snapped its jaw in pain, a steady drip of blood coming from its wound. Kiru's wolfish eyes saw the left head looking concerned at its counterpart but also noticed the subtle tension in one of its eyes and an almost imperceptible shift in the tension of its neck. Then, like a serpent, the left head struck out, intending to bite the psion in two. It would've caught Kiru by surprise, had he not noticed the minute changes in its posture. Because of that, it was the turtle croc who was surprised.

Kiru shifted to the right and used Clean the Hoof, aiming the pointed tip of his hook up and swinging, guiding the sharp point into one of the croc's vital spots. His Fu Tao bit into the softer scales of the reptile's exposed neck, tearing through the flesh and lacerating the turtle croc's jugular. The left head cried out in pain as it reflexively pulled in its neck and swiped a claw at Kiru. The psion wasn't ready for the fast speed of the retaliatory strike and so was sent rolling back some ten feet.

Fueled by adrenaline and William's continuous encouragement for more bloodshed, he got back up to his feet in an ungraceful roll. His yellow eyes widened as the two-headed creature charged at him. *Mutt was right. These things move fast in the daytime!* His sharpened sight was able to tell the creature's left head was close to death, its scales paler from its blood loss. Sensing a weakness, Kiru ran right at the crocodilian. Both heads roared with open mouths, but he noticed the turtle croc's right head withdrawing a little. That was the one that was going to strike.

As he ran, Kiru morphed his malleable weapon into that of a short spear. Using his enhanced connection with his Psyslime since ascending to Ruby, he threw his weapon forward, guiding it with his mental mana and perfectly controlling its trajectory. As the head struck out, the Psyslime went straight into its open mouth. The turtle croc's momentum was abruptly halted as Kiru's weapon impaled its fleshy throat.

The right head gagged and coughed out blood as the two-headed turtle croc collapsed against the sand. Both heads cried out in bloody pain, but Kiru wasn't done. If there was anything he learned in Imakandi, it was that a wounded animal—even a fatally injured one—could still kill. Using Telekinesis, he threw himself upward to land on top of the beast's shell. The croc flailed as both heads struggled to survive.

Still, Kiru was close enough to his Psyslime weapon to use his enhanced connection to change its shape even from a short distance. With a flex of will, Kiru turned it from a spear to a circular-bladed saw. Then, he made it spin. *No way I could've done this as a Gold,* he thought. The right head's cries were quickly cut short as the weapon in its throat changed and rapidly decapitated it. The left head with the throat wound was barely alive itself, and it desperately began pulling its half-limp body into the water in a hopeless attempt to save itself.

Not having to fight to keep his balance since the croc was no longer flailing, Kiru easily directed the spinning blade over and decapitated the second head from the previous wound in its neck. Kiru then changed his Psyslime's form back to its normal state and sheathed both his weapons. He stood there on top of the mutant sacred beast that had tried to kill him and breathed heavily through his new mask.

The Mask of Fenrir truly was an amazing boon! Sights, sounds, scents—they were all so much more vivid than he'd ever experienced before. With the sun warming up its blood, the large turtle croc moved with impressive and surprising speed. Kiru could've been killed or at least severely injured had he not had the mask on.

First off, he wouldn't have noticed it on its way to ambush him. Second, when he was fighting the frighteningly fast reptile, his mask made it so that it was if the sacred beast was moving in slow motion, or at least, his perception of it made it seem so, which allowed him to pick up on the subtle cues of what the creature planned to do next, helping him end it with relative ease. How far had he come from that boy in Bristleton?

"Hahaha! Whoa! Master, that was awesome! That slow creature wanted to eat us. Now, we get to eat him, and make his strength our own. Flee in fear, you cowardly crocodiles!" William cheered.

"Thanks, William." Kiru replied, opting to speak aloud to spare himself the brief pain using Telepathy would bring. He was about to take off his mask when the smell of crocodile began to overwhelm his nostrils. His wolfish ears twitched repeatedly as the sound of the lake's waves began to increase. He looked up to see the doubly decapitated turtle croc's neck stumps oozing blood into the water, which was also now littered with countless forms moving toward him.

"Oh, shit," he uttered. "Everyone, get up! Get up now!" Kiru shouted to his friends. Mutt and Brunhilda groaned, but as soon as Kiru started frantically kicking each of them and saying they were in danger, the two quickly changed their tunes. "We've gotta go now!"

"What? What's going on?" Brunhilda asked as she gripped her shields, and then she caught sight of him. "Kiru! What be going on with yer face?!"

"It's the mask. I'll explain later, but I'm fine," he replied hurriedly.

In a display of great athleticism, Mutt kicked both legs and went straight from lying on his back to standing up. The orc raised his head and began to sniff loudly, his head quickly snapping down in the direction of the water. "Oh, yeah. We gotta move," he said, showing uncharacteristic concern given his penchant for a good fight.

"What enemy approaches?" Zhaden asked as he dismissed his Invisibility, blades at the ready.

"Four words: too many turtle crocs," the orc answered before hastily throwing all his stuff in an enchanted bag of holding. "Don't worry, guys. We just need to get out of their territory and—"

Both Mutt and Kiru's ears twitched as they picked up the sound of rustling tree branches rapidly approaching them. Then, a "normal," single-headed turtle croc leaped out from the brush. Fortunately, since the orc and psion had heard the creature's charge, they were ready for it. Mutt caught its open jaws with both hands, preventing the croc from snapping down on him. Meanwhile, Kiru rushed forward and sliced at the hinge in between the upper and lower halves of the croc's left jaws.

Mutt finished the job and ripped out its lower jaw. To be safe, Kiru finished the job and stabbed the croc in between its eyes with the pointed pommels of his blades. Both the orc and psion turned back to see their friends already heading up and out toward the edge of the crater.

"Run, ya idgits!" Brunhilda shouted as her short legs pumped for all they were worth.

More rustling came from behind the pair, and they both quickly followed the dwarf's advice. All four of them hustled up the crater as fast as they could. Meanwhile, a horde of angry turtle crocs pursued them. In between heavy breaths, Mutt said that, as long as they got out of the turtle crocs' territory, they would no longer be in pursuit. They were extremely territorial creatures. Kiru just hoped that their territory was the edge of the crater, or they all might have wound up as some beast's breakfast.

As they got nearer to the crater's edge, Kiru could hear the sound of the rushing wind more and more. To their great relief, none of the turtle crocs had pursued them. They turned to face the crater and had their weapons ready just in case, but the most they saw was a flicker of a pair of jaws cresting the edge. When the scaled muzzle was struck by the wind, it flinched and let out a low growl before going back down and descending into the safety of the crater lake.

The party stayed quiet for a few minutes, not wanting to tempt any crocodiles that may have been lingering nearby. Feeling more secure, Brunhilda looked to the party. "So, we go east then?"

Kiru nodded, but then the direction of the wind suddenly changed. He still hadn't taken off his mask yet, so his nostrils and enhanced sense of smell were beset by all the scents from the new northerly wind. There were the expected smells—horse, grass, and orc—but he detected some unusual scents as well, namely stone, metal, and . . . something else.

"Mutt, do you smell that?" Kiru asked.

The blind orc sniffed. "Yeah, Boss."

"What is it?"

"It's dwarf, Boss, and that's not just any dwarf. I remember it. It was that weird laughing one who used earth mana."

Kiru idly wondered why, if the scent was that of a dwarf, he couldn't distinguish it himself. Brunhilda was a dwarf and was around them all the time. He should easily be able to notice the scent. The psion sniffed a couple more times to understand why that was the case. Brunhilda smelled different, not as earthy but more . . . *damp*, for lack of a better term. It was as if she smelled of a moist cave covered in moss. Then Kiru understood. Brunhilda smelled different because of her Trollblood. A few times, Mutt had said the paladin smelled like a troll, but Kiru hadn't really comprehended what he meant until that moment. While the scent wasn't bad, he should probably have told the orc to stop saying his girlfriend smelled like a troll. Even if not intended as an insult, it still wasn't a flattering statement.

"That deranged killer has come to finish the job. Let us lie in ambush and bring vengeance upon him," Zhaden hissed angrily.

Kiru shook his head and put a hand on his friend's shoulder. "Zhaden, we can't."

The assassin pulled his shoulder away from Kiru, looking both hurt and confused at the psion's words. "But why? We have the advantage. We can ambush them and get justice for Ebysso."

Kiru shook his head sadly. He really wanted to help bring justice upon the Inquisition, especially for his friend to hopefully get some closure. Doing it at this time, though, was reckless.

"It's more than likely that he has brought reinforcements. If he's somehow informed Van Blaine that I'm a psion, he won't hesitate to send forces after us that we can't handle."

"I do not see how running would be wise, Kiru. If he's tracked us this far, will he not be upon us soon?" Zhaden asked.

Kiru shook his head. "With the wind this strong pushing against us, the Inquisition has to still be miles away."

"Well, then we need to get going," Brunhilda urged. "We need to go west to the reach the coast and find a ship."

"We can't do that, either." Kiru replied. He sighed as he realized their situation was more dire than they'd hoped. "If they're tracking us this quickly, nowhere in the Great Alliance is safe. We won't make it before we're caught."

He turned away to face south. "So, we're going to have to get out of Alliance Territory, at least for a little bit."

William, sensing what was about to come, desperately asked Kiru to reconsider, *"Master, please don't. There's gotta be a different way."*

Kiru ignored his familiar's pleas and looked to the gold drakonid. "Zhaden, we're going with your idea from last night," he said, then took off his mask, gazing back south toward the way they would now go. "We're going to The Torn Empire."

About the Author

Maxwell Farmer is the author of the Ashen Plane, Dr. Druid, and Last Psion series. He spent his youth in Metropolis, Illinois, the home of Superman. There, the seeds of his love for fantasy and science fiction blossomed. Like the man of steel, Farmer dons an alter ego: During the day, he's known as Dr. Farmer and treats the ailments of all the local cats and dogs. At night, however, he works hard to write captivating stories full of action and adventure with the goal of transporting readers to new and magical worlds. Farmer lives in the Great White North of Wisconsin with his wife and two children. To learn more, visit his website at www.maxwellfarmer.com.

9 781039 455191